Civvy Street

FIONA FIELD

HEAD
ZEUS

First published in the UK in 2016 by Head of Zeus Ltd

9 7 5 3 1 2 4 6 8

A catalogue record for this book is available from the British Library.

Paperback ISBN: 9781781857786
Ebook ISBN: 9781781857779

Typeset by Adrian McLaughlin

Printed and bound by CPI Group (UK) Ltd, Croydon, CR0 4YY

Head of Zeus Ltd
Clerkenwell House
45–47 Clerkenwell Green
London EC1R 0HT

WWW.HEADOFZEUS.COM

To Ian, who still *believes in me*

Acknowledgements

I need to thank, in particular, John Backley who is the emergency planning officer and facilities manager for the South Oxfordshire District Council. He was amazingly generous both with his time and information and I am really grateful for what he told me about flood management and related issues. However, I need to stress at this point that Winterspring District Council bears *no* relation to *any* local government organisation I have *ever* had dealings with – the fictional council in my book is a total figment of my imagination and was created in that vein entirely for dramatic reasons. I have never met a 'Rob' or anyone quite like him, and sincerely hope that no one of his ilk is involved in that sort of work at whatever level!

I also need to thank my lovely agent, Laura Longrigg, for her continued support, and the team at Head of Zeus who look after me so well. In particular, I need to thank Rosie de Courcy who is a stunningly fabulous editor and makes me write the best book I can.

Chapter 1

Major Mike Collins walked into the adjutant's office feeling relaxed and reasonably cheerful. It was almost the weekend, tomorrow the kids were going to come home from boarding school on an exeat and the weather was lovely. All in all, life could be a lot worse.

'Go right on in, Mike,' said Andy, the adjutant. 'The CO's expecting you.'

Mike nodded, crossed the office to the adjoining door and knocked. He'd been summoned by the new commanding officer of 1 Herts in a phone call a few minutes earlier. Jack Rayner wasn't his favourite person – in fact, thought Mike, a more ambitious, back-stabbing, self-seeking officer would be hard to find. His predecessor, Tony Notley, had been pretty pushy and ruthless when it came to furthering his own career but nowhere near Rayner's league. It was like comparing a Vauxhall Conference football player with David Beckham or Ronaldo. Still, Mike was due a posting in the not too distant future – probably to some staff job somewhere – so, in all likelihood, he wouldn't have to suffer Rayner for much longer.

'Come.' Lieutenant Colonel Rayner's voice rang through the solid oak.

Mike pushed the door open, saluted as he stood on the threshold and then shut the door behind him. He wasn't concerned about this summons. No doubt the CO wanted to discuss how members of his company were shaping up: who might be a suitable candidate for this or that course; who might have the potential for promotion; which of his junior officers ought to be posted out to a staff job to broaden their experience. Or maybe that posting Mike was expecting had come through. Or if not that, perhaps he had a job for Mike: some committee to chair; an inquiry to lead; maybe a board to sit on. That was the thing about being in an infantry regiment; if you weren't actually doing what infantry soldiers did – fighting battles, killing the enemy or romping around the ranges on exercise – then the days had to be filled by training, courses or just being kept occupied in one form or another.

'Have a seat.' The CO nodded towards the armchair to the side of his desk.

Mike removed his beret and sat down.

The CO looked at him and sighed. 'Look, Mike...' He bit his lower lip and paused. 'There isn't an easy way to say this.'

Mike felt the first twinge of apprehension. What the hell was the CO finding so hard to spit out?

'The thing is...the thing is...I've had the list of names of soldiers in the battalion who are being made redundant.' There was another pause. 'And, the thing is, you're on it.'

If Mike hadn't been sitting down he'd have reeled and staggered. Then he cleared his head. Surely he'd misunderstood. He'd *thought* the CO had said he was being made redundant but he must have got hold of the wrong end of the stick. He was a career soldier. He had a regular commission. Provided that he kept breathing and stayed alive he had a job for life. He did, didn't he? The CO was still speaking but Mike realised he hadn't heard a word.

'Sorry, Colonel,' Mike said, shaking his head, completely puzzled. The CO fell silent. 'Sorry, could you say that again?'

'You're being made redundant.' The CO didn't meet Mike's eye. 'Sorry, Mike, that's how it is.'

Mike's shoulders slumped. His head rang and he felt dizzy. Redundant? There had to be a mistake. 'But I can't be. I'm on a regular commission. I've got years left to serve.'

'I'm afraid the nature of your commission has got nothing to do with it.'

'But...but...'

The CO shook his head. 'Look, Mike, no one is sorrier than I am to be the bearer of bad news. I was devastated when I read the letter from the MoD.'

Mike stared at his boss. For someone who professed to be 'devastated' he looked remarkably sanguine. A bit embarrassed maybe, but not gutted.

'Really, sir?' Mike felt cold anger start to consume him.

'I was shocked when I saw your name.'

Not half as shocked as me, thought Mike, bitterly.

'You're a valuable officer,' continued the CO.

'But not valuable enough, eh?'

'It's not like that, Mike.'

'Isn't it?' Mike sank back in the chair as he tried to come to terms with the awful enormity of what he'd just heard. Sacked. Chucked. On the scrapheap. The army could dress it up however they liked but the cold, stark reality was they didn't want him. A thought struck him. Important stuff from the MoD always got sent out to commanding officers well ahead of time – generally it was embargoed till the due date but that didn't necessarily stop the recipients opening it for a sneak preview. And Rayner, for a bet, would have been unable to resist the temptation. 'How long have you known about this, Colonel?'

'I...well...'

Mike stared at the CO coldly. No further confirmation of his suspicions was required. 'And you didn't fight it? You didn't tell the MoD that, seeing as how I am so "valuable", they ought to look at someone else to cull?' Mike shook his head. 'Obviously not.'

'Mike, Mike, it's not like that. This isn't how these things work.'

Mike snorted. 'Really.'

'And there'll be a redundancy package. It's very generous.'

'Generous enough to pay for the twins' boarding school fees for the next seven years?' He glared at the colonel who remained silent. 'No, I thought not.'

'No...Mike...I mean, I don't know the exact details of your personal package but...but...'

Mike shook his head, bringing the CO to a stuttering silence. 'But with all due respect, Colonel,' his tone clearly implying he had no respect for his boss whatsoever, 'whatever it is, it's going to be crap when compared to my potential earnings from the army for the next twenty years, and you know it.'

'But you'll get another job, have another career.'

'I don't *want* another job. I want this one.' He stopped. He sounded petulant and he felt his emotions were on the brink of getting out of control. And no way was he going to lose it in front of Rayner. 'If you'll excuse me, Colonel, I ought to go and tell Susie. I think she should get to hear of this before the regimental grapevine gets to her first.' Mike replaced his beret on his head and, with a perfunctory salute, left the office.

'Mike...?' Andy began, as Mike swept through his office, his expression thunderous.

'Not now, Andy,' Mike snapped at him, over his shoulder.

Andy stared after him in bewilderment and wondered what the hell had gone on between him and the colonel.

Susie heard the door slam and the sound of her husband's footsteps thump along the hall.

'Mike? You're home earl—' The rest of the sentence was forgotten when she saw the look on her husband's face as he pushed open the sitting room door. 'Dear God, what on earth is the matter?'

Mike stared at her, his mouth working.

'Mike?'

'Redundant. They're making me redundant.'

'But...but they can't.'

'Apparently, they can.' For a second, Susie thought he was going to cry, but then he straightened his back and took a deep breath. 'The CO told me a few minutes ago.'

Susie stared past him as she tried to take in the news. 'When? When will you have to leave?'

Mike shrugged. 'I don't know, I didn't ask. I had to get out of his office. If I'd stayed there to ask questions I think I might have been tempted to punch him.' He slumped into an armchair. 'Arrogant, fucking bastard.'

'Oh, darling.' She knew her husband hated Rayner, but she hadn't thought it was this bad.

'You know what he's like. He didn't give a toss about me. He's only ever been out for his career, worrying about his own back. I've never liked him, never trusted him. Right back when I first came across him at Sandhurst I always thought he was a slimy shit.'

'Mike!'

'Come off it, Susie. You know as well as I do what he's

5

like. He's hell-bent on getting to the top and he doesn't care one iota about who he has to trample on to get there. I wouldn't be the least bit surprised if I found out he'd actually put my name forward for redundancy.'

'Surely not.'

'I wouldn't put it past him. Of course he gave me a load of bollocks about being devastated that my name was on the list. Well, I can tell you something... he didn't look fucking devastated.'

Susie nodded. 'Do you think that if Tony Notley had still been in charge he would have fought to keep you?'

'I dunno.' Mike put his elbows on his knees and rested his chin on his hands. 'And to think about all the years I've given to the army, all the loyalty... and for what? All the shit that we've had to put up with, the postings, the short tours, the separation, the crap housing and then they kick me in the teeth with this.'

'How long have you got left?'

'Dunno, told you, I didn't ask. A few months. Well, one thing's for sure, from now till I go, they're not getting anything out of me. From here to the end I'll be spending my days in the office sorting out my future and my next job. Much as this'll put a burden on Seb and the others in the company they'll just have to get over it. As far as I'm concerned the army can sod off.'

Susie nodded. Why should he carry on busting a gut for an organisation that had done this to him? 'They can shove those committees that I'm on too. In fact, first thing in the morning I shall take great pleasure in going round to Camilla Rayner's and dumping the files in her lap.'

'So,' said Mike, 'I suppose I need to start looking for jobs and you'd better get out there and start house-hunting. Where do you fancy living?'

'Here,' said Susie, without hesitation. 'Our friends are here. It'll be bad enough having to start over without losing all our friends too.'

'Fair point,' said Mike. 'I'd better find out how quickly we need to get our act together and how much I'm going to get. One thing's for sure, unless I get a staggeringly well-paid job, we won't be able to afford the fees for Browndown.'

'We'll have to take the twins out of boarding school? But they're so happy there.'

'I suppose we could ask if there are any grants or bursaries going...'

Susie got to her feet. 'I suppose we could.' She didn't like the idea of asking for charity. It was all a bit demeaning.

'Your parents couldn't tide us over...' Mike's voice faded into silence before he finished the sentence properly. He pretty much knew the answer.

Susie shook her head. 'You know how tight things are for them with interest rates being so low; their savings are hardly bringing them in any income at all. And Mum is still thinking about moving back to the UK and if they do it'll take every last penny they have. I always thought going to live in Spain was a mistake.' She sighed heavily. It certainly had been a mistake in her view, but not as bad as the one Mike's parents had made, investing in a dodgy equity release scheme, which had meant that they'd died with hardly a penny to their name, not even the value of their house. But now wasn't the moment to rake all that up again. She dropped the subject. 'I'm going to make us a cuppa. Things always look better over a nice cup of tea. Well,' she smiled ruefully, 'less ghastly, maybe.'

Mike looked at her. 'I tell you, this is an occasion when I really regret being on the wagon. The temptation to hit the gin...'

'I know,' said Susie. 'But it won't help or change things.' Besides, there wasn't anything to drink in the house anyway – nothing alcoholic, at any rate. They hadn't had a drop of the hard stuff in the house for a couple of years now – not since that episode when she and Mike had been so pissed the girls, left very much to their own devices, had found one of Mike's more dubious 'adult' DVDs they'd failed to hide properly. The twins had then copied it and flogged the copies to their friends at prep school. The fallout from that affair had been what had finally convinced Susie and Mike to sign the pledge, once and for all.

She went into the kitchen and plugged in the kettle. Christ, it wasn't just Mike who wanted a drink, she did too. Good job they had none in the house. It was all very well staying strong on the outside but on the inside her willpower was crumbling to bits.

Mike had followed her and was leaning against the doorjamb. 'Why me, Susie, why me?'

He stared at her as if by doing so the answer would magically materialise but Susie couldn't think of a reason – or not one she wanted to admit to him...or herself. Maybe those years when her drinking had been pretty much out of control had put a black mark against Mike's name. Nothing had been said officially, that much she was sure of, but the army's rumour machine was second to none. Maybe the word had got about, reached the ears of people in high places...

'Tea or coffee?'

'I don't want fucking tea, I want a drink.'

Susie shook her head. 'We mustn't...' Although, God knew, she was gagging for one too.

Mike rubbed his face with his hand. 'No...no, you're right, tea's fine. Sorry.' He paused and gave her a tight-lipped smile. 'Just a bit overwrought here. This doesn't rank as one of my better days.'

'So, who else is for the chop?'

Mike pulled out a chair from under the kitchen table and plonked down onto it. 'Didn't ask that either, but when I came out of Rayner's office there wasn't a queue of other officers waiting for their turn to hear the glad tidings, so it might just be me.'

'It can't be, that would be *so* unfair. God knows but there are some officers in this battalion who are a complete waste of space.' Mike nodded in agreement – his own second in command was a case in point, and everyone knew it. She got a couple of mugs out of the cupboard above the counter. 'Can you appeal?'

'I don't know but I'll have a go, though. It isn't as if I've got anything to lose. What's the worst they can do? Sack me?' Mike laughed without mirth. 'I know one thing, though, I've had it with Rayner. If he wants me to do anything, *anything at all*, he can shove it.'

Susie wondered if that was altogether wise; after all, the CO would still be the man to write Mike's final confidential report and give him references. However satisfying it would be to piss off Jack Rayner, it mightn't be the best course of action. But given the mood Mike was in, Susie decided it would be a waste of time to point this out. Maybe later, when he'd calmed down a little.

Maddy Fanshaw was bathing the children when her husband, Seb, got home from work. She heard the front door slam followed by him bounding up the stairs as she lifted her youngest, Rose, out of the tub and wrapped her in a towel.

'You'll never guess,' said Seb as he stood by the bathroom door.

'Never guess what?' said Maddy as she levered herself to her feet and then sat on the edge of the bath to dry Rose.

'Mike Collins.'

'What about him?'

Seb drew a hand across his throat theatrically as he said, 'He's got the chop.'

'Don't be silly,' said Maddy, rubbing Rose's fine blonde curls. Rose giggled and squealed with pleasure and was rewarded with a kiss from her mother on the top of her fluffy head.

'God's honest. He went to see the CO just after lunch, came back to the office to pick up his briefcase, snarled at everyone and then stormed off home. I had to go and see Andy Bailey later about a cock-up on the duty officer rota and he told me what was behind it all.'

Maddy stopped drying Rose and stared at her husband. 'Hell's teeth,' she whispered.

'That was pretty much my reaction.'

'But why?'

Seb shrugged. 'Well...' He made a drinking gesture with his hand.

Maddy shook her head. 'Surely not. They've been on the wagon for yonks now.'

Seb shook his head. 'But if it's on his record...'

Maddy put Rose on the changing mat on top of the bathroom cupboard and deftly fitted her with a clean nappy. Then she grabbed a babygro and started threading Rose's arms and legs into the right holes. 'Scary to think something like that can come back to bite you on the bum though, isn't it.' Behind her, their son Nathan splashed noisily in the water. Maddy handed the baby to Seb and lifted out Rose's big brother and pulled the plug. The bathwater slurped noisily down the drain. 'Come on, young man. Time to get you in your jim-jams.' She wrapped him in a towel and cuddled him.

'It was hardly a momentary aberration, though, was it? I mean, they were knocking back the sauce like there was no tomorrow for years.'

'I wouldn't know – you've known them much longer than me.'

'Take it from me, they were.'

'Even so, you've always said you've got a lot of time for Mike.'

'He was never drunk at work – or at least, I'm pretty certain he wasn't. He was...*is*...a bl—' Maddy shot him a warning glance. Nathan had got to the stage when he hoovered up new words into his vocabulary like a Dyson on steroids. 'A *blooming* good officer.'

Still holding Nate, wrapped in his towel, Maddy got to her feet. 'You get Nathan ready for bed and read him a story. I'll put Rose down. We can talk some more over supper.'

Twenty minutes later Maddy was in the kitchen stirring Bolognese sauce to go with the pasta, two glasses of gin and tonic on the table and the radio playing some music quietly when Seb came in and looked at the drinks.

'Makes you wonder if we oughtn't to cut back a bit,' he said.

'I don't think we're in the Collinses' league. Not yet, anyway.'

'Maybe not. Cheers.' Seb picked up a glass with a grin and took a swig.

'So who do you think will take over from Mike as company commander?'

'I don't really care, just as long as they don't promote Craig to fill his shoes.'

Maddy took her drink and stared at Seb. 'Craig? No way.' Craig was the B Company 2IC and was, by common consent, an old woman and a waste of space. He was always flapping about health and safety, about Queen's Regulations, about doing things by the book and, above everything else, had no sense of humour whatsoever.

'He *is* the second in command.'

Maddy raised her eyebrows. 'I suppose. But even so...'

'No, it's unlikely. But I wonder who they'll pick to take his place?'

'We'd better just hope it's someone we like,' said Maddy, sipping her drink thoughtfully.

'We needn't worry about that though, just yet. It'll be months before Mike and Susie have to leave.'

'I'm not sure if that doesn't make things worse. It'll be like having some terrible dark cloud hanging over us – like some sort of terminal prognosis.' Maddy sighed. 'And what'll I say when I next see her? Poor Susie. She must be gutted.'

By the following evening, as Mike had pretty much predicted, the regimental grapevine had disseminated the news of the redundancies throughout the battalion. The living-in officers were gathered around the bar mulling over the casualties on the list. Naturally, Mike Collins was the main candidate for the 'why him?' speculation but there were others whose numbers were up: a sergeant major from C Company, the RQMS, Sergeant McManners who was the officers' mess manager, some corporals and half a dozen privates who had outstayed their welcome and who had failed to get promoted – or who *had* been promoted and had been busted once or twice too often. The atmosphere was subdued as everyone came to terms with the fact that while they had planned on a career for life in uniform, the army wasn't necessarily in agreement.

'So,' said Samantha Lewis, the REME officer in charge of the battalion's workshop, 'I suppose all of you lot,' she gestured to her mess mates who were all junior officers serving in the 1st Battalion of the Hertfordshire Regiment, 'are waiting to see who gets promoted into Mike's place. I mean,' she said, taking a sip of white wine, 'isn't this a case of an ill wind...?'

A couple of the men shuffled uneasily and it seemed to Sam that was exactly what they thought.

'Not really,' said James Rosser, who was one of Sam's best friends and had been since she'd arrived in the battalion some eighteen months previously. 'Anyway, knowing the army, they'll probably parachute an officer in from our sister battalion. You know what the postings branch is like – it seems to be their *raison d'être* to piss off the maximum number of officers as often as possible.'

Sam laughed. 'Cynical but true. Anyway, it's nothing to do with me since my little empire is almost autonomous, but I just hope for everyone else that whoever they choose is popular with the troops.'

Chapter 2

Horrified by the bombshell their parents had just dropped, Ella and Katie Collins, home from boarding school for the weekend, stared at each other and then at their mum and dad.

'It's only a possibility,' said Susie, placatingly. 'If Daddy gets a really cracking job then we'll be able to keep you at Browndown. But, darlings, the fees are ridiculous and without the army's help...'

Ella narrowed her eyes. Both she and her twin sister, for eleven, were remarkably astute. 'So where *would* we go to school?'

'Sweetie, it depends on where we buy a house.'

'You know what I mean,' she snapped.

'It'd have to be the local school,' said their father.

'You mean a comp,' said Katie with a sneer.

'There are some very nice comps. Honestly,' said Susie.

'Really?' said the twins in unison and in disbelief. Then they looked at each other again and left the room, slamming the door behind them.

'That went well,' said Susie, quietly.

Mike sighed. 'We knew they wouldn't like the news. Maybe we shouldn't have told them. Or not just yet anyway.'

'Like they wouldn't have heard about your redundancy

from other kids on the patch? And then they'd have done the sum and worked out for themselves that their chances of staying at boarding school were minimal. Besides, if they're not being moved from pillar to post, why would they even *need* to board? I suppose there's just a possibility we might be able to afford to get them into a half-decent private day school.'

'The fees are still crippling for anything that's worth its salt. Anyway, it's better they are faced with the worst-case scenario so if things aren't quite as bleak they'll be pleased rather than horribly disappointed. But it might not come to that. It isn't a completely impossible idea that they'll be able to stay put.' Mike tried to look hopeful.

Susie sighed. 'Come off it, Mike. Without the army's support we'll have to find over fifty thousand a year of taxed income. I know you're a clever and resourceful man, darling, but will you really be able to land a job that'll earn that sort of dosh? And of *course* I'm going to get back into harness but a year at a finishing school, learning to cook and how to get in and out of a sports car gracefully, isn't the best qualification in the world. We have to be realistic and accept that our lifestyle might be very different in the not too distant future.'

Mike smiled reassuringly. 'We'll muddle through.'

'But that's just it, Mike. I don't *want* to muddle through. I want order and security and...' Susie felt a pricking at the back of her nose and tears start to form in her eyes. She stopped and breathed deeply to regain her self-control. Now was *not* the moment to feel sorry for herself or go blaming Mike, or the system, or her parents for squandering her inheritance with a hare-brained scheme to up sticks and bugger off to Spain, or his for getting duped by a smarmy so-called financial adviser. It wouldn't do anyone any good and would just be a pointless exercise. They were where they were.

And furthermore, the last thing she should do right now was make Mike feel worse; as if he didn't have enough on his plate he certainly didn't need a dollop of guilt, ladled on by her, to add to everything else. Susie might have her faults but she was loyal and supportive and she loved her husband deeply.

The doorbell rang.

'What now?' Susie pushed herself out of her chair and went to answer it.

'Maddy. How nice,' she lied, when she saw who the caller was. She liked Maddy, she really did, but Susie didn't feel like receiving visitors. It was hard enough holding herself together in front of her family without having to put on an act for her neighbours too.

'Susie, I've heard the news and I want to tell you how shocked I am.'

Susie raised her eyebrows. 'I dare say I was more shocked.'

'God, yes, of *course* you were. I didn't mean...' Maddy ground to a halt. 'I just want you to know that Seb and I think the whole thing is appallingly unfair and if there's anything we can do...'

Susie held the door wide to allow Maddy to step inside. 'Maddy, much as I appreciate your support I don't think there's much you *can* do.'

'No...well. But you know what I mean.'

'I do. But, and let's be brutally honest here, I bet it's tempered by a large dose of "thank God it's them not us".'

'Susie, of course I didn't think that.' Maddy held her friend's gaze for a second or two before dropping her eyes. 'Well, it never crossed my mind that the redundancies would include any officers from here. And it was awful when I found out that it did and that you and Mike were the casualties.'

Susie led the way into the sitting room.

'Hi, Mike,' said Maddy. 'I just came to say how sorry I am about the news.'

'Tea?' offered Susie.

Maddy nodded. 'But only if you and Mike are having one.'

Susie went into the kitchen.

'Have a seat,' said Mike.

Maddy perched on a nearby chair.

'Thanks for coming round,' said Mike. 'Susie and I are feeling a bit bereft at the moment, as you might imagine. Being told you're being made redundant is a bit like being told you've got a terminal illness – people don't know what to say, so they ignore you rather than risk saying the wrong thing. Which is daft. As far as I can see the only "wrong thing" you might be able to say is "hooray and good riddance".'

Maddy grinned. 'No one would say that.'

'I think Jack Rayner had to hold back.'

'Yeah, but that's Rayner for you, isn't it,' said Maddy.

'Indeed.'

'Seb's gutted.'

'I suppose he doesn't fancy getting used to a new boss.'

'No, he likes you and the way you do things. Besides, he's worried it might be Craig.'

'No way. He's already over-promoted, in my opinion.'

Maddy nodded. 'And I'll miss having Susie as a neighbour.'

'We're not going just yet.'

'No, I know, but all the same...'

'Thank you, it's appreciated. Susie and I were thinking we might try and stay in the area. At least if we do that we can still see our old muckers from time to time.'

Susie reappeared with a tray of mugs. 'And house prices aren't completely ridiculous around here.'

'Although the job prospects might be a bit iffy,' said Mike.

'Still, I could easily commute to a bigger town... Salisbury or Trowbridge or somewhere.'

'But you'll find something,' said Maddy, accepting a mug from Susie.

'Yes,' said Mike. 'Of course I will.' But his words showed far more confidence than his tone of voice suggested.

After the hiatus of the news of the redundancies, life at 1 Herts settled down for the ensuing weeks. Speculation as to who would fill the vacancies ground to a halt and, for those officers and men not directly affected, the news receded into the background. In fact, for the vast majority of the 1 Herts' soldiers who subscribed to an I'm-all-right-Jack mentality, the whole business was largely forgotten. However, this was not the case in the Collins' household where matters were getting increasingly tense.

Mike had been on a course run by a recruiting agency designed to teach the redundant officers the best way to present their CVs, how to market themselves, how to write really excellent letters when applying for jobs and how to conduct themselves in interviews. It was, Mike had told Susie on his return, mostly basic common sense but it had been useful all the same. Armed with his new skills and fired with enthusiasm, Mike had scoured the appointments sections of the quality papers and fired off loads of applications. And now they were waiting for the replies.

Mike returned home from work at lunchtime as he usually did. After dropping his beret onto the hall table, he picked up his post; three letters, personally addressed to him so not spam. His heart rate quickened; he knew what these would be. Eagerly he ripped open the first envelope.

Dear Major Collins, We regret to inform you...

Fuck. He opened the next.

Dear Major Collins, While Bingham and Co appreciate your eagerness to work for this company, it is with regret...

Shit. He opened the last.

Dear Major Collins, We are sorry...

Bollocks.

He felt his shoulders slump. He had been sure he'd been in with a cracking shot for all of those positions. He'd had the qualifications, the experience, the know-how. And he wasn't over the hill. He was still young; he was only in his mid-thirties, for heaven's sake. Wasn't that the perfect age; young enough to still be open to new ideas and working practices but old enough to have plenty of experience? Angrily he screwed up the letters and stamped into the kitchen.

Susie looked up from the pan of tomato soup she was stirring. She saw the look on Mike's face. 'What's happened now?'

'Rejections. Three of them.'

Susie walked over to her husband and gave him a hug. 'There's other fish in the sea. It's early days yet.'

Mike sighed. 'I just... Well, I thought I'd be beating offers off with a stick.'

'You will be, I'm sure of it. So who's turned you down?'

Mike uncrumpled the letters and smoothed them out on the table. 'This lot.'

Susie glanced at the letterheads. 'Obviously companies with no taste and possibly worse management skills. You've probably had a lucky escape.'

She turned back to the stove and began to dish out the soup. 'Anyway, I've been thinking...' she said as she ladled their lunch into a couple of bowls.

'And?'

'You know McManners, the mess manager, is being given the heave-ho too?' Mike nodded. 'Supposing I applied to do his job.'

Mike shook his head. 'No.'

Susie put both bowls on the table and sat down. 'Why not? I understand basic accounting having run the thrift shop, I understand about catering and, God knows, I understand about 1 Herts. I'd be perfect.'

'It wouldn't be appropriate. It's not a job for an officer's wife.'

Susie raised an eyebrow. 'I hate to tell you this, sweetie, but when this job falls vacant I won't *be* an officer's wife.'

Mike stared at her, his spoon halfway to his mouth. 'That was a bit of a low blow.'

'Don't be so touchy, it's the truth.' She stared at Mike. 'I'm going to apply.'

'I'd rather you didn't.'

'It's a job. It's income. Anyway, I may not get it.' Susie tucked into her soup.

Mike considered what Susie had said about not getting the job and wondered if he could make sure she didn't. It wouldn't be ethical but it might be possible. It was a sergeant's job, not one for a major's wife. It would be demeaning. And how would she cope with complaints from junior officers – officers who had once held her in esteem and now she'd be their paid lackey? He turned his attention back to his soup and carried on eating. Not worth kicking off a row about it now, the job hadn't even been advertised. Maybe when it had been and *if* Susie applied for it, maybe he'd try and get her to see his point of view then. And if she didn't? Well, maybe then he'd try and kibosh her plans.

‘You're late,’ said Maddy as Seb arrived home for lunch fifteen minutes after she'd been expecting him. She was in the kitchen clearing up the mess left from the kids' lunches.

‘Had to see Rayner.’

‘Poor you. What about?’

‘That's the thing...’

Maddy looked at him expectantly. ‘What's the thing?’

‘I'm getting acting rank and taking over from Mike.’

Maddy's eyes widened. ‘You! Bloody hell. No, I mean congratulations and clever, clever you.’ She put down the dishcloth and gave her husband a kiss. ‘Craig must be pissed off. He must have thought he was in with a shout.’

‘It's not common knowledge yet, so don't say anything.’

‘Does Mike know?’

Seb shook his head. ‘Rayner's telling him this afternoon.’

Maddy took a loaf out of the bread bin and began buttering slices to make them both a sandwich. ‘How do you think he'll take it?’

Seb shrugged. ‘Badly, I should think.’

‘You reckon?’

‘It's a bit of a kick in the teeth, in my view. I'm not exactly his equal, am I? I think if he'd been getting replaced by a senior major he might feel a bit more valued but as it is...’

‘Oh God, and Susie won't be happy either, will she, with me usurping her as the OC's wife.’

Seb shook his head. ‘No, I shouldn't think so.’

Susie had spent the afternoon in Warminster trawling round estate agents. She knew what she wanted: four bedrooms, gas central heating, south-facing garden, off-street parking, good local schools and within a ten mile radius of where she lived now. She was hardly asking for a ridiculous amount, was she? And it seemed not because with the redundancy package they would have a decent deposit, and with Mike's projected earnings there were a fair few properties to choose from. She came home laden with particulars of possible houses to show Mike. She parked the car outside the house and let herself in. She could hear movement coming from the kitchen.

'Mike?'

'Where have you been?'

He sounded in a right grump, she thought. She wondered what had happened now. She walked down the hall, into the kitchen and dumped the sheaf of papers on the table.

'Just popped into town see what the estate agents have got to offer.' The look on Mike's face told her he didn't want to talk about houses. 'What's the matter, hon?'

'The last fucking straw.'

'What?'

'I've just been told who is replacing me.'

'Not Craig, surely.'

'No, although I almost think that would be better than who *is* getting the job.'

'And that is?'

'Seb.'

'Seb? But he's a babe in arms. How can he possibly command a company? He hasn't even gone to Staff College yet. And Maddy is hardly OC's wife material. I mean she's a nice kid but...' Words failed her.

'I know.' Mike looked at her bleakly. 'It seems to me that the army thinks so little of me that I can be replaced by someone who has got almost no experience and zero seniority. Well, thank you very much. And it's pissed off Craig so much he's talking about resigning. Honestly, if he goes, it'll be like the Night of the Long Knives in B Company.'

Susie gave her husband a hug. 'With Seb emerging out of the chaos and carnage smelling of roses.'

'I know it's not his fault, said Mike, morosely, 'but with this sort of HR bloodbath going on it makes me think I'm better off out of it.'

'Maybe.' Susie didn't look convinced.

She was about to put the kettle on to make them both a cup of tea when the phone rang. She picked up the kitchen extension and an unknown voice asked to speak to Major Collins. 'For you,' she said, handing the receiver to Mike.

She listened to Mike's side of the conversation with half an ear as she made the tea. Whatever it was, it sounded quite serious and Mike didn't look happy. Wordlessly she put his tea in front of him and waited patiently for the call to end.

'What was that all about?' she asked.

Mike stared at her. He opened his mouth and then closed it again. Susie felt worried.

'It can't be that bad, surely?' said Susie, hiding her fears with a light tone.

'I...I don't know how to put this.'

'Put what?'

'That was the mortgage broker.'

'And?'

Mike swallowed and looked down at the table. 'And...and they won't give me a mortgage.'

'What? Why?'

'It's my credit rating.'

'What about it?'

'That's the thing, Susie.' He still wasn't looking at her. 'I've found it a bit tough to meet the kids' school fees on a couple of occasions so I bunged them on a credit card. And then...and then I couldn't make the repayments so I transferred the debt to another card to give myself some breathing space.' He glanced up at her. 'I never meant to let it get out of hand.' He stared at Susie beseechingly. 'But I honestly thought it wasn't that bad. That it wouldn't have an impact.'

'How bad? How out of hand?' Susie tried to keep calm.

'Twenty thousand, give or take.'

'Pounds?'

'It's not fucking Smarties, is it?' he snapped. 'Sorry. Sorry, Susie.' He rubbed his face with his hand. 'Sorry,' he said a third time. 'I'm a bit stressed.'

'You're a bit stressed?' Susie breathed in and out twice before she said, 'Shit.'

Twenty thousand pounds of debt and no mortgage. How could he? How fucking could he? She looked at the pile of properties she'd been planning on showing Mike. Not much point in that now. Wordlessly she gathered them up and chucked them in the recycling bin. She wanted to cry. 'Mike, why didn't you tell me? I could have got a job ages ago. I could have earned some money to help out. Once the kids went off to boarding school I could have managed.'

'I thought *I* could manage. I thought *I* could sort it and I didn't want you to worry.'

'No.' She sighed as she bit her tongue. There was no point in getting angry. Neither of them could turn the clock back, so that was that. And he might not have wanted her to worry back then but there was no denying she was bloody worried now.

Silence fell and lengthened. Susie considered their options and decided there were precious few. She sighed as she came to terms with the stark grimness of their position. Finally, she spoke again. 'That's it then. I've got to get that job in the mess.'

'Susie—'

'Don't you *dare* say it isn't appropriate,' Susie snapped, worry, anger and emotion finally getting the better of her. 'We're running out of choices. It's a job I can do and probably do well...if I get it. And if I don't, I'll go and find something else. It may be that the best I can get is as a checkout girl in the Spar but, as things stand, I have to have *some* sort of income if we're going to have a house of our own in the near future.'

Mike looked shamefaced. 'Kick a man while he's down, why don't you?' he muttered.

'Darling, I didn't mean it like that but renting sucks – it's dead money. We have to face reality.'

'And the reality is that I'm a dead weight; no job, no prospects and no credit rating, my wife is being forced to go out to work and I'm being replaced by a man who has no experience and less seniority.'

Susie's heart went out to her husband and she wrapped her arms around him and held him tight.

Chapter 3

Mike sat in his office with the door shut and stared sightlessly out of his window. He'd told his office staff that he didn't want to be disturbed under any circumstances and when they saw the look on his face they all knew he meant it.

No job, no credit rating, no boarding school allowance for his daughters and soon, no roof over his family's head. How had it come to this? he wondered. The feelings of desperation and despair welled up inside him. He'd been so full of hope and ambition when he'd left Sandhurst, then he'd married Susie and they'd produced the twins and still everything seemed perfect. When had it all started to go so drastically wrong?

There was a knock at the door. Angrily he turned towards it.

'Come,' he barked.

Seb put his head around the door.

'Mike?'

'What? I said I didn't want to be disturbed.'

'I know. Sorry.'

'Well?'

'Mike...look, I just want to say that if there's anything, *anything* I can do to help...you only have to ask.'

Mike felt like asking Seb if he had a spare twenty grand to get him out of the hole.

'Really.' It came out in a more sarcastic tone than he meant. Mike shut his eyes and took a breath. 'Sorry, I didn't mean it to sound like that, it's just everything is a bit tricky right now.'

'I can imagine.'

'Really?' This time it came out exactly as Mike intended. 'Seb, you've got an Oxford degree, you've just been given your acting majority at a ridiculously young age, your future is secure, you haven't got twins at a school with fees you can probably no longer afford... No, Seb, I don't think you have can *possibly* imagine what life is like for Susie and me right now.'

Seb looked like he'd been kicked. Well, tough. Mike had too much to worry about without pussyfooting around the feelings of others. And Seb had come into his office when he'd asked *not* to be disturbed. If you stick your head into a lion's mouth you are asking for it to be bitten off.

'The offer stands, Mike. And any time you want me to cover for you in the office, you know, for job interviews and suchlike...'

Ha, job interviews? That was a joke. If Seb only knew how his job hunt was going so far. But best he didn't. Mike liked Seb but he had a suspicion that his subordinate's caring exterior was there to disguise a rather more smug interior. Maybe he was being unfair but it was a feeling he just couldn't shake.

Maddy wheeled Rose into the coffee shop on the High Street and looked about her for her friend. She spotted Jenna sitting in the corner, texting with the thumb of one hand while with the other she rocked the pushchair and lulled her baby.

'Hiya,' said Maddy when she got close enough to call out without fear of waking her own sleeping child.

Jenna looked up and smiled. She glanced down at one-year-old Rose and then across to her own baby – a boy, called Eliot, who was also sleeping.

'Hey, ain't this handy; both of them asleep at the same time. Maybe we can have a good old chinwag without getting interrupted.'

'It would make a great change,' said Maddy. 'So, what can I get you? Skinny latte as usual?'

'It's my turn,' said Jenna.

But Maddy dismissed Jenna's offer with a wave of her hand as she extracted her purse from her handbag hanging on the back of the stroller. She went to place her order with the barista. A few minutes later she was back with their drinks.

'So what's the hot goss?' said Jenna as Maddy seated herself on the sofa next to her.

'Well...' said Maddy. 'You'll never guess...'

'So tell me,' said Jenna sipping her coffee. 'From your expression it's got to be good news so it's not Seb playing fast and loose again.' Jenna was nothing if not blunt.

'Don't,' said Maddy with a grimace. 'Not that he'd dare, not a second time.'

'So?'

'Well, it *is* Seb, but this time it's a good thing.'

'Oh, come on, Maddy, quit with the riddles. Spit it out.'

'He's going to command B Company.'

Jenna's eyes widened. 'Get away.'

'Seriously.'

'I mean, but *why*? No, strike that, it sounds so rude but isn't he a bit...well, young?'

'I know. It's come as a complete surprise but I can't say I'm unhappy because it's quite a pay hike. Of course,' added Maddy, 'we can't be certain that he'll keep the rank or get the job on a permanent basis, but what the hell? It's still an unexpected bonus.'

'Lucky old you. What does Susie think about it?'

Maddy picked up her cappu and stared at the foam. 'I dunno. I haven't seen her for a few days.'

'You're avoiding her, then?'

Maddy nodded, guiltily. 'Wouldn't you?' she said quietly. 'I mean, it isn't like Seb and I angled for this. It was a complete bolt from the blue, but Susie has enough to cope with without trying to look happy on our account. Especially when it's come at her and Mike's expense.'

'Tricky. But you've got to face her at some point. You can't keep avoiding her – not when she was so good to you when Seb was...'

Maddy groaned. 'I know, I know. But what can I say? "Hey, Susie, I know life is shitting all over you, but do you want to come and help Seb and me pop the champagne corks?"'

'No, but you could explain that you'd rather it hadn't had to happen this way.'

'Maybe.' Maddy wasn't convinced. 'But you're right. I can't keep ignoring her. Better I go and see her and face the music – or whatever – sooner rather than later. If I leave it, it'll only get worse and harder.'

'Attagirl,' said Jenna. 'Hey, though, fancy you being the OC's wife. Think of all those committees you'll get to sit on.'

Maddy groaned again. 'Don't. Camilla Rayner's already been round to welcome me to the...' She did aerial quotation

29

marks with her fingers. '...Senior officers' wives' club. I mean, I ask you?'

'You lucky, lucky cow,' said Jenna, barely controlling her laughter.

'And she's already told me I'm going to be her deputy on the new community centre project.'

Jenna hooted. 'Oh, this gets better and better.'

'I don't mind doing my bit for the battalion, truly I don't, but Camilla is such a patronising bitch. Every time she speaks to me I feel as if I'm in primary school and I'm about to have to go and stand in the naughty corner. It's not her fault that she once *was* a primary school teacher but it gets on my tits that she treats everyone she meets like they're about five. And that sing-song voice of hers...'

'I know what you mean. So effing twee and babyish.' Jenna took a slurp of her latte. 'There's a lot to be said for living off the patch – I can avoid most of that sort of shit. Not that Mrs Rayner would have anything to do with the likes of me.'

'Wish it was the same for me,' said Maddy, gloomily.

'Still, if you want me to look after Rose while you have to cope with all of Camilla's crap, you just sing out. Anything I can do to help...'

'Thanks, Jen, you're a brick. But, as I'm going to *have* to do stuff to please Camilla, one of the first things I'm going to do is to try and get something sorted to please me too! I want to try and organise a proper crèche for the littlies, so the wives don't always have to rely on favours from neighbours if they want an hour to get their hair done or go shopping without dragging their kids along too.'

'I'm all in favour of that,' said Jenna with feeling. 'Especially the bit about having "an hour to go and get their hair done".' She was, apart from being a friend of Maddy's, also her hairdresser and the thought of anything that made it easier for her customers to make appointments was very appealing.

Susie pulled up on the wide gravel sweep outside the imposing grey-stone, Jacobean front of Browndown School and yanked on the handbrake. She was feeling nervous. Since Mike had broken the news to the girls that they might have to leave Browndown there had been a smidgen of hope that it might not come to pass – but since the bombshell about his debts, all hope had been totally and utterly snuffed out. And now Susie had the task of formally giving Miss Marcham, the head, official notice that the girls would not be returning in the autumn, before she collected her daughters and took them home for the summer half-term. Unless, of course, the school fancied offering the girls a stonking great bursary each.

She got out of the car and gazed at the beautiful building. She and Mike had chosen this school with such care; a place they both felt would nurture and educate the twins in equal measure before they went off to university in some six years' time. She'd taken a look at the local comp during the previous week and the austere brick, glass and concrete of that place was nothing like this.

She sighed. The girls would have to get used to it, that was all. There was nothing wrong with their new school – but on the other hand there wasn't much right with it either; not when compared to this place. Never had the old adage 'you get what you pay for' been more true. Twenty-five grand a year *each* at Browndown, or free at the comp. And didn't the price difference show.

Susie shoved thoughts of how the girls would cope in the far less rarefied environment of their new school to the back of her mind and made her way towards the head's office. The school bursar showed her in.

After an exchange of greeting she took the chair offered to her, opted for coffee, which the head ordered from her secretary via an intercom, and then the pair made polite but meaningless chit-chat about the weather and the impending holidays before the secretary appeared carrying a tray laden with delicate porcelain cups and saucers, a brimming cafetière and a plate of shortbread.

'So,' said Miss Marcham, as she handed Susie her cup, 'I gathered from your phone call that this isn't an entirely social visit. Not,' she added, 'that I don't always appreciate the chance to chat to the parents of my girls.'

'No. I mean yes,' said Susie. She put her cup down on the edge of the desk. 'The thing is that Mike...Major Collins...is being made redundant from the army. Without the army's contribution to the fees, the sums don't stack up. There's no easy way of saying this but we just can't afford to keep the girls here.'

Miss Marcham was impassive. 'I see.'

There was a silence. Susie wondered how she might broach the subject of the school handing out some sort of cash to keep the girls on. Maybe if she started by telling Miss Marcham how much the twins loved being at Browndown.

'I suppose,' said Miss Marcham, 'you are hoping I might be in a position to offer the girls a bursary or a scholarship.'

'I...well...' Susie smiled ingratiatingly. This was exactly what she was hoping for. She felt a little bubble of relief expand in her chest because she hadn't had to bring the idea of getting a charitable handout up herself. 'Well...it might make the difference,' she said. She gave Miss Marcham a beaming smile. A scholarship might make *all* the difference.

'Frankly...' said Miss Marcham, in a tone that made Susie's smile turn into a rictus grin. She lowered her glasses and fixed Susie with a look that made her wonder if she was about to be given detention for being insolent. 'Frankly, given the twins' behaviour this last term, I'm quite relieved they're going.'

Susie had thought that Mike telling her he had twenty grand's worth of debt had been the worst moment in her life. She'd been wrong – this was.

'I'm sorry.' Susie shook her head. 'I'm not with you.' She swallowed as she regained her composure. 'I'm sorry, Miss Marcham, I don't know what you mean.'

'I think you do, Mrs Collins. The girls arrived here from their prep school with a fairly dubious report.' Miss Marcham gave Susie a significant look. 'Their behaviour there left a lot to be desired and matters haven't improved here. They seem to think that because there are two of them they deserve to be treated differently from everyone else, that the rules don't apply to them, but let me tell you, they do.'

'But...' Susie felt her face flaring. Of course there had been the episode with the porn, but it had been a one off and they hadn't made a habit of doing that sort of thing. And they'd been punished. Susie felt her face burn even hotter as the memory of the event rolled through her mind. Not that the porn had been that bad, not really. Just a mucky video really. Nothing illegal...'What they did was naughty,' conceded Susie, 'but it was a one-off. It wasn't criminal.'

'No? Selling pornographic DVDs to their fellow pupils? Exposing nine-year-olds to *filth*? That might not be criminal in your eyes but it's a very close-run thing in mine.'

Susie felt her face redden further. She wanted to squirm. Instead she said, 'But we've been repeatedly told how bright they are.'

'Really? They lack focus, they lack self-discipline and they question everything – including authority.'

'But that's good. It shows they are naturally curious.'

'It shows they have no respect for their elders and betters,' snapped back Miss Marcham. 'And since they joined us they might not be selling dodgy DVDs to their classmates but their teachers tell me they are frequently rude, opinionated, their work is often below standard and they are disruptive. I gave them the benefit of the doubt in their first term; lots of girls take a while to settle down, get used to the ethos of this school, but during this last term there has been no obvious improvement and frankly I am beginning to doubt they'll ever fit in. They are *not*, Mrs Collins, Browndown material.'

Susie was lost for words. Rude? Opinionated? Her daughters?

Shit.

She sat in silence for a few seconds as she gathered herself. She knew they could be difficult but weren't they popular? Didn't the fact that they'd had loads of invitations to spend exeats at friends' houses prove that? They weren't *that* bad, surely? Except Miss Marcham and the other staff seemed to think they were. She took a deep breath and said, as calmly as she could, 'Maybe this parting of the ways is for the best then.'

'Correct. Naturally we, at Browndown, will continue to give your girls the best possible education and we will look after their needs both socially and physically until they leave but, to be honest, if you hadn't come to me to tell me their stay here is being curtailed I would have felt forced to approach you to suggest that it should be.'

Susie drove the car home in virtual silence while, strapped into the back seat, her two daughters chatted and gossiped as if driving meant their mother had been struck deaf. Susie listened to their tales of their own exploits and those of their peers and nothing they spoke about seemed to corroborate what Miss Marcham had said. She longed to tackle the girls with the accusations that had been levelled at them about their behaviour but she was already upset and she suspected that passing on Miss Marcham's comments would only upset the twins too. What was the point in ruining their day as well as her own?

A couple of hours later she drew into the drive by their quarter. Across the road she spotted Maddy, planting out trays of summer bedding plants in an effort to make the dreary beds that framed the patch of moth-eaten grass look more appealing. On the lawn Rose was sitting placidly on a travel rug playing with some toys in the warm May sunshine and Nathan was zooming up and down the drive in his red and yellow plastic pedal car. As she got out of her own vehicle she heard Maddy call, 'That's far enough, Nate sweetie. Come back to Mummy, please.'

The sight of Maddy playing happy families when her own was falling to bits, caused something to snap inside Susie.

'Go in and say hello to Daddy,' she instructed Ella and Katie, as she opened the front door to let the girls in. Then she stormed across the road.

'Well, look at you,' she sneered.

Maddy looked up, startled by the aggressive tone.

'Susie?'

'Isn't this cosy; the perfect officer's wife and her perfect kids, making her bloody garden just perfect.'

Maddy's forehead crinkled and she shielded her eyes from the sun as she looked up at Susie. 'Susie?' she repeated.

'Don't you "Susie" me like I'm some sort of friend; not after what you and Seb have done to my family.'

'But Susie—'

'But *nothing*. Would he jump into Mike's coffin as quickly?'

'But Seb's promotion wasn't our idea. We didn't angle for it, we didn't ask for it—'

'You didn't turn it down, though, did you?' she snarled.

Maddy got to her feet. 'Like that would have changed what's happening to you?' She sounded perplexed and angry. 'Your situation is horrible but it isn't anything to do with Seb and me. Don't take it out on us just because you've been dealt a dud hand.' She glared at Susie.

'After all I did for you.'

'I know, and I am grateful, I always will be, but what good would it have done if Seb *had* turned down the promotion? The army wouldn't have given Mike his job back.'

'It was still a kick in the teeth for Mike. I mean, Seb? Seb of all people, taking over from Mike. Come on, Maddy, even you must see it.'

Maddy shook her head, and scooped up Rose, then she pulled Nathan out of his pedal car. The child yelled in protest.

'Time to go in.' Her voice was falsely bright for the benefit of her children as she carted them indoors, Nathan protesting loudly.

'Run away from the truth, Maddy,' Susie shouted at Maddy as she shut her front door.

Susie felt the fight in her fade as suddenly as it had arisen. What had she done? Maddy had been her best friend and now…Susie shut her eyes. If Maddy never spoke to her again she wouldn't blame her. Wearily, she turned away and made her way back across the road to her own quarter. She'd have to apologise but first she needed to give Maddy some space, let everyone calm down a bit.

Maddy was close to tears as she poured out weak squash for her children. What had she done to deserve that onslaught? And from Susie? By her knees Nathan was tugging at her trousers and demanding to go back out. Back out? That was the last place she was going. No way was she going to risk another unfair and uncalled-for tongue-lashing from her neighbour. Nathan got more insistent, more whiney.

'Oh shush,' she snapped at him. Instantly, Nathan's face crumpled. God, now she was taking her own hurt out on her kids. 'I'm sorry, sweetie.' She knelt down and gave her son a cuddle before handing him his beaker. Then she rummaged in the biscuit tin for a digestive. 'Here,' she said as she thrust the biscuit into his pudgy hand. The tears stopped and he toddled off to the sitting room to find something to play with. Rose, in her high chair, was banging the tray with her palms. Maddy handed her a drink and a biscuit too before she sat at the table and wondered why on earth Susie had lashed out at her like that. She knew things weren't perfect for the Collinses, far from it, and Susie must be stressed out, what with house-hunting and Mike needing to find a job and looking for a school for the girls, but Susie was an army wife – she could cope with all this sort of shit, surely? Maddy shook her head. Maybe it was down to straws and camels' backs. Maybe she ought to go round with some sort of peace offering – show there were no hard feelings, show she understood. But she'd give it a while, let Susie calm down a bit. She wanted to pour oil on troubled waters, not chuck it on an already incendiary situation.

She was still wondering how long to give it when Seb came home from work. She was occupying herself with cooking a chicken fricassee, rather than address how she was going to handle a rapprochement with Susie.

'Hiya, hon,' said Seb as he strolled in, chucking his beret on the hall table.

'Hiya,' she replied.

'Good day?' He gave her a peck on the cheek.

'Oh, all right. Curate's egg, you know...' Maddy wondered about telling Seb about her run-in with Susie but decided against it. Seb had enough on his plate, what with his own tricky situation at work; Mike had given up on doing any work in the office at all and Craig seemed to be working to rule in protest at being passed over for the top job so, from what Maddy could gather, Seb was having to run just to stand still. 'What about your day?' she asked, knowing he'd tell her, which he did.

'...And I've had to bring home a pile of NCOs' confidential reports to finish drafting. I'll have to get on with those after supper.'

'Poor you,' said Maddy. Really, given how hard he was working at the moment, the last thing he needed were any gripes from her.

By the time he'd finished with the lowdown on his day and Maddy had put her casserole in the oven it was time for the children's baths and, after that, any interest Seb might have had in her day had long gone. On the other hand, Maddy mused, she hadn't thought about Susie and that row for the best part of an hour.

It was as Maddy was tidying up the kitchen after supper that the doorbell rang.

'I'll get it,' she called to Seb, who was beavering away at

the confidentials on the dining room table. She shut the dining room door so he'd not get disturbed by their visitor and then opened the front door.

'Oh.' Susie. What now?

Susie smiled at her, somewhat sheepishly. 'Maddy... look...' She thrust a box of posh biscuits towards Maddy. 'Peace offering.'

Maddy felt a wave of relief that Susie wanted to make up, not dish out more awful accusations. 'Oh, Susie. That's not the least bit necessary.'

'I think it is.'

Maddy stepped forward and hugged Susie. 'Shhh,' she said. 'I'd have lashed out if I was going through what you are.'

'But you didn't, did you? Not when...'

'Not when...' Maddy looked over her shoulder at the shut dining room door and dropped her voice to the faintest whisper. 'Not when Seb was shagging Michelle, you mean?' She returned her voice to its normal level. 'I was just about to make Seb and me a coffee. Do you fancy one?'

Susie nodded. 'I'd love one. Actually, I really fancy neat gin but coffee would be just fine.'

Maddy got the kettle on and turned her full attention to her neighbour. 'So what's up?'

Susie sighed and rubbed her face with both hands. 'The girls' headmistress is what's up. I went to see her today to tell her we can't afford to send them back in the autumn.'

'And she kicked off?'

'Au contraire – she put out the flags.'

'She what?'

'She basically told me that if I wasn't taking them away she'd have had them excluded.'

'No!'

39

Susie nodded.

'But...but that's awful.'

'Just when you think you've hit the bottom and things can't get worse...'

For a moment Maddy was lost for words. Then, 'Stuff her, the mean old cow. I shan't send Rose there, that's for sure. *And* I'll tell other people the head is a nasty, bitter old spinster who should be avoided at all costs.'

'I wouldn't,' said Susie, wryly. 'I expect she's a nasty bitter, *litigious* old spinster and she'd have you up for slander before you could say "not guilty, m'lud".'

Maddy giggled and Susie followed suit.

'Thanks, Maddy,' said Susie.

'What on earth for?'

'For being you, for being kind, even when I said some unforgivable things.'

'Hey, if you think what you said is unforgivable, you have a *very* low forgiveness threshold.'

'Even so.'

The kettle clicked off and Maddy made the coffee and passed a steaming mug to Susie before taking one through to Seb. On her return, she said, 'Changing the subject, are you going to the curry lunch on Sunday?'

'And give Camilla the chance to patronise me? I don't think so.' Susie put on a sing-song voice and did a remarkably accurate impression of the CO's wife. 'Ooh, Susie, you must be finding life *so* exciting at the moment. Fancy being able to choose your own home instead of relying on army housing.' She gave Maddy a wry grin. 'If only it were like that.'

'It must be quite nice, though, to choose what sort of heating your house has, or just have the opportunity to paint the walls some colour other than magnolia.'

'If only.' Susie took a deep breath and stared at her mug. Then she raised her gaze to meet Maddy's as she made up her mind to share with her friend what the score really was. 'This is strictly *entre nous* but Mike has run up some debts so his credit rating is through the floor. The mortgage broker won't touch him with a bargepole.'

'No!'

Susie nodded. 'So, if I'm the only one being considered for a mortgage I've *got* to get a job or we'll be renting till the crack of doom.'

'Oh, Susie, I am *so* sorry.'

'Yeah, well...don't be too kind or I might cry.' Already Susie felt tears in her eyes. She swallowed. 'In the great scheme of things it's not the end of the world...'

'No,' said Maddy, reaching across the table and putting her hand on Susie's. 'But it's a total bugger all the same.'

Susie nodded. 'Only, can I ask a favour...don't tell Seb. I don't think Mike would forgive me if he knew I'd told you, but I had to tell someone. Do you mind?'

'Mind? Of course not. And no, Seb will never hear of this from me. Trust me.'

'Thanks.' Susie went quiet for a second or two. Then she added, 'There's another thing...'

'What?'

'I want McManners' job in the mess.'

'Oh?' Maddy's eyebrows shot up.

'Don't sound surprised. The pay's not bad and I used to be in catering before I married Mike. Not canteen stuff, either – posh dinner parties, that sort of thing.'

Maddy looked dubious. 'But will the mess committee...?' She stopped, looking a little embarrassed.

Susie came to her rescue. 'Employ me?'

'Well, you know,' said Maddy, diffidently. 'Being an officer's wife and everything.'

'That's exactly what Mike said. But I told him I completely understand the 1 Herts' ethos and I understand about catering.'

'I suppose.' Maddy didn't sound convinced. 'And is catering the right background? I'm not being mean, Susie, but as manager you won't be doing the actual cooking, will you?'

'No, but I understand the principles and I can do accounting. OK, not like a proper accountant but I can do basic bookkeeping. All those hours of running the sodding thrift shop might finally pay off.'

'There has to be some payback for doing *that* job,' said Maddy, with feeling. 'Camilla is already trying to rope me into running it.'

'Run . . . run away!'

Maddy laughed. 'You see, there'll be lots of things about being an army wife that you won't miss.'

'And being at Camilla's beck and call won't be one of them.'

'So why don't you cock a snook at her and come to the curry lunch? Just think, you could cut her dead or tell her to get stuffed.'

'Actually, that's really, *really* tempting.'

Chapter 4

Sam was standing at the bar in the mess as the married pads, looking forward to the Sunday ritual of a curry lunch, began to drift in; some herding reluctant teenagers, some hauling in babies and toddlers and all their paraphernalia. Slowly the bar filled and the noise level crescendoed and Sam spotted Maddy, pushing Rose in her buggy, making her way over towards her.

'Good to see you,' said Maddy, when she was in earshot.

Sam felt a twinge of guilt at seeing her – she still hadn't got over the fact that it was her best friend who had had an affair with Maddy's husband. Not that she could *ever* be held responsible for Michelle's actions but somehow there was a bit of her that still felt she should have worked out what was going on and put a stop to it. As always, when Maddy spoke to her, Sam wondered if Maddy had some sort of agenda. Was she reminding Sam that she hadn't forgotten about Michelle's appalling behaviour, or was she signalling that she didn't bear Sam a grudge? And, as always, Sam longed to ask which it was but didn't quite have the nerve to do so, in case it was the former option not the latter.

'Hiya, Maddy,' she said, pushing her guilty feelings out of sight. 'Gosh, Rose is growing, isn't she?'

'It's what babies do best – only I think she's almost a toddler now, rather than a baby. How are the wedding plans?'

Sam shook her head. 'A nightmare. And worse, I invited Luke over for lunch today and he thought it would be nice if his folks came along too. I didn't have the heart to tell him I'd rather drink drain cleaner.'

'Poor you. It can't be easy.'

Sam shook her head again. 'Anyway, let's not talk about them. Oh – I haven't congratulated Seb on his promotion. You must be thrilled.'

'I'm afraid the jury is still out on that. I think promotion at such a young age mightn't be so popular amongst those with much more seniority.' Maddy glanced about her to see who might be eavesdropping. 'And over and above that we've yet to see how I get on with Camilla.'

Sam groaned. 'Oh God, Camilla! I know *exactly* what you mean. The other day she said she wanted to put me on the flower rota. When I asked her if all the living-in officers were going to take their turn, she went a bit funny on me. She seemed to think that just because I'm a woman I'm not really an officer and so I ought to be on one of her bloody committees.'

'That sounds like her,' said Maddy with feeling. She glanced over to her husband who was having a hard job restraining Nathan from climbing on the furniture. 'I think I'm needed – I ought to rescue Seb before Nate has a proper tantrum. Nice to talk to you and good luck with Lady Pemberton-Blake.'

As Maddy disappeared to the other side of the room Sam saw Luke and his parents make an appearance. With amusement, she also spotted Camilla Rayner do a double-take before she almost broke her neck to get across the room and greet General Sir Pemberton-Blake and his missus. The CO's wife's voice – even more high-pitched and sing-song than normal – cut across the hubbub as she bowed and scraped to the visiting VIPs. Sam went to greet her fiancé and his parents and felt, as she always did, that she ought to be dropping Lady Pemberton-Blake a curtsy rather than kissing her offered cheek.

Camilla looked daggers at her. 'You didn't tell me *they'd* be here today,' she muttered into Sam's ear. 'As a common courtesy I should have known.'

Sam was about to say that she herself hadn't known until the day before, and anyway they were *her* guests and hadn't come to see the CO and his wife, when Amanda Pemberton-Blake took her arm and drew her towards her, neatly cutting Camilla out of the conversation.

'Now, Sam, I've found the most divine website that sells wedding napery.'

'Can't we just hire the stuff?' blurted Sam. 'I only want to get married once so I'll hardly be using it again.'

Amanda gave her a rather withering look. 'But we'd have no idea who'd used it before.'

Sam wondered if Amanda insisted on new sheets when she stayed in hotels or friends' houses...if she *had* any friends, which, frankly, Sam doubted right now.

'You must tell me all about it,' gushed Camilla, wheedling her way back into the conversation.

Sam stood back. If Camilla wanted to talk about wedding arrangements she could be Sam's guest.

Across the room Maddy parked Rose in her chair by a nearby coffee table, scooped up Nathan and sat him on her hip. Seb looked relieved as Maddy's actions stopped Nathan from whinging.

'I've just heard a great piece of news,' said Seb.

'Good news? Blimey, that'll make a change around here,' said Maddy with feeling.

'Andy's just told me.'

'Told you what? Spit it out.'

Seb drew Maddy closer. 'Will's going to be my 2IC,' he said, quietly.

'Will?' squealed Maddy, only to get loudly shushed by Seb. Maddy glanced about to see if anyone had overheard her exclamation. She lowered her voice. 'You mean, Will Edwards, as in Caro-and-Will Edwards?'

Seb nodded.

'But won't he mind being your subordinate?'

'According to Andy, he's utterly delighted to be coming back to the battalion. He doesn't care what post he's given as long as he gets away from being a Whitehall Warrior.'

'All the same...' said Maddy.

'And Caro, apparently, is just thrilled too. Can't wait.'

But, Maddy thought, it still didn't address the problem that Will would be Seb's subordinate and while it was all fine and dandy in theory, the practicalities might prove to be somewhat different. After all, Will had been commissioned several years prior to Seb and being overtaken by a junior was never an easy pill to swallow.

Miles away in Surrey, Caro Edwards was dishing up roast chicken and preparing to carry the plates filled with Sunday lunch through to the sitting-dining room of her poky MoD quarter. Will and her two boys were already sitting at the table. She managed to balance three plates to take through to her hungry and expectant family.

'There you go,' she said as she put them down in front of them before she went back into the kitchen to fetch her own and her glass of wine.

'Well,' she said to her husband as the two boys fell on their food like they hadn't been fed in a week, 'I can't say I'll miss this place.'

'It's not that bad,' said Will.

Caro raised her eyebrows. 'It's nice for the kids. It's great that just about all their friends from school live locally, it's grand that there are so many young families here so they never have a shortage of playmates, but I am *not* going to miss that dreadful kitchen, nor the damp in the bathroom, nor the lack of double glazing...'

'Enough,' said Will.

'Just saying,' said Caro.

'You'll miss being close to London.'

'Really?' Caro's eyebrows went up again. 'Yeah, *really* going to miss you coming home every night in a vile mood because you've had a dreadful day at work and a worse commute. Or never being able to park in town unless I get there at about seven in the morning. Or the traffic jams which hold us up for hours if we want to go anywhere. Or the pollution. Or the joke of a garden.' She shot a look at the tiny square of paving at the back of the house which just about allowed a rotary drier the space to open out.

'It's not that bad,' said Will again.

'Wiltshire will be better,' said Caro, firmly. 'And I'll be back with all my friends.'

'You've got friends here.'

'But not mates like Maddy.'

'Have you told her yet?'

'I need to see the posting order in writing yet. You know what the army is like – being warned for a posting, particularly one you'd *really* like, isn't the same as actually having it in the bag. Besides, I don't want to jinx it.'

'Mummy, can I have some more please?' Oliver held out his empty plate to his mother.

'Just wait till everyone else has finished,' said Caro, realising she'd barely touched her meal. She started to attack her roast with gusto. 'But as soon as you get the order in your hand,' she said, speaking with her mouth full, 'I'm going to ring Maddy and give her the good news.' She swallowed. 'Second in command of B Company, eh? I hope Seb doesn't mind you being his boss.'

'Hardly,' said Will. '2IC doesn't mean I'm anyone's boss – general dogsbody, more like.'

'Still...he'll just be a platoon commander though, won't he?'

Will nodded. 'But I *am* a couple of years senior to him so, y'know, it's how it should be.'

'So that's all right then.'

Fifteen minutes later, while Will took Oliver and his brother out to the play park at the end of the road, Caro was in the kitchen with the last of her glass of wine and the washing up. As always the kitchen was in chaos – with a tiny work surface, minimal cupboard space and no dishwasher, clearing up after any meal was always an ergonomic nightmare. And as always, Will had offered to help but it was much easier to get him and the boys out of the house and tackle it, in the minute space, on her own.

She was just getting to grips with the burned-on fat in the roasting tin when the phone rang. Wiping her hands on a tea towel she went into the sitting room to answer it.

'Hello.'

'Caro!'

She recognised the voice. 'Maddy, how lovely. Were your ears burning?'

'Why, were you talking about me, you old moo?'

Caro could hear the laughter in Maddy's voice. 'I certainly was.'

'Snap then because Seb and I were discussing you. Look, I can't be long as I'm at a curry lunch but Seb told me earlier that you're getting posted here.'

'Yeah.'

'You don't sound wild about it.'

'Oh, but I am. Truly, I'm thrilled. Honest. I just wasn't going to tell you till I had it in writing. But if you know about it, then I suppose the battalion does so it *must* be official.'

'Woo-hoo. But that's brilliant. I am *so* pleased.' There was a pause. 'Will doesn't mind being 2IC?'

'Mind? Why should he? He'll be back in the same company as Seb and that's all he cares about. He adores Seb, as you well know. No, they'll be as happy as sandboys to be working together.'

'Phew. So when are you moving?'

'As soon as I can get packed, if I had my way.'

'But in reality...?'

'In reality, sometime in the summer holidays.'

'Not long then. Look, you keep me in the loop about your move and I'll make sure I'm around to help out as much as I can. If nothing else I can have the boys to stay for a night if that would make life easier for you.'

'Maddy, you are *such* a star. I might hold you to that.'

'Do. Look, I've got to go; I've left Seb with the kids and told him I was just popping to the loo so I can't chat for hours.'

'No, I completely understand. We'll talk more another time.'

'Byeee.'

Caro put the phone back on its stand. She couldn't wait to get back to 1 Herts and all her friends. With a happy heart she went back to the kitchen to finish the washing up.

Chapter 5

Seb sat in the armchair in Colonel Rayner's office feeling more than a little awkward. Mike Collins was still, technically, the OC of B Company and Seb didn't like the fact that the CO seemed to be sidelining his boss before the bloke had even gone on his terminal leave. Yes, they both knew that Mike had made it perfectly plain that he was going to concentrate on sorting out his future and his family (and why shouldn't he since he'd been so comprehensively shafted by the army?) but the fact that Rayner was being so obvious about bypassing the proper chain of command was very disconcerting. Seb just had to hope that the other officers in the battalion knew he wasn't conniving in the situation or, still less, approving of the CO's behaviour.

'So,' said Rayner, steepling his fingers, 'I think we need some innovation in the battalion.'

'Sir?' said Seb cautiously. He didn't like the sound of this. What sort of innovation? The phrase about new brooms sprang into his mind and from past experience he'd found that 'new brooms' rarely swept clean but just stirred up a load of shit which others then had to deal with.

'I want you to take over as PMC of the officers' mess.'

'Oh.' Bloody hell. Then Seb quickly added, 'I see, Colonel.' Although he didn't. He was going to be pushed to his limit as OC of B Company given his youth and inexperience; to be given *another* major role in the battalion, that of being the officer who oversaw the day-to-day running of the mess, was surely potty. And worse, with McManners being made redundant too he wouldn't even have an experienced manager as his right-hand man.

'Indeed,' said Rayner, with enthusiasm. 'Out with the old, in with the new.'

'But with McManners going...' Seb wondered how he could voice his concern that it might all degenerate into rat-shit with a new manager and an inexperienced PMC.

'It's the perfect time to make changes.' Rayner gave Seb a smile that resembled more a baring of his teeth than an encouraging grin.

'If you're sure.' Seb certainly wasn't.

'Excellent. I knew you'd see it my way.'

Seb suddenly felt empathy for the lone Chinese man who'd tried to face down the column of tanks in Tiananmen Square decades earlier – any show of resistance was utterly pointless. He smiled weakly at his boss and hoped his internal panic wasn't showing.

'So,' continued Rayner, 'how's it hanging in B Company?'

How's it hanging? Oh, for fuck's sake! Who on earth did this man think he was? Did he think he was 'down wiv da kidz'? The squaddies would laugh him off the parade square if he ever came out with stuff like that in public. Seb wondered if he ought to say something to save his boss from himself but then his dislike of the man got the better of him. Let the twat make a fool of himself.

'Well...it's awkward.'

'How come?' Rayner put on his caring face.

Seb felt like gagging. For a split second he thought about

fudging the issue but then decided it would do no good. 'Sir, I can't go and sit in Mike's office because, de facto, he's still OC, so I'm still very much a platoon commander and besides, I don't have a replacement yet. Craig isn't talking to me because he feels overlooked and blames me for making him resign and on top of that, everyone in B Company thinks the army is wrong to be getting rid of Mike so there is a certain amount of resentment about the changes taking place.'

Rayner's eyes hardened. 'Thank you for your honesty, Seb. I appreciate it.'

No, you bloody don't, thought Seb.

'Of course, if you don't think you're up to the promotion...'

'Sir, I can assure you I am capable of doing the job. It's the interregnum that's proving tricky.'

'You want me to tell the postings branch to arrange for Mike's redundancy to be brought forward?'

'No!' Shit, that was the last thing Seb wanted. As if he didn't feel guilty enough about taking over from Mike. He couldn't bear the thought he might be responsible for elbowing him out early.

'It would only be an administrative arrangement,' said Rayner, silkily. 'He wouldn't suffer a financial penalty, if that's what's worrying you.'

That put a different spin on it. But not different enough. Mike would still feel even less loved and wanted. Besides which, the clock would start counting down even earlier to when he and his family would have to vacate their quarter. They had enough on their plate without that too. 'I can cope, sir.'

'Good.' There was a pause. 'I'd like you to take over as PMC with immediate effect.'

'Oh.' Was this some kind of test? Seb wondered. And it also flashed through his mind that Maddy mightn't be overjoyed at being the wife of the PMC but before he had time to consider all the implications of the offer the CO carried on speaking.

'Yes, I don't think Alan Milward is up to the job. Very old school. To be honest the mess operates more like the sergeants' mess than the officers' one and it certainly looks like one. That's the problem with having a commissioned warrant officer do the job of PMC – old habits die hard.'

Hardly, the mess was beautiful and comfortable, and Milward had done a sterling job but Seb stayed quiet.

'Yes, I think the furnishings need updating. Let's get rid of all that dreary mahogany and damask and start again with some clean lines and modern textiles, linens and beech, for example, instead of that tatty, old-hat stuff.'

Seb was appalled. The lovely old furniture was part of the charm of the mess; 1 Herts had spent centuries acquiring the antiques in the building. OK, most of the better bits were the spoils of battles – looted by them, the victors, back in the eighteenth and nineteenth centuries. Some of the stuff was priceless. And as for the silver...did the CO think it would be properly set off in a bunch of Ikea Billy bookshelves rather than on the wonderful pair of French Empire-style side tables that 1 Herts had 'liberated' in the Peninsular war? 'I think, sir,' said Seb carefully, 'the regimental association might have a view on your plans.'

'If they feel strongly, tell them they can have it for their museum. Most of that stuff belongs in one anyway. I want you to come up with some ideas for renovations. Maybe Maddy can help, sound her out for ideas; she's young and on-trend.'

On-trend? Maddy?! Seb loved his wife to bits but he'd never known her take the least interest in fashion and trends.

'Come to me in a few weeks with your ideas. Let's say mid-July. But don't go talking to the other officers yet, eh? I don't want this to go off half-cocked. I want to be able to present them with a comprehensive plan. That way they'll more than likely agree that my idea is for the best. And I mean it, Seb, nothing to be said about this to anyone with the exception of Maddy. You understand, don't you?'

His way or the highway, and everything to be done in secrecy. Just great. Talk about a poisoned chalice. The trouble was, now he'd accepted the job of PMC he could hardly hand it back, Seb thought as he left Rayner's office.

But, as Seb knew, it wasn't just the mess that Colonel Rayner seemed to want to change. He'd allowed a short period of grace after the departure of his predecessor but as soon as a couple of weeks had passed he'd set about changing things left, right and centre in the battalion.

'It needs shaking up,' he'd told the officers.

It didn't, most of them had thought, but the CO had carried on anyway. The RSM, Mr Jenks, who had been as popular with the troops as an RSM was ever likely to be, had been posted out with unseemly haste and replaced with a man who had been universally loathed from the outset. The new RSM, Mr Horrocks, had come from one of the TA battalions and the *on dit* was that he'd spent most of his career with the TA because none of the regular battalions would have him once they realised what a useless NCO he was. And, since the quickest way to get rid of a dud soldier was to promote him beyond the unit's establishment, he had to go somewhere where there was a vacancy for that rank. Horrocks had hurtled up to the top and was now a warrant officer class one – and with nowhere else to go, 1 Herts was stuck with him. But he and Rayner obviously got on well enough, to judge by the amount of time they spent in each other's offices.

And with the arrival of a new RSM, the mood of the regiment shifted. The discipline had, apparently, been allowed to get exceedingly lax. Not that anyone had noticed but they certainly noticed the new regime; soldiers were picked up and charged for the least peccadillo, and the duty officer rota went out of the window as the junior ones found they were constantly picking up extras for the least thing.

Still, thought Seb, as he went back to his office, he was obviously doing *something* right if the CO had chosen him to be PMC, although at the back of his mind he had a faint niggle that he'd been given the post because Rayner thought that being such a junior major he might roll over and do as he was told.

Surprisingly though, when he told Maddy about being made the PMC, she seemed rather pleased.

'I didn't think you'd like the idea,' he said. 'I didn't have you down for wanting to be the PMC's wife; having to deal with the flower rota and make sure wives and girlfriends don't violate the dress code.'

Maddy shuddered. 'Gawd, spare me from the flower rota – although if you're in charge I won't be…spared it, that it. But as for the dress code…are you sure anyone at all cares about that these days?'

'Maybe not, but if some girlfriend did come in wearing something completely awful and inappropriate, I think it would be up to you to have a word.'

'Or you could tell her partner to put her straight? Your mess, your rules…'

'I suppose.' Maddy had a point. No, it shouldn't be down to her to enforce the rules. 'Anyway, you don't mind about me being PMC?'

'No, not really. In fact it might be a good thing because Su—' She stopped suddenly and changed tack. 'I'm not sure about the modernisation though. I can't see that going down a storm.'

Why on earth did Maddy think it might be advantageous for him to be PMC? Although, he was in agreement with her about the CO's plans for updating the building and he was going to do all he could, short of disobeying the CO about telling others, to procrastinate over the project. He told Maddy as much.

'Good plan. With luck, if you can procrastinate long enough, Rayner will have moved on before he can wreck everything. Or you'll have come to the end of your term as PMC and someone else will get the job.'

'So,' he said, 'I'm amazed you think me being PMC is a "good thing".'

But instead of answering him, Maddy said, 'Oops, forgot. A letter came for you today.'

She reached for a stiff white envelope that was sitting by the clock on the mantelshelf. 'Looks rather posh,' she said as she handed it over. 'Don't recognise the writing though.'

Seb took it from her and examined it.

'You won't find out who it's from just looking at it,' said Maddy, impatiently.

Seb slipped a finger under the flap and tore it open. He scanned the letter. 'Bloody hell.'

'"Bloody hell", what?' said Maddy, almost beside herself with curiosity.

'It's from Rollo.'

'Rollo! You mean, rowing-Rollo?' Rollo had rowed with Seb at their old Oxford college.

Seb nodded.

'What does he want?'

Seb read the letter in double-quick time, then reread it. 'He wants to come and stay.'

'Here? Why on earth?'

'He's house-hunting, apparently.'

'But why us?'

'Don't you want him to come?'

Maddy looked puzzled. 'Yes...no...I mean, I don't really care, per se. It's just, wouldn't he be more comfortable in a decent hotel than in a grotty quarter with two tiny kids?'

'But it'd be nice to catch up.'

Maddy nodded. 'I suppose.'

'You liked him well enough when we were all up at Oxford.'

Even Seb knew that 'liked' might have been a bit of an overstatement. Seb had been part of Rollo's circle because they were all in the same college eight and trying to get a seat in the Blue Boat – to row in the Boat Race – and Maddy was mad about Seb, so she hung around the same social set. But they'd never been bosom buddies.

However, Maddy said, 'What wasn't to like? He was loaded and threw great parties. On the downside he was a bit of a lech and a lush. Not that he leched after me much,' she added hastily.

No, Seb didn't think Rollo had. Although it was hard to remember. Rollo had leched after almost everything in a skirt and with a pulse. He laughed. 'Remember that party at his parents' gaff?'

Maddy raised her eyebrows. 'As you know very well, it's a bit – ahem – of a blur. I remember arriving and the hangover on the second day...'

She had got spectacularly drunk and passed out shortly after the dinner on the first night of a weekend house-party.

And Seb remembered why...He moved away from the subject of the house party.

'Rumour has it that Rollo's calmed down a lot since those days. I think winning that medal at the Olympics made him grow up.'

Maddy looked sceptical. 'Rollo? Grow up? You're having me on.'

'Seriously. He's dropped the double-barrel and everything. Plain old Rollo Forster, now.'

Maddy snorted. 'Rollo...plain? Seb is plain, *James* is plain. *Mark* is plain. Rollo...? Rollo is a toff's name.'

Seb ignored her. 'And does a lot of motivational speaking to schoolkids in his spare time, to get them to work hard and not get into drugs.'

Maddy started to properly laugh. 'So, he doesn't tell them about when he was a gold-medal-winning drinker and shagger?'

Seb couldn't stop a grin. 'I think he focuses on being an Oxford Blue and a rowing gold-medallist rather than his racy past.'

'Bloody good thing too. I hope the kids don't find out about that side of him – hardly role-model material.'

'Maybe not. But I bet he's good at it. He's a good laugh – always was – so I bet he's great with kids.'

'So when does he want to come over?'

'In a couple of weeks. You don't mind, do you Mads?'

She said she didn't but she didn't look wildly enthusiastic.

It was just for a weekend, thought Seb. What could go wrong?

Chapter 6

'Come on,' said Maddy, 'chop chop.' She picked up Seb's bowl and whisked it away as soon as he'd laid his soup spoon back in it.

'But...'

'But, you'd finished.'

'Only just. What's the hurry?'

'I need you to hurry up and get out of my hair. I'm off out with Susie in a little while.'

'Going somewhere nice?'

'There's a house in Winterspring Ducis she wants to look at so I've promised to drive her over for a viewing. Mike's in Salisbury...got a job interview.'

'Finally.'

Maddy nodded. 'I know. I mean we all thought he'd get snapped up but...' Maddy shrugged.

It was Seb's turn to nod.

'By the way...'

There was something in her tone that put Seb on his guard. 'Yes?' he said warily.

'Don't sound so suspicious. I was just wondering when McManners is going?'

'Next month. Why?'

'No reason, beyond that as PMC I think you ought to

organise a whip-round for him. He's done everyone proud over the years.'

'That's a good idea. He ought to get something nice from the mess members for all his efforts.'

Maddy preened. 'When are you interviewing for replacements?'

'Next week.'

'I haven't seen it advertised.'

'No, well...it's a sort of an in-house thing.'

'What if someone from outside wants a pop at that job?'

Seb's suspicions were really aroused. 'Why, you're not thinking of doing it, because—'

Maddy held her hand up to silence him. 'Me? Don't be daft, of course not. I just thought in the interests of equal opportunities and all that guff...Aren't there rules about advertising jobs?'

'Maybe. I'm sure it's all been done properly and with proper compliance to all the rules and regulations.'

'I'm sure. Anyway, I need to get the kids ready to go out with Susie.'

Seb stared after her as she left the kitchen. He been married long enough to know she was up to something, he just didn't know what it was – except, of course, that it concerned McManners in some way.

As Susie got in Maddy's car Maddy said, 'I think we need to go via the mess.'

'Why?'

Maddy started the car and pulled out onto the main road through the patch. 'Because, if you want McManners' job, you need to pull your finger out. He's going next month and they're interviewing next week.'

'No! I didn't know. I didn't even know they'd invited applications.'

'Exactly. Seb says it's in-house, which means they're probably after another time-serving sergeant. It's more than likely they advertised the post in the regimental magazine or on orders which is why neither of us spotted it.'

'Do you think I'm too late to apply?'

'Got to hope not.'

A couple of minutes later Maddy parked up outside the mess and Susie belted in the front door to talk to the mess manager. To pass the time she put a CD of nursery rhymes on for the benefit of Nathan and programmed the satnav to take her to the postcode on the house particulars that Susie had been sent by the estate agent. The picture on the details showed the sitting room, which looked bland but no worse than most of the quarters Maddy had seen. However, it didn't take long to read through the estate agent's blurb and, by the time Susie returned, and Nate had demanded 'The Wheels on the Bus' for the sixth time, she was almost catatonic with boredom.

'Success?' she said as Susie slid into the passenger seat.

'Well, the application is in although McManners was very sceptical about whether or not I was eligible for the job.'

'Not that it's up to him.' Maddy slipped the car into gear and headed back out of the barracks.

'No, but I bet he's got some sort of say in who takes over from him.'

Maddy glanced across at her. 'But it's Seb who's going to have the final say. He's been made PMC.'

'No!'

Maddy nodded. 'And I think Seb owes me, don't you?'

'Maddy?' Susie searched Maddy's face.

'Look, he still doesn't know that I know about his affair with Michelle – in fact I still don't even know for definite if he actually *had* an affair. For all I know that awful Michelle-woman was delusional and made up the whole scenario. But, on the other hand, there's no smoke without fire. But even if Seb has the squeakiest of cleanest pasts I've put up with an awful lot of shit as an army wife, as have you and, if nothing else, we deserve a break now and again. If he's got any sense of decency, he'll give you a proper crack of the whip. And I intend to make absolutely sure that you get it.'

They drove on towards the village that Susie's prospective house was in. It was, they discovered when they reached it, very chocolate-boxy; lots of thatched cottages, a proper village green and even a pub.

'Ooh,' said Maddy. 'I could live here. Very pretty.'

The satnav directed them away from the green and up the hill behind the village and suddenly the chocolate-box veneer began to come off. Up this side road the houses were 1960s semis with clapboard cladding, with some of the cladding falling off and almost all of it in need of urgent repainting. The gardens were unkempt and one even had an old caravan that was green with mould and moss parked on the drive. 'Squalid' was a word that sprang into Maddy's mind.

'Want to live here now?' said Susie quietly.

The satnav took them round another corner and back downhill. *Springhill Road* said the dirty black and white sign on the corner. Next to the sign was a dark green BT junction box on top of which sat a couple of youths, probably about thirteen years old, both swigging from cans and smoking rollies.

'They should be in school,' said Susie, in an appalled whisper.

'What number?' asked Maddy to distract her.

'Fifteen.'

The pair peered at the numbers on the shabby front doors as Maddy drove slowly along the road.

'There,' said Maddy as she pulled up behind a shiny BMW.

'At least the estate agent is here,' said Susie.

Maddy stared at the dispiriting exterior. No wonder the estate agent's particulars hadn't featured a picture of the outside. 'Looks just like a quarter,' she joked. She saw the bleak look on Susie's face. 'It'll be transformed with a coat of paint and a bit of a tidy-up in the garden.'

Susie didn't say anything.

They got out of the car and extricated the kids from the back seat; Susie grasping Nathan firmly by the hand while Maddy settled Rose on her hip. They could hear a dog barking its head off in a nearby house. It sounded big and ferocious although Nathan insisted he wanted to 'go see the nice doggy'. Maddy didn't think German shepherds or Rottweilers generally came under the heading of 'nice doggy'.

The front path had to cross over a narrow concrete bridge that spanned what looked like a drainage ditch, only it would be pushed to drain anything as it was completely overgrown with weeds and brambles. Maddy vaguely thought that if the undergrowth was cut back and the banks laid with turf it might look quite nice if planted with spring bulbs – but right now it was just one more eyesore amongst many others.

The front door opened and out bounced the estate agent, all dapper suit and beaming smile. He glanced from one woman to the other. 'Mrs Collins?'

Susie extended her free hand. 'Susie. And this is my friend who has kindly given me a lift – Maddy Fanshaw.'

'And I'm Damien. OK, so the house is ready for you to view.' He turned and led the way up the cracked concrete path. 'The village is lovely isn't it?'

Susie and Maddy exchanged a look before Susie said, 'The centre is, certainly.'

'Very sought after,' continued Damien. 'In the catchment area for a good comp, on a bus route and only five miles from Warminster. What more could you want?'

A house a bloody sight nicer than this one, thought Maddy, but she didn't voice her opinion.

Damien threw open the front door and led them inside. The house was cold, despite the fact that outside it was a warm summer's day. And it smelt weird...not disgusting weird but of cheap scented candles or air freshener or stale pot-pourri – something unidentifiable and sickly sweet and quite overpowering.

'Poo,' said Nathan, loudly. Maddy giggled.

They were in a big sitting-dining room with open-plan stairs heading up to the first floor. In the corner of the L-shaped room was a door to the kitchen.

'Nice room,' said Maddy. 'Double aspect.'

Susie gave her a look before she walked across the tatty, stained carpet and checked out the kitchen. Damien hurried after her.

'It does, of course, need updating,' he said.

It *needs*,' said Susie, firmly, 'ripping out and burning.'

Even by the standards of the crap army kitchens that Susie and Maddy had been used to, this one was eye-wateringly awful. One of the cupboard doors had fallen off and had been replaced by a tatty piece of now-grubby fabric stretched across the opening on a length of washing line. The flooring was cracked and worn lino and the counter tops were covered with scorch marks and stains. The oven was revolting. Had it *ever* been cleaned?

In silence they traipsed upstairs to find the bathroom suite, beneath the years of accumulated limescale, was avocado green and the surrounding tiles dark brown, and the four bedrooms were done out in a variety of shades of pink, ranging from salmon to magenta, which clashed with the turquoise carpet that covered the entire first floor.

'It makes you realise the army is wise in painting everything magnolia,' said Susie, with a shudder.

'But,' said Maddy, 'rip out the carpets, paint everything cream, redo the gloss and this place could be quite sweet.' She looked out of the window. 'The view is stunning.'

And it was. The back of the house looked over rolling hills and downs, dotted with sheep, an arc of clear blue sky providing the perfect backdrop to a scene of rural tranquillity. Springhill Road lay in a shallow valley that ran behind the main village and it was, despite being a pretty run-down area of ex-council and current social housing, remarkably peaceful. Or it was at this time of day.

Susie joined Maddy at the window and looked out too. 'But you can't live on a view,' she said, tonelessly. 'A view doesn't pay the mortgage.' She fingered the frame of the bed. 'But,' she sighed, 'it could be worse. At least both the girls' rooms are the same size so they won't kill each other over who has which and we could probably just manage to squeeze a double bed into the fourth bedroom. It'll do.'

It'll do? thought Maddy. Surely, if you were escaping from army housing into your own, forever home, surely you didn't want a house that *would do*? Or maybe it was just her.

Maybe other people didn't set such store by a house feeling right, hugging them from the get-go, making them want to put down roots...

Susie looked down at the floor. 'And the village is pretty,' she repeated. Swiftly she turned away and dragged a hanky out of her sleeve. Maddy looked out of the window again. Susie wouldn't want her to see that she was crying.

Ten minutes later they were loading the children back into the car as Damien locked up behind them. Maddy breathed in the fresh air deeply as she slammed the car door shut. The lads from the corner wandered past on the pavement, as Maddy tried to get the awful smell of the house out of her nostrils. As she sucked in the clean country air she caught a whiff of another smell. Pot? She glanced at the lads and at the rollie they were sharing and then at Susie. Susie, thankfully, seemed oblivious to the situation. Maddy wondered if she ought to tell her about it. On the other hand, it was only pot. The lads weren't mainlining heroin...

'I'm worried I won't get approved for a mortgage in time,' said Susie as they drove back to the patch. 'I know that house isn't up to much but it's a roof...'

'There'll be other houses,' said Maddy, stoutly.

'But we haven't got time to wait for "other houses" – not by the time we've got everything in place and arranged to move and got the mortgage sorted. And anyway, we can't afford anything better. That's the bottom line. If you want "pretty" or "desirable" or anything like that then you have to pay for it. Mike and I can't afford to be picky and that place has got four bedrooms. Maybe I should insist that the twins share or give up on the idea of having a spare room...but is it so wrong to want to keep just a fraction of the lifestyle we've got used to?'

Maddy was about to open her mouth when Susie held up her hand. 'And don't you *dare* say anything about cutting coats according to cloth.'

'I wasn't going to,' protested Maddy.

'Sorry. Sorry. Just a bit defensive here. You know...when you're on the way down you assume everyone's going to take a pop at you.'

'Why? Why would they? No one would do that, surely?'

Susie shrugged. 'Maybe I'm just being oversensitive.'

'I think you are. But if they do, they'll have me to answer to.'

Susie put her hand over Maddy's. 'Thank you, hon, but if you can persuade Seb to give me the job in the mess, you'll have done more than enough.'

Chapter 7

Maddy was unloading the children out of the car and was about to invite Susie in for a cuppa when she saw Camilla Rayner bearing down on her, a file tucked under her arm, an air of purpose about her and an inane smile on her face.

Susie leaned in and gave Maddy a quick peck on the cheek. 'Thanks for the support. I think I'll make myself scarce before I need to be nice to That Woman.'

Maddy grinned. 'I don't think that option is open to me.'

As Susie high-tailed it over the road to her own quarter, Maddy turned to Camilla. 'Hello, Camilla,' she called. 'Coming to see me?' Camilla, thought Maddy, might be a royal pain in the arse but at least she didn't insist on everyone calling her Mrs Rayner. The previous incumbent would only unbend as far as allowing a few favourites to call her 'Mrs N' but the rest weren't invited to address her as anything other than Mrs Notley. And while that had been faintly irritating and sometimes almost amusing, it came nowhere close to the amount of annoyance Camilla Rayner could generate in Maddy before she even opened her mouth.

'Coo-ee, Maddy,' she trilled. 'Yes, so glad I've caught you. I need to have a word if you can possibly spare me a little tick or two.'

Maddy hitched Rose up on her hip and led the way to the front door, herding Nathan with her free hand.

'Actually, if the kiddies—'

Kiddies? thought Maddy, her teeth starting to itch. Jeez...

'—can stand it, I'd like you to come with me to view the community centre.'

'Now?'

Camilla smiled her saccharine smile. 'Please.'

'OK. I'm sure the *children* will be fine for a minute or two.'

'Oh that's so wonderful,' chirruped Camilla. 'Only I know how bored little people can get and we don't want that happening, do we?'

Maddy had to grit her teeth to stop herself from responding inappropriately. As she trailed down the road with Nathan and Rose she began to wish she'd grabbed the pushchair but it wasn't far and Nathan was, at the moment, behaving.

They reached the old brigadier's residence – a throwback to the days when the army was much bigger and had far more senior officers who, in turn, needed housing that was concomitant with their status.

'It's a shame this lovely house isn't still being used as a quarter,' said Camilla.

Maddy reckoned that if it had been, Camilla would have done her level best to get it allocated to herself. Nothing if not pushy was that woman. Beneath that sweetness-and-light exterior beat a heart of absolute steel.

'Of course,' she continued, 'we've all reaped the benefit of the cuts in one way or another.'

'Really? I don't think Susie would agree.' Oops. That remark earned her a stony stare. Lucky not to be shoved on the naughty step too.

'The cuts,' continued Camilla with a note of frost in her voice, 'are the reason we're lucky to have such smashing quarters here.'

Maddy managed to keep her mouth shut this time. OK, her quarter wasn't completely rank, but 'smashing' wasn't the adjective that sprang to mind. 'Adequate' might cover it, at a push.

'Yes, we all got bumped up a level here. The reality is your quarter is a major's quarter and you shouldn't be entitled to a fourth bedroom.'

'Just as well Seb's getting promoted then, isn't it? We wouldn't want to have perks we're not entitled to, would we?' Oh, God, and now she was even starting to sound a bit like Camilla. Shoot me now, thought Maddy.

'Indeed.'

Camilla opened the box file and took out a key. The front door needed a lick of paint and dead leaves had blown into the porch.

'Here we are,' sang Camilla as she pushed open the door.

The quarter was almost bare though it still boasted, noted Maddy, a superior grade of carpets and curtains. One of the privileges of rank, obviously. There were still some pieces of issue furniture in the building including a telephone table in the hall. Camilla put her file down on it.

'So,' she said, 'while the army has agreed in principle that we should have this house for use by the 1 Herts families, we have yet to work out exactly how we are going to keep everyone happy. And we don't want anyone being left out, now, do we?'

Maddy shook her head. Oh no, that *would* be a disaster. She put Rose down so she could crawl about on the carpet while Nathan had stomped into the kitchen and was amusing himself by opening and closing cupboard doors. It was pretty irritating but not as irritating as Camilla Rayner.

'Who wants to be accommodated?' asked Maddy.

'The thrift shop, Mothers and Toddlers, the book club, Bitch and Stitch – although I *wish* they'd call themselves something more appropriate. Really!'

'Anyone else?'

'The gardening club, but they'll just need a greenhouse, if we can raise the funds, and the choir.'

'The only group that needs a permanent space is the thrift shop. And anyway, why do they want to move from where they are now? I'd have thought that room behind the housing commandant's office was perfect.'

'He's intimated he'd like it back. With the drawdown from Germany and more families moving into the garrison, he's getting more staff. He needs the space.'

'Fair enough. But even so, they'll only need the one room, everyone else can take turns using the other rooms. We'd just book them in to the available space on a rota system, surely. None of those groups meets more than once a week, do they?'

'The choir meets two nights a week to rehearse, but no, you're right about the others.' Maddy wandered into what had once been a dining room. 'There's acres of room here,' she said, her voice echoing slightly in the empty room. 'Plenty of room for the thrift shop. All we need is to get a lock put on the door.'

She strolled into the drawing room. 'If we built cupboards in round the edge of this room, each group could have their own storage space for any kit specific to them.' She went into the kitchen, where she scooped up Nathan – the incessant banging of cupboard doors had got too much, even for her high-tolerance threshold – and looked about her. The kitchen was big, twice as big as hers, and it had a huge utility room opening out from it. 'We could make this into a little café and meeting place.'

Camilla looked unconvinced. 'And who would run it? And what about food hygiene?'

'I bet there's an enterprising wife who would jump at the chance – especially if she was allowed to turn a profit. Anyway, it's just an idea.'

Beyond the kitchen was a snug or den. It was a reasonable size and had the downstairs loo leading off it. It also boasted a door into an old conservatory. Maddy unlocked it and went through. An idea began to form in her head. She turned back to Camilla. 'What's upstairs?'

'The master suite with its own dressing room and bath-room, five other bedrooms and a second bathroom.'

'Six bedrooms, blimey.'

'It *was* a brigadier's house,' said Camilla.

Maddy thrust Nathan at her. 'Can I just have a quick look, if you don't mind...' She glanced at Rose who was, as always, being angelic. 'If you could just keep an eye on these two.'

Maddy didn't wait for an answer as she bounded up the stairs. It certainly was pretty palatial. She had an idea about a use for that 'master suite' and she wanted a quick look to suss out the possibilities. She threw open the doors on the upstairs landing one after the other before she found the right room. Wow! A big bay window flooded it with light and the room was huge, far bigger than the poky bedroom she had in her quarter. She crossed the empty floor to one of the two doors on the far wall and investigated what was behind it – the en suite. Dated and tatty but big enough for what she had in mind. The other room, the dressing room, was more of a cubbyhole with a built-in wardrobe but still a useful space. Delighted with her find, Maddy skipped downstairs to relieve Camilla of a struggling and uncooperative Nathan who was hell-bent on following his mother upstairs.

'OK,' said Maddy, 'I've got some ideas. We'd be better off discussing them back at mine, if you'd like to come back for a cuppa.'

Camilla nodded. 'Oh, that's such a charming offer.'

Maddy held her tongue – again. 'Charming offer'? It was only going to be a mug of tea, when all was said and done.

They trailed back to Maddy's with Nathan, now bored and tired, wanting to be carried, even though he could see his mum was holding his sister. Camilla, Maddy noticed, didn't offer to take either Nathan or Rose. They finally reached Maddy's front door and she was able to herd the group in. Nathan, once home, made a remarkable recovery, his tiredness forgotten, and ran off to find his toys while Maddy dropped a protesting Rose in her playpen before hurdling the stairgate across the kitchen door to go and put the kettle on.

'A sensible mother,' said Camilla. 'I do so approve. It's so easy for accidents to happen and we wouldn't want that to happen to your kiddies.'

Maddy gritted her teeth. 'Actually, I got the tip about stairgates from Caro Edwards. She's posted back in here – her husband is going to be Seb's 2IC.'

'I don't think I've come across her. Of course Jack hasn't done that many tours with the battalion. The army always thought he was so gifted as a staff officer he spent a lot of time at the MoD and other HQs.'

More likely, thought Maddy, they knew how unpopular the pair of you were and did their level best to keep you away from the battalions to spare the other officers the awfulness of serving with you. But she smiled at Camilla as if she concurred with the analysis. She bustled about in the kitchen and made the tea, found a packet of biscuits which she decanted onto a plate and then led Camilla into her sitting room.

'Sorry about the mess,' she said, although she wasn't, as Camilla picked her way disdainfully across the toy-strewn floor.

'Tell me about your ideas,' said Camilla, sipping out of her mug, pinkie half-cocked as if she didn't know whether she should or not.

Maddy put her mug down on the desk beside her. 'So, I think we ought to use that room off the kitchen, and the conservatory, as a crèche.'

'Crèche? Why would we need a crèche when we've already got the Mothers and Toddlers?'

'But this is so the mums can *leave* their kids. Get a few hours to do their own thing: have a good rootle around the thrift shop; get their hair done; go shopping. And while I'm on the subject of hair, at our last barracks the garrison had its own hairdresser and it was so useful. We could turn the master suite upstairs into one. Get a backwash unit put in the en suite bathroom, use the bedroom as a salon and the dressing room as a store cupboard. We could even plumb a washing machine in the dressing room, joining up to the pipework in the bathroom and so the hairdresser could wash and dry the towels there too.'

Camilla looked indifferent. 'I suppose.'

Don't knock yourself out.

'These ideas are all very well,' Camilla continued, sounding utterly unenthusiastic, 'like your one for a café, but who is going to run them? I, for one, don't have the time or the inclination to take on any more little jobs for the battalion. There

74

are quite enough calls on my time as things stand.' She gave Maddy a stern look but Maddy refused to be intimidated.

Bossy old bat, she thought, before she said, 'Camilla, there are wives brimming with talents here. Their only problem is getting paid jobs. Caro is a trained nursery nurse, or nanny or something... anyway, she got all the qualifications. I know a wife who is a hairdresser and I am sure there's loads of other wives with catering experience and they'd all love to do something that was on their doorstep, and which might earn them a bob or two. Honestly, Camilla, I am sure we could do this.'

Camilla looked sceptical. 'And what about the finances?'

'People pay for the services they use and we pay the workers out of that. Any profit can go to the upkeep of the community centre or to service charities.'

'And if the enterprises don't make enough money?'

'Then we have a rethink.'

Camilla sniffed. 'I can see you are very enthusiastic but I have my doubts.'

'Let me see if I can find people qualified to run these ventures and see what they think. How about that?'

'It can't do any harm, I suppose.'

Damned with faint praise... 'Leave it with me,' said Maddy firmly. Besides, it wasn't just her ideas she wanted to get off the ground; if she could pull this off she'd be giving a leg up to two mates: Jenna and Caro. The only worry was that Camilla might have heard about Jenna's other enterprise at the previous posting and so veto Jenna having anything to do with this plan. However, there was no reason why Jenna's illicit hairdressing salon would have come to Camilla's notice so that wasn't likely to be a problem. No, the real problem was Jenna's affair with Dan Armstrong when her husband

75

Lee had been out fighting in Afghanistan. It hadn't made her the most popular wife on the patch, that was for sure. But it had been over two years previously, Lee was now happily married to another woman and a lot of water had flowed under the bridge. And Jenna was a bloody good hairdresser. Maddy rather hoped that the combination of the wives' desire to have a decent haircut, and the passage of time, would mean that Jenna wouldn't get blackballed if she opened a salon. Only one way to find out.

Chapter 8

'How did it go?' said Susie, when Mike got back from his interview.

Mike looked exhausted. 'I don't know. No idea. I did everything that recruiting firm told me to do: I told the company how much I loved the idea of working for them, I was geared up to talk about their products, their ethos, even their bloody history, but the spotty youth interviewing me wanted to know if I sucked sweets or crunched them!' Mike looked despairingly at Susie. 'I mean... what the fuck was that about?'

Susie shook her head. This didn't sound hopeful. Could she pile on the misery more by telling him just how dire the house was she'd been to visit? Or how hideous the neighbourhood? She decided not to mention it just yet.

'I applied for McManners' job today.'

'You did what?' He sounded horrified. It was almost as if she'd announced she'd gone on the game.

'Mike, don't start. It's a job and, God knows, I need to get one just as much as you do.'

'I know but—'

'No buts, Mike.'

'I don't know why I'm worried, anyway. I doubt if they'll give it to you.'

'Thanks for the vote of confidence.'

'I'm sorry.' Mike looked contrite. 'I didn't mean it like that. What I meant was they'll choose some ex-senior NCO. Stands to reason, doesn't it. It's what they always do.'

Susie nodded, non-committally. 'Maybe,' she murmured.

'Seb?' said Maddy as the pair relaxed in front of the box after supper.

'Hmm?' said Seb.

'Can I ask a favour?'

Seb took his eyes off the TV and looked at his wife. 'It depends what it is.'

'You know the CO's been badgering you about updating the mess?'

'Yes?' said Seb cautiously.

'Well, supposing you broke the mould.'

'What mould?'

'The mould of appointing a senior NCO to run the place.'

There was silence for a few seconds. 'Why?'

Maddy took a deep breath. 'I want you to give the job to Susie.'

'Susie? *Susie?!*'

Maddy rolled her eyes. She had a bet with herself that Seb would react like this. 'Yes, Susie,' she said, trying to stay calm. She started to count points off on her fingers. 'One, she needs a job; two, she understands everything about 1 Herts and their traditions; three, she has done catering; four, she understands basic accounting; five, she's the most honest person I know; six, I'm asking you nicely.'

'And seven, she's completely wrong for the job.'

'No, she's not...for all those reasons I've just given you.'

'Why? Why on earth do you want me to do this?'

'Because she's Mike's wife. Because you've got his job and I think you owe him one. Because he hasn't yet got a job and Susie is getting desperate...because...because...'

'"Because" bollocks. It's not an officer's wife's job.'

'But she won't be, will she? Think about it. And Seb, I've never asked for anything before. I've put up with you being away rowing, I've put up with the moves, with my career going tits-up, with everything, but I am asking for this. This *one* thing. Please, Seb. Please?'

'It's not in my gift.'

Maddy gave Seb a hard stare. 'Really? I'd say it's very much in your gift. You're the PMC. You'll be in charge of the interview panel and you know as well as I do that if you say that you think she is the woman for the job to the rest of the guys they'll all tug their forelocks and agree with you. Won't they?'

'Not necessarily.'

Maddy just narrowed her eyes.

Seb shuffled. 'I'll see.'

Maddy kept staring at him.

'If she doesn't measure up though, I will have to sack her.'

'Just as long as you give her a chance to prove herself, that's all I'm asking.'

Seb sighed heavily.

'Thank you, darling. Now, to change the subject...'

Seb looked at his wife, wary of what else he might have to agree to. 'Yes?'

'About Rollo's visit.'

'And?'

'Well, you're pretty much OC B Company and—'

Seb put up his hand. 'Not so fast. I'm not yet.'

'Details, details...Anyway, you *are* the PMC and I

thought we ought to have a bit of a party in Rollo's honour. Let's face it, he's a bit of a celeb – how many others on the patch can boast having an Olympic gold medallist to stay? – and he's pretty good fun so I think we ought to have some of our mates along to meet him.'

Seb considered the idea. 'I suppose. It might be politic to ask Rollo first. I mean, he might not want to be trotted out as main attraction.'

'Rollo?' spluttered Maddy. 'Not want to be the centre of attention?'

Seb conceded she had a point. 'But we ought to tell him – just as a courtesy.'

'OK, I'll do that.' She smiled. 'I'm so glad you agree. It's about time we did some more entertaining. It'll be fun.'

'Just one thing,' said Seb. 'You do realise we'll have to invite the Rayners?'

Maddy sagged. 'Must we?'

'We must.'

'If they come there's every chance Susie and Mike won't, you do realise that, don't you?'

'They don't have to talk to each other.'

'No, I suppose not.' But Maddy didn't think the possibility that the Rayners and the Collinses might be in the same room boded well.

Maddy threw open the front door as the engine of Rollo's powerful sports car rumbled into silence. Bloody hell, he still knew how to make an entrance. In a road where almost every car, including theirs, was an estate or a sensible four-by-four, his fire-engine red Jaguar F-type stood out like a ballerina in a rugby scrum. And what extravagance! This was an expensive car and no mistake. But that was Rollo – never subtle or understated.

Rollo threw open the car door and unravelled himself from the driver's seat, then stretched. As he did so he caught sight of Maddy.

'Mads! Darling Maddy.' He bounded up their front path and enveloped her in a hug before planting a kiss on the top of her head.

Clasped against his chest, barely able to breathe, Maddy wondered when she'd been promoted to 'darling Maddy'. They'd got on reasonably well at Oxford but he'd never called her 'darling' before.

He grabbed her shoulders and held her away from him.

'You are glowing,' he said. 'Being married to Seb obviously suits you. And being a mother!'

Maddy grinned. Rollo's bonhomie was infectious. He enveloped her in another bone-crushing bearhug.

'And what's this I hear about Seb giving up rowing?'

Behind her Seb boomed, 'You heard right.' Seb, carrying a sleepy, pyjama-clad Nathan, leaned over Maddy and clapped Rollo on his shoulder. Maddy, a respectable five feet eight, but squashed between two guys who grazed the six foot four mark, felt like the meat in a sandwich and a huge wave of claustrophobia engulfed her. She elbowed them both in the solar plexus.

'Oi, you two. I can't breathe.' They moved apart. 'And Nathan needs to go inside before he catches his death and I expect Rollo wants a drink.'

'Drink?' said Rollo. 'You know the way to a man's heart. Just give me two ticks.'

Seb bounded into the house to finish putting Nathan to bed while Rollo returned to his car, popped the boot and hauled out a small overnight bag and a large Fortnum and Mason carrier bag. He slammed the boot shut and then opened the passenger door and collected a vast bouquet of pink roses. 'Can't come empty-handed,' he said as he gathered everything up and walked up the path.

'But you're only staying for the weekend,' said Maddy, overwhelmed by his generosity. 'Honestly, Rollo, it's just lovely to see you again. You didn't need to bring all this.'

They may have had their ups and downs at Oxford but Rollo had grown up a lot since he'd graduated and was now the epitome of a suave and charming man.

'Here.' He handed her the roses and Maddy inhaled their scent.

'They're beautiful, Rollo. I just hope I can find a vase that can do them justice,' she said as she ushered him into the house. 'Seb isn't one of life's great romantics. His attitude to flowers is why would I want a gift that I am going to watch die?'

Rollo laughed. 'Ever the pragmatist is our Seb.'

He dumped his case at the bottom of the stairs and then carried the Fortnum's bag into the kitchen and put it on the table there. 'Nothing perishable,' he said. 'Just some treats.'

Maddy peered in; wine, tea, chocolates, honey, a jar of pâté. 'Gosh, thanks, Rollo.' She moved the bag off the table and into a corner. She'd unpack it later when she'd got supper on the go.

Seb thumped down the stairs. 'Nathan wants a goodnight kiss, Maddy. You do that while I get Rollo a beer.'

Maddy popped upstairs to check on the children, give Nathan his goodnight kiss and tuck him in, switch on the hall nightlight then she returned to the kitchen and a glass of gin.

The two men were already sat either side of the table, halfway down their first beers, talking about the old days, the rowing, the boat club at the college and past acquaintances. Maddy listened in as she began to make their supper.

'So, you're still not married? I thought you and Tanya would wind up together,' said Seb.

'Tans? Great girl,' said Rollo, 'but I don't think I quite fulfilled her ambitions. She was after a title as well as money. I could only ever give her the dosh and I think she's still looking for a suitable victim – er – I mean life partner.'

Maddy remembered Tanya who had also been a rower and thus one of their set, and, like Rollo, from a vastly wealthy family, although she'd not been her favourite woman. Tanya had been, and maybe still was, a woman whose idea of fun was to try and snare other people's boyfriends, just to see if she could. And having snared them, she'd chuck them back, not caring that in the process she might have ruined a relationship irreparably. She'd had a go at Seb once, at that house party of Rollo's, which was the reason Maddy had wound up so utterly plastered – drowning her sorrows – while Tanya had made off with a man she didn't really want, the man Maddy was insanely in love with, Seb. Still, I got him in the end, she thought, and Tanya was still, it seemed, on her own. Oh dear.

'So what's she up to now?' she asked, trying to sound casual and not let the last vestiges of her antipathy show.

'Last I heard she was in The Priory. I think her coke habit got the better of her.'

Maddy concentrated on slicing mushroom. She tried not to feel *too* smug. 'Poor Tanya.'

'So,' said Seb, 'this house-hunting of yours.'

Changing the subject, Seb? thought Maddy. You don't want to talk about Tanya? There's a thing.

'Maddy knows all about it,' continued Seb. 'A neighbour of ours is looking for a place and Maddy's been going to viewings with her.'

'I've been to one, Seb,' Maddy corrected as she swept the chopped mushrooms into a sizzling pan. She didn't add that what Susie could afford and what Rollo was after were probably planets apart. She began chopping onions.

'Anyway, she's up to speed on the desirable villages, that sort of thing. What's your budget?'

'I dunno,' said Rollo. 'A few mill.'

Maddy's knife slipped and she just escaped from cutting her finger. 'A few *million*?'

'Will that be enough?' asked Rollo.

Was he serious? She checked out his face. Shit, he was. Maddy shook her head. You could probably buy a whole *village* for that sort of money, let alone a single house. And how unfair was that? Susie would kill to have a tiny percentage of the money Rollo was thinking of throwing at a house, and he didn't even have a family to support.

'I should think you might be able to find a suitable place for that money.' She tried to keep the irony out of her voice. 'So why the move down here?' She added the onions to the mushrooms and gave everything a stir.

'The company I'm working for is relocating, moving out of London. To be honest I was in two minds about staying with them, under the circs. But then I thought, what the heck? My old mates are down there and I can still drive up to the Smoke if I want a taste of the high life. And if I'm not cut out for the country, I can probably sack this job and get a post back in the old man's bank – I didn't make a complete arse of myself the last time I worked for him and besides, he's a bit better disposed towards me since I got that gong at the Olympics.' Rollo grinned disarmingly. 'Anyway, enough about me, I want to hear all your news. All I know is you've got kids and you live here.'

So while Maddy finished off making a beef Stroganoff and Seb kept himself and Rollo topped up with beer, he also filled in their guest with most of what had happened in the years since they'd left university. He finished up with the news that he'd come out of the last round of redundancies and defence cuts smelling as sweet as Maddy's roses.

'Promotion, eh?' said Rollo. 'Congratulations.'

'And supper's ready,' said Maddy, plonking the big pan of beef on the table. 'Budge up,' she told Rollo.

'I say,' he said. 'I'd have thought now you're a field officer's wife we'd be dining more formally than this.'

'Fuck off,' said Maddy, amiably. 'This is us you're talking to. You should know us better than that. And Seb, crack open a bottle of wine, would you?'

'Just the one?'

'For the time being.'

Chapter 9

The next morning Maddy awoke to the sound of Rose crying lustily and Nathan yelling that he needed to do a poo.

She turned her head to look at the alarm clock and instantly wished she hadn't. God, she had the hangover to end all hangovers. She cracked open an eye and saw the clock read six thirty. Drinking and small kids was not a good combo – not the morning after the night before, at any rate. Oh God, and tonight she had that party to cater for. What had she been thinking about when she'd had those last glasses of wine? Beside her Seb slumbered on, oblivious to the demands of parenthood and the forthcoming drinks party. Typical.

Maddy swung her feet out of bed and slowly levered herself into a sitting position. She stayed perfectly still, like that, for half a minute, until her head stopped banging. Gingerly she rose to her feet and headed for Nathan. Dealing with shit and a hangover...it was her punishment for enjoying herself the night before. And she only had herself to blame; the third bottle had been her idea.

Twenty minutes later she was downstairs with Rose and Nathan washed and dressed and, more importantly, a cup of hot sweet tea and a packet of ibuprofen. The weather outside was glorious, perfect for a walk to the play park. She'd give them their breakfasts, sort herself out and then head out with the kids. It would also mean the guys would have a chance to sleep off their hangovers without the kids making a racket and waking them. Not, she thought, that they particularly deserved such kindness from her but the fresh air might help clear her head and if she could wear Nathan out with some exercise there was a fighting chance he might be persuaded to take a nap when Rose went down, mid morning. She left Rose strapped in her pushchair and Nate happily playing with his bricks on the sitting room floor while she shot upstairs and got herself washed and dressed in record time, despite tiptoeing around the still-sleeping Seb.

The patch was quiet and most bedroom curtains were still drawn as Maddy wheeled Rose along the road and Nathan skipped along happily beside her, chattering incessantly in the way that almost all three-year-olds do. Maddy tried to sound engaged and interested but the reality was that she wanted to die. When they reached the park she stared longingly at the bench there but knew she wouldn't get a chance to sit down and bask in the early morning sun and instead she pushed Nathan on the swing and then provided the counter-balance at the other end of the see-saw.

'More, Mummy, faster,' demanded Nathan as Maddy pushed the see-saw down, time and time again.

She swallowed as bile rose briefly in her throat. God, she mustn't be sick, not in front of the kids.

'Go and sit down.'

Maddy spun round. 'Rollo!'

'Sweetie, you look terrible.'

'I don't feel too bright,' Maddy admitted. 'The mother of all hangovers.' She gazed at Rollo who looked disgustingly chipper and bouncy. She relinquished her see-saw duty to him and tottered off to the bench. 'Anyway, what are you doing up so early? I brought the kids out so you and Seb could have a lie-in, in peace and quiet.'

'Very noble,' said Rollo. 'We didn't drink *that* much last night.'

'Three bottles,' said Maddy, wishing her head would stop throbbing.

'Is that all?'

'*All?!*' Maddy regretted her outburst instantly. She shut her eyes as her head reeled.

'Lightweight,' said Rollo.

She opened her eyes to see him grinning at her. 'Wait till you have kids,' she grumbled. '*Then* call me a lightweight. And you still haven't answered my question, why are you up so early?'

'I heard movement and I saw you going out for a walk. I thought I'd join you.'

'Sorry, I tried to be as quiet as possible.'

'You were. You didn't wake me, I was already awake, looking at property websites.'

'Find anything?'

'Lots.'

'I would imagine the world's your oyster when you've got your sort of cash to chuck at a place.'

'I'm very lucky.'

'You are.'

Rollo stared at her. 'That was said with feeling.'

'Sorry. It's just I've got a friend who is house-hunting right now and her budget is much more limiting. The amount of choice she's got is almost zero.'

'I'm sorry.'

Maddy shrugged. 'Don't be, it's not your fault.'

Rollo carried on amusing Nathan with the see-saw and then the swings again until Rose began to get restless.

'I think it's time we returned and woke Sleeping Beauty,' said Maddy. 'And I expect you'd like some breakfast.'

'Sounds good to me.'

'Full fry?'

'You sure? I mean if you're not feeling well...'

'I'm feeling a lot better. The painkillers have kicked in and the fresh air has worked wonders.' But she was still looking forward to the moment when Rollo and Seb took themselves off to go and see the estate agents in town and then go off on some viewings that Rollo had already arranged. A quiet day, cooking canapés and finger-food, and looking after the kids, was exactly what she needed.

It was nearly four when Seb and Rollo got back from their day out, trawling Wiltshire for the more desirable properties available and which might suit Rollo's requirements, and Maddy was at the end of her tether. Far from having a lovely, quiet and peaceful day looking after the kids and rustling up tasty nibbles, Nathan had decided that being difficult, truculent and throwing himself on the floor, screaming and crying at hourly intervals, was the only way to behave. Nathan, usually good and relatively placid for a just-three-year-old, seemed to have decided that he was about to miss out on his quota of toddler tantrums and he needed to bank a few before he was deemed too old to get away with it. And what a day to pick, thought Maddy as she battled with him, the last vestiges of her hangover and the clock that ticked on relentlessly as the hour of the party approached and the plates she'd put out for the food remained empty. So when the boys barrelled through the front door they found that Maddy was stressed out to breaking point.

It didn't take long to discover why she was so close to either bursting into tears or putting Nathan up for adoption, at which point Rollo took charge and demanded to know where the nearest Waitrose was.

'But I don't understand,' said Maddy. 'Why do you want to go shopping? Why now?'

'Because,' said Rollo patiently, 'while you feed the kids an early supper, I am going to buy the party food. And after – when everyone has gone home – we'll get a takeaway delivered. Think of me as your fairy godmother – only without the fairy bit. Think I'm a bit too hetero to be a fairy.'

Maddy stared at him. 'But you can't buy the food. You're the guest of honour.'

Rollo shook his head as he pulled his car keys out of his jacket pocket. 'Just shut up and sort out the kids, Mads. This is the least I can do to repay you for lending me your husband all day and putting me up.'

'But... but...' But the front door had already slammed.

By the time Rollo had got back, laden with carrier bags containing mini pork pies, frozen vol-au-vents, blinis, smoked salmon, cream cheese, crackers and dozens of other things that could be turned into delicious bite-sized snacks, Nathan and Rose had both been fed fish fingers and chips and were being bathed by Seb. Both of these things were treats in the kids' eyes and so Nathan's tantrums had been replaced by giggles and smiles while Rose, always a cheerful child, was even sunnier than ever. Maddy had wondered why she never seemed to reap the benefit of having perfect, happy, smiley children when it was she who spent her life looking after them. However, she hadn't been able to dwell for long on the unfairness of motherhood as she had had to whizz round the sitting room, tidying up the toys, then pushing a hoover round the ground floor to make the downstairs look more like a home and less like the council tip.

With fifteen minutes to spare before the first of the guests was due to make an appearance the children were tucked up in bed, snacks were warming in the oven, Rollo had made three jugs of Pimm's and Maddy had managed to change into a pretty dress and put on a lick of make-up.

'Phew,' she said, with feeling, as she looked at her tidy house and saw the trays of glasses standing ready.

'Don't know why you were so worried,' said Rollo, grinning.

'I was worried because I didn't know you had a magic wand.'

Rollo waggled his eyebrows suggestively. 'Never heard it called that before.'

'Grow up, Rollo,' said Seb, coming down the stairs.

'Killjoy,' countered Rollo.

'Nathan wants a goodnight kiss,' said Seb. 'Rose is already spark out.'

'You're a star,' said Maddy, giving Seb a peck on the cheek as she headed for the stairs. From being stressed and anxious she was now, suddenly, rather looking forward to the party.

Thirty minutes later, everyone had arrived, Rollo was lapping up the attention just like the guests were lapping up the Pimm's and the beer, and Maddy was chatting happily to her friends as she passed around the plates of food. It was obvious to Maddy that her party had already developed into two camps: at one end of the room were the Rayners where the conversation was polite and restrained, and at the other end of the room were the Collinses and Rollo and from where guffaws of raucous laughter billowed. Those with the Rayners cast occasional, envious glances at the other group but seemed to be trapped from abandoning the boss and his wife by politeness and protocol. Even Maddy, circulating as she was with the nibbles, found herself drawn to Rollo's group rather more often than to the Rayners' end of the room. As she offered her guests some mini sausage rolls she eavesdropped on what Susie was saying to Rollo.

'So,' she said, 'what was it like standing on the podium?'

'It's all a bit of a blur,' said Rollo. 'The whole event was just so bonkers: the noise as we got to the grandstands; the media circus; the interviews; that thing in Trafalgar Square afterwards...I mean, don't get me wrong, it was fab but the whole thing blew my mind a bit.'

'That, and the drink he consumed celebrating,' added Seb.

Maddy pushed the plate of warm sausage rolls into the little group and everyone took one.

'And who could blame him,' said Mike, taking a bite of his. 'I knew some army rowers – pretty serious ones who did Henley. Their training regime seemed bloody harsh – all the things they were and weren't allowed to do. I seem to recall that drinking was one of the proscribed things.' He finished his sausage roll and took another one as Maddy was still holding a half-full plate.

'I don't recall that ever applying to Rollo,' said Seb.

'Oi,' said Rollo, 'I'll have you know that when we went to the training camp barely a drop touched my lips for weeks. And talking of drink...?' He nodded at Susie and Mike's empty glasses.

'Oh, just fruit juice or lemonade for us,' said Susie.

'You sure? You can't be driving, surely. Don't you live on the patch?' said Rollo.

Maddy shot Seb a significant look. He picked up her silent message that the conversation was straying into dodgy territory. 'I'll get the drinks,' he cut in before Rollo could try and force Mike and Susie to reveal the reason for their abstinence.

'So,' said Susie, 'what brings you to this neck of the woods – apart from visiting Seb and Maddy?'

'House-hunting.'

Bugger, thought Maddy, another minefield. But there was nothing she could do about this new conversation, not without looking crass and obvious.

'What a fantastic choice there is round here,' Rollo was saying. 'All those wonderful villages and some of those old farm houses and barn conversions...'

Maddy glanced at Susie; her mouth was set in a tight line.

'Mind you,' continued Rollo, oblivious to Susie's discomfiture, 'there's a place I saw today which knocks the spots off almost everything else – a bit outside my budget but worth it, in my opinion. It's an old manor in Ashton-cum-Bavant, right on the village green. Jacobean and an absolute beaut of a place. Seven bedrooms, the most wonderful staircase and it's even got a ballroom. OK, not a very *big* ballroom, but how many houses do you come across that even have one to start with?'

Susie forced a smile and took her refilled glass from Seb with a brief nod of thanks.

Rollo turned to Seb. 'I was just telling Susie and Mike about that manor house we saw today,' he said. 'You know the one. Tell them what a fab place it is.'

Maddy looked at Seb again. Nooo.

'Well, I think it's probably a bit over-the-top for us ordinary folk,' said Seb.

'Come off it,' said Rollo. 'You lot must be in the ideal position to buy a nice pad – jobs for life, fat government pension guaranteed at the end of it, renting quarters at a very non-commercial rate. You'd be bonkers not to take advantage of all that.'

Maddy glanced at Susie, who looked stricken.

'Hey,' said Rollo. 'Just remembered, Maddy says some of her friends are house-hunting. I ought to meet them, exchange notes. You've got to introduce me when you get the chance, Seb.'

Seb mightn't know about the Collinses' dire financial situation but he did know that Mike was struggling to find work and that having Rollo banging on about his multimillion-pound house budget was hardly tactful.

'Actually, talking of introductions...' Seb grabbed Rollo's arm and tugged him away from the group.

Rollo looked a little surprised but followed Seb like a lamb – not without grabbing one of the last sausage rolls as he left.

Maddy shoved the two remaining sausage rolls under the noses of Susie and Mike as if giving them something to eat would take away the awkwardness of the situation.

Susie shook her head. 'Actually, Mads, I hope you don't think I'm horribly rude,' she said, 'but I've got a terrible headache starting. I'm sorry but I'm going to be a real party-pooper and crash out.'

Maddy gave Susie a sympathetic smile and pretended she believed her friend. 'Oh, no. Susie, can I get you a painkiller?'

Susie shook her head a second time. 'I've got loads at home. Sweet of you to offer, though.'

'But you can stay, Mike?'

'I think I'd like to make sure Susie's all right.'

Maddy looked from one to the other. No, they wanted out. She didn't blame them; it couldn't be much fun to be surrounded by people who could drink themselves silly without risking a trip to rehab, nor having to listen to someone without a financial care in the world. 'OK, if that's what you'd like.' She put down her plate of food and escorted them to the door. 'Thanks for popping round,' she said. 'I'll catch up with you in the week, Susie. Hope you feel better soon.'

'Night, Mads,' the couple said as they headed down her path and across the road to their own quarter.

Maddy watched them go and gave them a last wave as they went in their own door. How she wished she could magic things better for them.

Chapter 10

Susie leaned against the inside of her own front door and rubbed her face with her hands. 'I'm sorry, I couldn't keep up the pretence any more.'

Mike put his arm round her. 'I know, I know,' he said as he rubbed her shoulder. 'It's all my fault.'

'No, it isn't. It's no one's fault; it's luck, it's circumstances, it's... oh, I don't know what's to blame but I do know it isn't *you*.' She made her way into the sitting room and Mike followed.

As she flopped onto the sofa Mike looked at her with disbelief. 'Don't be so naive, Susie. We both know that, somewhere along the line, I fucked up my career. Fucked it up big time.'

Susie sighed. 'OK, so you *and I* made a few errors but we don't deserve this kind of shit. I keep thinking that things have got to turn a corner sooner or later.'

'It'd better be sooner,' said Mike with heavy emphasis. 'I don't think I can cope with pretending that things are all rosy for much longer. Thank God no one on the patch knows what the real situation is.'

Susie looked at her feet and could feel her face was flaring.

'Susie?'

She looked up.

Mike's eyes narrowed. 'So who have you told?' Susie said nothing. 'You've told Maddy, haven't you. How much?'

'Only that there's a bit of a hitch on the mortgage front.' She looked up at Mike pleadingly. 'She'd have guessed anyway as soon as she saw the sort of budget we've got for a house. And I needed her onside about the job in the mess – with Seb being the PMC I wanted her to put in a word for me.'

'So Seb knows.' Mike's voice was icy. 'Well thank you very much.'

'No, no he doesn't. I'm sure of that. Maddy promised not to tell him and I'm sure she hasn't said a word. Mike, I'd trust Maddy with my life – if she promised not to then that's that.'

But Mike didn't look convinced. 'You'd better be right. Let's face it, I mightn't have much pride left but I'd like to keep the last trace of what little remains.'

A few days later, Jenna parked her little Corsa outside Maddy's house and got out. She grabbed her big box of hair products and went to the front door to ring the bell. She looked about her. Despite the fact that it had been almost two years since her adulterous affair that had taken place when her then-husband had been out in Afghanistan, she was still wary about spending time on the married patches. Her name had been mud back then and, even though she had helped Maddy when baby Rose had arrived prematurely, Jenna had a feeling it still was where some of the wives were concerned. Most of Maddy's close friends had accepted her back into the fold and were her customers, but that left an awful lot of other wives who still loathed her. However, as it was much easier for Maddy if Jenna came to her house to do her hair, Jenna, being a good mate, was happy to oblige.

'Come in, come in,' said Maddy brightly. 'Fancy a cuppa before we get started?'

Jenna nodded. 'Coffee please. Are we in the kitchen as usual?'

'Yes, go on through. I'm just going to put Rose down for her nap and stick *Peppa Pig* on the DVD for Nathan.' Maddy followed Jenna into her kitchen, put the kettle on and then darted off to sort her children out.

'Now,' said Maddy, on her return. 'I've got some news.'

'Good, I hope.'

Maddy nodded, her eyes shining. 'It's brilliant. Well, I think it is.' She spooned coffee granules into two mugs.

'Spit it out then,' said Jenna.

'Remember Zoë's salon?'

'Yeah,' said Jenna, warily. Zoë's was the salon where Jenna had worked at the battalion's previous barracks until she'd set up as a direct rival. Her relationship with Zoë had, unsurprisingly, ended badly.

'Well, I've got the authorities to agree to the wives setting up a salon in the new community centre and it'll be properly kitted out and everything. *And*, and this is the best bit, Camilla Rayner says you can run it. How about that?'

'What?' This wasn't good news, this was awful.

'Yes, really – your very own, official salon.' Maddy's enthusiasm for her project was palpable. She passed Jenna her coffee.

'Hang on...'

'Why?'

'I think I should have a say in this, and my say is no, no way.'

'Oh.' Maddy looked surprised. 'But... but I thought you'd be pleased.'

'Setting up again? Here? Like that's going to go down well with the wives. It'll be as popular as a bucket of cold sick.'

'No. Everyone loved having Zoë's. It was so convenient. And you're a fantastic hairdresser.'

'Mads, I know you mean well, but no one'll come and get their hair done with me. I'll be blackballed, won't I?'

'Of course you won't.'

'I don't want to find out that I'm right. I love doing your hair and your friends' hair but you're all officers' wives, you're different. I don't go to the sergeants' mess because I'm pretty sure no one'll talk to me and I'm not prepared to find out if it's the same with the soldiers' wives. But a pound to a penny says it is.'

'But supposing you're wrong?'

'And supposing I'm right?' Jenna glared at Maddy, willing her to see it from her point of view.

'But I went right out on a limb for you. It took me ages to convince Camilla that it was a good idea. And I've got the funding out of the garrison welfare fund. I've worked so hard for this – for you.'

Jenna felt like a heel. 'I'm sorry, Mads, really I am, but I wished you'd asked me first.'

'I wanted to surprise you.'

'You did that all right.'

'At least think about it.'

Jenna shook her head.

'Why don't I canvass opinion?' said Maddy.

'You'll be wasting your time. And, to be honest, I'd rather you didn't. It'd just draw attention to the fact I am here. Living off-base means that an awful lot of people have no idea.'

Maddy sighed. She looked fed up. 'You'd better get on with my hair then, before word gets out you're here and the lynch mob arrives.'

'Don't be like that, Maddy. I didn't ask you to go to all that trouble on my account.'

'No, I'm sorry. I'm being a cow. But think about it...please?'

Jenna sighed. 'OK, I'll think about it but I'm making no promises.' She lifted a lock of Maddy's auburn hair. 'Right...the usual?'

Seb sat in the mess ante-room with the regimental admin officer, Sergeant McManners and the mess secretary ready to interview the prospective candidates for the post of mess manager. They'd all studied the applications and they'd all agreed there wasn't a stand-out contender. Susie, like the others, had her good points and was definitely in with a shout, thought Seb, except...except he was really worried about the appropriateness of selecting her. But if he didn't swing it with his fellow interviewers he'd have Maddy to answer to, to say nothing of the guilt he'd carry at making life even harder for the Collinses.

One by one the applicants trooped in to be quizzed about their previous experience, their knowledge of running events and of accounting and catering. And one by one they were given hypothetical problems regarding complaints or protocol or etiquette. To Seb's relief, Susie seemed to have the most comprehensive knowledge of the more ceremonial side of mess functions. Not entirely unexpected given that she'd attended a fair few in her time as an officer's wife but it was definitely a point in her favour.

'So,' said Seb, 'moving on. How would you cope if the staff complained to you about abuse from a mess member?'

Susie considered this for a moment. 'First, I would want to find out if there were any witnesses and I would gather any evidence I could, whether it supported or refuted the claim. Then I would come to you.'

Seb nodded. Textbook answer, in his opinion.

'And how,' said the admin officer, 'given that you are friends with the officers, would you address them?'

'I would call them sir or ma'am, just as Sergeant McManners does now, and I would expect them to call me Mrs Collins, just as we all call Sergeant McManners, Sergeant McManners. I wouldn't dream of letting things slip in that department. Besides, in a few years the people who live in the mess will have changed, there'll be a new crop of junior, single officers and my past will become irrelevant.'

'Good point,' said Seb. 'Now then, catering. Your application says you have experience.'

Susie explained about the small catering business that she'd run. 'I understand how to put together interesting and innovative menus, I can do economical as well as elaborate and I can cater to a budget.'

Out of the corner of his eye he saw the RAO nod in approval. Seb thought it mightn't be as tricky as he'd first thought to get the other board members to agree about Susie's suitability for the job.

After a few more questions, Susie was shown out of the room and left Seb and his colleagues to their deliberations.

'So,' said Seb, 'thoughts?'

As he expected they agreed with him that Susie was possibly the strongest candidate but they were all adamant that the fact she was a major's wife was a real sticking point.

'But, as Mrs Collins herself pointed out, in a few years no one will know or care.'

Sergeant McManners wasn't to be swayed but Seb was pretty sure he had the other two onside.

'Let's vote. Those in favour of employing Mrs Collins...'

He put his own hand up and the admin officer followed suit and after an agonising couple of seconds, so did the mess secretary.

'Sorry, Sergeant McManners,' said Seb.

'It's no skin off my nose,' he said cheerfully. 'I'm out of here, remember. By the time Mrs Collins is properly in post I'll be running my own little pub in Wales.'

'You're all sorted, then, Sergeant?'

'Oh yes, sir. The army did me a big favour when it decided to have done with me. I'm not complaining. I know there's plenty who aren't happy but I'm not one of them.'

Unlike the Collinses. Although, thought Seb, he hoped that now Susie had got the job she wanted, things might be looking up for them.

'You could at least look pleased,' said Susie.

Mike shook his head. 'It's not right.'

'Mike, whether it's *right* or not is irrelevant. It's a *job*. We can get a mortgage now, we can buy that house.'

'But I don't want that house.'

Susie banged the kitchen table with the flat of her hand. 'We don't have a choice.'

Mike glared at her. 'So rub it in, why don't you? Rub it in that this is all my fault.' His voice got louder. 'I'm the one to blame, I'm the one who is going to be on the dole and,' he was shouting now, 'I'm the one with the fucking awful credit rating.'

'I didn't say that,' Susie shouted back at him.

'You didn't have to.'

The doorbell rang.

The pair stared at each other across the table, like two cats about to fight. 'I'll go and see who it is,' said Susie.

It was Maddy with a bunch of flowers. 'Is this a bad time?'

Had she heard the row? wondered Susie. Given how jerry-built these quarters were it was quite likely. Still, never complain, never explain, as Disraeli had once said. She smiled and shook her head.

'Seb's just got home from work and told me the news,' continued Maddy. 'I am so pleased. Here,' she said as she thrust the flowers at her neighbour. 'To say congratulations.'

'Thanks. It's quite a relief.'

'Let's hope it means your luck is getting better.'

'It can't get any worse.'

'No... well. Anyway, I just wanted to give you the flowers.'

Maddy turned and went back to her own house as Susie shut the door.

'At least Maddy is pleased for me,' she said to Mike as she found a vase and put her flowers in water.

'She isn't being viewed as a total dead loss though, is she? Not like me.'

'And feeling sorry for yourself isn't going to make things better.'

Mike stared at her. 'No? You apply for one job – one miserable job – and you waltz straight into it and I... how many applications? Dozens? Scores? And I've had three interviews. And don't tell me that these things take time or any other crap platitudes. We both know it's because I'm not good enough.' He got up and stormed out.

Susie watched him bleakly as he slammed the front door behind him. Should she have stopped him? Should she have handled things differently? She pulled out a chair and slumped down onto it. God, she wanted a drink.

Chapter 11

Mike stormed through the patch, angry with the world, angry with Susie and angry with himself. If only... if only... But wishing things were different wasn't going to alter anything. Whatever Susie had said the other night he knew he'd fucked up somewhere along the line and now he was paying for it. Along with his family. He couldn't bear the idea that they were going to have to live on that tip of an estate in that appalling house. The place was a dump. It didn't matter that the village centre was pretty, because where they were going to live was anything but. And he dreaded to think what the neighbours were going to be like – out-of-work layabouts with addiction issues. The irony of his assessment wasn't lost on him. He was going to be out of work and he'd had his own battles with drink in the past... but he was an army officer. He wasn't exactly a contender for *The Jeremy Kyle Show*.

His mind roamed over and over the general unfairness of life as his footsteps took him through the patch and towards the barracks. When he looked up and took note of his surroundings he realised he was walking towards the mess. He *knew* he should keep on going, he *knew* that he shouldn't go in, but what the hell? His life was in such a shit state it couldn't get any worse. Besides, one drink wouldn't hurt.

He walked into the bar where many of the living-in members were enjoying a post-work-pre-supper drink.

'Hi, Mike,' said a number of them as they saw him.

'Hi,' he returned. 'Dawkins, get me a large gin, please.'

He ignored the surprised look he got from both the mess barman and the other officers present and he also ignored the subsequent awkward silence.

Dawkins pushed a mess chit and pencil over with the drink so Mike could sign for it but Mike ignored the slip of paper and grabbed, greedily, for his gin. He took a large slug before he picked up the pencil and scribbled his name.

'That sort of day, was it, Mike?' said James.

Mike took another gulp and nodded. 'Pretty much.' He drained his drink. 'Same again, please.'

The officers in the bar exchanged glances and Sam Lewis looked at her watch. She might have arrived since Mike and Susie had both gone on the wagon but she was still aware of their past – pretty much everyone was.

'Think I might go and grab a quick bath before dinner,' she said. She put her glass on the bar and disappeared. There were other mutterings and mumblings from the others about things they needed to do or phone calls that couldn't wait and in another couple of minutes the bar was empty except for Mike and Dawkins.

Mike looked around him. 'Just call me Mr Popularity.'

'Sir,' said Dawkins.

'It's all right, Dawkins, you don't have to stay and talk to me, just because the others have high-tailed it. I imagine they're thinking that failure is catching – like the flu.'

'Sir,' said Dawkins again.

'But before you go back to your cubbyhole, I'll have another one. I'll ring the bell when I want you again.'

'Sir.'

*

Susie's phone rang. She stopped mashing the potatoes for a shepherd's pie and picked up the handset.

'Susie? It's James here.'

'Hi, James,' said Susie, putting on a cheerful voice. James didn't need to know how grim things were for her right now. 'What can I do for you?'

'Look, this is a bit tricky and I may be out of order but Mike's in the mess and by the looks of things he's on a personal mission to see how fast he can get through a bottle of gin.'

Susie shut her eyes and leaned against the counter. Dear God. Just when she thought it couldn't get worse... 'Thank you, James. No, you're not out of order at all, and I'm glad you told me. I'll come over.'

'It might be an idea to bring the car. He's pretty far gone.'

'Thanks. I'll be there as soon as I can.'

Susie grabbed the car keys and raced out of the house. Part of her wanted to cry and the other part of her was seething with anger. How could he? How *could* he? Like getting shit-faced was going to make anything better. Barely checking the mirror and before doing up her seatbelt, Susie backed the car out of the drive and then scorched up the road towards the mess. Breaking the rule about not parking near a building, left over from IRA car-bombing days, she abandoned her vehicle bang in front of the entrance and raced up the steps. James was waiting for her.

'How bad is he?'

James raised his eyebrows.

'That bad, eh?'

James nodded. 'He had two doubles in short order before I left the bar to do some admin. When I got back he was still drinking and I don't think he's slowed up any.'

'OK,' said Susie. 'Let's get him home while he can still walk to the car.'

She went into the bar. 'Come on, Mike,' she said quietly. 'Supper's almost ready.'

'Shusie,' Mike slurred. 'Wha' you doin' here?' His face was flushed and his eyes were bleary. 'You fanshy a drink too?' He waved his glass at her, slopping the gin over the side.

'No thanks, Mike.'

'Go on. Don't be such a shpoilsport.'

'I just think it's time you came home.'

'Why?'

'Because you've had enough,' said Susie.

'Of coursh I've had enough. I've had enough of you, I've had enough of not getting a job, of being on the fucking wagon...' He waved his glass around again and spilt gin over James's sleeve.

'That's enough, Mike.'

Mike leaned towards Susie. 'Don't you tell me what to do.' He prodded a finger at her. 'Jusht because you're so bloody clever and you got a job, doesn't mean you wear the trousers now.'

'Mike...come on,' Susie pleaded.

'Do as Susie says,' said James. 'You're drunk.'

'Yeah, and so would you be in my position.'

'Maybe, but we both know it doesn't help matters. Time to go home, Mike.'

'I tried being shober,' said Mike. 'Look where it got me.' He lurched off his bar stool. 'I know you don't want me here. I'm an embarrassment. A drunk and a no-hoper.' His eyes filled with maudlin tears.

'Come on, Mike,' said Susie, gently. 'The car's outside.'

Mike allowed himself to be led away. He and Susie got

as far as the entrance hall when he stumbled and sagged. He was a dead weight and Susie could just about support him but she couldn't propel him forwards and getting him down the steps and into the car was going to be impossible. Once again, James came to her rescue. Taking the bulk of Mike's weight he was able to help get him out to the car and then hold Mike up while Susie got the passenger door open. James bundled and folded Mike into the front seat and then got in the back.

'You don't have to, James,' said Susie, squirming with embarrassment at the situation.

'And how are you going to get him out again and back into the house?'

Susie looked at him and sighed. He was right, of course.

'Thanks,' she said as she got in and started the engine. She drove the few hundred yards back to her quarter. 'Thank God the kids aren't home,' she muttered as she went to open the front door.

James managed to haul Mike out of the car again and between them the pair managed to half drag, half carry Mike indoors. He was not completely out of it – he was just conscious enough to mumble incoherent words now and again but he didn't seem to have a clue about what his surroundings were or what he was doing. They managed to get him as far as the sofa in the sitting room and into the recovery position. Wordlessly, Susie went to the kitchen and returned with the washing up bowl which she placed on the floor beside him. James had wedged Mike with cushions to stop him rolling onto his back and had loosened his collar.

'Thanks, James. I owe you.'

'Any friend would have done the same.'

'Maybe.' She looked at the floor. 'James, can I ask you another huge favour? Can I ask you to have a word to any witnesses and ask them to be discreet? Things are bad enough without...'

'Without this being the hot topic of the day?'

Susie nodded. 'We all know what the mess and the patch can be like.'

'Consider it done. And if it's any consolation, Dawkins is the soul of discretion. I dread to think what he's witnessed in his years as the mess bar steward and I've never known him say a word.'

Susie felt huge relief. It would be bad enough if all the officers knew about Mike's bender but if the soldiers did too... Not that it really mattered, as they would soon be out of that world altogether.

James returned to the bar and to judge by the sudden silence as he walked in the topic of conversation had probably been exactly as Susie had feared. The mess members, having fled rather than witness the embarrassing scene, seemed only too happy to pick over the bones of it now the source of their discomfort had gone.

James passed on Susie's request. 'And,' he said, turning to Dawkins, 'I know I don't need to say anything to you.'

'Sir,' said Dawkins by way of acknowledgement.

'You probably know where more bodies are buried than the gravedigger at Highgate Cemetery.'

'Sir.' Dawkins chest swelled.

'Of course we won't say anything,' said Sam. 'Not to anyone who wasn't here.'

'Not to anyone *at all*,' said James, firmly. 'It'd be too easy to let something slip.'

Sam shrugged. 'If you say so.'

The others nodded in agreement and there were murmurs of 'none of our business, anyway' and 'you're probably right'.

James wasn't sure if the genie had been put back in the bottle but he'd done his best.

Maddy saw Camilla check her watch and gaze around the table in the dining room of the ex-brigadier's quarter and now soon-to-be-converted communities centre and at the wives she'd coerced or co-opted to be on her committee. The room was chilly, despite the fact that it was the beginning of July, and there was a faint smell of damp. It would be different when the building was in proper use again and the sooner that happened the better it would be for everyone in the battalion. If this meeting was going to move things along then Maddy was all in favour of it – even if she knew it was going to mean a shedload of unpaid work.

Camilla pushed an A4 pad of paper and a pen in Maddy's direction and said, 'And I'm sure you don't mind taking the minutes, Maddy, do you?'

Maddy was tempted to counter that she blooming well did, but instead she picked up the pen and quickly listed the names of the attendees she knew. There were a couple who she had to get to introduce themselves and then she was done.

'Right,' said Camilla. 'Shall we get on?'

There was a definite inference, thought Maddy, that she had deliberately held up proceedings by trying to do a proper job with the minutes. She resisted the temptation to hand the job back to Camilla but, instead, she sighed and gritted her teeth.

'As you know,' said Camilla, 'we've received funding from various sources and the garrison commander has approved the conversion of this house in principle, but before anything can go any further we need to be in agreement of what we all want from this amenity. I've had a number of suggestions and now I want to see if the wives, whom you represent, agree.'

The wives around the table, who had been drawn from a cross-section of the battalion, nodded. In addition to the wives, the regimental admin officer was present as he also had the role of paymaster for the battalion and if businesses were run in this centre he would need to oversee the accounting and auditing.

'So,' said Camilla, 'here are the proposals.' She ran through the ideas for a coffee shop and a crèche, both of which would be open every morning from nine o'clock till twelve thirty, plus the hairdressing salon upstairs, open for the same hours, and the general space where groups like the choir and the book club could meet which would be available to interested parties right up to ten in the evening. Then she showed them rough plans as to how the house would be divided up to accommodate them. There were nods of assent. 'All we have to do now is to find some lovely willing volunteers to run these facilities,' trilled Camilla, looking expectantly and significantly at those assembled around her.

Instantly the wives looked in any direction but Camilla's.

'Come on now,' she cajoled.

'I think I might have someone lined up for the crèche,' said Maddy.

Camilla nodded in approval before saying, 'How about the hairdresser? Any talented wives here?'

Still not catching her eye, heads were shaken.

'I think,' said Maddy, 'we ought to put an ad in the garrison newsletter. We may not have anyone who would like to do it from 1 Herts but I bet someone in the garrison could.'

'I'll leave that with you, Maddy, then.'

The saccharine sweetness in Camilla's voice made Maddy's toes curl.

'I'll get on the case.'

'And you'll talk to your childminder friend, too? She needs to see the regimental admin officer to get the paperwork sorted.'

Maddy nodded. 'It's Caro Edwards. She's the wife of B Company's new 2IC but she's not here yet.'

'Well, talk to her anyway. You don't mind, do you?'

This might be Camilla's committee and Camilla would get all the praise from the brass for setting up the community centre, but it seemed to Maddy it was she who was doing the donkey work. Ho hum.

Caro picked up the phone before Josh could get to it. The four-year-old thought it the best fun to shout 'smelly poo pants' followed by shrieks of high-pitched giggles to whoever the poor unsuspecting caller was. Of course, if it was some spammer Caro couldn't care less, but on a number of occasions it had been someone who mattered and who hadn't been amused.

'Caro, it's me, Maddy.'

'Maddy! How lovely to hear from you.'

'How's the move going?'

'Don't ask,' said Caro with a heartfelt sigh. 'But I'm getting the cleaners in. No way can I bring this place up to snuff with the kids underfoot. While it's going to be great for Oliver to change school in the summer holidays it doesn't make life easy for me.'

'No, I can imagine,' said Maddy. 'Anyway, I have a proposition for you – a job here.'

'I haven't been dicked for something already with the battalion? I haven't even left this place yet!'

'You guessed it, but it's a good dicked.'

'There is *never* a *good* dicked.'

'You'll get paid.'

'Oh. Well, that's different. What is it?'

Caro listened while Maddy told her about the new community centre and the proposal for a crèche and that Camilla Rayner thought that Caro was the perfect person to run it.

'So, this is going to be on a proper commercial basis?'

'Yes. The profits will go back to the battalion welfare fund – if there are any – but you'll get paid a wage. I don't know all the nitpicky details, the regimental admin officer is dealing with that side of things. I can let you have his number if you'd like to go over that aspect with him. And there's lots of form-filling to do, as you can imagine. Oh, and I'll email you the plans for the rooms being converted for the crèche. You may want to check they contain everything you'll need – you're getting a little bathroom and loo and a tiny kitchenette so you can heat up food and milk and stuff but I'm no expert as to what else you'll need.'

'Thanks, I'd like that – and that phone number. I have to say this is a first; to have a job ready and waiting for me. Are you thinking of going back to work?'

Maddy's sigh gusted over the connection. 'Honestly, what with the kids and one thing and another it just doesn't seem possible. Luckily, we don't need the money so much now since Seb's prom—'

But Caro didn't hear why Maddy didn't need the money because Josh chose that moment to fall backwards off the arm of the sofa and was screaming blue murder.

Caro said goodbye to Maddy hastily as she rushed to see

how badly Josh had hurt himself. After a cuddle and a biscuit Josh decided he was feeling sufficiently better for Caro to resume what she'd been doing before; working out the kit they'd need to have with them in the car for the trip to their new home and what could be packed by the removal men. Why, she wondered, didn't moving, even after half a dozen times, ever become any easier?

Susie was also thinking about packing but, unlike Caro who was looking forward to her move, Susie was dreading her own one. It wasn't just the hassle of the move, it was the change in lifestyle, the massive drop in income, the effect it was going to have on the twins, to say nothing of what it was doing to Mike's state of mind. Since his 'lapse' he had been completely down; beating himself up about getting so drunk, being a loser, being a burden...Susie tried to be cheerful, tried to be supportive, but the reality was she couldn't keep shouldering everything all the time. Him moping and moaning about how life wasn't fair was getting her down too, and she didn't have the time or the energy to waste on bitching about it or, alternatively, trying to look on the bright side to stop herself from wanting to take a leap off Beachy Head. Someone had to spit on their hands and crack on because Mike didn't seem to be able to.

As she was digging out her airing cupboard and piling the spare room bed high with linen she heard the rattle of the letter box. In need of displacement activity, she pottered downstairs to see what the postman had delivered; an envelope addressed to Mike and some bumph from a double glazing company. Ha! Like the army was about to invest in that. She sighed as she put Mike's letter on the hall table –

no doubt yet another rejection. She thought about just chucking it in the bin. The poor man didn't need yet another kick in the crotch.

She returned upstairs and carried on sorting and doing until she heard the front door slam. She glanced at her watch – lunchtime.

'Hi,' she said as she ran downstairs.

Mike was standing at the bottom, the open letter in his hand. Uh-oh.

'I don't bloody believe it. I don't!'

Susie was about to mutter something sympathetic when she saw the expression on his face.

'What is it?'

'I've got a job. I've only gone and got a bloody job!'

Chapter 12

'What? What?!' Susie felt ridiculously excited by this news.

'I'm emergency planning officer for Winterspring District Council.'

'Which means you'll be doing what?'

'Flood defences, that sort of thing. Setting up temporary mortuaries in the event of an airliner crashing in the area.'

'Oh, Mike. I am so pleased.'

'What? About the chance of an air disaster?'

'No, numpty. I'm so pleased about the job.' She gazed at him with real fondness.

'You're pleased?' Mike grabbed Susie round the waist and planted a fat kiss on her cheek. 'Maybe things are finally looking up.'

'What's the salary?'

Mike sighed. 'Well...not brilliant to start with; only twenty-eight thousand, but it'll increase over time.'

'Bit of a drop for you.'

Mike nodded. 'But with your pay...And it comes with a company car. I have to do a fair bit of travelling.'

'Hey, that's a perk and it really doesn't matter if you're earning less than you are right now. It's just wonderful you've got a job. A proper job.' Susie paused. 'Of course, with both of us working we'll have to budget for childcare. I don't think the twins are old enough to be left alone when they come home from school. But, hey, you've got a job and that's just brilliant and we can cross the childcare bridge later. When do you start?'

'In a few weeks. I'll still be on resettlement leave so I'll still be getting paid for this job. We'll be on double money for a bit.'

'Good,' said Susie, emphatically. 'Glad to know you can squeeze the last drops out of the army. Though, considering what they have done to us and the kids, they owe us. Big time.'

Mike laughed – laughed for the first time in an age. 'You sound like Don Corleone,' he said.

'If I could get my own back on the army and I thought it would do any good, I'd *behave* like Don Corleone!'

After Mike had returned to work Susie popped across the road to share the good news with Maddy who was, predictably, almost as chuffed as her neighbour.

'Oh, Susie, I am so pleased for you. That must be such a relief.'

'It wasn't just the money – because we'd be really struggling on just what I'm going to be earning,' Susie admitted. 'It was the whole macho, not-being-the-man-of-the-house, wearing-the-trousers, being-the-breadwinner thing that was getting Mike down. It didn't help that I only went for one job and I got it, while I dread to think how many he applied for.'

'But you can't beat yourself up about you getting lucky first time out.'

Susie looked Maddy steadily in the eye. 'We both know my *luck* had a helping hand.'

'Truly, Susie, if Seb hadn't reckoned that you can make a proper fist of the job, he wouldn't have given it to you.

You must have impressed him to have been right up there in the running.'

'Maybe.' Susie looked doubtful. 'Anyway, at least now we can start to move forward.'

'And talking of moving...?'

'All being well, we exchange contracts next week. The people moving out are going into rented accommodation and we don't have a place to sell so there's no chain and this is all very straightforward. The advantage is that we can probably get in and get everything straight before the girls come back from school.'

'Have they seen the house?'

Susie shook her head. 'It's going to be an interesting moment when they do. I mean a quarter is hardly palatial but...well, you've seen the place. And the estate.' Her happy mood evaporated. There was no getting over the fact that the place was a dump and their neighbours...Mike had called the estate ASBO Central. 'And then it's going to be even more interesting when I take them to see their new school which I'm going to do as soon as they come home for their summer hols. The comp doesn't break up till the week after Browndown so I've arranged for them to visit it and meet their head of year.'

'Where are you going to send them?'

'Winterspring Comp.'

'What's it like?'

'Modern, big. Nine tutor groups in each year.'

'*Nine?!*'

Susie nodded. 'I know...don't.' It was so far from ideal but they had no choice – not if they couldn't afford to pay for education. 'Over a thousand kids go there. Once you get away from the private sector you enter a whole other world.

But there's a bus from the village every morning so that means Mike and I don't have to juggle a school run along with getting to work on time. And going on the school bus should help them to make new friends. And they're bright girls so they ought to be in the top set for everything and there's lots of kids that go from the comp to uni so the move shouldn't wreck their educational chances.' Susie wondered if she was trying to convince herself as much as Maddy that she and Mike had made the right choice. And maybe she was exaggerating about the 'lots of kids that go from the comp to uni' bit. A few did, for sure, but from what Susie had ascertained it was a pretty small minority. Still, her girls would surely be amongst that minority – given the educational start they'd had. Susie was fully aware, though, that regardless of that start the comp wasn't going to provide the same social chances. Half the thing about going into private education was to do with the Old Boy or Old Girl network. There'd be precious little chance of a network of any description at Winterspring Comprehensive.

'I remember the school bus,' said Maddy. 'I used to get half my homework done on it before I got off. Of course, sometimes it bore a remarkable resemblance to my best friend's.'

Susie grinned. 'And talking about the bus journey home...' She paused. She needed to ask Maddy a monster favour but was this the right moment?

Maddy looked puzzled. 'Is there a problem? Surely there'll be a bus back for them.'

'Oh, there is. Except there won't be anyone in when they get back. I won't get away from the mess till five thirty at the earliest – much later if there's any sort of function, and Mike'll be working till gone five as well and the kids finish school at three. I really don't think they're old enough just yet to be left for well over two hours on their own.'

'What are you going to do?'

'That's the thing, Mads.' Susie looked her friend in the face. 'You said to me a while back that you couldn't see that you'd be getting back into the saddle any time soon regarding getting a job, what with being the OC's wife and with two tiny children...'

'Ye-e-e-s,' said Maddy, slightly warily.

'Well, there's a school bus that passes the barracks. If the girls caught that one, could they jump off here and stay with you till either Mike or I can pick them up after work? I'd pay you, of course,' Susie added hastily. 'The proper going rate and everything.'

Maddy considered Susie's proposition. 'Susie,' she began, 'can I think about it for a day or two? It's quite tempting, and you know I adore Ella and Katie but it *is* quite a commitment.'

'Yes, yes of course.' Susie hadn't totally expected Maddy to bite her hand off but she'd thought there might be a bit more enthusiasm.

'In fact, it might be worth getting hold of Caro. She's coming back to the battalion, she's qualified. You might be better off with her. Not that I wouldn't step in if you, or she, had an emergency.'

Dan Armstrong let himself into his flat and found Jenna, as usual, lounging on the sofa, reading a magazine. Eliot was on his playmat, under his activity centre, bashing the brightly coloured beads and bangles that were suspended above him. The flat, as always, was pristinely tidy and Jenna looked a million dollars so why, wondered Dan, did Jenna's lack of obvious activity annoy him so much? He knew he was being unreasonable; she *had* tried to get work as a hairdresser before she'd had Eliot, and obviously, now she was a mother, getting work when there were childcare considerations made things more difficult, but he couldn't help feeling resentment that he earned all the money and she spent it. Anyway, he had news for Jenna that might change all that.

'Hiya, babe,' said Jenna, looking up from her mag. 'Good day?'

Dan chucked his beret on the coffee table.

'Don't do that,' said Jenna. 'There's a hook in the hall.'

Dan ignored the comment. 'I've got something for you.'

Jenna brightened. 'Ooh, lovely.'

'It's not a present, it's this.' He pulled a thin magazine from his pocket.

Jenna's nose wrinkled. 'The garrison newsletter? What would I want with that?'

Dan opened it and folded the page then handed it to his partner. 'I thought you might be interested in this.'

Jenna scanned the page and handed the magazine back. 'Yeah, I know about that.'

'Jenna, they're advertising for a hairdresser for the new community centre. It's right up your alley. And I'm reliably informed there'll be a crèche there, right on the doorstep, so Eliot could be properly looked after while you do people's hair and if he needs you, you are right there. It's perfect.'

Jenna shook her head. 'Like the wives would come to me? With my reputation?'

Dan sighed, exasperated. 'No one remembers that now.'

'Wanna bet? I was hardly flavour of the month back at the old place, was I?'

'But that was ages ago.'

Jenna stared at him. 'And you think they'll have forgotten?' She snorted. 'I don't think so.'

'But when Maddy had the business with that mad stalker and the baby coming early and everything, you were the hero of the hour.'

'On the officers' patch, maybe. I didn't see any of the soldiers' wives patting me on the back. I don't suppose they even knew.'

'Don't be like that, I bet they did, you know what the rumour mill is like. But you wouldn't know because you never have anything to do with them. You never go to any functions, you never interact...'

'Don't meet trouble halfway, that's my motto. I don't want to give my old neighbours the chance to spit in my face. And they more than likely would.'

'You don't know that.'

'Huh.'

'Look, Jenna, I know my pay as a sergeant isn't bad but we're hardly flush.'

'We're all right.'

'If you worked we could afford to go somewhere nice on holiday – take Eliot to Greece or Spain for a proper holiday. You'd like that, wouldn't you; get a proper tan instead of having to spray one on.'

'You want me to get skin cancer now?'

Dan rolled his eyes. 'I wasn't suggesting that and you know it.'

'Anyway, I don't want no crèche looking after little Eliot. I'm his mum and looking after him is *my* job, not some stranger's.' Jenna narrowed her eyes. 'Are you suggesting I don't make a good enough go of it?'

'No, of course not. I'm just saying that here is a job that would be perfect for you, it comes complete with childcare and I really, *really* don't get why you're turning it down.'

With exaggerated slowness and enunciation Jenna said, 'I've just explained why.'

'OK,' said Dan. 'Then I'm going to explain things to you from my point of view. If you don't apply for this job, the next time you want a new outfit or to fill your car up with petrol, or get your nails done professionally, don't come to me for the money. You can have money for the groceries and stuff for Eliot but after that you're out of luck. This is a partnership and at the moment I'm doing all the heavy-lift.'

'You wouldn't?' said Jenna, looking genuinely shocked.

'Try me.'

'What if I apply for the job and don't get it?'

Dan knew just how good a hairdresser Jenna had been. 'You will,' he said. He handed the magazine back to her. 'I suggest you ring this number right now.'

Jenna snatched the magazine off him and picked up her mobile. 'Satisfied?' she said a few minutes later after she finished the call to Maddy. She glared at him.

'There, that wasn't so hard, now, was it?' he replied, refusing to rise to her belligerent tone.

'I can see it's going to be a right pain in the arse to get it off the ground. The place is half built and I've got to go and see the admin officer to get insurance and terms of trading sorted out. Honestly, Dan, it had better be worth it.'

'Of course it'll be worth it – it's a job.'

'Maybe, but once we take out the cost of Eliot's childcare and tax and national insurance there'll be precious little left.'

'Whatever it is it'll still be more than what you are earning right now.'

Jenna wasn't convinced and she certainly wasn't sure it was going to be worth the effort but Dan had made his point of view perfectly plain and she wasn't going to risk her relationship and her lifestyle by thwarting him. She flashed him a smile.

'You're right, hon.'

'Good.' Dan drew her to him and gave her a kiss.

'But I do worry about some of the wives.'

'It'll be a five-minute wonder – maybe not even that. Once they realise how good you are they'll forget all about your past.'

'Hey,' said Jenna, ruffling Dan's number two buzz cut, 'how do you know I'm any good?'

'Your mate Maddy rates you – that's good enough for me.'

Yeah, thought Jenna, Maddy did – but she was only one out of hundreds of wives.

Chapter 13

Susie drove the family estate up to the gravel sweep in front of Browndown School and stared at the beautiful building looking spectacular in the bright summer sunshine. The stands of mature chestnut trees that flanked the main house were a brilliant green, the lawns beneath were immaculate and the distant playing fields gave the impression that the school was set in acres and acres of parkland. It looked more like a stately home than a school – but then that was exactly what it had been once upon a time. Around her, other cars were drawn up – mostly top-of-the-range four-by-fours driven by mothers in designer clothes and carrying ridiculously expensive handbags. Susie glanced at her Marks and Sparks faux-leather bag and her Boden summer dress and tried not to feel envious. Still, they would fit right in where she was going to be living next – they might even be considered posh.

She opened the car door and stepped onto the crunchy well-raked gravel. She'd been dreading this. Despite what the vile Miss Marcham had said about Katie and Ella, they'd made friends at this place and had been happy here and taking them away from the school – which had pretty much been their home for a year – was going to be hard on them. Maybe they *had* been naughty but Susie wondered if it hadn't been more a matter of high-spirits, which would explain their popularity. Not that that dried-up old trout Miss Marcham would understand about popularity. Susie bet her bottom dollar that Miss Marcham had been Nora No-Mates when she'd been at school and consequently now resented those girls who weren't. Yes, that probably explained a lot, thought Susie. Still, Miss Marcham's past wasn't going to have any bearing on the twins' present and Susie suspected that it was going to be a very tearful end of year service in the school chapel and an even more traumatic departure. She checked her bag for tissues. Lots...good.

There was a steady trickle of parents – mostly mothers – heading to the chapel at the rear of the main building. The women, like Susie, were mostly in dresses, some in skirts and smart jackets, and the handful of men were dressed in business suits. Some of the parents were greeting each other like long-lost friends but most were just picking their way across the gravel, the women concentrating on not letting their high heels sink into the soft ground under the path. The herbaceous border that flanked the route was wonderful and the scent of roses and lilies was heavy in the air. Susie wondered casually how much the school spent on gardeners and groundsmen but, given the annual bill for fees, it was probably quite a lot. Not the sort of money that poor old Winterspring Comp could run to. No wonder the campus of the girls' new school mostly consisted of paving slabs and asphalt. The difference was going to come as such a shock to the girls after five whole years in the private system. No manicured lawns, no swanky sports pavilions, no soundproofed music rooms, no grand piano in the school hall... No, Winterspring Comp was all utilitarian and functional, all hard edges. And the words 'hard edges' probably applied to the pupils as much as their surroundings, thought

Susie as she pushed her worries as to how her daughters would cope to the deepest recesses of her mind.

She entered the cool gloom of the chapel and was handed her service sheet by a sixth-former who represented everything that Susie hoped her own daughters would become: self-assured, elegant, poised and, very possibly, given the school's excellent academic record, intelligent. Susie took her seat in one of the pews reserved for the parents, at the side of the chapel, and bent her head. She wasn't praying – she wasn't the least religious – but she knew it was important to observe the social norms in an environment like this. Although, since in about an hour she'd be an outsider to this exclusive group, she spent her time in this position wondering why she bothered. She sat up straight again and began to look at the other parents. She nodded at a few that she recognised and was rather shocked when one woman didn't return the silent greeting and deliberately looked away. Ah, thought Susie, the ostracism has started. Word has got out that we're no longer wealthy enough to afford the fees so now I am persona non grata. Still, as she didn't want to be friends with people that shallow, she didn't much care.

There was the sound of the approach of distant voices and the scuffing of crêpe-soled shoes on flagstones which gradually grew louder. The voices stilled as the girls began to file into the chapel and fill the central pews, form by form, the youngest girls – Katie and Ella amongst them – nearest the front. The sixth formers, the last in, made their way up the length of the aisle to the choir stalls and sat there. During previous services Susie had imagined her girls in that lofty position, but it was never going to happen now.

The school chaplain made his entrance, everyone stood and the first hymn began. 'I Vow to Thee, My Country', the school hymn, had always moved Susie but this time it seemed especially poignant and before they'd got halfway through the first verse she found that she was unable to sing properly because of the lump in her throat. She struggled on as best she could, till the last verse when she reached into her handbag and dabbed her eyes, hoping no one had noticed. She glanced around, feeling faintly foolish about her display of emotion. Luckily no one had been looking at her – no one, that was, except Miss Marcham, who was at the lectern and who was looking at Susie with a sneer of disdain as she waited to read the first lesson. Susie narrowed her eyes and stared back till Miss Marcham dropped her gaze. Rancid old bag. Susie wouldn't miss *her* when the kids left.

Packing everything the girls had with them at the school took an age and filled every inch of space of the car that wasn't to be occupied by Susie or the twins. Other children could leave a sizeable proportion of their personal kit at the school till the autumn term but not Ella and Katie. The fact that the girls were taking everything just served to make their departure even more public and, as Susie spotted the conversation between the mothers, followed by the glances in their direction, even more humiliating.

And then came the moment when the two girls had to say goodbye to their friends. Their tears were heartbreaking as they hugged their classmates and made promises to keep in touch, and Facetime or Skype or text all the time. Susie watched, wondering just how long these friendships would last when the other children's parents realised where Ella and Katie were going to be living. Houses on an army patch mightn't be luxurious – and certainly not when compared with the homes of girls whose parents were in the 'super-rich' league – but at least the neighbours on the patch all had a respectable occupation, talked with the right sort of accents, sent their kids to the right sort of school and held political beliefs that were acceptable to the Rolex and Range Rover brigade. Susie didn't think they'd want their precious daughters visiting ASBO Central any time in the future. No matter what plans the children were making for the holidays, Susie didn't think any of them would come to fruition.

Everyone in the car was silent as Susie drove away from the school for the last time. Ella and Katie sniffed loudly as they bumped over the cattle grid at the end of the drive and out onto the main road.

The silence continued for some miles then Ella spoke from the back seat. 'Katie and I won't go to the comp, you know that, don't you?'

Susie glanced across at Katie, the front seat passenger, and then at her sibling in the rear-view mirror. 'You've got to go to school somewhere and I'm afraid that's the law.'

'We'll play truant. Run away,' said Katie.

'Don't be silly,' said Susie. 'Anyway, you haven't seen it yet, you might like it.'

There was a loud snort from Ella. 'Yes, we have.'

'Don't be silly,' said Susie again, trying to concentrate on her driving, and really not wanting to have this conversation right at this moment or even *ever*.

'God, Mum, of course we've seen it. What do you think Google Earth is for? And it's rank.'

'A shit-hole,' said Katie.

'Don't use that language,' said Susie, trying to keep her cool.

'Why not? It's the only word that suits it.'

Susie sighed. 'It's not as smart as Browndown, I grant you that. It's just modern, that's all.'

'It's a dump,' retorted Ella. 'You send us there, and you and Dad'll regret it.'

They were upset, thought Susie. And now was not the time to pick a battle with the twins. When they'd calmed down, when they'd seen the school in reality and not just trawled past it courtesy of Google Earth, they'd feel differently, she was sure.

Chapter 14

A few days later, Susie pulled the car up in yet another school car park but this one was a million miles away, metaphorically speaking, from the previous one. This was the car park for Winterspring Comprehensive School, with potholed asphalt, and litter piled by the wind into the corner of the tatty, battered, sagging chainlink fencing that surrounded it. It was a far cry from the raked and perfect gravel of Browndown.

'Told you it was a dump,' said Ella with a sneer in her voice.

Susie took a deep breath before she said, 'I am sure it's a perfectly nice school. They just don't have obscene amounts of money to spend on extras – like landscaping.' She turned to her daughters who were both sitting in the back seat. 'First impressions count and I am sure you have no wish to start off on the wrong foot so I suggest you keep your opinions to yourself when you meet Mr Rogers.'

'And who's he?' asked Katie.

'Your head of year.'

'What's that? Like a housemaster?'

'Something like that.' Susie hadn't yet told her daughters just how big this school was compared to Browndown and the exclusivity it offered. Now they were going to be in a school of well over a thousand children and where the sixth form formed a tiny proportion of the whole. At Winterspring, taking A levels was the exception not the norm, and older, high-achieving role models were as rare as rocking horse goolies. Most kids left at sixteen to take their chances in the job market so even if Ella and Katie stayed on to do A levels they were hardly likely to become clones of the poised and self-confident sixth-formers at Browndown. Maybe she and Mike could guide them towards the right path. Maybe...'Come on,' she said with forced cheerfulness. 'We don't want to be late, now, do we?'

In the mirror she saw the twins exchange a look. Susie sensed that this morning might be tricky.

They made their way out of the car park, following the signs to the main entrance, Susie walking briskly, the twins straggling behind her, shoulders hunched, feet scuffing, their body language oozing negativity.

'For heaven's sake,' said Susie, her exasperation boiling over as they reached the main path to the front door, 'just try and make an effort to look pleasant.'

'Why?' said Ella. 'We don't want to be here so why should we pretend we do?'

Susie stopped dead in her tracks. 'Now listen to me, you two. You've had every chance so far in your lives, you've had opportunities and privileges that kids at this school would give their back teeth for. And now things have hit the buffers. Daddy and I didn't plan it that way and we certainly wish things might have turned out differently. But they haven't so that's that. But when it comes to the bigger picture you're still incredibly lucky compared to half the kids on this planet. I am sorry you can't stay at Browndown and I'm sorry you don't think Winterspring is good enough for you but there is no choice. The law says you must be educated and that's an end to it.' She glared at them. 'Understand?' she snapped.

'Yeah, we understand,' said Katie. But she still sounded sulky.

'Good. Now walk tall and try and be pleasant.' Susie led the way through the front door and then to the reception desk in the big foyer. Just as they reached it earsplitting bells rang out through the school and a few seconds later kids poured down the stairs and along the corridors like a mass migration of wild beasts. The noise of shoes clattering and kids talking or shouting was deafening. As the pupils surged past them the three visitors pressed themselves against the reception desk. Susie was reminded of the line she'd read in *The Good Schools Guide* which had been her bible when she'd been choosing a boarding school for the twins: *You can tell the quality of a school by whether the teachers press themselves against the walls when the children go by or whether it is the reverse.* That said it all really.

'Can I help you?'

Susie spun round and smiled at the receptionist, hoping she didn't look quite as shocked at what she'd witnessed as she felt. 'Yes, thank you. Here are Ella and Katie Collins to meet Mr Rogers.'

The receptionist tapped at a computer keyboard and then looked up again. 'Yes, that's fine. He'll be in the staffroom in the Welwyn Block.' She picked up a map of the school and drew a couple of circles on it. 'We're here and this is the Welwyn Block. It's not difficult to find.' She handed over the map.

Susie studied it and got her bearings. 'Come along, girls,' she said and led the way back out of the building. They'd arrived at the start of breaktime, it seemed, as outside the reception area the place swirled with kids; girls walking arm in arm, lads kicking footballs around, some pupils swigging from pop bottles or scoffing crisps, others just hanging out, chatting or sharing images on phones. The noise in this courtyard area was mad – shrieks and screams and yells and cries. No one seemed to be speaking at a normal volume and the walls on three sides just made every sound reverberate and echo. It was completely unlike the atmosphere at Browndown and quite intimidating. No one took any notice of the newcomers as they made their way to their destination. Ella and Katie stared in boggle-eyed amazement at the crowds, the noise, the boys, keeping close behind their mother as they made their way along various paths between modern concrete and glass blocks.

'Here we are,' said Susie as she found the right building. She held the door open to allow her daughters to precede her. Ahead was a door marked 'Staff' and a bell on the wall with a sign telling them to ring for assistance. Susie pressed it firmly. The door opened and a young woman, who Susie thought looked barely old enough to be out of the sixth form, looked out.

'Yes?'

'The Collins family to see Mr Rogers.'

'OK.'

The door slammed shut. Hardly gracious. Prospective pupils and parents at Browndown weren't treated like this. But then prospective parents at Winterspring wouldn't be handing over upwards of twenty-five thousand pounds a year. They hung around in the corridor getting a few curious glances from pupils drifting in and out of the building. Finally Mr Rogers appeared.

'Hello, hello,' he said. He smelt of instant coffee and stale cigarette smoke and had biscuit crumbs on his sports jacket. He held out his hand to Susie. 'Pleased to meet you, Mrs Collins. And this must be Ellen and Kath.'

'Ella and Katie,' corrected Susie.

'Yes, yes.' He didn't sound as if he cared what they were called. 'And they'll be joining us in September?'

Susie thought she heard Ella whisper 'in your dreams,' but decided to ignore it. 'Yes, she said.

'Jolly good. Now, we can't put them in the same tutor group – it isn't school policy.'

'No!' shouted Ella.

Mr Rogers looked at her in surprise. 'I'm sorry, young lady, but we won't make exceptions. We always split up twins – we find they integrate much better when they can't rely on each other.'

The twins looked at each other in horror and then at their mother.

'Can't you make an exception, this once? It isn't as if they are joining the school with everyone else at eleven,' said Susie.

'Absolutely not,' said Mr Rogers. 'They'll be fine after a couple of days, trust me.'

The girls' expressions seemed to indicate they didn't agree.

'Now then, let's go to my office and have a chat,' said Rogers.

The three Collinses trooped after him, down the stark, soulless corridors, so unlike the wood-floored and panelled ones of Browndown, to an even starker and more soulless office.

Mr Rogers settled himself behind his desk and indicated the two chairs in front of it for his visitors. There was a third chair by the wall which Katie pulled over to sit by her sibling and her mother.

Mr Rogers opened a file on his desk. 'I see you've been studying Latin,' he said. 'I'm afraid we can't offer that here and we do combined science not chemistry, biology and physics as separate subjects. But other than that we can pretty much offer everything else you've studied up till now.'

'Lacrosse?' said Ella.

'Err, no. But hockey.'

'Fencing?' said Katie. 'Riding?'

Mr Rogers closed the file shut. 'There is plenty of sport on offer,' he snapped.

Susie shot the girls a warning look and Ella and Katie slumped back in their seats, arms crossed, sulky expressions on their faces.

'Of course, their marks seem to show your twins ought to be in the more academic sets. We'll test them ourselves, naturally, to make sure we haven't under- or overestimated their capabilities. We don't want them struggling, now do we?'

'Struggling? In a dump like this?' Katie might have meant to have kept her voice to a whisper but Susie and Mr Rogers heard her comment too.

Susie sighed and Mr Rogers stared at Katie in disbelief.

'You may not rate this school, young lady, but I do. Just because you've come from a private school doesn't mean you're better than anyone – just more privileged. And if that's going to be your attitude you're going to find that you could be making life much harder for yourself than necessary.' Mr Rogers leaned across his desk. 'Do you get my drift?' he ended, his eyes narrow and his voice low.

Katie rolled her eyes but Susie could tell he'd rattled her daughter. Not a good start – making an enemy of her head of year before she'd even started. Things didn't bode well for September. Mr Rogers mightn't have been able to recall their names this morning but Susie reckoned he wouldn't forget them again when they actually started at the school.

As soon as they got back to the patch Susie let the girls

into the house and then crossed the road to Maddy's quarter. The visit to the new school might have gone less well than she hoped but there was still something else she had to get sorted and now was as good a time as any.

She rang Maddy's doorbell and after a few seconds the door opened.

'Hiya, Susie. Lovely to see you. Come in.'

'I won't thanks, Maddy. I just wondered if you've thought any more about having the twins after school, in September.'

'Ah.'

Susie didn't think this sounded hopeful. 'It's only for a couple of hours. They won't be any trouble.'

'I know they won't, but it's a heck of a commitment. What if Seb and I want to go away for a long weekend or something?'

'Then I'd sort something out. Mike or I would take leave – or I'd twist someone else's arm.'

'I don't know, Susie. Nate is due to start playgroup in the autumn. I was kind of looking forward to having a bit more time with Rose.' Maddy gave a hollow laugh. 'That is, if bloody Camilla doesn't twig I might have a bit more freedom and muscle in on it first.' She saw the pleading look in Susie's eyes. 'Look, I'll tell you what, I'll take them if you absolutely can't find anyone else and you are desperate, but only if you promise to keep looking. I really don't think I'm the right person to do this. I'm sure there's rules and regulations and all sorts of red tape ... but, as I said, I can act as a safety net in the short term. You ought to talk to Caro, when she gets here – she knows all that stuff.'

Susie hugged Maddy. 'Yes, of course, but in the meantime I know I've got you ... just in case. Thank you. You're a total life-saver. And the twins'll love the idea of coming to yours, so they'll be happy.' She sighed. 'Which will make a change.'

Maddy looked at her questioningly. 'Have they got to that age?'

'Early-onset stroppy teendom? Well, quite possibly, but I think their general vileness is more to do with going to a state school. We went to visit it today and, let's just say, now they know about where they will be going in September hasn't made things better. Worse if anything,' she added gloomily.

'Oh, Susie. They'll come round when they're actually there.'

'You think? I wish I did. And I promise I'll look out for someone else but just knowing I've got you on standby, just in case, is a huge weight off. What with Mike and me both in gainful employment, the kids' school sorted and now this...suddenly things seem to be coming together. Maybe we're over the worst.'

Chapter 15

A couple of weeks later, after Mike had formally handed over B Company to Seb, had been dined out of the officers' mess and given his ID card in, he and Susie packed up and left the patch for good. Their removal van had barely driven away when Caro and Will's rolled in, followed by the Edwards family in their car.

Maddy, making lunch for the children while both Nate and Rose had their mid-morning naps, saw her best friend's car draw up and dropped everything to race out of the house. She hadn't seen them for almost two years and was instantly struck by how much the two boys had grown and how like their blond, blue-eyed parents they were. Not for the first time Maddy thought that eighty years previously they could have been a poster family for the Third Reich with their good looks, tanned skin and air of robust health.

'Caro! Oh, Caro, it's good to see you,' said Maddy as she wrenched open the car door on the passenger side to greet her new neighbour.

Caro got out and stretched and then hugged Maddy. 'This is brilliant. And I can't believe we got allocated a quarter so close to you.'

Will hauled himself out of his side of the car. 'God, I hate moving,' he said, with feeling. 'Hello, Maddy. Nothing personal in that statement – just an observation.'

Maddy went round the back of the car and hugged Will. 'No offence taken. It's just lovely that you're here. It makes up for the socking great hole left by Mike and Susie going.'

Caro laughed. 'That's a phrase I don't suppose you thought you'd say a couple of years ago. I remember you were distinctly unimpressed by Susie to start with.'

'No, well, I admit it, I was wrong and she turned out to be a cracking friend.'

Caro raised an eyebrow.

'Long story,' said Maddy.

'Oi,' shouted one of the removal men. 'You got a key to this gaff?'

'Excuse me,' said Will. He bounded off to open the front door and let the men in.

'And?' prompted Caro.

'She was a perfect brick recently – especially when the battalion was in Kenya last year and Rose arrived in a bit of a rush.' Maddy left it at that. Caro didn't need to know all the details of the story. 'Now then, I'll get the kettle on while you direct the men as to where to put the boxes. Would you like me to take Oliver and Josh? I can give them lunch and everything. Although they mightn't find our toys very interesting – a bit babyish.'

'No problem. I've a box of theirs in the boot. Plenty to keep the little buggers amused.'

Caro opened the tailgate and hauled out a plastic crate brimming with toys and games then she let the boys out of the car.

'Follow Maddy,' she instructed them. 'You remember Maddy, don't you?' Oliver looked as if he might but Josh seemed bewildered. 'Never mind, but she's a friend of

Mummy's and if you're very good for her she might be your friend too and find you a biscuit.'

'Ooh, I think I might have one. I might even find some chocolate ones if you are very, *very* good.' Maddy took Josh's hand and led him into her house while Oliver trotted in happily after her.

'I owe you for this, Maddy. Big time,' called Caro, dumping the crate of toys by the front door. 'I'll be round later with a bottle of something alcoholic to make up.'

Maddy went into the kitchen and found the promised chocolate biscuits which she handed out.

By the time Caro reappeared several hours later Maddy was on her knees, metaphorically and physically. Two lively boys plus two toddlers meant she had to operate at full throttle just to keep the tiniest smidgen of order. If two of the children were settled then at least one of the others wanted a drink or the loo. If Rose was quiet, Josh and Oliver were squabbling and, of course, all Nathan wanted to do was play with the Big Boys and playing with 'a baby' was the last thing they wanted to do. She got to her feet in relief when Caro rang the doorbell, very happy to hand over her charges.

Nathan and Rose were tired too, not being used to the stimulation provided by two boisterous boys. Maddy thought she'd give them an early supper and get them to bed pronto. She was in the kitchen making a cheese and tomato omelette for them both when Caro returned a few minutes later with a bottle of cold chardonnay. She cracked the screw top as Maddy opened the door and had the top off the bottle by the time Maddy had closed it. She ruffled the hair of the kids, sitting patiently in their highchairs.

'I told Will he could feed the boys a sandwich while you and I got outside of this.'

'That's not very fair,' said Maddy with a grin. She got two glasses out of a cupboard. 'I bet he's been working as hard as you with this move.' She stirred the omelette in the pan.

Caro raised an eyebrow. 'Erm...no. His hours at the MoD were insane, right up to the last minute. I can't remember the last time he got back before about eight o'clock, so muggins here did all the donkey work in that department. Besides, he's hardly seen the boys except at weekends and then he was too knackered half the time to really play with them. Honestly, I sometimes wonder if he knows which is which any more.' She poured the wine.

Maddy giggled. 'You're exaggerating.'

'Busted – but only about him not knowing which is which. The rest, Will not contributing to the move, et cetera, et cetera, is all true. Anyway, it won't hurt him to do a bit of parenting for a change.'

'Parenting isn't too bad, but childminding on top!' Maddy took a big swig of her wine and attended to the frying pan again before turning back to Caro and saying, 'Really, Caro, I don't know how you do it. Honestly, why on *earth* would anyone who has their own kids to look after ever go into childminding as well? It's a nightmare.'

Caro grinned. 'We all have our strengths and weaknesses. I couldn't analyse stuff in a lab. This game is just a matter of being organised, having a routine, setting boundaries...'

'I'm sure you're right and I feel I *should* be able to do it. I'm a mum, I should understand about kids but honestly, this afternoon was an eye-opener. I simply didn't have enough pairs of hands.'

'So will you and Seb have a few more or has this put you off?'

Maddy shuddered. 'No, absolutely not. What I've got is quite enough. Besides, he's been to the doc and has been "done".'

Caro giggled. 'You make him sound like the cat.'

Maddy was tempted to tell Caro the rest of the story she'd started earlier, telling her just how like a tomcat Seb had been and how she'd been sorely tempted to give him a DIY job involving a couple of bricks. But she stopped herself; perhaps the fewer people in the battalion who knew the better. And as Seb was about to be Will's boss maybe it wouldn't be wise to be so indiscreet to his wife.

Maddy removed the omelette from the heat, and decided to change the subject. 'Hey, I keep meaning to say that I am so pleased Will was cool about being Seb's 2IC.'

Caro looked a bit bewildered. 'Sorry, I don't get you. Will is 2IC to the company, not Seb's platoon.'

Maddy divided up the omelette and slid it onto two waiting plates. She stared at Caro.

'What's the matter?' asked Caro.

Maddy wasn't sure what to say for a second. Caro didn't know... but...? Maddy was certain she'd mentioned it. 'But I told you. I told you about Seb's promotion.'

'What promotion?'

'His acting majority.'

Caro put her glass down on the table. 'His *what*?' The atmosphere in the kitchen turned frosty. Rose gave a soft wail. Nathan also picked up that something was wrong and screwed his face up too.

'His majority,' said Maddy, quietly.

'That's what I thought you said.'

'But I told you. When I phoned you, weeks back, I asked you how Will felt about the situation, being Seb's 2IC, and you said both of you were just glad to be coming back to the battalion.' Both children were sobbing now.

Caro raised her voice to be heard over them, not caring that this upset the two little ones even more. 'Which we were...*then*. And when you said about Will being Seb's 2IC I *assumed* you meant as his superior, not his subordinate. You really, *really* didn't mention that Seb had just leapfrogged him. I think I'd have remembered that little fact if you'd bothered to mention it. I would have worked out that Seb had just pinched the job that should have been *my* husband's. Will's senior to Seb, if anyone should have got promoted to be the OC it should have been Will.'

Maddy put her hand on Caro's arm but it was roughly shaken off. 'We didn't ask for this, Caro. Seb didn't plan it.' She pleaded silently at Caro to believe her.

Caro looked disbelieving. 'Yeah, right. You and I know how the army works – a word here, a rumour there. So what did you and Seb say to fuck us over? And who to?' She glared at Maddy, waiting for an answer. 'Huh?' Caro picked up her glass and drained it before she slammed it back down again. 'I'm going. Call yourself a friend?' She picked up the half-empty bottle and stormed out, leaving Maddy with two yelling children to cope with.

Seb returned from work a few minutes later and order of sorts had been restored but Maddy still felt shaky, even if the kids were calmer.

'So,' said Seb, as he put his beret on the hall table, 'you've talked to Caro.' He came into the kitchen and kissed her then sat at the table while Maddy fed Rose some yoghurt and Nathan chewed on a bread stick.

Maddy nodded. 'How did you know?'

'Because I've just seen Will. He was coming over

to the office to confront me and cornered me just down the road.'

'And...?'

Seb shrugged. 'He's not happy. It was rather nasty *and* quite public.'

Maddy scraped the last of the yoghurt out of the pot and fed it to her daughter. She chucked the empty pot in the pedal bin. 'How didn't they know before they got here?'

'Search me.'

'I could have sworn I asked Caro if Will was all right with you being his boss.'

'Maybe she misunderstood.'

Maddy shook her head. More than likely Caro had heard what she'd wanted to hear – not what Maddy had actually said. 'So what does Will plan to do?'

'There's nothing much he *can* do at the moment. Craig has gone, the vacancy exists and the other OCs don't want to lose their own 2ICs in a game of musical chairs. I think, for the time being, Will is going to have to put up and shut up.'

'Ouch.'

'And I've just got to hope that Will and Caro realise that I had nothing to do with the situation.'

'Caro doesn't see it like that.' Maddy gave Seb an expurgated version of what Caro had said.

'Oh.'

'Indeed.'

Maddy felt like crying. She'd so looked forward to the return of her best friend and now the situation was just horrible.

Susie was feeling like crying too. The house was just as nasty as she remembered and the estate as grotty. And it still smelt.

The downstairs was piled with boxes as Mike didn't want any more clutter upstairs while he reconstructed the disassembled beds and wardrobes. The twins sulked on the sofa, fiddling with their iPhones and complaining that they were bored till Susie snapped.

'Then help me get the kitchen sorted. Sitting there on your backsides isn't doing anyone any good.'

The twins just gave her a look and returned to their phones.

Susie had had enough. She marched over to the sofa and, before the twins had clocked what was happening, she'd snatched both of their phones out of their hands.

'Hey,' they said but Susie shoved them into the pockets of her jeans.

'I said,' she said with menace in her voice, 'help me get the kitchen sorted.'

The twins glanced at each other and both clambered off the sofa. With bad grace they followed Susie into the kitchen where she handed them a box each.

'Cutlery in the top drawer, mixing bowls, pie dishes and the like in that cupboard, utensils in the middle drawer. Anything else, ask me.'

The twins put their boxes on the shabby work surfaces and began to unwrap the newspaper that protected every item. The pile of crumpled, discarded newsprint on the floor grew. Every now and again Susie bundled it up and stuffed it in a green recycling box. The twins grumbled as they worked but Susie ignored their gripes. If they wanted her to take pity on them and let them off, they were out of luck.

When the boxes marked 'kitchen' were all unpacked – which took a good couple of hours – Susie relented and gave them their phones back. They slouched off back to the sofa.

'Why don't you go and play outside?' said Susie.

'In this dump?' said Ella.

'Who with?' sneered Katie.

'Your bikes are in the garage. You could have a ride around the village, explore the area. It's a nice evening.'

'Suppose,' said Ella.

The girls left and Susie surveyed her kitchen. It was awful, and the oven was a joke, but the great thing about coming from an army quarter was she'd made do with kitchens and appliances almost as bad for most of her married life. The contents of the fridge in the quarter had been transferred via a cool box to the factory-new one that had been delivered that morning. The shiny new fridge looked out of place in amongst the tatty battered units but Susie promised herself that as soon as she and Mike were back on their feet she'd have a proper kitchen, a new one, one that was designed to meet her needs. It might take a year or two but she'd get it. Eventually.

Chapter 16

Jenna picked up Eliot from his pushchair and cradled him on her hip as she made her way through the open door of the proposed community centre and picked her way over the cables of the contractors working on the alterations. Somewhere a radio blared and there was the sound of hammering and drilling emanating from several of the rooms. A builder whistled tunelessly but stopped when he saw Jenna.

'Wotcha, love. Can I help you?' he said, looking directly at her tits.

Jenna pulled her cardigan across her chest with her free hand. 'I'm looking for the foreman. He asked me to come over to check the plans.'

The builder looked towards the kitchen and yelled at full blast, 'Oi! Greg! There's a lady to see you.' Having alerted his boss about his visitor he returned his gaze to Jenna's bosom. Jenna pushed past him so he'd only get her back view.

A middle-aged man with fox-coloured hair came out of the kitchen. 'Hello. Crèche or salon?'

'What? Oh...' The penny dropped. 'I'm here about the salon.'

'Follow me. Watch your feet.' He led the way to the stairs. 'I'm Greg by the way. And you are?'

'Jenna, Jenna Perkins.' She looked over the banisters as she picked her way up the stairs, littered with rubbish – the result of the wallpaper being stripped off. Below her the builder in the hall was staring up at her. Jenna was thankful she was wearing jeans and not a skirt. Perv.

'Right,' said Greg. 'Where do you want everything?

Jenna looked at the space she'd been allocated. It was wonderful. The bay window let in loads of light and there'd be ample room for several hairdressers to work simultaneously – assuming she could recruit more stylists. She peered into the bathroom which had been stripped out and then peeked into the dressing room. As Maddy had suggested the dressing room would make a perfect utility space to put a washer and a tumble drier to sort out the towels and also double up as a kitchenette to provide drinks for the customers.

Momentarily Jenna forgot her trepidation about how the wives might treat her and felt a burst of excitement about the project. Maybe Dan was right after all about how this might be the perfect opportunity to get her hairdressing skills back up and running, although she was still a bit narked about how he'd railroaded her into this so maybe she wouldn't share that with him just yet. She went through her requirements with the foreman; the backwash units, plumbing for a washing machine, a counter with a sink and cupboards under, several workstations with good lighting and electricity sockets and a window seat in the bay window where customers could wait in comfort. Greg made notes and took some measurements as Jenna spoke.

'All done?' he said, as Jenna finally ran out of ideas and steam.

She nodded. 'When's it going to be finished?' She jiggled Eliot on her hip. He was starting to get bored with being lugged around and was beginning to squirm.

'A while yet. Several weeks and that's assuming we don't get any hitches.'

A female voice called from the door, 'Hello, sorry to interrupt.'

Jenna spun round. 'Maddy.' Maddy was standing in the door and, like Jenna, she was encumbered by a child on her hip. 'And hello, Rose.' Rose rewarded Jenna with a smile revealing two top teeth.

'They said I'd find you up here.' She looked around the room. 'Exciting, isn't it?'

'It'll be better when it's finished.'

Greg interrupted. ''Scuse me, ladies, but I've got work to do.'

'Yes, of course, you get on,' said Maddy.

The two women were left alone.

'So,' said Maddy, 'is this the first time you've seen the salon?'

Jenna nodded. 'It's nice. Better than I thought it'd be. Big too.'

'Bigger than your bathroom, that's for sure.'

'We could have more than one stylist working here.'

'That's what I thought. Do you know of anyone?'

'No, but I could train people up.'

'That'd be fab,' said Maddy. 'I should think you'd be killed in the rush. It's such a useful skill. Someone who can cut and style hair can always find work.'

'Not necessarily,' said Jenna. 'Not if you piss off your past employer.' She shifted Eliot to her other hip.

Maddy grinned. 'Something you did monumentally.'

'Yeah, well...moving on...'

'Anyway, being a hairdresser is still a sight more use than being a biochemist.'

'Not as brainy though.'

Maddy shrugged. 'It's no good having a brainy qualification if you can't get work. People will always want hairdressers.'

'But will they want *me*? I'm still not convinced that any of the wives'll want to have me do their roots or give them a trim.'

'Look, I know this is the 1 Herts community centre but I don't think anyone is going to bitch if you take bookings from wives who are with other units in the garrison. We're not going to ask for ID on the door.'

'I suppose.'

The two women made their way down the stairs, past the lecherous builder and out into the garden where Jenna was able to put Eliot back in his stroller. She eased her back. He was getting too heavy to carry like that for long. Maddy put Rose down and she managed to stand, hanging onto Maddy's leg for support as Maddy put on Rose's sun hat. The weather was pretty lovely – even by July's standards.

'And I also suppose,' said Jenna, 'that with your mate Caro running the crèche it'll be easier for the wives with kids to make appointments.'

'Exactly, although...'

Jenna sensed not all was well. 'Although?'

Maddy took a breath before she started. 'Caro and I have had a bit of a falling out.'

Uh-oh. 'What sort of "falling out"?'

Maddy told Jenna about what happened.

'Doesn't sound ace.'

'That's a bit of an understatement,' said Maddy, picking up Rose again and sitting her on her hip.

'You know what I think?' asked Jenna. 'You need to get on the sidelines of this. You need to get Camilla to make sure Caro stays put. Let's face it, the whole point of this place is to make it a one-stop shop and without the crèche there'll be a hole in it you could see from space.'

Maddy couldn't help laughing at Jenna's exaggeration. 'You're right. Caro won't cooperate for me but she might for Camilla. Besides, she'll be earning good money so she'd be bonkers if she turns it down.'

'Right, I need to go back and feed Eliot or he'll be a right pain.'

'And I need to get Nathan from playschool.'

'Playschool? Already?'

'Just a taster day, to see how he gets on. He's due to start in September. Let's hope he had a good time and wants to go back.'

'Blimey, nursery school for Nathan. They do grow up fast, don't they?'

Maddy nodded. 'Soon we'll have to decide about prep schools and all that stuff.'

Jenna shook her head. 'I suppose you don't want him to go, do you?'

'Not really but in my heart I know it may be the only way. It's that or risking the poor little blighter having to change schools all the time.'

Jenna was silent for a minute. She hadn't even considered Eliot's education although she didn't think she and Dan would be sending him to swanky private schools. She just had to hope they wouldn't get buggered about by too many moves in the next sixteen years. Fat chance of *that* though.

'Talking of changing schools, have you heard how Susie's kids are taking it all?' she asked Maddy.

Maddy grimaced. 'I don't think it's going great, to be honest. I'm going to pop over later today and see how she is.'

'Give her my love. And if there's anything I can do...'

Maddy nodded but Jenna knew that the only thing that would probably make things better would be if everything reverted to how it was.

Maddy pushed Rose along the road towards the garrison playgroup, on her way to collect Nathan and wondering where the years had gone. It seemed no time at all since he'd been born but suddenly he was almost old enough to be at nursery school. OK, there were still another couple of months to go before he'd start properly and this was just a taster session to see how he got on, but even so it was yet another huge milestone that was whizzing by. She'd tried not to worry about how he might be getting on, had kept herself busy for the two and a half hours since she'd dropped him off to keep her mind from dwelling on it, but now it was time to pick him up she felt a surge of guilt at abandoning him with a roomful of strangers. She consoled herself with the knowledge that he'd been pretty good about her leaving him alone, but she couldn't help wondering if he'd missed her, spent the time sobbing. Leaving him with other mothers to babysit occasionally was one thing, leaving him with a roomful of children and a couple of nursery school teachers was rather different. She glanced at her watch – her anxiety was making her early. She had about ten minutes to kill before it was time to pick him up. Maddy decided that as she was passing the Spar she might as well pop in for some more bread and milk.

The doors swooshed open automatically and she went in from the hot July sun to the cool interior. She grabbed a basket which she balanced on the hood of the pushchair and headed for the groceries aisle. As she rounded the end of the shelves she met Caro, face to face, coming the other way.

Both women stopped in their tracks and stared at each other. Maddy was about to say something – *hello...sorry...*anything to try and make a start at a reconciliation – but Caro just looked away and swept past, leaving Maddy feeling cut to the quick.

Chapter 17

Susie walked through the back entrance of the mess – the tradesman's entrance – for the first time in her life. In fact, until Sergeant McManners had told her about it she hadn't known of its existence. She felt extraordinarily self-conscious about this change of status and hoped that none of the mess members saw her. Which was ridiculous, she realised. She was going to be the mess manager, she was going to be their employee so the sooner she got over herself the better. Of course, it didn't help matters that Mike still didn't approve of her working here. He'd made it more than plain when she'd asked him to wish her luck on her first day. Maybe, when he started work at his new job, which he was due to in a week, he'd have more to think about than how inappropriate he thought his wife's new career was. Susie sighed. For heaven's sake she was hardly standing on a street corner prostituting herself, but if Mike was to be believed she was only one step away from that.

'Ah, you're here,' said McManners who was sitting on a stool in the big, stainless steel mess kitchen. 'You found your way all right?'

'Yes, thanks.'

'Coffee?'

'Please.'

'Charlie,' called McManners across the kitchen to a steward, 'get Mrs Collins a coffee.'

'It's Susie,' she reminded him.

'Yes of course, ma'am...Susie.'

Susie smiled. 'And you are?'

'Scottie. Well, it's Robert really but I haven't been called that since I was a recruit.'

'Which would you prefer?'

'Och, Scottie'll do. When I'm a civvy I may try reverting to my given name but until then I think I'd be better saving my breath to cool my porridge.'

The steward brought over a steaming mug of coffee along with a carton of milk and a bowl of sugar that had seen a wet teaspoon dipped into it a few too many times. Susie took the milk but declined the sugar. Now she was one of the staff she didn't merit a salver and the silver-plate milk jug and sugar bowl. She smiled to herself.

'All set?' asked Scottie. Susie nodded. 'Follow me, then.'

Susie picked up her mug and followed him through the kitchen, out of the door into the main mess and across the entrance hall to his cubbyhole beneath the stairs.

He grabbed a spare chair and put it behind his desk. 'Right.' He plonked himself down and switched on the computer. 'I've made some notes about what routine jobs need doing and when. It's a bit like running a house – only on a grander scale.' He reached over to a bookcase beside his desk and grabbed a big A4 lever-arch file. He handed it to Susie.

Bloody hell. She stared at the wodges of paper between the stiff cover. How much had she to learn?

Scottie must have clocked her expression. 'Don't worry, ma— Susie. It's all quite straightforward. Most of that is what my predecessor did for me, and probably his did for him. I've just updated it for you – taken out the references to double-entry bookkeeping and proving balances and replaced them with examples of the formulae on the Excel program. It's great as a reference though, if you forget stuff.'

The computer bing-bonged into life and as Susie sipped her coffee, Scottie began to teach her about making up the members' mess bills, catering contracts, stock checks, extra-duty pay for the staff, dinner nights and the other matters that were involved in the running of the mess. By the time they got towards lunchtime her head was bursting with information.

She glanced at her watch, ten past twelve. Almost time for a break, she thought with relief. Not that she'd go home, she had things to do in her lunch hour – assuming she got a whole lunch *hour*.

'Scottie? I need to go out at lunchtime. Got something I have to do but I was just wondering how long our lunch break is?'

'That's the thing, ma'am...I mean Susie. Sorry, but after a lifetime of calling you "ma'am" it's blooming hard to switch.' He smiled apologetically.

'Not to worry. What's "the thing"?'

'Lunchtime is when the officers like to come and discuss their bills, or complaints, or ideas for the menu...that sort of stuff.'

Right on cue James peered round the door.

'McManners...oh, hi, Susie.'

'Captain Rosser,' said Susie, firmly. James looked puzzled. 'Now I am taking over as mess manager from Sergeant McManners it would be more appropriate if you and the others call me Mrs Collins. Let's face it, you don't call any other members of the mess staff by their Christian names. I'm not being stand-offish but it would be better all round in the long term.'

'Oh. Oh, OK.' he still looked a bit bemused though. 'Whatever you say, Su— Mrs Collins.' He flashed her a slightly embarrassed smile. 'Anyway, I've come to suggest that we might want to look at our subscriptions to newspapers and periodicals. I've noticed that some things are barely getting read and we could probably do with more than one copy of *The Times*; there's often a bit of a scramble for it at breakfast. Can we table it for the next mess committee meeting?'

'It's a matter for the PMC more than me,' said Scottie. 'You'd best take it up with Major Fanshaw, although I can make a note to remind him to add it to the agenda.'

'Would you? Ace,' said James. 'Sorry to interrupt.' He gave Susie a smile and left.

'See what I mean?' said Scottie. 'So I generally have a sandwich at my desk. You're not obliged to, of course, but I find it just makes life easier for everyone if I'm accessible around this time.'

'Not a problem,' said Susie. 'I see exactly what you mean. I'll bring something in with me tomorrow.'

Scottie nodded in approval. 'So, has Major Collins started his new job yet?'

'Next week. He's on resettlement leave at the moment, but he's not bothering with resettlement as such. He's using the time to redecorate our new house, and look after the kids while I'm here. Which is kind of the reason why I have to nip out shortly. I need to sort out some childcare because when he starts work...I mean, my two are almost old enough to be left to look after themselves but I'd rather not.' Not on that grotty estate, at any rate.

'Then you go right ahead, ma— Susie.'

'I won't be long, promise. Just a few minutes.'

Susie grabbed her handbag and left. She hoped to catch Caro before Will came home for his lunch. Susie didn't want to interrupt the Edwards' family meal but she had to pick Caro's brains about proper childminding. She knew she could fall back on Maddy's offer in the short-term but she needed to sort out something permanent – and legal.

Caro opened the door wide and Susie was assailed by the sound of small boys fighting, only, to judge by the volume, these small boys were a lot less small than they'd been when she'd last seen them, a couple of years previously, back at the old barracks. Now they sounded like proper bruisers.

'Hi, Suse,' said Caro. 'Come in, come in...if you can bear it.' She opened the door wide so her visitor could step inside. 'What can I do for you?' She reached behind her and shut the sitting room door which went some way to lessening the racket. 'Come into the kitchen so we can hear ourselves think.'

Susie followed her along the hall. She'd just sat down when Josh burst in.

'Mum, Mum, Ollie hit me.'

'Did he?' said Caro with a total lack of concern. 'Hit him back. In fact...' She went to the sitting room. '...I've had quite enough of you two squabbling and Susie doesn't want to be bothered with your racket so the pair of you can play outside. Get your bikes out of the garage and go and find some other kids to play with. It's a nice day, there's bound to be lots of your friends out and about. Shoo.'

'But Mu-u-um...' they both wailed.

'I'm not discussing this,' said Caro firmly. She opened the front door. 'Out. And if you stay out for at *least* half an hour you can both have a chocolate biscuit after your lunch.'

Ollie and Josh exchanged a look and obviously communicated to each other that the bribe was probably worthwhile. They ran off.

Caro slammed the door and returned to her visitor. 'You know, there's a lot to gripe about, living in crappy army housing on a patch, but the demographic is A Good Thing. Having loads of kids around for your own to play with almost makes everything else worthwhile.'

Susie nodded. 'I know. I miss it.'

Caro stared at her. 'Sorry. That was crass of me. I keep forgetting you've escaped from all this.'

'I wouldn't put it quite like that,' said Susie with a wry smile. 'And don't worry about pussyfooting around our situation. Let's face it, what happened to me and Mike was none of your doing.'

'No...well...' There was a short awkward silence before Caro added, 'How are you all settling into your new house?'

Did Susie tell Caro the truth? That the twins were the brats from hell? That they sulked around the house, complaining about every last thing: the village; the estate; the inhabitants; the lack of public transport; the lack of friends...the list went on and on. That Mike was sure their next-door neighbours were drug dealers? That someone had already keyed their car?

'Fine,' she lied. 'Although it's a bit different to living on a patch.'

'Really?'

'Yeah, very.' Again she was tempted to tell Caro what it was really like but she stopped, afraid that it would make her and Mike look like even sadder losers. Better to put a bit of a spin on things. 'Maybe I'm being over-cautious but is it OK to ask one's neighbours what they do for a living? Is it a question that might offend?'

Caro nodded, thoughtfully. 'I don't know, would it? But I can see what you mean. It isn't as if it's a question that's ever arisen on a married patch, is it? Let's face it, if you live in a Type IV quarter everyone knows that you've either got at least three children or you're a field officer's wife.'

'Exactly, that's my point. You can tell at a glance what the pay grade is. And let's face it, on a patch you're a bit unlikely to find that your neighbours are drawing the dole. Although,' she added with a raised eyebrow, 'we came perilously close.'

Caro reached across the kitchen table and gave Susie's hand a squeeze. 'But you didn't. That's the main thing.'

Susie brightened. 'Anyway, with both Mike *and* me in paid employment I need childcare. So, this is the reason I'm here – to ask you if you can help me. The twins are no trouble, honest, and they might even be able to lend a hand with Ollie and Josh. And I'd pay, obviously.'

Caro remained silent for a second or two. 'Susie...'

Susie picked up on Caro's tone of voice, and the hesitation. 'That's a "no" then, is it?'

'No. Well, a bit of a no. But not a complete one,' Caro added quickly.

Susie understood. Like Maddy, Caro would do it at a pinch but not as a permanent arrangement. 'But it's the same sort of "no" that I got from Maddy.'

'Maddy?' snorted Caro. 'There's a surprise. In fact, the only surprise is that now she's so grand she even bothered to talk to you.'

Susie was stunned. What was going on there? 'But you two are mates.'

'Not *are*...were.'

Susie's eyes widened. 'And Maddy's not grand.'

That comment got a derisory snort from Caro.

'What happened?'

Caro told Susie about the row. 'In fact,' she finished, 'if it wasn't for the fact that running the crèche in the community centre wasn't such a bloody good opportunity to earn some decent money, I'd tell her to shove that too. But running the crèche is *exactly* why I can't give you an unqualified yes. If I'm going to be doing that, I can't be certain that I'll have the energy left to take on private childminding on top.'

Susie shrugged. 'I see.'

'And, Maddy shouldn't even consider doing it, not unless she gets registered and checked and everything. It's the law. If she did, she could be in real trouble – and you too.'

'But she's a mate. I know her, I'd trust her with my life, let alone my kids.'

'Rules is rules, Susie.'

Susie rolled her eyes and wasn't sure, in the light of what Caro had just said about her and Maddy's relationship, if Caro mightn't be exaggerating things a little, just to spike Maddy's guns. But surely Caro wasn't like that...was she?

The boys barrelled back into the house insisting they'd been outside for 'hours and hours'. Caro gave them no truck and sent them packing again.

'The big hand has got to be pointing straight up and the little hand on the one before you can come back in. In fact, why don't you go to the end of the road and see if you can see Daddy coming home for lunch? When you see him you can come in.'

The boys scooted out of the house again and once more there was peace.

'So, when is the community centre going to be up and running?'

'In a few weeks.'

'So, could you help out till then?' pleaded Susie.

'I suppose. But I can't give you a definite promise once the crèche opens. Not until I see how it all pans out. Susie, I'm not being difficult but you need to have a back-up in place...just in case, and it can't be Maddy, not unless she's prepared to jump through a whole load of official hoops.'

'No, no, I completely understand. I'll see if I can find someone else – just in case, as you say. And someone who is properly registered, et cetera, et cetera. Promise. And one other thing, Caro. The Fanshaws...Mike wasn't best pleased when he heard that Seb was taking over from him.'

Caro snorted again and muttered, 'I bet.'

'Let's face it, promoting a pretty junior officer rather indicated to Mike that the brass felt that anyone could do his job, even a fairly junior captain. I mean, I don't think anyone, least of all Seb, expected him to take over from Mike. As you can imagine, Mike felt a bit undervalued as a result.' Caro nodded in sympathy. 'But Seb really didn't back-stab to get it. He was as gobsmacked as everyone else.'

'Really?' Caro sounded utterly unconvinced.

'This is Rayner's doing.'

'Pah, Rayner.' Caro's antipathy was almost tangible.

'You don't like him either?'

'Does anyone? I haven't heard anyone say a good word about him or bloody Camilla since they arrived. It really does beg the question as to why he got the job of CO.'

'Someone thinks the sun shines out of his backside.'

'Yeah, while the people below him know what is *really* coming out of it, because we're the ones, standing beneath, who it's landing on.'

Susie giggled then got serious again. 'All I'm saying, Caro, is don't blame Maddy.'

'Bit late for that now, though. I already have. So what do you think Rayner's master plan is?'

'No idea, but Mike is sure he's up to something – something that Rayner hopes, in the long run, is going to make him look like God's gift to the army.'

'Involving Seb?'

'Involving people who may not want to risk telling Rayner where to get off. Which, if Will had been made the OC of B Company, he might have done. Let's face it, Will's never been one to worry too much about rocking the boat, which I always found so refreshing. Seb is much more career-minded and is less likely to be stroppy.'

Caro smiled. 'No, Will's never been much of a one for forelock-tugging.'

Which, thought Susie, was all well and good, as long as it didn't lose you your job.

'I'll be in touch about the twins,' said Susie. 'And I promise I'll keep looking for childcare, just in case taking them on once the crèche gets going will be impossible for you.'

'Do that. I'm not saying a categorical no but you need to have a Plan B.'

As Susie left the Edwards' house she was drafting, in her head, an ad for a childminder to put in the garrison newsletter. Maybe in a year or so she'd feel they were old enough to look after themselves for an hour or so after school but not yet. Although she was sure they'd bitch about having a babysitter at their age. *Another* thing they'd bitch about. That was all they seemed to do these days, bitch about everything. She was deep in thought about her children and the toxic atmosphere that seemed to surround them these days when a greeting made her jump.

'Hi, Susie.'

'Oh, Seb. Hello.' Shit, should she have called him Major Fanshaw? After all, that was the agreement she undertook when she got the job working in the mess. Maybe off duty, outside the mess it was OK to be informal. Anyway, he'd called her Susie...

He stopped, he obviously wanted to talk. 'How are things?'

'Not too bad,' she said. 'I've started taking over from Sergeant McManners today.'

'How's it going?'

'I'm sure it'll all be clear by the end of the week. There's a lot of information to get my head around at the moment. And given how much I've got to learn, I must get on. Seriously, must dash. I promised Sco— Sergeant McManners that I'd only be gone for a few minutes. Nice to see you though. Bye, Seb.' Susie walked on. She wondered about suggesting that maybe he and Maddy ought to try and have a word with the Edwardses, kiss and make up and that sort of malarkey, but then decided that it wasn't her place to interfere. She wasn't the OC's wife any more, just the mess manager, and it would be, like a lot of things were now, inappropriate.

Chapter 18

Just a few minutes after Susie had gone, Will, with the two boys hanging off him trying to cadge piggybacks, thundered into the house and, once again, any semblance of calm was ruined. The boys demanded their lunch as fast as possible, 'pl-e-e-e-ease, Mum' as a lad down the road had, apparently, built a 'wicked den' and was allowing Ollie and Josh to play in it with him. They wolfed down the ham and chutney sandwiches that Caro had prepared, then demanded, got and snarfed the promised chocolate biscuits before racing back out again. The peace that descended on their departure was deep and gratefully received. Will and Caro sat at the kitchen table and munched their own lunch in appreciative tranquillity.

Will finished first and pushed his plate away.

'Enough?' asked Caro.

Will nodded and stretched. 'Yup, that'll keep me going till supper.'

'I saw Susie just now,' said Caro.

'Oh?'

'She's started work in the mess. She came asking if I'd do some childminding for her.'

'That's nice.'

'Only I can't really, or put it another way, I don't want to

166

take on more than I can chew. Not if I'm going to run the crèche properly.'

'I suppose.'

There was a silence while Caro twiddled the salt cellar on the table. 'How was work?'

'All right. Why?'

'I was just wondering how things are with you and Seb?'

Will studied his wife. 'Tricky.'

'Is it likely to get any better?'

'I don't find it easy to work for someone who I know has less experience than I have. I see him doing stuff, issuing orders, planning things and I know I could do it better. Once or twice I've made suggestions but he won't listen, so now I'm letting him dig his own grave.' Will shrugged. 'If he doesn't want advice from his elders and betters, why should I give a fuck?'

Except Caro could see that being rebuffed by Seb hurt him.

'I ran into Maddy in the Spar yesterday.'

Will raised his eyebrows and looked questioningly at his wife. 'And?'

'And I didn't have much to say to her. Just because her husband is your boss doesn't mean we have to be friends.'

'No, but it's sad that it's ended this way.'

'Maybe it means the friendship was never that strong.' Caro finished her sandwich and pushed her plate away. 'Friends don't do the dirty on each other, do they?' But she missed Maddy's companionship – even if she was denying it to everyone, including herself.

The following week Mike Collins had started work at the Winterspring District Council offices, Susie was flying solo running the officers' mess and the twins were being looked after by Caro.

Was this job, wondered Susie as she flopped into her office chair, going to be worth the money given the utter bloodiness of getting the twins up and dressed in time to leave the house at eight? She might have thought they had been sullen and sulky before, but the last couple of mornings, since the new routine had had to kick in, their truculence had hit new heights. And, of course, she couldn't threaten them with leaving them behind because that was *exactly* what they wanted her to do.

Everything about going to Caro's was wrong, as far as the girls were concerned although Susie knew for a fact that they had a perfectly lovely time with her old neighbour. Caro went out of her way to make their day fun and interesting; picnics, trips out, teaching them to make delicious treats in the kitchen... All the sort of things that really 'mumsy' mums did and which Susie had never quite found the time or the energy for. Naturally, when she'd picked the girls up the last thing they were going to let on was they might have had a good time, that, in fact, they'd had a zillion times better time than they'd ever had stuck at home with her or Mike. To do that would involve loss of face and would be uncool. Susie just had to make do with the crumb of comfort that while the twins were utterly vile to her, they did, at least, behave reasonably decently for Caro. It was better that way, obviously, but Susie did just wish occasionally that she reaped the benefit of their expensive education and her own efforts at proper parenting and teaching them half-decent manners and social skills.

Still, she didn't have time to worry about her kids; there was a mountain of work to be done. She drew the pile of chits, signed the previous night by officers who had bought drinks in the bar, towards her and began to go through them, adding up the drinks bought and putting the totals on the correct mess bills. Like many jobs that Scottie had taught her, it all seemed straightforward while he'd been there at her elbow but now she was on her own she kept finding she had to check and double-check, that she missed details, or entered figures in the wrong columns or did something that meant she didn't get it right first time. And it didn't help that she was subject to constant interruptions; the mess staff wanting keys to various store cupboards or asking her to approve orders for food or other stocks, or the phone ringing…By elevenses Susie's head was ready to explode. She took the phone off the hook and shut the door. Just five minutes, that was all she wanted, five minutes to finish the accounts so she could move onto the next job, the next job out of about thirty she ought to get through today or she'd still be at her desk come midnight. She got stuck in.

Seconds later there was a knock on the door.

'Yes!'

'Sorry, Susie…'

It was Maddy. Susie tried to look welcoming but this was the last sodding straw. She did not need a social call right now.

'Is this a bad time? It's just Nathan is playing at a friend's house and Rose fell asleep on the walk here,' she indicated the pushchair parked in the hall behind her, 'and I thought I'd grab a word with you while I've got the chance. Is that OK?'

'No, no, Mrs Fanshaw, what can I do for you?' The phone whistled an alarm to indicate it was off the hook and Susie silenced it by replacing the receiver.

'Mrs Fanshaw? What's this all about, Susie?'

Susie took a deep breath. 'It's protocol. I agreed with your husband, Mrs Fanshaw, that as a mess employee, I ought to treat the mess members with the same deference as Sergeant McManners did. In the mess, this is how it must work.'

'What? But that's daft.'

'It's appropriate.' God, how often had she used that phrase recently?

'Really?'

Susie nodded. 'It's for the best.'

Maddy looked unconvinced. 'If you say so. Anyway, I came to discuss the wives' coffee morning, next week.'

'Of course.' Susie reached up to the files stacked on the shelf above the desk and got out the relevant one. Not that she needed to open it – she'd run more officers' wives coffee mornings in the mess than Maddy had had proverbial hot dinners. 'What do you want to know?'

Maddy looked a little hesitant. 'So I just need to check the arrangements...The mess can let us have the ante-room from ten o'clock onwards and there'll be a crèche set up in the bar for the toddlers which is being run by a couple of the mothers.' Susie nodded. 'And the budget is two pounds a head to cover tea, coffee and cake plus fifty pence for each child's refreshments of juice and biscuits and a fee of a pound per child for the crèche to cover costs.'

'That's the way it usually works, Mrs Fanshaw.'

'When do you need numbers?'

'Two days before is ample. As long as the catering staff have enough time to bake the cakes.'

'Cakes...yes...'

'What sort would you like?'

Again Maddy hesitated.

Susie stepped in. 'I would suggest a coffee and walnut, a lemon drizzle and a Victoria sponge – that's assuming there'll be about thirty attendees.'

'Yes, yes, that sounds perfect.'

'I'll tell the chef.'

'Thank you. Susie—'

'I think we'd better stick to Mrs Collins here.'

Maddy shook her head. 'Susie...Mrs Collins...' Maddy shut her eyes and shook her head again. 'You're my friend, I can't do this.'

'When I'm at work you are just going to have to try. It's part of the deal. Mrs Fanshaw, you, of all people, know how the army is.'

'Yes, I see. It's just so odd...so formal.'

'We'll all get used to it in time.'

'I suppose. Look, Su— Mrs Collins, I have to ask because I really, *really*, need some advice but how did you cope as the PMC's wife? It's a nightmare. I haven't a clue what to do or where to start. May I come and talk to you one evening?'

'Maybe it would be better if I came to your house. Easier for you.' Susie didn't want Maddy to be reminded of how grim the estate was, how low she'd sunk. 'Anyway, off duty I think we can allow ourselves a little less formality. Out of this office, out of the mess we can all still be friends.'

'Oh, please.' Maddy looked pathetically grateful.

'Not this week though. I'm too busy running to catch up and getting my head around the job, but soon, I promise.' Susie smiled. Her phone rang and she put her hand out to lift the receiver.

'I've held you up enough. Bye.' And Maddy left, leaving Susie still wondering how she was going to get away on time.

Chapter 19

At the end of the day, with her brain still feeling fried from everything she'd had to deal with, Susie arrived at Caro's to pick up her daughters.

'God,' said Caro as she opened the door, 'if I didn't know better I'd say you were in need of a strong drink.'

Susie sighed heavily. 'There are occasions when not hitting the gin bottle is very difficult indeed. And today is one of them.'

'How is the new job?' Caro stepped back from the door-step and held the door wide to allow Susie into her house.

'I know I'll get used to it and I know it isn't terribly complicated but there is a lot to get my head round. And the fact that I am constantly interrupted by the mess members, or the staff, or the phone or something doesn't make life easy.'

'I can imagine. Look, the girls are watching a DVD with Josh and Ollie and it hasn't quite finished yet. Do you fancy a cuppa rather than drag them away before the end?' Caro looked at her watch. 'It can't have more than about thirty minutes to go, if that.'

In reality Susie just wanted to get home, get supper on and then, as soon as the family had been fed, get to bed. She hadn't felt this knackered in a very long time. However, she knew that dragging the twins away mid-film was probably unwise. 'Go on, then, that'd be lovely.'

She followed Caro into the kitchen and wearily plumped down on a chair while Caro bustled about getting out the tea bags and putting the kettle on.

'And how is Mike's job?' asked Caro.

'All right, I think.'

'What is it that he does?'

'He's emergency planning officer.'

Caro mashed the tea bags in a couple of mugs and then passed one of them to Susie. 'It sounds important.'

Susie shook her head. 'I think it's all a bit fiction-factory stuff. You know, imagining the worst that could happen, multiplying it by a factor of ten and then stopping people running around like headless chickens if the worst *does* happen by running exercises and having...' Susie held up both hands and dipped both index fingers, '...a Plan of Action.'

Caro giggled. 'I am sure there is more to it than that.'

'Oh, there is.' Susie assumed a serious face. 'He's in charge of sandbags too.'

'OIC sandbags?' Caro snorted with laughter.

'Exactly. OIC sandbags, only don't tell Mike I said that.'

'Why not, Mummy?'

Susie spun round on her seat so fast she slopped her tea. 'Ella.' She felt her face flare. She shouldn't have said what she had about Mike's job; he'd be so hurt if he thought she was taking the piss out of it.

'Why not, Mummy?' repeated Ella.

Susie tried to compose herself. 'Mummy was just being a bit silly. If there's a flood or a big crash or any sort of disaster, Daddy will be in charge of saving people's lives. It's a really important job.'

'Really?' Ella just stared at her, unblinking. She clearly didn't want to believe her mother.

Susie wondered whether she ought to make Ella promise not to tell but decided that the more she made an issue of it, the greater the likelihood of Ella doing something to spite her. With luck, if she just laughed it off, it would all be forgotten.

'So, is the film finished, sweetie?'

But Ella looked away from her and said, 'Please, Caro, may I have a glass of water?'

'Of course, Ella.' Caro got the water and handed it to her, then Ella disappeared but not before she'd given her mother another long stare.

'Anyway,' said Caro, apparently oblivious to the significance of the exchange between Susie and her daughter, 'with both you and Mike in work you must be almost back to where you were before...well, before Mike lost his job.'

Susie pursed her lips. 'Sort of.'

Caro raised her eyebrows. 'Sort of?'

Susie shook her head. 'I shouldn't be telling you this but our finances were a bit rocky before Mike's redundancy so...let's just say, him losing his job really didn't help matters. And that had all sorts of knock-on effects which means that the girls aren't happy.' She glanced towards the door and lowered her voice. 'They don't like the house, the estate, the fact I'm working so they need to come to you...To be honest, Caro, they're making life bloody awful. It's hell. So, having them kick off on top of everything else means that life isn't exactly peachy at the moment.'

'Oh, Susie. I had no idea.'

No, well...why should you.' She sighed. 'It's not as if it's the girls' fault either. It's probably hormones as well as the change of status and it's just unfortunate that it's all come at once. It'll get better. Once we get our finances sorted we can get a bigger mortgage and move into a nice house and eventually the girls will get used to the idea they're not spoilt little public school kids any more and accept that going to a comp isn't all bad.' Susie leant across the table. 'Caro, they haven't even started at Winterspring Comp and they've made up their minds that they hate it. I wish they'd go with open minds and give it a chance.'

Caro sighed. 'Well, I'll do what I can to help over the next couple of weeks; you know, send positive vibes to them about state schools, tell them how much I enjoyed going to my local high school and it didn't wreck my life.'

'Would you?' Susie felt a rush of gratitude. 'The trouble is that Mike went to Radley and I went to a minor public school and they seem to think that *not* going to a fee-paying school is some sort of ghastly social stigma that'll blight them for life and ruin their prospects. I keep trying to tell them that as long as they work hard they'll have just the same chances as anyone else but, of course, these days, they don't believe a word I say.'

'Unless,' said Caro, in a very low voice, 'it's something they want to believe – like you saying Mike is OIC sandbags.'

The summer continued and the weather, for once, was unbelievably good with hot days filled with sunshine even as August finished and September began. The community centre came on in leaps and bounds, Susie got to grips with her new job and life seemed to settle down for everyone. Despite the fact that she and Caro barely spoke to each other – and even then it was in cool but polite monosyllables – Maddy began to feel more comfortable about being the wife of the OC of B Company as well as being the wife of the president of the mess committee. And, of course, she discovered that having the wise hand of Susie – sorry, Mrs Collins – in the mess made life a great deal easier. Susie – she just could *not* think of her old friend in any other terms – Susie had been there, done it and got the T-shirt and there wasn't much she didn't know about the protocols of ladies' dinner nights or the flower rota or charity coffee mornings so Maddy was able to relax knowing that advice was always on hand. Or at least, she could relax on *that* front. Sadly, Camilla Rayner's relentless demands on Maddy's time and patience meant that she seemed to be run ragged in every other department.

'What's for lunch?' asked Seb one swelteringly hot day, as he came into the kitchen.

Maddy looked up from her laptop. She was working in the kitchen while Rose was in the playpen and Nathan watched *Peppa Pig...again*.

'How the hell should I know?' she snapped. She was too hot, she was fed up and she felt under ridiculous pressure to type up some minutes for Camilla before the end of the day.

Seb looked hurt. 'Sorry I asked,' he muttered.

Maddy felt contrite. 'No, *I'm* sorry. It's just Camilla's been on my back this morning and I've had it up to here.' She put her hand up to her eyebrows. 'And I really wanted to take the kids out for a nice walk this afternoon, let Nate burn off some energy, and I just can't see it happening.'

'Tell her where to get off,' said Seb.

'Oh yeah?' Maddy raised her eyebrows. 'And have her complain to Jack and then you get a crappy confidential report and your chances of going to Staff College go right down the loo.'

Seb shrugged. 'Going to Staff College isn't the be-all and end-all.'

'Really? Mike didn't go and look what happened to him.'

'I'm not Mike.'

Which was true but Maddy, along with the rest of the patch, had wondered if Susie's battle with drink might have played a part in Mike's sudden and unexpected departure from the army. Of course, Mike had had problems in that department too but Susie's had been rather more public. Wives were *told* that their actions didn't affect their husband's careers but most of them didn't completely believe it. And Maddy certainly didn't want to test things to breaking point, which she just might if she told Camilla Rayner where she could shove the minutes of the welfare committee.

Maddy hit save and closed her laptop. 'Right, lunch.'

'No,' said Seb, 'I can rustle something up. Have the kids been fed?'

Maddy nodded. 'How about a cold chicken and lettuce sandwich? There's some of Sunday's roast left over.' She got up and went to the fridge. She pulled out the remains of a chicken and some salad leaves.

'Sounds perfect.'

'And I got a tub of ice cream from the Spar.'

'Pudding? How come?'

'The kids get so cranky when they get too hot and there's only so much iced water they're prepared to drink.'

'The forecast is for thunderstorms.'

Maddy stopped carving off some slices of meat. 'Really? Much as I appreciate having a nice summer I could do with a night when I don't feel like I'm sleeping in a sauna. And the garden needs a soak. A real bobby-dazzler of a thunderstorm is probably what we need.'

'Be careful what you wish for,' said Seb.

Maddy grinned. 'I don't think a thunderstorm will cause a disaster, though, do you? And even if it does, we know we've got an A-grade emergency planning officer in the area.'

By mid afternoon the heat was stifling and Maddy had finished typing up Camilla's wretched minutes. She connected the laptop to the printer and while it spewed out page after page she got both the children ready to go out. She planned to deliver the minutes to Camilla and then take Rose and Nathan to the play park. All in all it would kill an hour, give the children some exercise and fresh air and, hopefully, make them sufficiently tired that, even given the sweltering temperatures, they would fall asleep as soon as she put them to bed. Maddy herself felt enervated by this relentless heat and didn't fancy spending an evening dashing up and down stairs dealing with sweaty, uncomfortable, over-tired and miserable children.

It took longer than Maddy imagined to get the children slathered in sunscreen and ready to go out. Nathan in particular was especially awkward, not wanting to wear his sun hat, kicking off his sandals as soon as Maddy got them on and grizzling about anything and everything. At one point she considered sacking the whole idea and staying at home but she was sure the kids would love the play park when they got there. Finally she was able to grab the bundle of freshly printed minutes, stuff them in a carrier bag, which she hung on the back of the pushchair, and head out. Once in the open Nathan seemed to forget his bad mood and was happy to trot along by Maddy's side as she pushed Rose. However, every few yards he found something to interest him – a fly on a fence post, a dandelion in the verge, the colour of a parked car – and they would have to stop until his curiosity or interest waned. Progress was slow but Maddy was in no particular hurry and it was too hot to rush anyway.

They dawdled along and Maddy thought she could hear the very faint rumble of a faraway storm. She looked at the sky but there was no sign of a cloud. The ground shimmered with heat haze and mirages but the sun blazed down with no sign of a thunderhead billowing upwards. Maybe she'd imagined it or perhaps it was a distant jet. It was probably wishful thinking, she decided, because she longed for some relief from the stifling heat.

They finally reached Camilla's quarter and Maddy handed over the promised minutes. There seemed to be precious little in the way of thanks, noted Maddy, and neither was any refreshment offered. Not that Maddy wanted it; Camilla had set views on children being seen and not heard, or climbing on the furniture, or walking around while munching a biscuit. Maddy certainly couldn't rely on Nathan to be on his best behaviour in Camilla's no doubt pristine quarter and she felt sufficiently pissed off with the CO's wife that there was every likelihood that she would have snapped if Camilla had criticised her son. No, not being invited in was completely for the best.

As they walked back down the path there was another faint rumble. If there was a storm brewing it must still be miles away. They continued their way to the play park where Maddy put Rose in a swing and Nathan was able to let off steam on the slides and the climbing frame. As Maddy wearily swung Rose back and forth she was amazed at Nathan's energy.

By the time Nathan had started to flag and Rose was sucking her thumb and looking a bit dozy, the rumbles were definitely coming closer. Maddy gathered the children up and started for home just as a terrific gust of wind came out of nowhere and blew dust and the odd piece of rubbish up high into the air. Nathan got grit in his eyes and began to bawl and Maddy had to spend the next few minutes calming him down and making sure he didn't rub his eyes before she got the muck out as best she could with the corner of a clean hanky. By the time they got going again the weather was definitely on the change and the temperature had started to drop. Maddy looked at the sky again – 'apocalyptic' was the word that sprang to mind. It was like the worst kind of bruise – purple and black and horrible.

'Come on, children,' she said, trying to chivvy Nathan along, but he was still grizzling about his poorly sore eye and, tired from running around the play park, he was dragging his feet.

The wind swirled again, causing the temperature to plummet further, and Maddy shivered in her thin dress. How could the weather change so dramatically and so fast? Then, splat, a fat raindrop hit the pavement by her feet. And then another and then, almost without warning, the heavens opened and lightning ripped across the sky, followed about two seconds later by a terrifying crash of thunder. As Maddy flipped the hood of the pushchair over Rose to protect her from the worst, Nathan screamed with real fear and stood stock-still, refusing to budge. Maddy tried to persuade him to run but it was hopeless. The poor little mite was utterly terrified so Maddy grabbed him and swung him onto her hip, and steering the pushchair with one hand, she headed for the nearest shelter she could find – the community centre. She could see the workmen's vans and cars parked in the drive so she knew it would be open. By the time she was through the front door she and the children were soaked.

She knelt by the pushchair, just inside the open door, and tried to calm her children while water, dripping off their sodden clothes, pooled around them. Luckily the old carpet had been ripped up and more hard-wearing, practical vinyl flooring had been laid in the hall. Rose was crying but her tears seemed to have been brought on by being bounced around in her buggy. Nathan, however, was almost inconsolable. Maddy cuddled him as the puddle around them grew. At least, thought Maddy, the new flooring meant that any mess she made would be easy to clear up. Behind her, in the kitchen and crèche area, she could hear a radio blaring – presumably where the workmen were now – and the old quarter reeked of paint. Glancing around her as Nathan sobbed against her shoulder she saw almost everything looked pretty much finished.

Outside, the rain bounced knee-high off the ground and the thunder and lightning crashed and flashed. She stroked Rose's cheek as she held Nathan tight and made soothing noises.

'Silly old storm,' she said, hiding her own fears. The thunder and lightning were now almost simultaneous and when the thunder cracked the noise was deafening. 'It doesn't frighten us, does it?' she said in a lull between the crashes.

Nathan looked at her, his lip trembling, and shook his head.

At least, thought Maddy, it had taken his mind off his sore eye.

'This is some storm,' said a familiar voice.

Maddy swung round. 'Jenna, what are you doing here?'

'Come to see the progress of my salon. It's coming on a treat. We'll be ready to open in a couple of weeks. All we need is the crèche ready to rock and roll and this place should start paying its way.'

'That's brilliant.'

Another crash of thunder made Nathan wail again and Maddy soothed him.

'Look at you lot,' said Jenna, 'you're soaked through.'

'Skin's waterproof,' said Maddy with a bravado she didn't feel. She was beginning to feel really cold, and if she did, so would her children.

'Wait here,' said Jenna. She disappeared up the stairs and came back a couple of minutes later with her arms filled with new fluffy towels.

Maddy wrapped up the kids and then herself and instantly she could see the kids were comforted.

'You are such a star, Jen.'

'Just as well I was here, eh? And as soon as this rain eases off I'll give you lot a lift back.'

Sometimes, thought Maddy, her friends were just the best.

Chapter 20

Susie was making a dash from the back door of the mess to her car and even though she was only in the rain for a few seconds, she too was soaked. She did think about waiting for the worst of the storm to abate but she'd promised Caro that she'd pick the kids up at five thirty and it wouldn't be fair of her to be late – just because of a drop of rain. Besides, how long was this storm set to last? The sky was still almost pitch black and there was no sign of it moving off.

Not, thought Susie as she reached her car, wrenched the door open and dived in, that this quite qualified as a 'drop of rain'. Tropical monsoon was nearer the mark. If it carried on like this, she thought as she pushed her dripping hair off her face, Noah would be getting his plans out again and ordering the lumber.

She started the car and, with the windscreen wipers working on full speed, she drove along the road, through the barracks and down to the patch. The gutters on either side were brimming and bubbling with water and some of the drains seemed unable to cope and puddles were spreading across the tarmac. Susie drove carefully – what with the reduced visibility and the amount of water on the road, driving conditions were far from ideal. It had got so dark that despite the fact there should have been several hours of daylight left, the streetlights had all switched themselves on. Truly, if four horsemen had galloped by, Susie wouldn't have been surprised.

When she reached Caro's she could see her friend at the kitchen window, silhouetted by the light she had on – at five thirty...in the summer. Caro waved and had the front door opened before Susie could ring the bell.

Susie fell into the house, shaking the worst of the rain off her clothes as she stood on the doormat.

'You should have waited till the worst was over,' said Caro. 'There was no need to get soaked. The girls are happy and an extra few minutes wouldn't have mattered.'

Susie shrugged. 'Hey, don't encourage me to take liberties.'

Caro grinned. 'Have a cup of tea, at least, before you go. Don't drag the girls out to the car in this – it can't go on for much longer. There's no point in getting wetter than you need to.' Which made sense.

Half an hour later, the worst of the storm had passed, going almost as suddenly as it had arrived. The sky was brightening, the birds were making an effort to sing again in the cool, calm evening and the deluge had fizzled out to a few spits and spots so Susie decided it was time to take her kids off Caro's hands.

They drove back towards their village along roads that were half flooded and covered in leaves ripped from the trees and other detritus the violent storm had washed into them. Even though the sun was trying to break through the thinning clouds, Susie still drove with extreme care, as they picked their way through the debris. In some places the road was flooded from kerb to kerb and she held her breath as she negotiated her way through, a bow wave preceding them as she prayed she didn't stall or the car didn't conk out.

The road at the bottom of the village was hubcap deep in water and the green seemed to have been transformed into a pond but once they turned up the hill that led to their road Susie breathed a sigh of relief.

Now they were heading for higher ground everything would be better, wouldn't it? Except the gutters that ran down the sides of the road were still brimming with water; it must all be running off the hill above the village. Susie turned into their road and gasped. The drainage ditch that ran parallel to their road and formed a boundary between the pavement and the front gardens was a raging torrent. How? Why? Where was this weight of water coming from? It was swirling across the path that led to their front door and it was brown and muddy and looked incredibly dangerous. Susie didn't like to think of the consequences if any of them happened to slip trying to cross the narrow concrete bridge that usually spanned the messy undergrowth.

'Just stay in the car, girls,' she said.

'This place is such a dump,' sneered Ella. 'Look, even the drains don't work.'

Susie took a deep breath. 'This is nothing to do with the estate,' she said. 'This is the result of a freak storm.'

'Yeah, right,' said Katie.

Susie ignored her. 'The water will soon go down. The rain has stopped so it's got to drain away shortly.' She sounded more confident than she felt and even as she looked at the water she could have sworn that it was marginally higher than it had been just seconds earlier. She assessed the situation. Would she be better going back down the hill, back through the flooded village road and back to Caro's or would she be better to stay put?

The water began to lap over the top of the flooded,

overgrown ditch and onto the footpath. It was definitely rising, no doubt about it now. But if it was bad here it would be even worse down in the village, Susie reasoned. She decided to stay put. A memory popped into her head of watching the news on TV and seeing a car being washed down the valley when the village of Boscastle had been hit by a similar freak storm. Susie looked around her and at the water swirling towards the car. Would she and the kids be safe? Ought she try to drive to higher ground? But where? Their road led downhill, not up, and if she wanted to reach higher ground she'd have to brave the flooded road in the village first.

Susie tried to control the rising panic and wished Mike was here to go through the options with her. Suddenly, the idea of having someone on hand who knew about floods and emergencies and sandbags seemed incredibly appealing. But no way would he be able to get away with this sort of stuff going on. Surely, as emergency planning officer, he'd be up the sharp end organising flood defences, or sandbags or rescue crews or...well, whatever he had to organise. She turned and looked out of the rear window at the filthy brown water pouring down the road, tumbling through the drainage ditch, lapping around the wheels of the car...She felt sick with worry. Were they in more danger staying put or was it worth risking crossing the bridge and trying to get to the house? And what sort of weight of water did it take to wash a car away? She wished she knew. She swallowed and tried not to cry with worry.

The girls seemed oblivious to the danger of the flood and after whinging about missing some TV soap or other they got their phones out and began to play arcade games. At least they were now less likely to monitor their mother's body language.

She told herself that if the water rose another couple of inches she was going to ring 999. Better to be accused of wasting the emergency services' time and of being a drama queen than do nothing and endanger her children. She got her phone out and held it in her hand while she watched the water level.

Movement in her rear-view mirror caught her eye. Mike? Oh, thank goodness. For a second relief flooded through her followed by a bolt of apprehension. Shit – maybe they *were* in real danger and he'd come to get them out. And he was now in danger too.

He got out of his car, waded through the now ankle-deep water and got into Susie's.

'Bloody hell,' he said as he slammed the car door. 'This is a bit of a turn-up. When the particulars said "hot and cold running water" I assumed they meant in the house,' he joked.

Susie's apprehension subsided a fraction at his attempt at humour, but it still didn't explain his presence, nor did it mean their predicament was any less serious.

As casually as she could, not wanting to display any panic in front of the twins, she said, 'I wasn't expecting to see you. I thought as the emergency planning officer you'd be up to your ears dealing with this.'

'I have been, but the fire brigades are all coping, any flooding is very localised and no new emergency calls have come in. But there'd been a report of flooding here so I thought I'd better check up on you. I'm on a mobile if they need me again.'

Susie shut her eyes in gratitude to that report. 'Mike, I am so pleased you're here. I did have a bit of a moment a while back.' *A bit?* She paused and stared at the brown, swirling water. 'What will we do if it gets any higher?'

'I don't see how it can. That mad thunderstorm has gone, the rain has stopped and I know it's caused problems with the drains and sewers across the county because just about every fire brigade we've got is either pumping out properties or clearing drains but they're winning the battles. Give it another half-hour and it'll all be back to normal.'

'Really?'

'Do you think I'd have been able to come back and check on you if the whole county was about to go under for the third time? No, honestly, the Met Office assures us the worst is over.'

With Mike being there Susie calmed down and she was able to observe the rushing water without feeling panicky. And, just as Mike predicted, it wasn't long before the water began to go down, receding first off the pavement, then off the footpath to the front door until, finally, the flood was confined within the drainage ditch itself. Their front lawn, which had been tatty and weed-ridden to start with, now had a brown slick of mud covering it, along with rubbish and other detritus that had been carried down with the torrent. The family got out of Susie's car and picked their way up the mud-slathered path.

'At least,' said Susie, as she opened the front door, 'the house didn't flood. That ditch served its purpose. Handy it was there, really.'

But the knowledge that another six inches might have caused a real problem left her with a nagging worry. Given what the weather gloom-merchants kept saying about climate change and a more frequent chance of extreme weather events, there was a distinct possibility that it might happen again, only next time they mightn't get away with it. Really, she thought, the sooner they could get Mike's credit rating back on track and move somewhere else, the happier she'd be.

Chapter 21

Susie was popping out of her office the following day when she met Sam crossing the lobby on her way to the dining room for lunch.

'Hi, Sus— Mrs Collins,' said Sam with a slightly self-conscious laugh. 'I'll get used to calling you that one day.'

'Afternoon,' said Susie.

'What was it I heard about you being involved in those floods?'

'It wasn't as bad as all that – just rather a lot of water got between where I'd parked the car and my front door.'

'Scary.'

'Well…it wasn't great but it could have been worse. The trouble is…' Susie paused.

'Is?' prompted Sam.

'Is that Mike…sorry, Major Collins…and I have just realised about the name of our road.'

Sam shook her head. 'Sorry, you've lost me there.'

'We live on Springhill Road. When we had that storm, the water that came down our road was more than just what fell from the sky. It seemed to come pouring out of nowhere. So Mike…Major Collins…asked around and guess what? There's a spring – a stream – that makes a seasonal appearance, which explains why we have a socking great ditch across our front garden.'

'But it hasn't caused a problem before?' said Sam.

'No, but then that storm was a bit out of the ordinary.'

'Well, then,' said Sam. 'It's not likely to be a regular event – or not on that scale anyway.'

'I know...I just worry about it happening again. Global warming and freak storms and all that. No, you're probably right, it was a one-off. Anyway, mustn't keep you...' She bustled off towards the mess kitchens.

'That must be a bit of a worry,' said Sam to herself.

Maddy was racing to the Spar to grab some bread for lunch before Seb came home and found that she had precious little to feed him with. She'd got all behind following a meeting with Camilla in her own house which had overrun by a whole hour and was feeling fed-up, pissed off and put upon in almost equal measure. It wasn't just that Camilla had dragged the meeting out interminably but it was also as if she thought she was her own personal lackey. And as for the way she'd caught Camilla running a finger over her mantelpiece, looking for dust...Maddy had been seriously tempted to march straight round to Camilla's place and do the same to her, see how *she* liked it. She stamped along the road, pushing Rose in her buggy and hauling along a reluctant Nathan, thinking about how she would treat wives if ever she became a CO's wife, and not really looking where she was going.

'Careful!'

Maddy stopped in her tracks. 'Caro.'

'Maddy.' Caro's voice was cool to the point of being frosty. The two women stared at each other before Caro side-stepped round the buggy and walked on. Maddy felt her eyes pricking with tears. How had it come to this? How had their friendship soured so quickly and so badly when she'd done nothing, *nothing*, to hurt her friend?

She turned and stared at Caro's retreating back view, longing to run after her, ask for an explanation or forgiveness or...something, make some sort of rapprochement. But the trouble was, Maddy knew what the explanation was, and that meant that she, personally, wasn't in the wrong so why *should* she beg for forgiveness? She sighed and squared her shoulders. No, fuck it; it was Caro's loss that they weren't friends any more. Besides, she had loads of friends – one less wasn't going to make any difference.

Except she knew she was kidding herself.

The next morning Susie had more to worry about than how the mess members addressed her or whether global warming was going to threaten her home, as Katie and Ella confronted her about their new school uniform.

'This is gross,' said Ella, tugging at her navy polo shirt.

Katie turned on her mother. 'You can't expect us to go around in public in *this*.'

'Why not? All the kids around here do.'

'But they're sad losers,' said Ella dismissively.

'No they're not. And don't be so judgmental.'

'God, Mother, you've only got to look at the kids on this estate to know that,' sneered Katie.

'Anyway, I think this is loads nicer than the Browndown uniform. Whoever thought that brown was an attractive colour for a uniform got it wrong, in my opinion.'

'Duh,' said Ella. '*Brown*down School.'

'Don't talk to me like that,' snapped Susie. She tried to be patient with the girls but it was a real struggle some days.

They were so negative about everything. It didn't matter what she said, did or suggested, they ganged up against her and it was grinding her down. It was as if they thought that everything was deliberately judged to piss them off when, in reality, she was busting a gut – and so was Mike – to try and keep life as close to how it had been as possible. The exception had to be, of course, their school. They could not stay in the private system and that was that.

Ella and Katie rolled their eyes and exchanged a look. Susie had to hold her hands tight by her side. She itched to slap them but, apart from being wrong on every level, it wouldn't help matters. Instead she counted to three.

'Right, well, if you are both ready you should head for the bus. You don't want to be late – not on your first day.'

Katie turned to face her mother. 'Like going to this school is going to make a difference to our lives. It isn't as if we're going to learn anything there. It's rubbish and you know it.'

Susie shook her head. 'We'll see, won't we. Now get going. Do you want me to walk to the stop with you?'

'We're not babies,' said Ella dismissively. She picked up her rucksack and slung it over one shoulder.

'And you'll remember to get the other bus at the end of the day. You won't forget you're going to Caro's? I'll pick you up after I've finished work.'

'God, Mum, we *know*,' said Katie, grabbing her own school bag.

The pair headed for the door.

'Have a good day,' Susie called after them as they headed out of it. 'Bye...' But the door slammed as she said it.

She turned away from it, trying not to worry how they would get on at their new school, how they would cope with being split up, how they'd integrate with their new classmates.

And then she worried that maybe, this first day, she should have taken them herself, instead of leaving them to catch the school bus. She sighed and pushed her worries away. She'd never worried like this when she'd sent them off to board when they'd only been eight. Well, she had worried a little, but the prep school had been so lovely and the staff so kind that she'd known that her twins would be happy. And then when they'd moved to Browndown the transition had been almost seamless and loads of their friends had moved with them so, again, Susie was sure they'd settle in quickly. Except that, of course, she now knew that their time at Browndown hadn't been a total success. Miss Marcham's words still echoed inside her head. Rude. Disruptive. Lacked focus.

God, what if their behaviour caused a confrontation with the staff at Winterspring Comp? Would the different standard of discipline at a state school intimidate Ella and Katie or make them even worse? Susie really started to worry. But what could she do about it? Time would tell, she supposed, miserably.

Time. She glanced at her watch. Hell, she was going to be late. She grabbed her car keys and raced out of the house.

As she drove down the road she saw her daughters standing at the bus stop, apart from the gaggle of other identically clad kids, and both looking apprehensive. The bravado and uncaring attitude at home had been a front; that much was blindingly obvious. Susie's anxiety rocked up several more notches. Would they fit in? Would they make friends? Would they get bullied? Dear God, she hoped not the last. And even more fervently she hoped they wouldn't be insolent to the teachers.

Chapter 22

Maddy pushed a contentedly sleeping Rose along the road to the community centre. She had a whole hour before she had to collect Nathan from his playgroup in the garrison church hall which he could now attend on three mornings a week, and she was keen to see the new amenity now it was up and running properly. It had been opened last week by General Sir Pemberton-Blake – Maddy reckoned that Sam had had her arm twisted by the CO to get her future father-in-law to agree to perform the ceremony – but now, four days after the formal shenanigans, the café, salon and crèche were all properly open for business. Having been in from the start of the project, Maddy was keen to see how it was all working now. And besides, she had business of her own there that she needed to do. She wasn't looking forward to the encounter she was about to have, but it had to be done.

She turned into the drive and was pleased to see a satisfactory number of empty pushchairs parked outside. The tiny ex-occupants were, presumably, now being entertained in the crèche and Maddy hoped that their mothers were either getting their hair done or relaxing over coffee and cake. She parked her own pushchair, extricated Rose, who mewled in protest before slumping sleepily over Maddy's shoulder, and went in. As Maddy pushed open the front door the hubbub of chat told her that the café was obviously doing a great trade – which was pleasing – but given the almost irresistible smells of freshly brewed coffee and baking cakes it wasn't surprising. And, over and above the delicious aromas from the café, Maddy could detect the scent of hairdressing products. Good, Jenna must have got a client too. Maddy so wanted the salon to be a success; partly because she wanted Jenna's skills as a hairdresser to get wider recognition but partly because she felt the salon was her idea and she wanted to see it do well as a matter of personal pride. There was a nagging doubt that this initial success might be down to the novelty factor but she had to hope that the community centre would become an established part of garrison life when that had worn off.

Maddy walked past the café to the crèche, and opened the door. Caro was there with a couple of helpers and the three of them were sitting on the floor playing with the children. In the conservatory were several cots, two of which contained sleeping children, but the other children were happily entertained by a selection of brightly coloured toys and seemed perfectly contented.

Caro looked up as Maddy entered.

'Maddy,' she said as she got to her feet.

Maddy took a deep breath. This was going to be tricky.

'Hi. I'd like to book Rose in for a morning, please.'

Caro stared at her. 'Really? When?'

'Thursday.'

'We're full.'

'Friday?'

'Nope, full then too.'

'Could you check, please?'

Caro picked up a desk diary off the counter. She barely glanced at it before she snapped it shut again. 'As I said, we're full.'

'When will you have a space, then?'

'I really can't say.'

So this was how it was going to be, was it? Maddy resisted the urge to grab the desk diary and prove that Caro was lying, but what good would it do? Better to walk away, her head held high. She'd survived without a crèche so far, she could manage without one for a bit longer.

'Never mind,' she said lightly. Behind Caro a toddler burst into tears. 'Mustn't keep you,' she said as levelly as she could as she left. She was *not* going to show Caro that she cared. No way.

She left Caro mopping up the tears and headed for the stairs and Jenna's salon. It wasn't exactly as if tumbleweed was rolling over the laminate floor but it was pretty darn close. Just the one customer, her hair in foils, sitting reading a magazine while Jenna sat at a desk and worked at her laptop.

'Hi,' she called across the room.

'Hi, Mads.' Jenna got up and walked across the big ex-bedroom to greet her. She looked very smart and professional in her white overall with its pink gingham trim.

'I can give you five minutes,' said Jenna, 'before I have to get those foils off.'

'I just came to see how it's going. How the bookings are.'

Jenna rocked her hand. 'So-so. Early days and I don't think I'll be rushed off my feet for a while but I've another couple booked in for tomorrow.'

'And no problems – you know…' Maddy lowered her voice, '…about your previous life?'

'You mean as regards my ex?' responded Jenna in an equally low tone. They both glanced at the lady in the foils who appeared engrossed in *OK*.

Maddy nodded.

Jenna shook her head. 'Mind you, my name isn't over the shop, is it? If this place was called Jenna's or something like it people might have worked out it's me running it. As it is, with a name like Hairs and Graces no one'll know it's my place till they walk in and see me here. Once they do and word gets around, well, then it might get tricky.'

'But it hasn't yet?'

'Come off it, Mads, this is the first day and I've only had the one client so far.'

'Oh well, so far so good. It'll be fine.'

Jenna gave Maddy a stare that implied she didn't entirely agree.

'And Eliot is OK in the crèche?' asked Maddy.

'Good as gold, apparently. I've popped down twice this morning to check on him and he doesn't seem to have noticed I'm not really around.' Jenna grinned ruefully. 'Nice to be appreciated.'

'Better that way than him crying his eyes out and leaving you feeling wrung out by guilt.'

'I suppose.' Jenna didn't seem to be convinced. 'So, it's nice being close enough to be on hand but it's even nicer being back in work. We've got to hope it all pans out. Dan was being a bit arsey about me not earning, if I'm honest.'

'Is that why you changed your mind about the job?'

Jenna nodded. 'Mind you, it could all go tits-up if the wives decide to boycott me.'

Maddy shook her head. 'They'll have forgotten what happened at the old barracks. Water under the bridge and all that.'

197

'Huh,' snorted Jenna. 'Anyway, we'll see who's right about that in a week or so, when I've had a few more customers. When the grapevine has spread the news that I'm back.' She laughed. 'Makes me sound like Arnold Schwarzenegger, doesn't it?'

'And all you now have to do is become as unstoppable.'

'That'd be good.' She glanced at her watch. 'Anyway, must go. Got to get them foils off.'

Maddy picked up Rose again and went back down the stairs. She glanced at the crèche as she made her way to the front door. If it wasn't for the Caro-sized fly in the ointment she'd be chuffed to bits about the way the community centre was working, because to judge by these early signs it looked as if it was going to be a success. And the crèche was a success – just not one she would be able to reap the benefit from. She had a feeling of satisfaction that this project that she'd worked so hard on had come together. It made it almost worth working with Camilla. Almost... but not quite. As Maddy pushed the front door shut behind her and posted Rose back into her pushchair she wondered if she ought to ask Seb to have a word with Will about Caro boycotting Rose from the crèche. Or would that be like taking a mallet to crack the proverbial nut? And Seb had told her that things in B Company offices weren't exactly tickety-boo; that he and Will were behaving professionally but no more than that. They certainly weren't best friends for ever, not any more, and Maddy was sure it would just make things worse if she told Seb about Caro and the crèche. No, better all round if she kept shtum.

When Jenna got home at lunchtime she was surprised to see Dan waiting for her. God, she hoped he wasn't expecting her to cook for him, she was completely knackered after working in the salon all morning. Well, 'working' might be a bit of an overstatement but she'd been at her place of work and mostly on her feet. It was just a crying shame she'd only had the one customer. But her morning hadn't been completely wasted, in her free time she busied herself making a poster to put up on the noticeboard, just in case it had passed anyone by that there was now a hairdressing salon open above the café. And, also on the positive side, her one and only client had been delighted with her cut-and-colour so she would be a walking advert for a week or two.

'How did it go?' asked Dan as Jenna took off her mac and hauled Eliot out of his buggy.

Jenna wrinkled her nose. 'So-so.'

'What does that mean?'

'It means no one tried to slap me or have words with me about my past, but that was only because hardly anyone came to the salon.'

'Oh.' Dan looked disappointed. 'But it's early days, love.'

She stared at Dan as she stripped off Eliot's all-in-one waterproof. 'So, is that "early days" till they find out who I am and send the lynch mob round or "early days" till I make enough money to make this all worthwhile?'

'Come off it, love, you know what it means. Any new business takes time to get going.'

Jenna put Eliot on the floor so he could crawl around and headed for the kitchen. 'Tea?'

'What's for lunch?'

'I was offering tea,' she countered. 'I wasn't expecting you back so unless you want to share a scrambled egg with your son…' Jenna opened the fridge to show Dan how empty it was, '…there isn't much else. I'm going shopping this afternoon.'

Dan frowned. 'What, nothing?'

'As I said, I'm shopping later. You can't expect me to run around after you, cooking, cleaning and skivvying now I've got a job. If you want a hot meal I suggest you go off to the sergeants' mess.'

'Is this how it's going to be from here on?'

'I don't know what you mean.'

'You working to rule? Because that's what it looks like from here.'

'Working to rule?'

'Yeah. You're punishing me for suggesting you ought to use your skills instead of sitting on your arse reading stupid magazines all day.'

'I did not read stupid magazines all day.'

'All right, half the day.' Dan gave her a wink and despite herself Jenna's mouth twitched.

And she couldn't deny it – she had read *a lot* of magazines. 'You're a bastard, Daniel Armstrong,' she said with a grin.

'Yeah, but you love me, admit it.'

Jenna gave him a peck on the cheek. 'Only sometimes.'

'Got any bread?'

'Half a loaf.'

'Then I'll pop a couple of slices on and have that and some peanut butter. I'd rather stop here with you than go back to the mess.'

'Have it your way.' Jenna got the egg out of the fridge and cracked it into a Pyrex jug.

'And tonight I'll get a nice takeaway and a bottle of fizz to celebrate your first day back in harness. How does that sound?'

'Sounds ace.' Jenna put the jug on the counter and gave Dan a hug. 'If you're going to treat me like this, maybe it's worth the hassle of working again.'

When Ella and Katie got off the school bus by the barrack gates, Caro was waiting for them with Ollie and Josh. The other kids tumbled off and headed towards the other ranks' patch leaving the twins to accompany Caro to the officers' one. They could see the looks the other kids were giving them as they turned right, not left, and they both knew that this would be yet another reason to be called even more names when they caught the bus again tomorrow.

'Hi, girls,' said Caro, cheerfully. 'How was your first day?'

The twins exchanged a glance. Did they tell her the truth?

'All right,' mumbled Ella.

'Bit different from your old place,' said Caro. 'Still, it must be nice to come home at the end of the day instead of having to board for weeks on end.'

Katie shrugged as Caro dragged her two boys along the road towards the patch. 'Suppose,' she said.

'Anyway,' said Caro, 'I suggest that when we get in you have a nice drink of tea or squash or whatever you like, and a biscuit or two and then get your homework done before you mum comes to pick you up. Does that sound like a plan?'

The girls nodded.

'Got much prep?' said Caro.

'A bit,' they admitted in unison.

'What have you got to do?'

Ella spoke first. 'I've got some French – just some sentences to learn.'

'OK. Well, if you need any help my French is not too bad. A bit rusty but I can still remember bits. What about you, Katie?'

'English. Got to write a story.'

'That's nice.' They turned into Caro's road. 'Nearly home,' she said.

The girls stared at their old home which was still standing empty. The grass at the front needed cutting and the window of their old bedroom looked blank with no ornaments arranged or books stacked up on the window sill.

Caro let them into the house and the boys raced into the sitting room and switched on the TV with the remote.

'I suggest you girls use the dining room to do your homework. You'll get a bit of peace and quiet.'

Silently the twins went through into the dining room and dumped their school bags down.

'Those bags look heavy,' sympathised Caro.

'Yeah, because it's a shit school and you can't have lockers or leave your kit there,' said Katie.

'Oh, it can't be that bad,' said Caro.

Katie stared at her. 'It's a dump.'

'Oh.' There was a pause then Caro changed the subject. 'Tea? Squash?'

The girls opted for squash and Caro brought their drinks to them, and a plate of digestives while the girls unpacked their bags.

'I expect,' she said, as she put the glasses on the table, 'that your new school won't seem so different from Browndown, when you get used to it.'

Ella shook her head and sighed. 'It's horrible. Rank.'

'You'll be fine in a week or so, when you've settled in.' Caro went back to the kitchen where the kids could hear the sound of her chopping something up.

'What's your tutor like?' Ella asked Katie, now they were alone. They both wanted to talk on the school bus but the behaviour of the other kids had left them so horrified they'd just huddled together in miserable silence. They'd both learnt separately and swiftly at school that the way they spoke made them the butt of bullying and unwelcome attention, so they didn't open their mouths when they could be overheard by their fellow pupils unless absolutely necessary. The whispers and the sniggers were almost unbearable.

Katie shook her head. 'She's all right, I suppose. We only saw her for register this morning. We get her for double science tomorrow. What's yours like?'

'I've got Mr Jakes. He's supposed to teach PE but I can't see how, 'cos he's fat and old.'

Katie stared at her sister. '*So* not like Miss Merry.' Miss Merry had been their housemistress at Browndown.

'No.'

They sighed in unison. They'd both had a bit of a crush on Miss Merry who had been young and slim and had taught tennis in the summer and lacrosse in the winter.

Ella opened her French text book. 'And there's a kid in my class who smells.'

Katie stopped rummaging through her exercise books to find her English one. 'Yuck.' Then she added. 'I hate it.'

Ella nodded. 'Me too. And the lessons are so babyish. We're doing stuff in maths we covered in prep school.'

Katie leaned in towards her sister. 'They're all mongs.'

Ella nodded. 'And we're in the top sets. Just how thick are the others?'

When Susie came to get them a couple of hours later they'd long since finished their homework and were watching TV with the boys while Caro was busy in the kitchen again.

'So how was your first day?' she asked breezily.

'What do you think?' said Ella.

'What do you care?' added Katie.

'Don't be silly, of course I care.'

'The kids there are rude, they smell and they're stupid,' said Ella.

'Don't exaggerate,' said Susie.

Ella and Katie looked at each other. What was the point?

Chapter 23

Mike looked at his local government colleagues in the big open-plan office. They were all so scruffy, he thought. No sense of pride in their appearance, no proper bearing with their slouching posture and hunched shoulders. Not for the first time he wanted to stand behind each and every one of them, put his knee in the small of their backs and pull on their shoulders to force them to straighten up. But it would be useless, they wouldn't understand that if they stood properly they would be doing themselves a favour, to say nothing of looking like professionals instead of a bunch of layabouts. He sighed and applied himself to the paperwork on his desk. The cut in the budget that his department was being forced to implement was going to be a bugger to apply. He'd tried explaining about risk management, putting lives in jeopardy, about short-term gain versus long-term consequences, but no one was really interested. Besides, the general attitude seemed to be that nothing was going to happen in their area. It wasn't a place where disaster was going to strike. What was the point in wasting any of the over-stretched finances on something that probably wouldn't happen? The whole point of *Emergency* Planning seemed to be lost on them.

Mike threw his pen on the desk, leaned back and ran his fingers through his hair. He admitted to himself that he hated the frustration of his job. No, that wasn't entirely true – he hated his job. Full stop. When he'd got it, back in the summer, he'd been thrilled and he'd come to it fired with enthusiasm, geed up with euphoria at actually, *finally*, landing a job, but then the day-to-day drudgery of it began to wear him down. That, and the petty office politics and the attitude of his workmates. God, he wished he was back in the army where there was a hierarchy and order and people did as they were bloody well told.

He returned to the budget cuts and resisted the temptation to scrawl 'You'll be sorry' across the proposals. Instead he began to work out a way of explaining to these morons, in words of one syllable, what *could* not be cut, what *should* not be cut and what, if it *were* cut, they might just conceivably get away with. He beavered away at the document, trying to implement as much damage limitation as was humanly possible, given the financial constraints.

The phone on his desk rang. 'Rob here. Can you come and see me?'

Mike looked across the office to Rob's workstation and hoped he was masking the feelings on his face. The git couldn't even be bothered to walk across the floor and make the request. 'Sure. I'll be over right away.'

At least the summons spared him from working on the finances for a few minutes. He hit the save button. He knew it would be just his luck, if he didn't, that something would happen and he'd lose the lot. He pushed his chair back and wandered over to Rob's corner of the office. Shit, he was getting as bad as his co-workers; he should be walking with a purpose, not loafing across like some idle teenager. He lengthened his stride for the last few paces.

'Rob, what can I do for you?' It irked him that this

twenty-something oik was his boss but Mike was savvy enough to keep that thought hidden too. In fact, the space where he kept his views about the local government offices and his colleagues hidden was getting incredibly crammed.

'Um...let's go somewhere more private, shall we?'

At the far end of the big workspace were a couple of private offices for interviews or small meetings. They made their way between the desks to one of them while Mike wondered what the hell Rob had to say to him that ought not be overheard.

Rob shut the door behind them and then turned to face Mike. No 'have a seat', he noticed. He felt a faint flicker of apprehension.

'I've had a complaint,' said Rob.

Oh, for fuck's sake, what now? 'Oh, really? I'm sorry to hear that.'

'You are not in the army now and you can't just order people around.'

'I understand but, with all due respect, Rob, I don't think I do. I am very careful to ask people nicely...say please and thank you.' He stopped himself from adding, 'that sort of crap.'

'It's your tone.'

'My *what*?'

'You see – you're doing it to me.'

Mike paused for just a beat before he spoke. 'I am really sorry, Rob,' he lied. 'Old habits. I'll try and do better.'

Rob put his hand on Mike's shoulder. Mike resisted the urge to shrug it off. Who was this little turd who thought he could be all chummy-chummy?

'We are all one big, happy team here,' said Rob. 'And I know we're a fair distance from the sea but we don't want anyone rocking the boat.' He laughed.

Pathetic, thought Mike.

'And your brusque tone and rather demanding style is rather alarming to some of the workers – especially the women. The women in the office are our equals, we're *all* equals and we must respect all the views, genders, ethnicities. I'm sure you understand that, Mike.'

He did, only too well. God, this lot needed to man up. Only he suspected that was yet another phrase he wouldn't be allowed to say. Too gender-specific, probably.

'Of course, Rob.'

Rob removed his hand and stared intently into Mike's eyes. Oh God, he was going to get all caring now. Mike wanted to gag.

'Thank you, Mike. I really respect the effort you are making to integrate with our team.'

'No,' said Mike, 'thank you for pointing out *my* errors.' God, his own hypocrisy made him want to vomit.

Rob opened the door and Mike went back to his desk. He glanced at the clock. Twelve thirty. He grabbed his sandwiches from his briefcase and made his way to the lift. It was nice enough to go and sit by the river to eat his lunch today. Besides, even if it hadn't been he needed to get out of the office before his feelings escaped. He could feel them writhing around inside him like the eponymous Alien and sooner or later they were going to bust out of him and rampage round the office uncontrollably. Jeez, if he heard any more of that politically-correct-caring-blue-sky-thinking-low-hanging-fruit-one-hundred-and-ten-per-cent-outside-the-envelope-buzzword bollocks he might be very tempted to punch someone.

He passed the Red Lion just as a burst of laughter and a waft of beer came out of the open door. He looked at his sandwiches. They'd slip down so much better after a pint. Just one wouldn't hurt – and he *so* needed it today.

Susie was making supper when he got back. He really had only had 'just the one' but he still muttered something about 'needing a slash' when he got in rather than kissing her. He dashed up to the bathroom where he had a quick swill of mouthwash – just in case – as he took a leak, before returning downstairs. He could hear the twins chatting in Ella's bedroom as he clattered back to the kitchen.

'Good day?' he asked casually as he pulled out a chair and sat at the table.

'Fine, thanks,' she replied as she half-filled a saucepan with water. 'You know, it's so nice still seeing the old friends. Maddy was in the office again today about the Ladies' Guest Night and we had such a lovely chat. It was great to catch up on all the gossip from the patch and hear what's going on in B Company. How about you?'

She had her back to Mike and didn't see the look of anguish on his face. He longed to be back in his old environment, where it was all safe, he knew his place in the scheme of things and he was respected.

'Oh, you know...' Actually, I had a patronising interview with a bloke who is my boss but I wouldn't have had as an unpaid acting lance-corporal, I was juggling figures that now make no sense because if the balloon *does* go up around here, fuck knows how we'll cope and I fell off the wagon *again* at lunchtime. 'Fine.'

'That's good.'

'Want a cuppa?'

'No, I'm fine,' said Susie. Mike stood up and went over to

the counter where he plugged in the kettle. 'The girls are still mutinying about Winterspring.'

Mike sighed. He didn't need any more problems. 'What's their gripe now?'

'Same old,' said Susie. 'They don't like the other kids, they don't like the tutors, the lessons are boring, breaks are awful because no one wants to be their friends...' She sighed. 'I think most of it stems from them being split up. Do you think we ought to ring the school and tell them they're wrong? Ask them to put them together?'

'Look,' said Mike, 'if we stir up a shit-storm we'll probably make things even harder for them. They'll get used to it.'

'You think?'

'Eventually.'

The two stared at each other.

'I hate this,' said Susie, 'the girls being miserable. It's breaking my heart.'

Mike nodded. And it was all his fault. If he hadn't been made redundant none of this would have happened. 'It'll get better, it will.' He had to hope so, because it was desperate as it stood.

Susie raised an eyebrow. 'And they're not yet at the stroppy-teenager stage. Getting there but not fully fledged. Can you imagine what they'll be like when they are?'

They stopped talking as they heard the twins thumping down the stairs; not that the twins were 'thumping' per se but in this house the thin walls made any noise echo and reverberate. Mike sighed as he poured boiling water into a mug and chucked a tea bag in on top. He took his drink to the table and sat down.

They slouched into the kitchen.

'Darlings, do stand up straight,' said Susie.

Ella gave her a withering look. 'Why? No one gives a shit at school about that crap.'

'Yeah,' added Katie with a sneer, 'we're not *young ladies* any more.'

'Don't talk to your mother like that,' said Mike. Maybe he did raise his voice a little more than he meant to, was more brusque than he intended but he'd had a shit day too.

'Or what?' said Ella.

The last straw. 'Or I'll take your mobiles off you and ground you,' he roared. 'I will *not* be spoken to like that. Understand?'

Ella gave her father a look of loathing. 'God, I hate you.' She stormed out of the room.

Katie followed but stopped at the door. 'Even Mummy thinks you're crap,' she flung at him. 'She says you're just OIC sandbags – I mean, how rubbish is that?' Then she flounced out of the door, slamming it hard behind her.

The silence that followed was ghastly and it seemed to drag on for ages as Mike waited for an apology from Susie, or an explanation, anything. He stared at her back view, willing her to say that Katie was being spiteful, that she'd made it up, but nothing. Silence. Eventually he pushed his half-made mug of tea away from him and stood up. 'I see.'

Susie spun round. 'Darling...I never meant...I mean...' She slumped against the counter. 'Oh God.'

'Even you think I'm a waste of space, a loser,' he said quietly.

'No, no I don't. I never have.'

'Really?' He gave her a long stare before he walked out of the kitchen. Five seconds later she heard the front door slam and the car engine rev. She thought about running after him but knew it was useless. By the time she got to the front door he'd have gone. Miserably she sat in the kitchen and wondered what she'd done to deserve this utter, total, downturn in her life.

Several minutes later she turned the gas off on the stove, abandoned preparing a meal and took herself up to her room. The silence that fell over the house was angry and toxic.

She lay on her bed, dry-eyed, going over and over the might-have-beens and the what-ifs and the if-onlys and examining everything that had happened since that late May morning when Mike had come home and dropped the bombshell about his redundancy. Should she have handled things better, could she have been more supportive, ought she not have taken the job in the mess... The light faded, the room darkened and the answers failed to materialise yet Susie felt sicker and sicker as time passed because over and above everything was the worry that the last row might have pushed her husband to the brink.

By ten Susie was out of her mind with anxiety. Her thoughts began to race with possibilities of things that might have befallen him and each scenario seemed worse than the previous one. She wondered about phoning the local hospitals or the police but knew she was overreacting. No one would be interested in helping trace a grown man who had been missing for just a matter of hours. She told herself to get a grip – not that it helped. Neither did telling herself that no news was good news.

Shit, if only she could turn back the clock and could erase that stupid, *stupid* glib comment about Mike being OIC sandbags. Still feeling sick with anxiety, shame and a host of other awful feelings she rolled over on her bed and sat up. And she hadn't fed the girls. Part of her thought, angrily, that they didn't deserve it and going supperless to bed for once in their lives wasn't going to kill them but she was being unfair.

They weren't to blame for that remark – she was. They were just hitting out because their world had gone tits up and they were in a frightening and unfamiliar place.

She crossed the bedroom and opened the door. Silence still prevailed but the lights were off. She didn't remember doing that. She went downstairs to find the kitchen had been tidied up; the half-cooked supper had been put into bowls, cling-filmed and put away in the fridge, the saucepans washed and the surfaces mopped. On the table was a note.

Sorry, Mum. We didn't mean to be so horrible. xx E and K
Susie sagged down onto a seat and began to cry.

Chapter 24

Seb, in his role as PMC, popped into the mess office to discuss the calendar of events with Susie...Mrs Collins. When would addressing her so formally come naturally? Maybe they ought to go for a slightly *less* formal approach, maybe he'd been too hasty in trying to erect a Chinese wall between her past association with the mess and her current one.

He knocked on the door and opened it.

'Susie?' he exclaimed when he caught sight of her. She looked ghastly. Normally she was so well groomed; her make-up perfect, her hair washed and brushed, her clothes pressed but this morning...'What the hell's the matter?'

Susie shook her head.

'Susie?' Fuck protocol.

She fumbled up her sleeve for a hanky and blew her nose.

Seb walked around the desk and hunkered down beside her. 'It's not one of the twins, is it?'

Again she shook her head. 'Not them,' she sniffed.

'Mike?'

She nodded. 'Oh, Seb.' She turned her stricken face towards him.

'Come on,' said Seb. He got to his feet and pulled on her arm until she stood next to him. 'You're coming with me.'

Meekly she allowed him to lead her out of the office but

when she discovered they were heading to the front door she drew back.

'Where are we going?'

'To see Maddy.'

'Oh.'

She didn't protest as Seb gripped her arm and walked her through the barracks and along the road to the patch.

He opened the door to his house and called to his wife. 'Mads, visitor.'

Maddy appeared on the landing and peered over the banister. 'Susie?' She disappeared and reappeared two seconds later with a sleepy Rose in her arms and ran down the stairs. 'Susie, what on *earth* is the matter?' she asked as she gave Susie a hug with her free arm.

This display of affection was too much for Susie and fat, silent tears cascaded down her cheeks.

Seb backed out of the house mouthing 'good luck' to his wife as he bolted. Hopeless, but typical man, thought Maddy.

She pulled Susie into her kitchen, popped Rose into her high chair and put the kettle on.

'Tea?' she said as she handed Susie the roll of kitchen towel. Susie nodded, tore off a sheet and blew her nose then sat in miserable silence as Maddy made the tea.

'So,' said Maddy, gently, as she handed over the mug, 'what is it?'

Susie lifted her eyes and stared at Maddy. 'Mike didn't come home last night. Or rather, he did, and then...then there was a row and he stormed off. I haven't seen him since.'

Maddy lowered herself onto a chair opposite Susie and reached across the table to hold her hands. 'Oh God, you must be so worried.'

Susie nodded, bleakly. 'I tried ringing him on his mobile but it goes straight to voicemail.'

Maddy was at a loss. 'Do you have a work number for him? Has he turned up at his desk today?'

'I tried a while ago and was told he wasn't in yet. I daren't try again...you know...in case...'

'In case?'

'Maddy, suppose he's done something desperate.'

Maddy froze then she quickly recovered herself. 'No, no, he's much too balanced for that. Anyway, I know things aren't perfect—'

She was interrupted by a derisory snort from Susie.

'—but you've got a house, you've both got jobs and things could be so much worse. He wouldn't do something that would really wreck the family. He loves you all too much for that.' Maddy hoped to God she was right.

Susie brightened fractionally. 'You think?'

Maddy nodded, trying to display a confidence she didn't entirely feel. 'Tell you what, would you like me to see if I can get hold of Mike at work? He might be there by now.'

'Would you?'

Maddy nodded again and picked up the phone. 'What's the number?'

Susie told her and Maddy dialled carefully. After a few seconds it was answered. 'Hello,' she said. 'Could you put me through to Mike Collins, please?...Yes, I'll hold.' She smiled at Susie encouragingly. 'Oh, hi, Mike.'

Beside her, Susie burst into tears.

'Look, Mike, I've got Susie with me and she's been a bit worried. I don't want to interfere but I think you ought to have a quick word with her.'

Maddy handed the phone to her friend, picked up Rose

and legged it out of the kitchen, shutting the door behind her. Whatever Mike and Susie had to say to each other, they didn't need her eavesdropping.

A few minutes later Susie found her in the sitting room where she was kneeling on the floor stacking beakers for Rose to knock over.

'I'm so sorry,' said Susie.

Maddy scrambled to her feet and hugged her. 'You have *nothing* to be sorry for at all. Nothing. Honestly. You and Mike have had so much to cope with recently and all that upheaval would make life tricky for anyone.'

'I know, and it's been hard on the girls too. I don't suppose it helps that they're getting to That Age.'

'A change of school, a change of lifestyle, a change of friends *and* a change in hormones...I can see it would all be very difficult.'

Susie shook her head. 'You have no idea *how* difficult it can be at home. It's awful.'

Maddy looked at Rose. 'I can't imagine this one being a stroppy teen but I imagine it'll happen.' She bent down and scooped up her daughter. 'More tea?'

Susie shook her head. 'I ought to get back.'

'Come on, one won't hurt. Besides, it was your boss who dragged you down here.'

Susie smiled. 'I suppose.'

'I'd say it gives you *carte blanche*.' The pair returned to the kitchen and Rose was popped back in her high chair and given some carrot sticks to chew on while Maddy slopped the dregs out of their mugs and put the kettle on again.

'I suppose I ought to tell you the gory details,' said Susie.

'Not if you don't want to.' She was gagging to know.

'Well, it all stemmed from something the girls overheard

me say...' And Susie recounted the awful cause of Mike's precipitate departure, and then the twins' heartbreaking attempt to make things better.

'Oh, Susie,' said Maddy, passing Susie her tea. 'Kids, eh? So where did Mike go?'

'Nowhere really. He spent the night in the car. Then he waited for me to go to work before he snuck back in to shower and change. He must have had such a miserable night.'

'Probably no more miserable than yours. At least he *knew* he was safe and well so he wasn't wracked by guilt and worry like you were.'

'I suppose,' said Susie, doubtfully. She sipped her drink. 'But what I said was so hurtful in the first place.'

'You didn't mean it to be. Susie, you were just making a bit of a joke.'

'A joke Mike didn't find funny.'

'No, but maybe under other circumstances...'

'Or maybe not.'

'Look, tell you what, how about the kids have a sleepover with me tonight?' Maddy held up her hand. 'And I truly don't think Ofsted will have a go at us about one night, and you cook something lovely for Mike and have a proper heart-to-heart over a nice meal.'

'He may not want to.'

Maddy raised an eyebrow. 'If you don't try you won't find out. The offer is there, let me know, and if the answer is yes, you can drop the twins over to me along with some overnight kit when it's convenient. It's Friday, they don't have school tomorrow, I can let them stay up and watch some DVDs, we can make popcorn, have a few treats, have a girls' night in. I'll send Seb off to the mess, get him out the way for an hour or so. Do think they'd like that?'

'It's so kind of you but I think we might be better having a nice supper together. The girls might feel we're trying to exclude them, like Mike and I don't want them around. They made such an effort to make it up to me last night, writing that note of apology and clearing up and everything, I need to meet them halfway.'

'If that's what you think. It's up to you but the offer stands and if you ever want to take it up, just give me a shout.'

Susie looked as if she might cry again. 'This is what I miss so much...the support of the patch wives.'

'We're still here, you're still one of us, really. Just because you live a few miles away doesn't mean you don't belong right here too. And if you ever need a shoulder to cry on again...well, you know where I am.'

'God, I owe you.'

'No, it just makes us quits. I haven't forgotten what you did for me when I had that mad stalker.'

'Quits then.'

Jenna was busy washing a client's hair in the converted bathroom of the master suite. She'd got to the stage of massaging the conditioner deep into the scalp of her newest customer. Soothing music played in the background, her customer sat, head back, eyes shut, enjoying the pampering while Jenna worked her magic with her fingers. She heard the door to the salon open and shut, and the creak of a chair in the reception area as someone else came in and took a seat. She wasn't expecting anyone – maybe it was someone wanting to make an appointment. It reminded her that she could really do with a receptionist but, frankly, given the turnover so far, there was no way she was going to be able to afford one for a bit. On the other hand the business was growing nicely and maybe, in a couple of months, it might be a real consideration. She mightn't be rushed off her feet but she was pleasantly busy and her client base was certainly increasing.

Still massaging she glanced at the clock on the wall – time up. Mrs Laycock had had more than her five minutes. She switched on the taps and began to rinse the conditioner out.

'Water all right, Mrs Laycock?'

'Lovely,' came the murmured reply.

Jenna rinsed and rubbed the hair until the water ran clear

then took a comb and made sure the newly washed locks were tangle free. After she had wrapped Mrs Laycock's head in one of the new towels she led her to a chair in front of the mirror. It was only then she turned to see who it was who had come in and sat down. A female soldier, and then she realised just which female soldier it was. Chrissie Summers – or Perkins as she was probably called now given that she was the new wife of her ex-husband. The husband she'd been unfaithful to while he'd been out in Afghanistan. The husband who'd been injured in a Taliban ambush while she'd been in bed with Dan Armstrong. The husband whose savings bank account she'd emptied to set up her own illicit hairdressing salon at her previous quarter.

'Bloody hell,' she whispered.

'Jenna?' Chrissie's eyes were wide with shock, disbelief and something that verged on dislike.

Jenna recovered herself a fraction. 'What...what are you doing here? You're up in Catterick, aren't you – you and Lee?'

'No, no. Lee got posted back here a couple of months back, but he's with A Company now, so there's no reason you should know. I'm surprised to see *you* here though – given your track record.'

Miaow. 'Dan, my new partner, is with the REME here. Technically we aren't part of 1 Herts.'

'I'd say that's probably for the best, wouldn't you?'

Double miaow. 'It works for us,' responded Jenna as calmly as she could.

'No, well...' Chrissie got up to go.

'Hang on, did you want an appointment?'

Chrissie looked at her. 'I did, but I've kind of gone off the idea now. Knowing, as I do, what you did to Lee I'm not sure I want to contribute to your profit margin, given the fact that

Lee and I don't have much in the way of spare cash – well, nothing in the way of savings, at any rate.' She gave Jenna a long stare before she left the salon, banging the door shut behind her.

Jenna, with a fixed, forced smile on her face, turned to her customer and whipped the towel off her head. 'Right, Mrs Laycock, what am I doing today?'

Mrs Laycock stared at her in the mirror. 'Wasn't that Chrissie Summers?'

'Might have been,' said Jenna.

'I remember who you are now,' said Mrs Laycock. 'I remember you from the old barracks. You know, I thought I recognised you when I walked in but I couldn't put my finger on it. I couldn't quite place you. Well, I never.'

Here we go, thought Jenna. She knew Mrs Laycock's sort and as soon as she got out of the salon she'd be telling everyone she knew about this little nugget of knowledge. It might have taken several weeks for Jenna's past to emerge but it finally had. Just as Jenna had predicted. She wondered what the repercussions would be. A boycott?

'Anyway,' said Jenna, firmly. 'Your style.'

It took several attempts to get Mrs Laycock to concentrate on what she wanted done with her hair and, as Jenna started to cut it, there was no chit-chat about holidays or her kids or any of the usual topics. Instead, Mrs Laycock had her phone out and was busy texting all and sundry. Even though Jenna couldn't read the texts from where she was standing, she had a pretty shrewd idea what the old bat was spelling out with her thumbs.

As soon as her last customer had left the salon, Jenna locked up, grabbed Eliot from the crèche and zipped round to Maddy's house.

'You'll never guess,' she said without preamble as soon as the door opened. 'I told you this would happen and it has.'

'Hello, Jenna. Never guess what? What's happened?' Maddy ushered her visitor in, helping Jenna get the buggy over the front step.

Jenna related the details of Chrissie's visit and Mrs Laycock's reaction.

'Was that Sergeant Major Laycock's wife?' asked Maddy.

'Search me. I don't know half the people who use the community centre. When I worked at Zoë's salon, back at the old barracks, I didn't know half the ladies because other stylists dealt with them, and then I didn't have my own place long enough to build up much of a clientele.'

'If it is who I think it is,' said Maddy, 'she may cause a problem or two. She's real old school, real dyed-in-the-wool career wife.'

Jenna rolled her eyes 'That's all I blooming need on top of Chrissie. You know she had the cheek to have a pop at me over Lee's savings!' She held up a hand. 'Yes, I know I was wrong, I know I shouldn't have taken his dosh but we *were* married and I honestly thought I could make a go of it. Anyway,' she said a bit petulantly, 'it's water under the bridge now, not that Chrissie seems to want to let it go,' she added darkly.

Maddy raised her eyebrows a smidge.

'Look,' said Jenna, 'I know what I did was out of order, but it was Lee's money I borrowed...' She saw the look on Maddy's face. 'OK, nicked. But it wasn't hers. I wouldn't mind Lee having a go at me, but I resent it coming from Chrissie.'

Maddy sighed. 'You may have a point, technically, but I wouldn't go taking the moral high ground over this.'

Jenna nodded. 'No, you're right. Of course you are. I'm just being a bit of a cow. But,' she added, 'Chrissie was too.'

Maddy grinned. 'I expect you weren't overly intimidated.'

'Nah...well...except I don't want to get involved in another cat-fight. Don't want to get too much of a reputation.'

After Jenna had gone Maddy had to get her skates on to get Nathan from his playgroup before racing home to make lunch for everyone. September had started off nice enough but now, as it was drawing to a close, it was decidedly autumnal but without the poetic mists-and-mellow-fruitfulness baloney. The icy north wind nipped at Maddy's ankles and rain spat at her intermittently from a sky that threatened worse. The trees, still laden with leaves, were thrashing about and no matter that Maddy had pulled her winter coat tight about her and was hurrying as fast as she could with Nathan standing on the buggy-board behind Rose's pushchair, she felt chilled through. Bugger it, she decided, when she got in she was going to light the gas fire in the sitting room and she and the kids could hunker down in the warm fug for the afternoon, playing games, looking at picture books, maybe watching *Peppa Pig* – again.

As she opened the front door she heard the phone ringing. It was a race to get the kids indoors and the front door slammed behind her before the phone stopped. She was panting slightly when the caller spoke.

'Maddy? It's Caro.'

'Caro?' Blimey.

'I need to talk to you.'

'What about?' Maddy wondered if she should sound more enthusiastic but she couldn't help feeling wary. After all, her last couple of encounters with her former friend had hardly been congenial.

'Look, can I come round?'

'Suppose so.' Hardly gracious but did she care?

'I'll be round in five.'

'See you then.' Maddy put the phone down. Bloody hell, she thought as she got Nathan out of his all-in-one and then lifted Rose out of the buggy, what was this going to be about? Another rant about Seb's promotion, maybe? Or had Caro found something else to have a go at her for?

The kids pottered off into the sitting room and Maddy went into the kitchen. She supposed she ought to offer Caro a cup of tea. Not to would be pointedly churlish – although given the way Caro had treated her when she'd tried to book Rose into the crèche she was sorely tempted to repay in kind.

The kettle had just clicked off when the doorbell rang. Maddy took a deep breath and went to answer it.

Caro came in, taking off her coat. 'Hello, Maddy.'

No 'how are you' or 'nice to see you', Maddy noticed. 'Caro,' she said, without any warmth. She took Caro's coat.

'Nice and warm in here.'

'I gave in and put the heating on.'

'Lucky you. Will won't hear of it, says we must put an extra layer on. Still, it keeps the bills down.'

Was that a dig that Maddy and Seb could afford to because of his promotion? Maddy refused to rise to the bait. 'The money from the crèche must come in handy,' she said.

'It's useful. And with everyone out all morning it doesn't matter if the house is a bit Baltic – that is, till I come back at lunchtime.'

Maddy led Caro into the sitting room and went to make tea for them both. When she returned Caro was sitting on the rug helping Nathan with a jigsaw with one hand while helping Rose post shapes into a box with the other. At least she had the decency to be nice to the children, even if she was no longer friends with their parents.

'Right, kids, you're on your own for a bit while I have my hot drink,' said Caro, getting up off the floor and plonking down on the sofa as Maddy handed her a brimming mug.

'I don't know how you do it,' said Maddy. 'My knees seize up after five minutes crawling round like that.'

'Practice,' said Caro. 'If you did it all morning, every morning, your joints would soon loosen up.'

'So...?' said Maddy.

'So? Oh yes, the reason why I'm here.'

Maddy nodded encouragingly.

'I'm worried.'

'About?'

'Ella and Katie.'

'Oh.' This wasn't what Maddy expected. She felt a small ripple of relief that Caro wasn't going to have another go at her over something she or Seb had done – or not done.

'You're friends with Susie; haven't you noticed anything?'

'Well, a bit. I mean, I don't see much of the girls these days but I know things aren't completely happy at home. I had Susie crying her eyes out here the other day.'

'Oh, no. Why?'

'She and Mike had a row. She said something inappropriate that the twins overheard and they threw it back at their dad. I think her comment was meant as a joke—'

'OIC sandbags?'

Maddy nodded. 'How...?'

'She made that comment to me when she didn't realise Ella was right behind her. And it was kind of funny at the time but I can also see how Mike might take it the wrong way.'

'Anyway, it seems that he feels he's let them all down, the twins are being horrible, they're miserable at their school, the other kids are ripping the piss out of them because they talk posh...'

'So the Collinses aren't playing happy families.' Caro took a sip of her tea.

Maddy shook her head. 'And I don't know what to do to help. I suggested that I should have the girls for the night, so she and Mike could have a proper heart-to-heart but she thought the girls might think they were being excluded, not wanted. The last thing she wanted was for them to feel they were being punished for causing the row.' Maddy told Caro about the twins' note of apology and the pains they'd taken to make up by tidying the kitchen.

'Bless them,' said Caro.

'I know. They're good kids really. They didn't mean to cause trouble, I'm sure.'

'Do you think I ought to try talking to them?'

Maddy looked doubtful. 'And say what?'

Caro put her cup down on the table beside her. 'I could tell them what a great guy their dad is, how much Will liked working for *him*.'

Was there a hint there that Mike was an OK boss but Seb wasn't? Maddy ignored it. 'I suppose. It can't do any harm, at any rate.'

'And I think they're lonely. Any friends they had on the patch are away at their own boarding schools so the only kids around in term time are far too little for Ella and Katie to play with. And as for their new school – they're very tiny fish in a very big lake.'

Maddy agreed. 'Winterspring Comp is huge. Susie told me that there are nine tutor groups in each year. Nine!'

'I hoped they'd get to know the kids on the school bus but it doesn't help that they get two different buses a day. And I don't think it helps that the other kids on their bus go to the soldiers' patch when they get off, while they come here with me.'

'So everything about them sets them apart.' Maddy shook her head. 'That's not good for integration.'

'But I don't want to worry Susie. I wondered...I wondered if you might have some ideas.'

Maddy stared at Caro. Was Caro – trained in childcare – really asking her advice or was she using her worry about the twins as an excuse to extend an olive branch? And if it were the latter, was Maddy prepared to forgive and forget the way Caro had treated her recently? She'd think about it. In the meantime, she needed to give Caro a reply.

'I think you're just going to have to give them as much support as you possibly can when they're at yours. And they may talk to you, more than they do their parents, you being an outsider and everything.'

'You think?'

Maddy shrugged. 'I'm not the expert. And I think you are going to have to tell Susie about your concerns. If the kids are really miserable at school, mightn't it be a symptom of something worse, like bullying?' She gave Caro a long stare. 'When someone thinks that someone else is being mean and unpleasant, just because they can be, it's very upsetting.'

Caro lowered her eyes. 'Indeed.' She picked up her mug and drained it. 'Well, I mustn't keep you, I expect you're busy. Thanks for the tea.' She stood up.

Maddy wondered about asking if the crèche was still fully booked but decided to leave it for the time being. A first, tiny, step had been taken. Maybe it was best to leave things as they were for the time being. Communications, of a sort, had been re-established and she ought to be grateful for that.

Later, when Seb came home, she told him that Caro had visited.

'And?' said Seb. 'That's news? You and she used to practically *live* in each other's houses.'

'That was then,' said Maddy.

Seb's brow crinkled into a frown. 'You've lost me.'

'You remember that row – when Caro discovered you'd be made OC?'

'That isn't still rumbling on? You are kidding me. Will and I managed to put most of our differences behind us weeks ago.'

'Well, Will obviously hasn't told Caro that. Or maybe he has – finally.' Maddy told Seb about the lack of space for Rose at the crèche.

'Oh, that's just plain childish. I'll have a word with Will.'

'No! No, leave it. I think this row may have run its course but if you criticise Caro to Will…well, it might all kick off again.'

'If you're sure.'

'Seb, I haven't wanted to burden you with stupid patch politics. You've got enough on your plate, what with being OC and PMC and having to jump through Rayner's bloody hoops and everything but I've hated falling out with Caro and if we can make up again, well, no one will be happier than me.'

'But you should have said something sooner. I might have been able to do something.'

'As I said – you've got enough to cope with. And I'm a grown-up, I can fight my own battles.'

Chapter 26

'Got any homework, girls?' asked Susie as they drove away from the barracks and back to the estate at Winterspring Ducis.

'No,' said Katie.

'What, again?'

'We do it at Caro's,' said Ella.

'Properly?'

There was a heavy sigh from the back seat, then Katie said, 'It's all baby stuff. The kids know nothing. We've done it all before, most of it at prep school.'

'Even so,' said Susie as evenly as she could, 'it won't hurt you to repeat things. Look at it as revision. Besides, it won't do you any harm to do really well at your new school.'

Beside her, in the passenger seat, Ella snorted. 'Oh yeah, like being the class swots is going to make us *so* popular.'

Susie dropped the subject and they drove the rest of the way home in silence. When they got back the girls banged up the stairs to their bedrooms and Susie was left feeling bereft at the continual lack of communication between her and the twins. Every time she tried to reach out to them they swatted her away – and it was worse with Mike. Even when she'd been super-kind to them and bought them a few treats to thank them for their apology for causing that awful row they'd seemed diffident and almost embarrassed. And since then they'd barely spoken to her. Maybe she ought to have a word with Caro? Maybe they confided in her.

The next morning, after she'd dealt with the previous night's bar chits and talked to the chef about menus for the following week, Susie locked her office and headed through the barracks to the community centre. It was noisy with conversations emanating from the coffee shop and over those could just be heard the noise of a hairdryer from Jenna's salon. She made her way along the main hall to the crèche at the back and leaned over the stairgate that blocked the entrance.

On the floor were two of Caro's assistants playing with some toddlers while other children were occupied in the Wendy house or were tearing around the big conservatory on scooters. Caro herself was sitting on the big comfy chair that she mainly used when it came to story time, feeding a small baby from a bottle.

'Can I come in?' asked Susie.

Caro smiled. 'Be my guest.'

Susie opened the stairgate and stepped through. Caro nodded at a stool beside her chair. 'Pull up a pew. What can I do for you?'

'Is this a good time?'

'As good as any. It isn't often I get the chance to sit down in this job.'

'I can imagine,' said Susie.

'So?'

Susie took a deep breath. 'I'm worried about the girls.'

Caro looked down at the sucking baby. 'You too.'

'So, I'm not imagining that things really aren't great.' Caro looked back up at her. 'I'm not being an over-anxious mother, am I?'

'No,' said Caro. 'And if I'm honest, I think things are getting worse not better. When they first came to me they used to settle down, do some homework, play with the boys, maybe help me in the kitchen but now...now they sit on the sofa, watch TV, barely speak. They don't want to talk about their day, they don't want to talk about any friends they might have...or not, they don't want to talk about school...or home for that matter. They seem to be unnaturally introverted.'

'And they're the same at home. They seem very unhappy. Caro, it's tearing me apart but they won't talk to me and they certainly don't talk to Mike. I was rather hoping they might have talked to you about it?'

'They barely say a word to me these days. I *do* ask them, Susie, but when you keep getting stonewalled it's really difficult to keep asking. After a bit it stops looking like casual interest and more like prying.'

Susie nodded. 'So you've got no more of an idea about why they seem so unhappy than I have.'

Caro shook her head. 'Although I do wonder about bullying. They stand apart from the rest of the kids – their voices, their previous school, the fact their dad was an officer. I know most of the kids at that school have nothing to do with the army but there are a few off the soldiers' patch and they might make life difficult.'

'I thought about bullying too,' said Susie, quietly. 'But if their lives are being made miserable why don't they say something?' She felt stricken for them. Then she said, 'You say they watch TV. Do they do their homework?'

'They tell me they'd rather do it at home.'

'They tell me they've done it at yours.'

The two women gazed at each other.

'I think,' said Susie, 'I need to talk to their head of year. Things aren't right; in fact, things are probably worse than I thought.' She stood up to go. 'Don't tell the girls I came to see you. I don't want them to think that you and I are ganging up on them too; I think they've got enough to cope with at school without thinking that we are swapping stories about them.'

'Which we are,' said Caro.

'Yeah, but only because we care about them.'

Susie returned to the mess but found it hard to concentrate on her work. In the end she gave up and rang Seb.

'Major Fanshaw,' she said when he answered his phone.

'Mrs Collins. Problems?'

You don't know the half of it, she thought. 'Not with the mess. I just wondered if I could have a half-day off.'

'Of course. When?'

'I don't know yet. I need to go into Winterspring School. I wanted to get agreement in principle before I make an appointment.'

'God, Su— Mrs Collins, you really don't need to ask my permission for something like that.'

'Maybe not, but I don't want to take liberties.'

'That's not a liberty. Just let me know when you're off.'

'Thanks.' She hung up, dialled nine for an outside line and then dialled the school.

'I had Susie on the phone today,' said Seb when he got home at lunchtime.

'So? You're her boss.'

'She wants time off to go into the girls' new school. But it's not a parents' evening interview, she's making an appointment to see someone there.'

Maddy put the knives and forks she was holding down on the table. 'Is she now.'

Seb nodded.

'I had Caro round here the other day because she's worried about the girls, she's got a suspicion they're being bullied. She wanted to know if I'd picked up anything from Susie, seeing as how we used to be so close. But what with that and the row Susie had with Mike I'm beginning to think things are far from happy for them all.' Maddy picked up the cutlery again and began to lay the table. 'I wish I could do something for them.'

Seb shrugged. 'I'm sure you're being very supportive.'

'Fat lot of good *that* does though.'

She turned to the counter and began cracking eggs into a bowl.

'In other news,' said Seb, 'I saw Jack Rayner this morning.'

'Oh yes. What did he want?'

'He wants to know how I'm getting on with his plans to modernise the mess.'

'And you said...?'

'I gave him the same story that I have done since he first mooted it – that Susie and I are still finding our feet as the new team in charge of running the joint and to embark on any major change will probably mean we'll be biting off more than we can chew.'

'Did he buy your excuse...again?'

'Not really. He's getting impatient. Muttered stuff about me not being up to the job.'

'The bastard.'

'I've put him off for quite a while now – three whole months.'

'Pah, that's no time at all.'

'I can't do it for much longer. And then...?' Seb looked rightly worried.

'But he can't railroad his mad scheme through, though, can he? I know we've been told not to discuss it with anyone yet but at some point he's going to have to get the mess members' agreement.'

'I think his attitude is this is *his* battalion now, *his* toy, *his* rules.'

Maddy thought about things for a while as she beat the eggs and then got out a saucepan. 'I suppose going over his head – having a word with General Pemberton-Blake – would be career suicide.'

Seb snorted. 'What do you think?'

'But I still don't see how he'll get everyone to agree to stripping out all that beautiful furniture and making the place look more like a Premier Inn and less like an officers' mess.'

'He writes all our confidential reports.'

'Oh, come on! There's laws against that sort of workplace bullying.'

Seb raised an eyebrow. 'There may be, but I think you'll find there will be quite a few who aren't prepared to risk jeopardising their careers for a few Empire style side tables and some leather armchairs.'

Maddy snorted in disgust. 'There's got to be something we can do to stop him.'

Seb shook his head. 'Maddy, promise me you won't let it even cross your mind about dropping hints to outsiders. With only us and the Rayners privy to this potty scheme, if it gets out, I know who he'll blame and, unless you want to find yourself neighbours of Mike and Susie, you've got to keep shtum.'

'All right,' agreed Maddy with bad grace. 'But I'm not happy. And there has to be a way to stop him. We just need to think of it.'

Supper at the Collins' house was the usual subdued affair with the twins barely talking and Mike answering monosyllabically Susie's questions about his day. She tried to lighten things by recounting news of their old friends in the mess but Mike didn't seem to be interested in that either. Finally the girls finished their shepherd's pie and escaped upstairs and as soon as they had gone, Susie crossed the kitchen and shut the door behind them.

Mike looked at her. 'What's up?'

Susie sat down next to him in the seat Ella had just vacated. 'Mike, we need to talk.'

'Sounds ominous.'

'I think it might be. I'm really, *really* worried about the twins. I saw Caro today and she is too. They barely talk to her—'

'It's probably their age,' interrupted Mike.

Susie shook her head. 'They're not doing their homework at hers and I'm pretty sure they're not doing it here either.'

'So? They keep telling us how far ahead they are – that most of the stuff is a repeat of what they've already covered at Browndown.'

'Mike, that really isn't the point, is it? And if they're *not* doing it, why isn't the school telling us they're failing to hand work in?'

'I suppose.'

'And Caro thinks... well, I do too... we think they might be getting bullied.'

At this Mike really paid attention. 'You think?'

'Why not? We both know how vile kids can be to each other and Ella and Katie are different: they talk differently, they went to prep school and then boarding school, all the sort of things other kids will pick up on and use against them.'

'I suppose.'

'And they don't seem to have any friends.'

'Well, you don't want them to make friends on this estate, do you?' Mike sounded incredulous.

'Do you know, I think that even if they did that it would be better than nothing.'

Mike looked sceptical.

'Maybe not,' admitted Susie. 'Anyway, I rang the school this morning and asked for an appointment to see the head of year. It's the day after tomorrow. Seb's given me the morning off but is there any chance you can come along too? I think you should.'

Mike groaned. 'Not a snowball's chance. I've got a meeting with the local water authority and Defra. I can't bail out of it at this late stage. People are coming from London and all over – hotels have been booked, the works. Can't you rearrange things?'

'I suppose I could. Or I could go along on my own – find out how the land lies. There's a chance Caro and I are both wrong, in which case...' She shrugged.

'Let's hope that's the case. You go on your own. If things are really terrible...' Mike ran his hand across his face. 'Let's just hope we're both wrong and it turns out to be a waste of your morning.'

Chapter 27

Susie drew her car up in the visitors' car park at Winterspring School and gazed at the main building. God, it was a dispiriting place. Perhaps if she wasn't tempted to compare it to Browndown it mightn't have been quite so bad. Actually, no, it was awful...depressing.

She climbed out of the car and made her way over to reception.

'I have an appointment with Mr Rogers, head of Year Eight.'

'I know who Mr Rogers is,' the receptionist responded tartly.

Jeez, thought Susie, what happened to civility and good manners? Maybe they got beaten out of you at a place like this – which didn't bode well for the kids.

'He's expecting you. If you make your way across to the Welwyn Block, he'll be in the staffroom.' She reached for a school map.

'I know my way,' said Susie. Two could play at being snippy, she thought rather childishly as she swept off.

As before, she stood outside the staffroom and rang the bell. As before, someone, another someone who looked young enough to be a pupil not a teacher, appeared, took Susie's name and scuttled back inside. As before, Susie was left waiting on the threshold. Finally, Mr Rogers deigned to make an appearance.

'Ah, Mrs Coulson.'

'Collins.' Susie had to make an effort not to roll her eyes.

'Yes – of course. Follow me.'

They reached his office and he ushered her in.

'What can I do for you?' he said as she sat down.

'I'll come straight to the point. I am worried about my two girls – Ella and Katie.'

'Oh, yes, the twins. In what way?'

'Where do I start? They aren't making any friends, they aren't settling, they aren't happy and I worry about the attention that is being paid to their well-being because of everything I have just said.'

'I see.'

Mr Rogers, thought Susie, didn't sound in the least bothered. 'Aren't you concerned?'

'Mrs Collins, I am responsible for nearly three hundred children, many of who come from families far less stable than your own, children with far less parental support than your girls presumably get, and to whom I must devote more time and energy.'

'So you're not worried that I think my two daughters are being bullied?'

'Have you any evidence? Have they said anything to you?'

'No, but I am sure this is the case. They're miserable, they're becoming introverted and I think they're underachieving.'

Mr Rogers steepled his fingers and stared at Susie. 'They might achieve better, Mrs Collins, if they bothered to do any work in the first place.'

Susie felt her face redden. 'I haven't had any complaints from the school.'

'You're getting one now.'

'I see.' She felt stung but she recovered. 'The trouble is, Mr Rogers, they're bored. They've covered a lot of this work at their previous school and they're no longer being stretched.'

'So, instead of making any attempt to integrate in class, or maybe offering to help some of their less able classmates, instead of making any sort of contribution, they sulk in silence at the back.'

'Well...'

'"Dumb insolence" is the phrase most of their teachers seem to use to describe your daughters, Mrs Collins.'

'But that's...they're not...in the past they haven't behaved like that,' she finally managed to enunciate. No, Miss Marcham had called them 'rude, opinionated and disruptive', but she wasn't going to share that fact. And now they were insolent and sulky. And how often, when she'd wanted to criticise the below-par behaviour of other children, had the phrase 'I blame the parents' been on her lips?

'Really? Maybe, when you are paying very expensive fees, the staff are more inclined to give your daughters the benefit of the doubt. Here, at Winterspring, we will help, we will encourage, we will even cajole – but when pupils flatly refuse to play any part in the curriculum we haven't either the time or the energy to spend on them when we have other children who want to, and who are willing to learn.'

Susie sat, ramrod straight, trying desperately not to show how she was reeling from the onslaught.

'I still think they are being bullied,' she insisted, not wishing to address Mr Rogers' other comments.

'I will ask the staff to keep an eye out for any signs. But I suggest, Mrs Collins, that you ask your daughters yourself that question. I don't want to spread scarce resources even thinner if your assumption is incorrect.'

Susie knew when she was being given the brush-off.

'And,' he continued, 'while you are at it, you should also ask them to consider their behaviour and attitude in school. Now, is there anything else?'

Susie felt humiliated and angry in equal measure and, head held high, she left the head of year's office without another word. Why, whenever she thought the family had hit rock bottom, did she find they could descend yet further?

Susie waited until she got the girls home after school and they'd all had a cup of tea before she broached the subject of her trip into Winterspring Comprehensive.

'So, I had a word with Mr Rogers.'

'You did what?' snapped Ella.

'Darling, I am worried about you and Katie. Caro is too.'

'You've been talking to her about us?' said Katie.

'Have you been talking to *all* your old pals?' added Ella.

Susie got defensive. 'No! And I only had a word with Caro because I'm worried about you. You don't seem to be happy at school.'

'Well, whose fault is that?' shot back Katie. 'You and Dad sent us to that dump.'

'It's not a dump,' said Susie.

The twins' sneering look told her they disagreed.

'Look, whatever you think about the school, you have to be educated somewhere and Winterspring is all we can afford. I wish it was otherwise but that's that. And the reason I went to see Mr Rogers was to try and find out why you seem so miserable. Even Caro thinks you're not happy.'

She gazed at the twins but they didn't make eye contact back. 'Are you being bullied?'

'Is that what Rogers said?' muttered Katie.

'No.' Susie didn't add that their head of year, the man responsible for their pastoral care, didn't say anything much and what he had said had been less than favourable.

'So, what's your problem?'

Ella's comment verged on the insolent and Susie, only wanting to help, felt stung. She took a slow intake of breath. 'My problem is that I love you, that I can't bear the thought of you being unhappy, that I want the best for you—'

'So why send us to Winterspring?' said Katie.

Susie felt she was going round in circles. 'You know why. And you're not answering my question.'

Katie looked up. 'Well, we're not... being bullied. Happy now?'

Susie wasn't sure she believed her daughter but what could she do? 'I'm glad. You know, if you've got any friends you'd like to have over for a sleepover...'

'Here?'

'Why not?' said Susie.

The girls just shook their heads and shrugged, then Katie muttered, 'No thanks.'

So did that mean they didn't have any friends to ask for a sleepover or they didn't want to ask their friends to come back to this house? Susie didn't dare probe further. 'OK, but the offer is there if you want it. So...' She tried to sound bright and cheerful, 'What homework have you got tonight?'

'Nothing.'

'But you must have. Caro said you just watched TV at hers.'

'You checking up on us now?' accused Ella.

'Of course not. I just asked her what you'd got up to.'

'Well, don't.'

'But you didn't do any homework.' Susie's tone was harsher than she meant.

'And?'

'And... you should both be getting about an hour a night, *and* I haven't seen you do any for a while now *and*, more's the point, neither has Caro.'

'There's no point in doing any. The lessons are rubbish and we're not learning anything,' countered Katie.

'So is that why Mr Rogers told me you both sulk at the back of classes?' Susie stopped. She wished she hadn't said that but they'd pushed her.

'He's lying,' said Ella.

Susie remained silent.

Katie pushed back her chair and stood up. 'Except you seem to want to believe him not us, don't you?'

'Not at all.'

'Yeah right,' said Ella, following suit.

'You don't trust us, you don't believe us. You're as bad as Dad.'

'But...' said Susie. She put a hand on Katie's arm but Katie batted it away.

'Just leave us alone,' snarled Katie.

She and Ella stormed out of the kitchen and a few seconds later the front door slammed.

Susie sat at the kitchen table wondering how she'd got it so wrong. She'd just got her and Mike back on an even keel and now she'd wrecked her relationship with the twins. How? She shut her eyes for a second, willing herself not to give in to the tears that were just under the surface. After a few seconds she opened them again. This wasn't getting supper made and the girls would be back shortly, she had no doubt.

It was getting dark, the weather was chilly and they'd want something to eat in a while. Besides, where would they go?

She got up from the table, fished some spuds out of the veg rack and set about peeling them. She'd just run the water into the sink and picked up the peeler when the phone rang.

'Hello?'

'It's me,' said Mike. 'Just ringing to say I'm probably going to be late.'

'I'm sorry.'

She heard him sigh. 'That meeting I had went on longer than I expected so I've only just got back to the office and I have to write up my notes before I leave.'

'Can't you do it at home?'

'No, I need some files here. How did *your* meeting go?'

Susie groaned. 'Don't ask.'

'That bad?'

'Worse. And now I've just had a row with the girls.'

'Welcome to the club.'

'Only this time it was them who stormed out of the house, not one of their parents.'

'Hey.'

'Sorry...'

'Where've they gone?'

'I don't know. It can't be far and it isn't as if it's late. I'll get supper on then go to look for them.'

'Hmm. Don't leave it too late, it'll be dark soon.'

'I expect they'll be at the bus shelter or somewhere like that.'

'OK – but even so...'

'Mike, they're together, they're twelve and it's still after-noon. You wouldn't have worried about them on the patch.'

'Exactly – but this isn't the patch.'

Mike's words stuck in Susie's brain for a while after she

put the phone down and when she'd finished the potatoes she put them in a pan of water, grabbed her keys and coat and headed out of the front door herself. She took a punt on them going to the end of their road and down the hill towards the village. As she neared the junction she heard laughter. She listened. Laughter and voices. She stopped walking and listened even more intently. Yes, she could hear Katie and Ella's voices but she couldn't make out what they were saying although it was clear that they weren't alone and they seemed fairly relaxed. That was something to be grateful for. Maybe they did have some friends in the area and her interview with Mr Rogers had been unnecessary. She headed back to the house feeling happier; they hadn't gone far and they were with friends. She could get on with supper. If they weren't home by the time supper was ready she'd go out and call them in.

Half an hour later that front door banged open.

'Katie, Ella?' she called from the kitchen.

Footsteps thumped up the stairs. Two pairs. They were both in, good.

Susie went into the hall. 'Katie, Ella?' But still silence.

She followed them upstairs. 'Katie...? Ella...?' she called tentatively. The last thing she wanted to do was spark another row.

'Yeah? What do you want?' said Katie from her room.

'I just wanted to tell you that supper'll be about fifteen minutes.'

'Whatevs.'

Susie didn't rise to the bait and tell them she'd rather they said 'Thank you, Mum.' Pick your battles, she told herself.

When the girls came down to eat she noticed they'd changed out of their school uniforms. Odd, they didn't usually bother, but she didn't comment: to ask was to risk another altercation. The meal was a fairly silent affair. Susie thought about asking them where they'd been but she knew she'd only get accused of prying and she certainly couldn't ask who they'd met. The girls uttered a couple of things like 'pass the salt' and then, as soon as they'd finished, they shot back up to their rooms. Morosely, Susie cleared up their plates, dished up Mike's meal and covered it in cling film ready for his return, and then loaded the dishwasher.

At least, she thought, being able to tell Mike that the girls seemed to be, at last, making some friends, would counter the dismal interview with Mr Rogers. Maybe there was light at the end of the tunnel.

Chapter 28

As October headed towards Hallowe'en and then bonfire night, the weather took a turn for the worse and refused to budge. It seemed to rain almost every day; not in great cloudbursts, like the one in the summer, but constant, dreary drizzle, falling from leaden skies. Even when it wasn't raining the air was cold and damp and the sun rarely, if ever, seemed to shine. It was dispiriting and depressing and everyone began to feel beaten down by the dreariness of it all. Caro found the kids in the crèche cranky and difficult, the bookings in Jenna's hairdressing salon took a dive, but Jenna couldn't be sure if that was down to the weather or because the wives had worked out about her past, and Maddy, trapped indoors with two small children, began to go stir-crazy. Morale everywhere in the 1 Herts barracks appeared to be at a low ebb and, lately, even the normally buzzing coffee shop in the community centre had been pretty quiet. In fact, because the takings had dropped, Camilla had demanded a meeting with Maddy at the shop to discuss its viability.

'Just what I need,' she muttered to Seb over breakfast. 'A morning with bloody Camilla.'

'It's not like you've got much else to do,' said Seb.

Maddy glared at him. 'Like that's my fault. You try to

keep a career going with two small children in tow and three house-moves in as many years.'

'I'm sorry,' said Seb. 'I didn't mean it like that.'

'You'd better not have done.'

'I just meant that...' He stopped. 'I'm in a hole, aren't I?'

'And I'd stop digging if I were you.' She glowered at him. 'Sorry, I shouldn't be so tetchy but the prospect of being patronised by Camilla for an hour or so is more than flesh and blood can stand.'

'I sympathise. I've got a meeting with her husband again.'

'About the mess?'

'I should imagine so. And I think I'm going to have to either stand up to him and refuse to carry out his plans, or tell him he's got to involve all the members. He and I can't act unilaterally in this matter.'

Maddy stared at Seb. 'I don't envy you that.'

'No. So, I think today is going to be the Fanshaws versus the Rayners.'

Maddy sighed and pulled a face. 'And I think I can guess which team will come off worst. Let's just hope we don't get completely thrashed by them.'

'Let's just hope I still have a career at the end of the day.'

'On the positive side, when I asked Caro if she could take Rose for me at the crèche, she managed to find a space.'

'That's a step forward.'

Maddy nodded. 'We're still not back where we were but...' She shrugged. 'Hey, I think solving that little problem is going to take a bit of time.'

But, she thought, her problems were nothing compared to Susie's, although if she and Seb both fell out with the Rayners, they might move easily into Susie's league. She hoped not.

The last thing she wanted to do right now was join Susie on Civvy Street – or Springhill Road.

If it weren't for the fact that she was meeting Camilla, Maddy would have looked forward to the excuse of having a coffee and cake at the café – a bit of a treat. Oh well, she thought as she made her way to the coffee shop having dropped off Rose, she couldn't have everything.

'Hello, Maddy.'

Oh God, thought Maddy. Bloody Camilla was early. That was all she needed.

'Hello, Camilla,' she said, trying to sound welcoming. 'Let me get you a coffee.'

'Lovely. Black, no sugar.'

'And something to eat?'

'Oh, I don't think so, but thank you.'

Was it Maddy's imagination or did she look at Maddy's hips?

Maddy fetched the drink and then settled down at the table. An hour later, after a guided tour of all the community centre had to offer, meeting Jenna, Caro and the ladies who ran the coffee shop, Maddy had persuaded Camilla that the place wasn't about to bankrupt the battalion, that it was being run as efficiently as was humanly possible and that judging its performance after a paltry three months was hardly fair.

'If you say so,' she'd finally and grudgingly agreed. 'Now, I think we need to have a little chat.' Camilla looked about her. 'But not here. Maybe we could go over to The Residence?'

Come into my parlour, said the spider to the fly... Maddy felt uneasy. 'If you wish. But I won't be able to stay long. I've got to pick up Nathan from playgroup in about forty minutes.'

'I don't think you need worry about the time. This won't take long.'

Maddy felt really apprehensive now. Unhappily she trailed after Camilla and down the road to the CO's residence. Of course, until the Rayners had moved in, the house had just been 33 Arnhem Avenue. It was just a matter of days after their arrival that it had been redesignated Hertfordshire House and referred to by them, but no one else, as The Residence. For a few days it had seemed amusingly pretentious – little had they all known that it was a first indication of how much the Rayners wanted to put their stamp on the regiment, turn the battalion into their own personal fiefdom. Maddy might have felt anxious about this summons to a private interview but she was also curious as this was going to be the first time she'd been invited inside Camilla's quarter. As yet, she'd never stepped over the threshold – not sufficiently worthy, she imagined.

Camilla opened the door and ushered Maddy in. The house smelt of lilies and furniture polish, which reminded Maddy of visiting the undertaker, years back, when a maiden aunt had died. She'd thought the smell creepy and cloying back then. But the smell of flowers and polish was about the only traditional thing in the Rayners' quarter. Maddy clocked the modern art on the walls, the objets d'art on the floating, asymmetric shelves and the garish rugs covering up the drab issue carpet. It was striking – if you liked that sort of decor, which Maddy, frankly, didn't.

Camilla opened the door to the drawing room and beckoned Maddy to follow.

'Take a seat, Maddy.'

Maddy perched on the edge of a modern designer sofa – all geometric shapes and corners and, she decided as she sat down, as uncomfortable as it looked. The other chairs didn't look much better and the whole room, with its stripes and angles and bold, clashing colours, made Maddy think she'd been sucked into a Bridget Riley painting.

'I'll come to the point, Maddy,' said Camilla sitting on a hideous, lime-green bucket chair.

'Please do,' she murmured.

'As we both know, women can have a great deal of influence on their husbands. A word here, a hint there...' She smiled but there was no friendliness in it.

Maddy didn't say a word. She thought she knew what was coming.

'Now, Seb has been asked on a number of occasions, by Jack, to work out a strategy to update the officers' mess. You should be aware of this because Jack told Seb he could talk to you about it, and, let's face it, husbands tend to tell their wives about the important things going on in their lives.' She smiled archly. 'Pillow talk.'

Maddy shuddered inwardly.

'However, nothing much seems to be happening on that front and Jack is getting very frustrated. Maddy, you must understand Jack's point of view; that the army is a twenty-first century organisation and yet we seem to insist on surrounding ourselves with nineteenth century trappings. I am sure you agree with me and Jack that the mess is more of a museum piece than a living space.' Camilla smiled her winsome smile at Maddy, who felt her gorge rise.

She took a deep breath. 'Actually, I rather like it as it is. Very country house hotel.'

'I think,' said Camilla, a little steel in her voice, 'the look I would prefer is *boutique* hotel – *modern* boutique hotel. The Downton Abbey look is so passé, don't you think?'

'Not at Highclere House it isn't,' muttered Maddy.

Camilla glared at Maddy. 'I don't think you quite understand, Maddy. Jack wants things to change and I agree with him. So...as Seb seems to be dragging his feet, I'd like you to persuade him that, in all our best interests, he does what Jack has asked him to do. I'm sure you get my drift.'

Maddy certainly did. Shape up or ship out. Maddy knew that Jack Rayner wouldn't be able to get rid of Seb from the army but he could get rid of him from his battalion and how would that play with Seb's future career? For a start he'd probably be posted without his acting rank of major and the pay drop would come as a blow. He and Maddy had got used to the extra bunce in his pay packet at the end of the month and losing it would be tough.

On the other hand, was the money worth being threatened by Jack and his obnoxious wife? Maddy thought not. Besides, she wasn't in the army. She didn't have to toe the line, obey Queen's Regulations, or kowtow to the CO and she wasn't about to start now.

'I'm sorry, Camilla. I don't know how *your* marriage works but Seb is very much his own man and I don't burden him with the day-to-day running of the house and in turn he doesn't burden me with the day-to-day machinations of his job. I hardly know anything about your plans for the mess – apart from what you've just told me now,' she lied, and pretty fluently at that, she thought, 'and with two small children I haven't the time or the energy to take on any sort of project you may have in that regard. If you and Jack want to ruin a beautiful building with some fashion statement that will probably be out of date before the paint is dry then I suggest you sort it yourselves.' She stood up. 'Now, if that is everything, I have to collect my children.'

Without waiting for Camilla to show her out, Maddy left. As she shut the front door behind her she leaned against the porch. Her legs were shaking so much she thought they might collapse under her. What had she done? Dear God, of all the people to pick a fight with, Camilla was not the one to choose.

Chapter 29

When Seb got home for his lunch, Maddy still felt sick with nerves at what damage she might have done to his career.

'Hi, sweetie,' he said, giving her a peck on the cheek as he came into the kitchen. 'You all right? You look a bit peaky,' he added as he ruffled Nathan's hair and brushed Rose's cheek.

'Seb, I've got a confession to make.' She stopped stirring the chicken soup on the hob and turned to face him.

'Oh yes. What have you done? Embezzled the flower arranging fund?'

'Worse than that. I told Camilla to fu— I told Camilla where to shove her ideas for the mess.'

Seb's mouth twitched. 'Really?'

Maddy nodded miserably.

'I wish I'd been there to see it.'

'But Seb, there are bound to be repercussions.'

'Quite likely, but probably no worse than the ones that'll follow from me telling Rayner much the same thing.'

Maddy's eyes widened. 'You did *what*?'

'I told Rayner I wasn't going to get rid of any of the mess furniture – or the silver, or the soft furnishings for that matter.'

'But why? I mean . . . what about your career?'

'What about it? I had a long hard think about things when I got to work this morning and then I had a telephone conversation with Tony Notley.'

'Tony?'

Seb nodded. 'I asked him for some hypothetical advice – you know, in the event of an officer going against some Machiavellian plan of his commanding officer and getting a completely dud confidential report as a result.'

'And?'

'And he said the hypothetical officer ought to be bullet-proof as his past CRs would show him to have been a good officer up to that point. Notley also added that he's heard rumours that Rayner has previous in trying to wreck other officers' careers and that, if said officer suddenly got a crap CR he should demand a redress of grievance from the brigadier. And if that officer did, Notley would back him up.'

'Wow.'

'So when I went to see Rayner I told him that I couldn't, in all conscience, carry out his plans for the mess.'

'And he said?'

'Not a lot, to be honest. I think he was quite surprised I stood up to him. He seems to be the sort of bully-boy who is used to getting his own way and when he didn't he didn't know what to do.'

'Oh, Seb, I am so pleased you did that. I saw the inside of the Rayners' quarter this morning and it's awful. Well, maybe it's the height of fashion but it was garish and uncomfortable and absolutely loathsome.'

'And that's probably what Jack wants for the mess.'

Maddy went back to the stove and stirred the soup before pouring it out into four bowls.

'So have you shot his fox?' she asked.

'Time will tell. In the meantime it'll be interesting to see what happens.'

Maddy put the bowls of soup on the table and began blowing on Rose's to make it cool enough for her.

The phone rang. Maddy sighed and went to answer it.

'Caro. What can I do for you?'

'Maddy, what's been going on?'

What do you mean?'

'I've just had Camilla on the phone. She wants me to take over from you on a couple of committees. Have you resigned?'

'I think,' said Maddy, 'I've just been sacked, although it's news to me. Look, I can't talk now; I'm dishing up lunch for the family. Come round this afternoon and we can talk then.'

As she turned back to the table Seb raised his eyebrows. 'Trouble at mill?'

'Looks like it. It seems Camilla doesn't want me on her committees any more. Mind you, little does she know that sacking me is the answer to my prayers. The thought of not having to be patronised by her again is just wonderful.'

'Anyway, to make your day even better, I've just heard from Rollo. Remember that house he liked?'

Maddy did, only too well. She remembered, even more clearly, the squirming embarrassment she'd felt as Rollo had described it in loving detail to the Collinses of all people, and then suggested that given how well-off army officers surely had to be that they ought to join him as property tycoons. OK, she exaggerated, but it had still been a horrible moment. No wonder Susie had pleaded a headache and fled.

'Well, he's only gone and bought it. He'll be living almost on our doorstep.'

'Really? Where was the house again?'

'Ashton-cum-Bavant.'

'Oh, yes.' Maddy remembered now. So Rollo had a perfect house in a perfect village. It was a totally picture-book one with a green, a pond and a small stream and some of the prettiest houses in the area. It was the sort of village that featured in calendars and was used for jigsaw puzzle pictures. The sort of village people longed to end up in, the sort of village Maddy was sure she and Seb would never be able to afford to move into, and which was as far removed from where Susie and Mike lived as to be almost on another planet. 'Lucky old him.' She tried not to feel jealous – and failed miserably.

As Seb was leaving to go back to work and Maddy was clearing up the kitchen, Caro rocked into the house.

'So come on,' she said, as soon as Seb had shut the front door, 'what happened? Why has Camilla sacked you? What on *earth* have you done?'

Caro, noted Maddy, wasn't crowing or pleased at her apparent downfall but curious as to the reason why. Which was pretty normal, she thought. If the tables had been turned it would have been how she'd have reacted. So this was yet another baby-step towards normality again, another bit of the olive tree being held out. Maddy took it.

'Well,' she said, wiping down the highchair, 'let me put you in the picture. Camilla and Jack want to strip out the mess and put their stamp on it.'

'No!' Caro sat down on a chair. 'But that's awful. Have you seen her idea of interior decor?'

Maddy nodded. 'I have.'

'It's like some mad film set for a James Bond baddy. It's ghastly.'

'Tell me about it. Anyway, Seb was tasked with finding a home for all the old furniture and getting interior designers in and, naturally, he's been dragging his feet about it, so Camilla told me to tell Seb to get a move on.'

'She never.'

Maddy nodded. 'She did. And I told her that I wouldn't.' Maddy then recounted what she'd actually said.

Caro looked at Maddy with an expression that combined admiration with respect. Maddy grinned back. *Normality* had been achieved. It had taken months for Caro to get over her rage at Seb's promotion but at last it had happened. Thank goodness.

'Oh, Maddy, I wish I'd been there to see her face, it must have been a picture.'

'I don't know. I was so shattered by what I'd actually said I had to get out of her house before I changed my mind and apologised.'

'Shit no, that would have been bad. But it's really nasty that she's now canvassing behind your back for people to take over from you on those committees. She obviously doesn't want to give you the push until she's got replacements lined up.'

Maddy shrugged. 'You know, I just don't care. There's no kudos in being at her beck and call, just a shedload of hard work and precious little thanks.' 'You can't recommend it then.'

'No way.'

'Good, then telling her I didn't want the jobs was the right move.'

Maddy nodded. 'You did? Oh, well done you. Do you think she'll find anyone mug enough to take over?'

'Not if they've got any sense.'

'What do you think she'll do, if she draws a blank?'

'Don't know, don't care,' said Caro.

Maddy felt much the same. 'At least I know I'm not battling alone against bloody Camilla.'

'No way. I'm right there with you.'

Chapter 30

'Did you get them?' asked Ella.

Katie nodded and drew a half-empty packet of cigarettes from the pocket of her school trousers. 'Got to hope Old Rogers thinks he dropped them out of his jacket somewhere.'

'And no one saw you?'

Katie gave her twin a quick shake of her head. 'No, I was alone in his classroom and I'm sure no one else was anywhere near.'

'Well done.' Ella gave her sister's arm a squeeze of appreciation. Katie tucked the fags back into her pocket.

'And it's not raining. We can meet the others on the corner, like we planned.'

They giggled with excitement at the prospect of meeting their new acquaintances from the estate, the ones they'd fallen in with the night they'd rowed with their mother. The ones who'd been smoking and drinking cider from cans. The ones who said they would teach the twins how to smoke but they had to produce the fags first. Their mother, they knew, would have a fit if she knew about the kids they'd taken up with, but that only added to the thrill of it all.

Throughout the rest of the school day Katie oscillated between terror at having her crime discovered and a feeling of delicious naughtiness at what she'd done. When she was sure she wasn't being observed she fingered the little cardboard carton in her trouser pocket and wished the hours to pass as quickly as possible so she and Ella could escape to the end of their road and spark up with their new mates. Finally, school was out, and then two whole dragging hours later they were picked up from Caro's by their mum and taken back to Springhill Road.

The twins hurtled upstairs as soon as they tumbled through the front door and then were back downstairs less than five minutes later changed into jeans and hoodies.

'We're going out,' said Ella as she tugged on her shoes at the bottom of the stairs.

'Where?' asked Susie.

'Going to see Ali,' said Katie.

'Who's Ali?'

Katie rolled her eyes. 'A kid from school.'

'Lives at the end of the road,' said Ella.

'OK, but don't be late. Supper'll be at seven. And if you've got any homework...' But Ella and Katie didn't hear what their mother wanted to say on the subject of homework as they were out of the house with the door shut behind them.

'Just had a thought,' said Katie.

'What?'

'We shouldn't have changed out of uniform.'

Ella stopped and stared at her twin. 'Why on earth not?'

'Because we can't change our clothes *again*, not like we did last time because we smelt of smoke. Mum'll smell a rat.'

Katie considered her sister's point. 'Mum'll smell more than that. Bugger. We'll just have to cross that bridge when we come to it. We'll think of something. I wonder what it's like.'

'What?'

Katie shook her head at her sister and rolled her eyes. 'Duh. Smoking, of course.'

'Oh...yes.'

'You're not getting cold feet? Not after I nicked the cigs.'

'Course not. Show me them again,' said Ella.

Katie pulled the packet from her hoodie pocket and flipped open the lid. Inside, the filter tips of fifteen smokes were crammed together. 'We've got loads,' she crowed.

'Gotta hope Ali's got a lighter.'

'Don't be a dumb-ass, course he will.'

The pair ran up the road to the junction to the agreed rendezvous with their new friends at the dark green BT junction box there. Ali, short for Alastair, and his three cronies, Tom, Dylan and Jezza, were leaning against the fence by the road sign, swigging Strongbow out of cans.

'What kept ya?' sneered Ali.

Katie felt nettled. 'We came as fast as we could. Got these,' she added, offering up the fags.

'Give 'em here.'

Katie willingly handed over her prize.

'Where d'you get 'em?'

'Rogers left his jacket hanging on the back of his chair at break. I pinched them out of his pocket.'

Ali looked at Katie with something that might have been respect and Katie felt a glow of pride. 'Nice one.'

Ali took a cigarette and handed the packet round. Eagerly Katie and Ella took one each too. Jezza produced a lighter and the lads lit up, blowing long streams of smoke down their noses.

Jezza proffered a flame in Katie's direction. She took a tiny sharp inward breath, just enough to get the cigarette to light and then quickly exhaled. Ella did likewise. Katie could feel her eyes stinging with the smoke but managed to swallow down a cough. Out of the corner of her eye she could see Ella's shoulders jerking as she almost choked, although, like her sister, she tried to do it silently.

The boys laughed. 'Lightweights,' said Ali. 'Have another drag. You'll get used to it. Just takes a bit of practice.'

Katie took another tentative puff and this time she dragged the smoke a little deeper into her body. This time her cough reflex seemed less trigger-happy but the rush of light-headedness was most disconcerting. She grabbed onto the junction box to steady herself as the world spun around her. Her ears rang and for a few seconds she felt nauseous but then both feelings passed. Feeling cocky, she took another puff. A big one. Huge mistake. The smoke went far too deep; she gagged, she coughed, she damn nearly choked, her eyes watered and she began to retch. The boys leapt backwards – no way did they want to be in the firing line if she hurled. And far from looking concerned, they seemed to find her reaction to the smoke hilarious.

Finally she got herself and her breathing under control. 'Like you were so good at smoking the first time you tried,' she wheezed.

'We were better than that,' said Ali. He eyed her fag. 'And if you're not going to smoke that, give it here.'

Katie snatched her hand away as he reached for her ciggie. 'Gonna have a last go,' she said. She took a puff, inhaled and then blew smoke down her nose. 'Nothing to it.' Although, despite her bravado and her new-found expertise, her ears rang and her head spun, but once again, it settled down after a shortish while.

It took Ella rather longer to get the hang of it but by the time they had to go home for their supper they were both smoking like old hands.

Ali, keeping the cigarettes, drifted off with his mates, leaving Katie and Ella shivering slightly in the chill autumn air – although they were grateful that, for once, it wasn't actually raining.

'We'd better go in,' said Ella. 'Don't want Mum coming looking for us.'

'Do you think we smell of smoke?' asked Katie.

Ella sniffed the sleeve of her jersey. 'Can't tell. Let's walk really slowly. The fresh air might blow the smell away.'

'We could always say Ali's folks smoke, if she mentions anything.'

'Genius,' said Katie.

The two girls loped back towards their house. 'Hi, Mum,' they called in unison, as they let themselves in.

'Hi,' said their mother from the kitchen. 'Supper's in ten minutes. Your dad should be home by then.'

They scuttled upstairs and collapsed on Katie's bed in her room.

'So how are we going to get more cigs?' asked Ella.

Katie shrugged. 'Don't think I can risk nicking too many off Rogers. And we don't really know anyone else who smokes. Maybe we could get someone to buy them for us.'

Ella shook her head. 'Like who?'

'Maybe we could ask a sixth former. We know there's a bunch who head off into town every lunchtime who light up when they get to the path across the rec. Maybe if we offered them a bribe...'

'Using what?'

'Money, of course, stupid,' said Katie.

Ella shook her head. 'Like we get enough pocket money to do that.'

'No, we don't. But Mum's always leaving her bag lying

around and I bet, half the time, she hasn't a clue how much she's got in it. You know as well as I do she just goes to the cash point whenever she gets a bit short. Come on, she won't miss it. And think what we're saving them now we're not at Browndown. They owe us the odd quid for that, at the very least.'

Ella didn't look completely convinced.

'You got a better plan?' said Katie. 'Anyway, I think Ali really likes us. We don't want to look like lame losers in front of him so we've got to.'

'I suppose.'

Katie narrowed her eyes. 'We can't back out now. Not without looking like mongs.'

Ella nodded.

'Anyway,' continued Katie. 'If Ali thinks we're cool, the other kids might leave us alone.'

They heard their dad come in and call hello. Then they heard him come upstairs and go to the loo and then clean his teeth, like he did most nights.

A couple of minutes later he clattered downstairs and they heard him and their mum chatting in the kitchen and then they were called to the table.

They took their places opposite each other and their father looked from one to the other. Their mother dished up shepherd's pie and told them to help themselves to the peas from the dish in the centre.

'Have you two been smoking?'

Katie felt her face flare but Ella, as cool as anything said, 'God, no, Dad. Whatever gave you that idea?'

'I can smell it on you.'

'Really?' said Ella. In an exaggerated way she pulled the hood of her sweatshirt round to her nose and sniffed it.

'I can't smell anything. It must be 'cos we went to see Ali, from school. His mum and dad smoke.'

There was a snort from their mother. 'I'm surprised the sort of people who live on this estate can afford to.'

'People like us, Mum?' said Katie forking some mince into her mouth.

'Don't be cheeky. You know exactly what I mean. And anyway, I thought this Ali person was a girl.'

'No, Alastair.'

Their mother narrowed her eyes. 'I'm not quite sure I want you hanging around with boys.'

Katie slumped in her chair and chucked her fork onto her plate. 'What do you think we do at that crappy school you sent us to? Half the kids are *boys*, half the kids on the bus home are *boys*. What do you want us to do? Burka up?'

'That's enough,' roared their father.

The girls exchanged a look.

Katie stood up. 'I'm not hungry.' She left the kitchen followed by her sister and together they stormed back to Katie's room.

'That settles it,' said Katie. 'Next time Mum leaves her bag lying around I'm going to pinch a tenner. That'll pay her back for letting Dad have another go at us.'

Chapter 31

'OK,' said Seb, as he dropped his briefcase by the front door and took off his beret, 'who did you tell?' He shook the worst of the rain off his combat jacket and hung it on a peg.

'Tell what?' said Maddy indignantly. She put down the slice of bread she was about to butter.

Seb sighed. 'About Rayner's plan for the mess.'

'Oh, that. Just Caro.'

'But I told you not to tell *anyone*. It was one thing telling Camilla that you wouldn't twist my arm to rip out the existing decor; it's another thing entirely passing on stuff that I told you wasn't for general publication. And telling Caro is like taking out a double page ad in the local paper.'

'Look, she asked why Camilla was trying to find people to take over from me on her blasted committees . . . what was I supposed to say? Besides, does it matter any more? We've both told them we're not having anything to do with their mad scheme and even madder ideas about interior design so, presumably, it's all dead in the water anyway.' Maddy went back to buttering bread.

Seb shrugged. 'We can but hope. However, it's the talk of the mess and the fact that it's now common knowledge is bound to get back to him. I popped across there this morning and got

267

waylaid by two of the residents and got given the third degree. I know no one talks to Rayner if they can help it, but even he is going to get wind of the mood amongst the mess members.'

'You can't blame them. What Jack Rayner wants to do to the place is monstrous.'

'Indeed, but he is the CO here and as such if he wants to run things differently from the way they have been in the past, as long as he doesn't break the law, he can.'

'He can, if he doesn't piss everyone off. And let's face it, that's exactly what he and Camilla seem to be doing. No wonder everyone is up in arms.'

'By the way, in other news, he's called a snap exercise. We're all off to play on Salisbury Plain next week.'

Maddy frowned. 'How long for?'

'Monday to Friday. We're deploying first thing Monday morning and should be back in barracks sometime after lunch on the Friday.'

'And what's this in aid of?'

'Rayner's idea of keeping us on our toes. Or maybe he wants to prove to the brass how proactive he is. Or maybe he just wants to bugger all his soldiers about.'

'Ha,' said Maddy. 'That's the most likely reason.'

'Enough of that,' said Seb. 'How was your day? How are the kids? And what's for supper?'

Maddy laughed. 'Fine, fine, although Rose is teething again, and it's chicken in barbecue sauce. Only the kids get their chicken without the sauce. I'm not sure they're quite up to the addition of chilli powder into their diet just yet.'

'Yum,' said Seb. 'I'm starving.'

'Good,' said Maddy, 'I think I might have over-catered.'

'And I could fancy a glass of wine with it,' said Seb. 'How about you?'

'I could, totally. There's just one snag.'

Seb glanced across the kitchen to the wine rack on the counter. 'I see what you mean,' he said as he saw the empty pigeonholes. 'How about I pop across to the mess and buy a couple of bottles?'

Maddy stood on tiptoe and kissed him on the cheek. 'Oh, do. And while you're doing that I'll get the kids fed and bathed. Make sure you're back for seven. I know what you're like when you get chatting to your mates over there.'

'Promise,' said Seb, heading for the door. 'Cross my heart.'

Across the barracks in her office, Sam heard the news about the exercise with a leaden heart. That was another weekend about to be buggered up. With the battalion crashing out of the barracks first thing on the Monday, Rayner had just cancelled all leave for the weekend – he wasn't going to run the risk of some of his soldiers failing to get back in time to deploy with everyone else. And that meant that, once again, her chance of seeing Luke had just been completely and comprehensively scuppered. She threw her biro onto her desk and sighed. Thanks, Rayner, she thought. Thanks a bunch.

The urge to work deserted her. She yawned and stretched and looked at her watch. Five thirty. Sod it, it was time to call it a day. She picked up her filing trays and stuffed them in the secure cabinet at the back of her office and locked it, switched off her computer, made sure the windows were closed tight and then took her office keys along to the duty clerk's office up at battalion HQ.

'Night, Williams,' she said to the clerk as she hung her keys in the key press.

'Night, ma'am.'

She left the office block and pulled her combat jacket collar up. Raining again. When hadn't it? she wondered, as she trudged through the steady drizzle back to the mess. The rain just added to her low mood. Nothing seemed to be going right at the moment. And no one else seemed to be enjoying life either. There was no doubt about it, morale – and not just hers – was at rock-bottom.

The rain's intensity suddenly increased from drizzle to full-on downpour and, head down, she ran the last hundred yards to the front door and careered into a shape by the porch, someone who was frantically pressing the keypad in order to get inside and gain shelter from the storm.

'Whoops,' shouted a voice.

'Sorry,' said Sam taking a pace back.

The figure flung the door open and they both piled into the warm, dry lobby.

Sam clocked who she'd run into. 'Sorry, Seb. Didn't mean to bowl you over.'

'No harm done. God, it's filthy out there.'

Sam began to take off her soaking combat jacket. 'Vile. I am fed up with being wet and cold.'

Seb snorted. 'And if it's like this next week...'

'Don't,' said Sam with a groan. 'The idea of spending five days in a slit trench in this...' She shook her head.

'Call yourself a soldier...' joked Seb.

Sam sighed. 'You know, there are days,' she said, hanging her dripping jacket on a hook in the alcove that passed as a cloakroom, 'when I sometimes wonder if I'm in the right job.'

'That was said with feeling,' said Seb.

'Sorry, crap day.'

'Come on. Let me buy you a drink. Things may look better after a stiff gin.'

'Doubt it,' said Sam, gloomily.

'It *was* a bad day.' He led the way to the bar. 'What's your poison?'

'Actually, a gin sounds lovely,' said Sam.

'Dawkins,' said Seb to the steward, 'a large gin for Captain Lewis and a pint for me. Oh, and two bottles of the house red.' He picked up a mess chit and wrote down his order before signing it while Dawkins sorted out the drinks. 'Tell Uncle Seb what the problem is.'

'In the great scheme of things it's nothing, but I was planning to nip over to see Luke and the CO's cancelled all leave.'

'That's a bummer.'

'Tell me about it.'

'What about Luke coming over here?'

'It's just...it's just I don't fancy him staying in the mess – it isn't exactly private, is it? – and with leave cancelled I can't book into a hotel off base.'

'I see your point.'

'Anyway, it's not the end of the world except there always seems to be *something* that mucks up our plans.'

Dawkins put their drinks on the bar along with the wine Seb had ordered.

'Cheers,' they said and clinked glasses.

'And thanks for the drink and the chance for me to sound off.'

'All part of the service.' Seb grinned at her.

'Hey, and what's this I heard about the CO wanting to turn the mess into some sort of Ikea showroom?' said Sam changing the subject.

Seb shook his head and ran his hand through his hair. 'It's something and nothing,' he said non-committally. 'It's an idea he's got but it probably won't come off.' Not now the cat's out of the bag, he thought.

'It won't if the livers-in have got anything to do with it. They're livid at the thought of him chucking out the furniture.'

'Hmm,' said Seb. 'I don't think he was going to *chuck*.'

'Whatever. It may be a bit shabby and the armchairs have seen better days but it's comfortable. Who wants cutting-edge design when you can sink into an armchair with an arm wide enough to rest a cuppa or a drink on?'

'No, well...Anyway, the CO's plans may not come to anything.'

'They better hadn't,' muttered Sam. She sipped her drink again and other officers began to appear in the bar, ready for a quick drink before going to their rooms to wash and brush up, catch up on emails and square away any personal admin before dinner at seven thirty. The noise level rose and Seb found himself explaining several times that the rumoured plans for the bar were nothing to do with him and he was not to blame for any of it. He thought about staying for a second pint when Sam offered to buy him a drink, but he felt a bit picked on by the residents and called it a day, shortly after six. Picking up his bottles of wine he set off back home, dodging the rain as best he could.

'You're early,' said Maddy. She was sitting on the sofa, with the children, pink and scrubbed, beside her in their pyjamas as she turned the pages of a picture book about an elephant.

Seb explained the reason. 'And I got my ear bent by all of them.'

'Can't say I'm the *least* bit surprised.' She turned her attention to Nathan. 'Where's the elephant in this picture, sweetie?'

'Even Sam, who's not exactly a fully paid up member of the Hertfordshire Regiment, felt the need to have a go at me.'

Nathan found the animal and was rewarded with a kiss on top of his head.

Maddy turned the page. 'And how is Sam?'

'Pis— hacked off. She was planning on seeing her man this weekend and with leave cancelled her plans have been scuppered.'

'Can't he come over here?'

'I don't think she fancies staying with him in the mess.'

Maddy considered the situation. 'I can see her point. What about the Old Bell?'

'Because with leave cancelled she can't go off base.'

Maddy wrinkled her nose. 'Duh, silly me.'

Nathan began to wriggle and Maddy turned back to the book. It was later, when the children were tucked up in bed and she and Seb were eating their supper, that Maddy suggested that Sam could stay with them for the weekend.

'You sure?' said Seb. 'It'll be work for you.'

'The spare room is made up and I expect they'll be out a lot of the time – romantic dinners, that sort of thing.'

'If you're sure.'

Maddy nodded. 'Ring the mess and tell her – before she goes putting off her bloke.'

Chapter 32

Mike sat at his workstation in the council offices and earwigged some of the conversations going on between his colleagues. They were, he thought, all unutterably dull – and stupid. Really, was the high point of these people's lives watching stupid videos about cats on YouTube, because that's what it seemed to be. There were occasions when he despaired of the human race. Of course, the calibre of his colleagues in the army had been high; they'd almost all seen active service, had had to make life and death decisions under trying circumstances, many of them had seen tragedies and destruction on a scale this load of muppets wouldn't be able to envisage, let alone cope with, and yet, almost to a man, they remained balanced individuals who didn't moan, didn't complain and who worked hard. And yet, this lot... Mike cast his eye around the office. There were the spotty youths who shirked jobs whenever they thought they could get away with it; the time-servers who had 'always done it this way'; the thirty-something job-sharing mums who had one eye on the clock and the other on their mobile; and the sharp-suited thrusters with their buzz-words and Estuary English who strutted like starlings but never seemed to do a hand's turn. Once again, Mike felt he had nothing in common with any of his colleagues. They didn't share a work ethic, politics, interests... even their choice of daily papers differed.

And tonight they wanted him to go out with them for a drink after work. A drink, a meal and some team bonding. The last two Mike dreaded; he dreaded the pointless chit-chat, he dreaded trying not to be rude to his vacuous workmates but he was excited about the prospect of a legitimate social occasion where he could have a couple of drinks. And the breath freshener he now kept in the glove compartment of the car should hide any evidence before he got home.

However, a niggle worried him. So far he'd managed to keep his regular clandestine lunchtime pints under control, but he'd been drinking on his own with no one to suggest 'one for the road' or shout that they were buying the next round. Besides, with only an hour for lunch, a pint – or sometimes two – were all he could down in the time. But an evening 'bonding with the team', as that oily git Rob put it, was going to test his resolve. Of course, he'd have the car so he really shouldn't have more than two drinks – or he wouldn't be OK to drive, not legally – but when was the last time anyone out here in the sticks had seen a police patrol? He could probably risk having twice that amount and still get home with his licence intact, and that very tempting bit of knowledge was deeply unsettling.

Mike rubbed his hand over his face and turned back to his filing tray. He pulled the next document towards him; a briefing paper on the proposed dredging of the Winterspring river – or rather the postponement of the proposed dredging. Mike began to read but as he did his mind kept wandering to that night's meeting in the pub. Maybe he could pretend the car broke down and book into the Red Lion. If he rang Susie at around eight, maybe nine o'clock, and told her he couldn't get home he could stay and make the most of the evening. Even considering the company he'd be keeping, it would be good to have a proper drink. And Susie needn't be any the wiser. He'd get home the next morning, tell her the car was covered by the council's AA policy and that they'd been able to send a team out first thing to fix it. Maybe that was a plan. Mike, his mind not on the job, skim-read the rest of the document, signed it off and chucked it into his out-tray and then rang the Red Lion.

'Can I have a word, please, Maddy?'

Maddy turned round, her heart sinking fast. She recognised that stupid, trilly voice. She'd been out for a walk with Rose and had only dropped into the Spar for a couple of essentials before taking Rose home for her nap. She hoped Camilla's 'word' was going to be a quick one – Maddy had every intention of putting her feet up for an hour before getting Nate from playgroup.

She fixed on a smile. 'Of course, what can I do for you?'

Camilla didn't return the smile. 'Not here.'

Maddy's heart, already sinking, headed for her boots. 'You'd better come back to mine then. Rose needs a nap.' She knew she sounded graceless. Well, tough.

'Fine.'

Maddy walked around the shelves of the little store, picking up the things she needed before heading for the checkout. She stuffed the milk and bread in the tray under the buggy then wheeled it to the front door of the shop where Camilla was waiting for her. She wasn't physically tapping her foot in impatience but she gave every impression that she was about to.

Maddy led the way up the road to her quarter and opened the door.

As Camilla stepped over the threshold she sniffed.

Yeah, it's a mess, thought Maddy defiantly. Like I care. Except, of course, deep down she did rather mind an outsider seeing her house at less than its best.

She unbuckled Rose who slithered out onto the floor and toddled away into the sitting room.

'Tea?' she offered, hoping to God it was going to be refused.

'This isn't a social call.'

Nope, Maddy had guessed that much. She knew exactly why Camilla wanted a word.

'In which case, I hope you don't mind if I put Rose to bed for her nap before we talk.' Ignoring whatever answer Camilla had given her, Maddy followed Rose into her sitting room, picked up her daughter who squirmed in protest in her arms and took her up to her cot. She eked out the time as much as she dared, considering her responses to what Camilla was bound to say to her, before she came downstairs again to find Camilla installed on the sofa.

'So,' said Camilla. 'What did you hope to achieve by telling Caro Edwards about Jack and my plans for the mess? I thought Jack made it plain to your husband that, while he was at liberty to discuss the matter with you, it wasn't to go any further.'

Maddy had had enough of Camilla. 'It may have escaped your notice but the last time I paid any attention to things military, army wives didn't seem to be required to sign the official secrets act.'

Camilla snorted. 'That's got nothing to do with it. You were told something in confidence and you spread the information around like a common gossip.'

A common gossip?! Now Maddy really saw red. 'I think your idea that your neighbours are here to be at your beck and call is not only outdated but out of order. I haven't signed the secrets act, I haven't signed a confidentiality clause and I am pretty sure that in this country I am not subject to military law either. Consequently, when Caro asked me why you are looking to replace me on your committees – and I notice you haven't bothered to inform me of this fact as common courtesy might dictate – I told her the truth. And why shouldn't I?' She stared at Camilla until she dropped her gaze.

Maddy stood up. 'So, if there's nothing else...'

Camilla's eyes narrowed. 'No, that's it. But let me just tell you that I am *very* unhappy. *Very*.'

'Fine.' Maddy moved to the front door and held it open. 'Good day.'

Camilla swept out. As soon as the door was shut Maddy sank onto the chair by the hall table and put her head in her hands. What had she done?

After a couple of minutes had passed her heart rate subsided to something resembling normal and Maddy picked up the phone and dialled Caro's number.

'Caro,' she said as soon as it was answered. 'Can you come round? I've just had the most appalling row with Camilla and I need a shoulder to cry on.'

Caro was ringing the bell almost before Maddy had filled the kettle and plugged it in.

'What? Why? What about?' she squawked as Maddy opened the door.

As they went back into the kitchen and Maddy made the tea she relayed the story to Caro.

'The old cow. She had no right to call you a common gossip. The cheek.' Caro's voice was almost a bat-squeak with indignation. 'You're a very refined and well-brought-up gossip.'

Maddy gave her a rueful grin before saying, 'Maybe I overreacted.'

'I think an overreaction would have involved an actual physical slap to wipe that self-satisfied smirk off her face. Anything less shows a degree of restraint, in my view.'

Maddy grinned. 'Maybe.' She was so glad she had Caro for a mate; she could always be relied on to talk sense and be cheerful.

'Have you told Seb?'

'Not yet.'

'Don't you think you ought to before he gets hauled into Rayner's office for an interview without coffee? I bet Camilla will have gone bleating to him straight away.'

Maddy nodded. 'You're right.' She picked up her mobile off the coffee table and tapped the screen a couple of times.

'Seb...Oh. You're on your way there now. Yes...Do you want the details? No, no, I wasn't very rude. I just told her I hadn't signed the official secrets act and I wasn't at her beck and call...Yeah, sorry...Love you.'

Maddy tapped the screen again.

Caro looked at her with raised eyebrows. 'Let me guess...?'

'On his way to Jack's office now.'

'Dear God, but that woman is poison.'

'Jack can't sack him for something I've done, though, surely?'

Caro shook her head vehemently. 'No, of course he can't.' But Maddy could hear a hint of doubt in her friend's voice.

Mike leaned against the table and regarded his co-workers. Maybe they weren't so bad after all. He took another slurp of his pint. In fact, he might have got them wrong. For a start they'd been pretty darn generous when it came to getting him drinks. He'd bought a round at the start of the evening but he'd not had to go to the bar again, not once. No, they were all right. Definitely all right.

One of the women – Jane? Janine – got up to leave. 'Gotta go, folks. Hubby'll be wondering where I am.'

Hubby? Hubby! Mike revised his opinion of her in a heartbeat. The others were OK. In fact, some of the others could be his new best friends.

Then he remembered. Fuck, what was the time? He had to ring Susie and tell her...tell her...? He concentrated on the problem; that's right, tell her the car was kaput. That was what he had to do. He gazed blearily at his watch, willing his eyes to focus on the face. What had happened to his vision? It was all blurry. But with both hands pointing somewhere north of the nine it was gone eight o'clock, that was for sure, only he couldn't quite work out whether it was ten to nine or quarter to ten. Not that it really mattered.

He stood up to go outside and ring his wife and banged into the table. The drinks slopped but it wasn't his fault, the bar staff shouldn't have filled the glasses so full.

'Sorry,' he slurred.

'You all right, Mike?' asked Rob.

'Jusht gonna ring the wife,' he answered.

'Do you want a lift home?'

'Nah. Need to tell her the car's fucked.' Rob didn't seem to understand what on earth Mike was going on about because he shook his head and shrugged, while a couple of his female colleagues frowned at his fruity language. 'Shorry, ladies. Shouldn't have said "fucked".'

Mike reeled out of the bar and into the drizzly night. He sheltered under the smokers' refuge and got out his mobile.

It took several attempts to get his pass code accepted by his phone. What was the matter with the stupid thing? Finally he was able to access his address book. He pressed the icon that read 'home'.

'Shusie. Shusie, listen to me. I gotta stay overnight in town. The car won't go.'

'I can come and get you,' she replied. 'No problem.' There was a pause. 'Have you been drinking?'

'Me, drink, corsh not. What makes you think that?' Mike leaned against a wall for support.

'Because you sound pissed.'

'Well, I'm not. It's just the car's fucked...buggered...The AA will come and sort it. They promished.'

'When?'

'Tomorrow.'

'Then I'll come and get you tonight.'

'You can't. The girlsh. You can't...you can't leave the girlsh.'

'They're in bed asleep. I can pop out for a short while.'

'It's all right. I've got a bed. I'll stay over.'

There was a pause. Then Susie said, 'OK then. I'll see you tomorrow.'

'Night, Shuse.'

'Night, Mike.'

Mike ended the call and staggered back into the pub.

'Who's for another drink?' he said, waving his arms around expansively.

The others, gathered around a big table, looked at each other.

'Actually,' said Rob, 'we're all thinking of calling it a day. Work again tomorrow and all that.'

'Don't be spoilsports,' said Mike. 'It'sh still early.'

'Mike, it's almost ten. Enough's enough.'

Fuck 'em, thought Mike. He could get another drink at the Red Lion. A nightcap before bed. The party broke up and Mike wove his way, bouncing off the occasional wall and sometimes off another pedestrian, as he stumbled his way along the town's narrow pavements to his hotel. He grabbed his key from reception and then made his way to his room, stopping at the bar en route to grab a double Scotch to take up with him.

After several attempts he managed to get his key in the lock and then blundered into his room, slopping some of his drink as he cannoned off the doorjamb. He put the remains of his drink down on the bedside table while he lay down – just for a minute – before he got undressed. Yeah, he'd have that last drink in just a minute...

Chapter 33

Susie had had a bad night. It wasn't that she wasn't used to Mike not sharing her bed. Was there an army wife on the planet who got to sleep every night in the year with their husband? No, it was worry that he'd had a skinful that caused her to toss and turn throughout the night. She'd drift off for a few minutes but then something in her subconscious would jerk her awake again. As a consequence she felt light-headed with exhaustion and knew that her mood was not going to be the best when the alarm finally told her the long night was over. As she rolled over in bed and pressed the off button, she wondered about ringing Mike. No, there wasn't time and besides, if he *had* been drinking she didn't think she had the energy for a row – not and get the girls off to school on time.

Wearily, she hauled herself out of bed, grabbed her dressing gown and went to wake the girls. Katie's room, when she opened the door and stuck her head around it with as cheerful a 'Wake up, Katie, dear,' as she could muster, was a total tip. Katie didn't acknowledge the call so Susie tiptoed her way as best she could across the floor to the window and drew back the curtains. Not that it made much difference; it was only just getting light and the relentless rain and low cloud seemed to negate any effort the sun might have been trying to make.

'Come on, Katie. Wakey, wakey.' Susie shook Katie's shoulder hidden under the duvet.

'Gerroff,' was the response.

'It's seven thirty. Time to get up.'

'Yeah, yeah.'

Susie gave up and went across the landing to her sister's room where a similar scene was played out. As Susie was heading back across the messy floor something crunched under foot. Bugger, what had she trodden on? She hoped, as she scrabbled through the layer of discarded clothes, that it wasn't anything important – or precious. And under a school sweatshirt she found a packet of cigarettes.

Susie sagged. So was this why they were so keen to high-tail it out of the house every evening and meet their friends? Smoking? As if this family hadn't had enough trouble with addictions without the girls adding smoking to the list. And the penny dropped as to why, for the last week or so, the girls raced upstairs to get changed as soon as they got back in again – they knew that their clothes would reek and the excuse that they'd been to a house where the parents smoked would wear a bit thin with constant use. Oh, for fuck's sake, she thought angrily. She slipped the carton into her dressing gown pocket and went back to her room wondering how they could afford them and how they managed to obtain them. Jeez, as if she didn't have enough on her plate and this was going to mean another row – a row that would have to wait until Mike got home.

Then she remembered that she was angry with him too. Bollocks, first him and now the twins. What the hell was wrong with her sodding family? She felt close to tears of self-pity as she began to get ready for the day. What had she done to deserve this? she asked herself as she stepped into the shower. But she knew the answer to that. She and Mike hadn't exactly been shining examples to their children and their problems had probably tipped the balance against them when the redundancy notices had been handed out. As she lathered her body with shower gel she wished – pointlessly, she knew – that she could turn back the clock. Well, she couldn't, and now she'd just have to make the most of this shit-awful situation.

In the Red Lion, Mike was coming round. He groaned as he forced his eyes to open. For a second or two his situation made no sense and then slowly bits and bobs of memory kicked in; office drinks, his plan, his phone call to Susie. He lay on the bed contemplating what he'd done and wondering quite how much he'd drunk. Outside his room, in the street, he heard a car horn toot and the deep throbbing purr of an idling bus engine. Shit, what was the time? He reached out to fumble on the bedside table for his watch and felt his hand connect with a glass which tipped over, soaking his hand with liquid. The smell of whisky assaulted his nostrils. He flicked the drops off his skin and sat up. For the second time in as many minutes he felt bewildered. He wasn't under the covers, but fully clad in slacks, shirt, tie, sports jacket...the full works, lying on top of the bed. And now the cuff of his shirt and jacket were soaked in Scotch. He pulled back the sleeve of his jacket and stared at his watch. Eight thirty? Shit a brick.

Suddenly wide awake he tumbled off the bed and caught sight of himself in the full-length mirror on the wardrobe door. Horrified, he stared at his reflection. He looked like an unmade bed. His trousers and jacket were creased and rumpled, his eyes bloodshot, his hair tousled and that, together with a five-o'clock shadow, made him look like some sort of tramp. He dashed into the bathroom and grabbed the razor and travel-sized can of shaving foam he'd had the foresight to buy the previous day, before he'd checked into the hotel. Quickly he stripped off his jacket, shirt and tie and then lathered his chin and had a rapid shave. He damped his hands under the tap and smoothed his hair down. There was, he thought, a lot to be said for a short back and sides; not much styling required to make it look half decent. He replaced his shirt and tie, tucking his shirt in firmly to his trousers which straightened out some of the creases. Finally he put on his jacket. He stared at himself critically in the mirror. It was an improvement but he still looked pretty terrible. It'd have to do. Furthermore, he had to hope that the fresh air on his walk from the hotel to the council offices would dissipate the smell of Scotch from the sleeve of his jacket.

Feeling considerably below par, Mike went downstairs, paid his bill at the reception desk and set off through the crowded rush-hour streets to the modern block housing Winterspring District Council offices. Predictably, of course, it was pissing with rain when he left the hotel. Now he was going to be unkempt and bedraggled when he arrived at work. But he had to hope that having a soaking jacket might explain away the creases. And another bonus was that the rain might help wash the smell of alcohol out of the fabric. Maybe, he thought as he trudged along the sodden streets, the rain on this occasion was a good thing.

He arrived and swiped in through the front door just a few minutes after nine; certainly, he thought with relief, not late enough to cause any comment. Taking the stairs rather than the lift – he was wary of being trapped in a confined space with a work colleague in case the smell of whisky still hung around him – he made his way as swiftly as possible to his workstation, took his jacket off and hung it up on the hanger he kept in his filing cabinet for such occasions – got his head down and began to work. Behind him he could hear a rhythmical *pat...pat...* as the water dripped out of his jacket and onto the thin carpet. Maybe the wet and the warmth of the office would allow the creases to drop out. And if they didn't he could explain getting soaked as the reason for the state of his clothing if Susie asked when he got home that night. All in all, Mike felt as if he'd got away with his excesses of the night before.

The office, he noted thankfully, was pretty quiet. Maybe he wasn't the only worker who was feeling the effect of the previous night. Thank God it was Friday and he could go home later in the day and collapse till Monday. As it was, he thought that today was going to be a struggle. And he was proved right – by eleven he was starting to flag, big time, so he got up and went to the hot drinks dispenser in the corner of the office to get himself a coffee. He rarely used the machine because the drinks it produced were generally awful but today he needed the caffeine boost. He noted that his jacket was still looking rumpled but was almost dry and, glancing at his reflection in the office window, he reckoned he looked better, *much* better than he deserved, considering he'd spent the night in his clothes.

When he got back to his desk his phone was ringing.

'Collins,' he said into the receiver as he answered it, still standing.

'Mike.' He recognised Susie's voice instantly. 'Good, you've sobered up.'

'I...I don't know what you mean,' he said, defensively.

There was a short silence, then, 'Look, I don't have the

time or the inclination to argue the toss, but you will be home tonight, won't you?'

'Of course. I would have been home last night except the car went kaput and I had to get it fixed.'

'And has it been?' The scepticism in her voice was clearly evident.

Mike played it cool. 'I don't know. I haven't been down to see if the RAC has been out to it yet.'

'Oh? I thought it was the AA that you'd called out.'

Shit, had he said AA last night? He couldn't remember. 'AA, RAC, one and the same,' he blustered.

'Really?' Susie sounded far from convinced.

'Anyway, why are you asking if I'll be home tonight? Why wouldn't I be?'

'You tell me. I want you home because you and I need to have a word with the girls. I think they're smoking. In fact, I am pretty sure of it.'

'What?' Mike's exclamation of horror came out far louder than he intended and heads popped up over the workstation divisions across the office. He sat down. 'You've got to be mistaken,' he hissed.

'Then why did I find a packet of Benson and Hedges on Ella's floor this morning?'

'It doesn't mean they belong to the twins.'

'Oh, come off it, Mike. What else can it mean?'

She was probably right, he thought. Bollocks.

'OK. Do you want me to meet you at the mess, before you get the girls?'

'I think that might be for the best. I'll see you sometime before five. I'll ring the guardroom and ask them to have a visitor's pass ready for you.'

Mike replaced the receiver of his phone. Things were

going from bad to worse. Why was life so intent on kicking him in the teeth?

Maddy hummed as she made sure her spare room was neat and clean. She was looking forward to having Sam and Luke to stay although she didn't know Luke terribly well. He'd been a corporal when he'd been stationed with 1 Herts and since he'd got commissioned he'd been posted to another unit. Maddy was sure he'd be nice – after all, Sam was a sweetheart.

Shutting the door on the bedroom Maddy ran lightly down the stairs, stepped over the stairgate and went back to the kitchen to carry on making that night's supper. Sam had told her that Luke was due to arrive at their quarter around six in the evening. Perfect, thought Maddy, as it would give them all time to have a drink together and get to know each other before the meal. She just hoped that the kids didn't play up. It would be nice for once if Nathan didn't throw a strop. She'd like her visitors to think her family was adorable rather than the spawn of the devil himself – because Nathan was more than capable of doing a very passable impression of being possessed by evil spirits, especially when he was tired at the end of the day. Maybe this time he would be sweet and adorable and lovable – like he could be. OK, she was very biased when it came to her kids and maybe not everyone thought he was as sweet and adorable and lovable as she did, but all the same, she could do with having a child who showed its best side to outsiders rather than the opposite. Were kids, she wondered idly as she chopped onions, programmed to be naughty, to push the boundaries, or did they pick it all up as they grew up? Because if Nathan's naughtiness carried on developing at the rate it had been of late, by the time he was a teenager he was going to be a right handful.

Half an hour later, still faintly musing on how her kids might turn out, she left the house with Rose in her pushchair to pick up Nathan from playgroup. Rose was snuggled up in her thick fleecy foot muff and sheltered under the clear plastic rain-canopy while Maddy, unable to hold an umbrella, had to cope with the rain that drizzled constantly from the low cloud and trickled down the back of her neck. Waiting outside the playgroup which took place in the garrison church hall Maddy grumbled with the other mothers about the shocking weather and wondered, as they all did, if it was *ever* going to stop raining.

After what seemed like an eternity to those getting cold and wet – although it was bang on the dot of midday, the allotted time for the playgroup to end – the playgroup leader finally opened the door and the toddlers surged out, all dressed in their raincoats or anoraks and wellies. Nathan proffered a still-wet painting to his mother which Maddy exclaimed over before putting it in the buggy's tray for safe keeping.

'Right,' she said, as Nathan stood on the buggy-board, 'let's get home.'

They scooted along the road, Maddy walking as fast as she could, head down against the miserable weather.

'You're in a hurry.'

Maddy looked up. It was Jenna, coming out of the community centre.

'Hi, Jen. Yeah, I want to get this pair home before they get soaked through.'

'Miserable, ain't it?'

Maddy nodded. 'You busy? Only if you fancy coming back to ours we could have a bite of lunch. Seb is working through today – he took in sandwiches. I expect your Dan is busy too, isn't he? What with this wretched exercise next week.'

Jenna nodded. 'If you're sure?'

'Totally. I'll be glad of the company, if I'm honest.'

'Great.' Jenna fell into step beside her friend, her high heels clacking manically on the asphalt as she pushed Eliot in his buggy.

Maddy had her keys out as they turned onto the path to her front door and she had the door open as fast as possible. A few minutes later she and Jenna had the kids out of their wet things, the gas fire lit in the sitting room, a big pan of soup heating up on the hob and a glass of wine poured for them both.

'This is a bit naughty,' said Jenna, accepting the glass.

'I know, but I'm so sick of the weather I need cheering up.'

'Know how you feel.'

Maddy stopped stirring and looked at her guest. 'You sound proper fed up.'

Jenna sighed. 'Business isn't going that well, if I'm honest. I get one customer a day if I'm lucky. A few weeks back, before that sergeant major's wife—'

'Mrs Laycock?'

'That's the one. Well, before she witnessed Chrissie and me having that spat, it was all going swimmingly. I was even thinking I might need a receptionist. But now...' Jenna sighed. 'Now, honestly, some days I don't get a single customer.'

'That's not right,' said Maddy. 'We need to do something about that.' She went back to stirring the soup while Jenna sipped her drink. 'Maybe,' she said after a minute or so, 'we ought to leaflet all the houses in the garrison. I mean, the 1 Herts wives know about your salon and we advertised in the garrison newsletter for a stylist, but do the wives from the other units know that you've opened for business or where to find you?'

'I suppose.'

'And the big advantage of doing that is the other wives aren't aware of...' Maddy paused, slightly unsure as to how to put her thoughts.

'My past.'

'Exactly. So, after lunch I suggest you and I get busy on my laptop. I'm sure, between us, we can come up with a flier that'll drive some business your way.'

Jenna smiled. 'What would I do without you, Mads? You're such a mate.'

'It's payback for what you did when I had to deal with Seb's Other Woman.'

Chapter 34

Mike had managed to survive the day at work despite a thumping headache that kicked in mid-morning and the worry about his daughters. Why were they growing up to be so bloody difficult? Why did they think that alienating their teachers and their parents was cool? And why on earth had they taken up smoking? he kept asking himself. In order to take his mind off his children he looked at the briefing papers from the local water authority about flood defences along the Winterspring and Bavant rivers and their costings. Given the reaction that moronic little shit Rob had had to the comments he'd made some weeks earlier about the cuts to the emergency planning budget, Mike had no faith that there was the least chance of these flood defence measures being adopted but he'd have to try and make the case. Wearily, he drafted a report to Rob pointing out all the pros and the very few cons and summed up his findings in a conclusion that would leave even Rob in no doubt as to the folly of failing to implement the recommendations. Mike knew he really ought to take the file over to Rob personally, to explain to him the foolishness of opting for a short-term saving over the long-term risk, but he didn't have the energy. Not today. He chucked the file in his out-tray, flagged up for Rob, and pulled the next piece of work that needed his attention towards him.

It was with relief that he shoved everything back in his filing cabinet and switched off his terminal at the end of the day and made his way to the staff car park. As he plipped his car and the indicator lights flashed in acknowledgement he offered up a small prayer that it was going to start. There was no reason at all why it shouldn't but having lied about its reliability, given his recent luck, it would be sod's law if it had *really* broken down now. He slipped into the driver's seat, glad to get out of the rain that had been falling all day – when were they going to get a day when it *didn't* rain? he wondered – put the key in the ignition, and with a quick prayer, turned it. The engine fired first time. Thank God.

Mike drove out of the district council offices' car park and headed towards Warminster. On either side of the main road the fields, now devoid of crops, were glistening with standing water and the roadside ditches were almost overflowing. Everywhere Mike looked the countryside looked sodden and waterlogged. And not surprising, he thought. He reviewed the weather since that torrential thunderstorm and it seemed to him that it had rained almost every day since. There had been a couple of nice summer days immediately after the cloudburst but shortly after that it was as if the taps had been turned on and left running. So much, he thought, for the gloom-and-doom predictions of depleted aquifers and the need for water management. Still, as long as the weather didn't get worse, the drainage system and the rivers across the county seemed to be coping and it couldn't keep raining like it had for the *whole* winter, could it?

Before long Mike pulled up at the guardroom at the barracks, parked in the visitor's lay-by and went to book in.

'Oh, hello, sir,' said a soldier he recognised. Mike felt a

294

little puff of pleasure at this show of deference. He hadn't had that in a very long time.

'Hello, Corporal. No need for the "sir" bit now. I'm a civvy these days.'

'Sorry, sir, but old habits and all that. Mrs Collins phoned down. Here's your pass and if you'd just like to sign for it here and remember to hand it back in on your way out.'

'Sure thing,' said Mike.

He took the proffered pass and the pen, scribbled his name in the visitors' book and then returned to his car. The barrier raised, he drove up to the mess. It seemed far longer than just a few months since he'd last done this, in uniform, being saluted, entitled to be there. He sighed – so much had changed and almost all of it for the worse. He drove to the back of the building and parked his car next to the Grundon bins. Gone were the days of being able to use the mess members' spaces at the front, now he was reduced to parking by the rubbish skips. What a comedown.

Susie was waiting for him and let him in the back door. If she noticed his rather dishevelled and unkempt appearance she said nothing about it, to Mike's relief. At least he was pretty sure his jacket no longer smelt of Scotch, which was something to be grateful for. His wife led him to the staffroom beside the main kitchen which was silent.

'We've got the place to ourselves for a bit. The staff don't come back on duty till five thirty to clear up the tea things and get ready for the evening meal.'

'Best you tell me what you know then.'

'There's nothing to tell really, beyond what I told you this morning. I found a packet of fags in Ella's bedroom and it was half empty. What we need to talk about is how we handle things.'

'Ground them?'

Susie nodded. 'We could but seeing as how they are utterly bolshie I think they'll just ignore it. Realistically, I don't think I'll be able to prevent them from going out of the house when we get back in the evening if they are determined.'

Mike looked at her, she had a point. 'I suppose we could deadlock the front door,' he offered.

'They'd climb out a window.'

'We could stop their allowance.'

'That might certainly have an impact. I'll keep on thinking – we'll come up with something, but before we can do any of that we are going to have to confront them with the evidence.'

'That's not going to be an easy conversation,' said Mike.

'Easy or not, it's got to be done. Do you think they'd have started smoking if they'd stayed at Browndown?'

'Who's to know? If we start down the "what if" route I think we might end up going potty.'

'I often wonder...' mused Susie.

Mike put his hand on her arm. 'Me too.' They looked at each other, both knowing what the other was going to say. 'But what's done is done. We are where we are.'

'Very profound, Mr Collins,' said Susie wryly. 'And while we've got a moment to ourselves – about last night.'

Mike felt his heart rate increase; he knew what was coming next and guilt swept through him.

'You were drinking, weren't you?'

Busted. He nodded. 'Yup, fell off the wagon. I'm sorry and I won't do it again.'

'Oh, Mike.' Susie's disappointment was tangible. 'That's twice. If only your stupid car hadn't broken down.'

Mike couldn't meet her eyes. Lie upon lie... Not just the car but the fact that it was *a lot* more than twice, although it was only twice he'd been shit-faced. Besides, a pint or so at lunchtime hardly made him a lush – not like he'd been back in the old days, and if she had to work with the twats he was lumbered with, she'd be driven to drink too. At least she didn't think he'd had his binge all planned, that he sorted things so he could fall off the wagon. In fact, he hadn't *fallen* so much as actively jumped but as long as Susie was in ignorance life would be easier all round.

'It won't happen again,' he promised. Although, internally, he was thinking that he wouldn't get *caught* again. He just had to be more careful if he was going to have the occasional drink.

'OK,' said Susie, 'let's forget about it. Back to the girls. How about confiscating their iPads and phones?'

'It would certainly hurt them. We can't do it without giving them a chance of redeeming themselves. We have to have a carrot available as well as a stick.'

Susie nodded. 'So, if you go straight home while I get the girls, you can raid their rooms for their iPads. As soon as I get back with them, we can tell them we know about the smoking and ask them to hand over their phones as punishment. They mightn't mind too much if they think they still have their tablets, which they won't – assuming you can find them.'

'Sneaky,' said Mike.

'Off you go then. You'll probably find their iPads on their desks or by their beds. That's where they usually are.'

Mike splashed out back to his car, wondering when his wife had learned to be quite so Machiavellian. He had to hand it to her, she was in a class of her own.

*

Ella and Katie had spent most of their breaks huddled together in sheltered corners of the school playground, wondering what had happened to their precious stash of cigarettes.

'You can't have looked properly,' Katie kept insisting.

'But I did, I know I did. I *know* I had them when we came in from meeting Ali, they were in my sweatshirt pocket.'

'Then they must have fallen out.'

'But where?'

'I don't know,' said Katie. 'You had them. They must be on your bedroom floor.'

Ella sighed and looked exasperated. 'But I told you, I looked. I picked everything up and they weren't there.'

'When we get home we'll have a proper look.'

Ella had shrugged. She'd *had* a proper look but if Katie wanted to waste her time doing it again, it was up to her. 'Anyway,' she said, 'what are we going to tell Ali?'

'Maybe he'll lend us a ciggie. We can pay him back tomorrow.'

'Maybe.' But Ella wasn't convinced. He smoked far more of their fags than they ever got off him. But in his favour, life on the school bus, now he allowed them to sit with his crew, was much easier. It was worth hanging around in the cold and wet by the junction box or huddled in the bus shelter for that alone.

When their mother came to pick them up from Caro's everything seemed pretty normal. It was only when they got home and saw their dad, waiting for them to come in, that they began to twig that not all was right.

'I want a word with you two,' he said without preamble.

The twins exchanged a nervous glance and felt their anxiety levels and heart rates soar. They both had a horrible idea they knew where this was going. They followed him into the sitting room. Their mother trailed in last and stood by the front door. To stop us escaping? wondered Ella, nervously.

'Sit down,' he ordered.

They both dropped, side by side, onto the sofa. Ella wanted to hold Katie's hand for support but knew it would show weakness.

'What's the meaning of this?' Their father brandished the missing packet of smokes.

'I don't know what you mean,' blustered Ella.

Her father's eyes narrowed. 'Don't lie,' he said. 'Your mother found them on your bedroom floor this morning.'

Instinctively, Ella glanced at Katie.

'Yes,' said their father. 'You may well look to your sister for support. I imagine she's in on this too.'

Ella stared at him defiantly. 'They're not ours.'

Their dad just stared at them and sighed. 'Really. So whose are they? And why would you have them in your possession?' He patently didn't believe a word she'd said.

'They're Ali's...or his mum's. I...I must have picked them up by accident.'

'Really?'

'Yes.'

Well, as you insist on lying to me as well as smoking I am forced to take action. Not only are you grounded but I want your mobile phones.'

'No!' The girls spoke in unison.

'Yes. Hand them over.'

'You can't make us,' said Katie.

Their father looked at them and held his hand out. 'I think I can. I am your father,' he suddenly thundered, 'and I will *not* be disobeyed.'

The girls both jumped at his change in tone of voice.

Wordlessly they reached into their school bags and handed them over.

'Thank you. And don't think you'll be going out to meet your friends this evening or any evening for the foreseeable future. You're grounded till further notice, so I suggest you go to your rooms and think about your behaviour.'

Ella felt a wave of rage against her father. What right had he to treat them like this? He was hateful and mean and...and...suddenly she felt tears welling up. She jumped up off the sofa, barged past her mum and raced up the stairs. Katie followed a second later. A door slammed upstairs.

Susie stared at her husband. 'Thank you. They may not like it but it had to be done.'

Mike sank into the armchair next to him. 'I feel a heel.'

'Parenting isn't easy. It's tough love.'

Mike breathed deeply. 'I sometimes think tough love is tougher on us than it is them.'

They heard a bedroom door open upstairs.

'You've taken our iPads!' screamed Ella.

'Yes,' shouted back Susie.

'I hate you. I hate you both.'

'And I do too. I wish you were dead,' added Katie.

The door slammed again; this time the windows rattled in the sitting room.

'That's it,' muttered Susie. She flew up the stairs. She flung open Ella's door and saw the twins huddled together on Ella's bed. They were crying but her heart didn't soften. Serve them right, she thought.

'You can shout at your father and me as much as you like,' she said in a dangerously low and quiet voice. 'You can call us names. But if you start damaging property with your stupid, spiteful behaviour, by slamming doors and the like, the loss of your iPads and phones will seem like nothing compared to the sanctions I will impose. Do you understand?' She glared at them till they both dropped their defiant stares. 'Do you understand?' she repeated.

'Yes,' mumbled Ella sulkily.

'Katie?'

'Yeah.'

'Good. And if you think you can stay up here and sulk, you've got another think coming. I expect you at the supper table at the normal time.'

Ella looked at her with a cold hard stare.

'Your choice,' said Susie. 'If you don't come down you can go hungry.'

'That's child abuse,' said Katie.

Susie leaned forwards. 'No, it's discipline. The food will be there for you, downstairs on the table. Your choice.'

They thought about it.

'When can we have our iPads back?' asked Ella in a more conciliatory tone.

'When I say so,' said Susie. She backed out of the room and shut the door.

Round one, she thought, had been won on points by her and Mike. Not that she felt she had the energy for any further rounds in the foreseeable future.

As she went downstairs she wanted a drink more than anything. Like that was going to help. One of the family had to stay strong but she wished that, just for once, it wasn't her.

Chapter 35

When Maddy met Luke again she remembered how much she liked him at their first brief meeting at the officers' mess summer ball, well over a year previously. He had classic good looks with dark hair, a wide smile and brown eyes. Kind eyes, too, she thought. No wonder Sam had fallen for him. In fact, if she didn't love Seb so much, she might have taken a shine to him herself. And over the course of the evening, Luke had made them all laugh and had been charming and entertaining; he'd even helped with clearing the table – the perfect houseguest.

The next morning he and Sam appeared at the breakfast table looking as if they hadn't slept a wink. Maddy smiled inwardly and pretended not to notice the dark shadows under Sam's eyes, her tousled hair and her tendency to yawn every few minutes. And why not? thought Maddy. When was the last time she'd seen her fiancé?

Breakfast was in the dining room because there wasn't room for the four Fanshaws and their houseguests around the kitchen table so Maddy had been busy ferrying what was needed from the kitchen while Sam and Luke made calf's eyes at each other, when they weren't being interrupted by Nathan asking them what they knew about *Peppa Pig*. Give them their due, thought Maddy as she plonked a jug of orange juice down, Luke and Sam were very patient, which made her warm to them even more. They were all settling down to coffee and toast and Maddy was just about to pour the orange juice when the phone rang.

Maddy frowned. Who on earth...? And at this time on a Saturday morning. She put down the jug, pulled her dressing-gown cord tight about her and went to answer it.

'Will? What can I do for you?'

'Can I speak to Seb?'

'Of course.'

Maddy went to fetch her husband and then carried on serving breakfast.

She'd barely finished pouring coffee for everyone when Seb returned. 'Wouldn't you know it,' he said, shaking his head.

'Know what?'

'Will's got it on good authority that that wretched exercise is going to kick off today with an emergency crash-out.'

'Really?' said Maddy. 'Who's his source?'

'He was duty officer again last night.'

'Again?'

'He got a bunch of extras.'

'More extras?'

'Mads, the CO and RSM give them out for almost anything these days. Anything at all.'

Maddy shook her head. 'Poor Will.'

'Anyway, the poor old duty clerk was called in to open up battalion HQ for the CO and when Will went to do the midnight check on the guardroom he saw the light on and went to investigate. The poor old duty clerk was having to type up a bunch of orders for *today*.'

'Bugger,' muttered Maddy.

'Bugger, bugger, bugger,' crowed Nathan, delighted by a new word.

Maddy rolled her eyes. 'Sorry,' she said to no one in particular.

'Precisely,' said Seb. 'So that's the weekend fu— ruined.'

'Right,' said Sam, 'I'd better get dressed and get down to the workshop. I don't suppose Will knows when we're all going to get crashed out?'

'No, the duty clerk said it would be more than his life was worth to pass that on. And knowing how Rayner likes to behave as if he were Hitler, no doubt if he found out what the clerk has already let slip, he'd have the poor guy shot at dawn.'

Seb and Sam both disappeared to get themselves over to the barracks and to do as much as possible – while not appearing to be doing anything – to prepare for the CO's surprise crash-out.

'And don't expect us back for lunch,' said Seb as he left the dining room. 'If we haven't been called out by then we'll grab something in the mess.'

Which left Luke, Maddy and the kids and the remains of breakfast.

'Tell you what,' said Luke.

'What?' said Maddy helping herself to a slice of toast.

'Why don't I treat you and the nippers to a pub lunch?'

'You can't do that, you're my guest.'

'I think I can. Call it a thank-you present for having me and Sam to stay.'

'But it's been lovely.' Maddy finished buttering the slice, cut it into fingers and gave them to the children.

'It certainly has,' said Luke with feeling. 'And it might have been lovelier if Rayner hadn't stuck his oar in.'

'That's Rayner for you.'

'So, after we've finished breakfast and I've helped you clear up...' Luke saw the look on Maddy's face. 'No, no arguments, this is how today is going to roll. After that, I shall Google some nice pubs in the area – ones that are properly child friendly – and we'll treat ourselves to a slap-up lunch.'

'OK,' said Maddy, grinning. 'Sounds like a plan.'

A couple of hours later Maddy loaded the kids into her car and they set off, the windscreen wipers flick-flacking as they drove out of the garrison. Luke programmed the satnav as she backed out of the drive and ordered her to follow it.

'That way it'll all be a surprise.'

'I like surprises,' said Maddy. 'Just not the sort that Rayner springs.'

'No. I don't think you're alone there.'

Fifteen minutes after that, Maddy was driving through the little village of Ashton-cum-Bavant.

'Oh my God,' she said as she drove past the village green. 'So that's the house.'

'What house?'

Maddy stopped the car and pointed through the rain-flecked glass to a beautiful three-storey Georgian house with a shingle tied to its ornate, wrought-iron fence declaring it to be 'Sold STC'.

'A mate of Seb's has just bought that place.'

'Bloody hell,' said Luke. 'How does he make his cash? Robbing banks?'

'Sort of – his dad runs one. Ever heard of Forster's Bank?'

Luke whistled. 'I'm impressed.'

'I'm jealous,' admitted Maddy.

'It'd be hell to heat. Think of the bills.'

Maddy laughed. 'Yeah, I'd forgotten that. Puts you right off it, doesn't it.'

She turned the key in the ignition and set off again following the directions on the satnav but when she got to the next junction there was a sign: *Road closed. Flooding.*

She stopped and pulled on the handbrake. 'OK, which way now?'

'Just keep going straight on, the satnav will recalculate. And if it doesn't, well, maybe we can find another pub. There doesn't seem to be a shortage around here.'

'No, although whether we'll find one as appropriate as your carefully researched child-friendly one, I don't know.'

'And we have to hope the pub's open. It's called the Ferryman so it suggests it's by the river and it might have trouble with floods too.'

But the other way to the pub was fine and the car park was surprisingly empty for a Saturday lunchtime.

'I suppose people coming from Salisbury might be put off by the road closure. Still, it's an ill wind and all that,' said Luke, cheerfully.

Maddy looked at the Bavant river racing past the far end of the car park – a brown maelstrom, lapping right at the top of the bank – and wondered how often this pub got flooded. It wouldn't, she thought, take much more rain to make this place go under, and it was still coming down in buckets with no sign of it letting up in the near future.

As Maddy, Luke and the children were settling down at their table in the pub and starting to peruse the menu, Seb and his sergeant major were in B Company stores checking the equipment that company HQ would need out in the field when the CSM's phone rang.

''Scuse me, boss,' said Sergeant Major Riley, pulling his mobile out of his pocket.

Seb listened to him take the message and then end the call.

'Flash message from the CO,' said the sergeant major. 'All personnel to be on parade with all kit and vehicles as soon as possible. You were right about the exercise being called for today. And the stopwatch is running. Apparently there is an "optimum time".'

'And no doubt there'll be sanctions if we don't hit the mark.'

The CSM nodded. 'Extras all round, no doubt.'

'Any idea what the "optimum time" is?'

'Nope, not a Scooby, sorry, sir.'

'Never mind. We'd better start the cascade. You ring the company duty clerk; I'll ring the platoon commanders. Let's see if B Company can be first to be ready. I'll stay here till the CQMS gets here to issue the kit and I'll meet you at the vehicle garages in an hour.'

'Sir.'

Seb got ringing, setting off a cascade of calls that would have everyone back in barracks as soon as possible. Luckily the personnel he had to ring were, like him, pretty much expecting the call and picked up instantly and, with everyone confined to barracks, when CQMS arrived at the stores and Seb could make his way to his quarter to collect his Bergen the entire barracks was already a scene of manic activity. And as a bit of a bonus the rain had eased off slightly so the soldiers weren't getting completely soaked.

Seb let himself into the empty house, sent a quick text to Maddy telling her what was going on and warning her that he and Sam might not back for supper, then he changed into his multicam, picked up his kit and raced back to the barracks.

His sergeant major was several minutes behind him but his excuse was more than valid.

'I took the liberty of getting your personal weapon out of the armoury,' he said, passing Seb his gun. 'Stupid for both of us to have to queue up.'

'Thanks,' said Seb, shoving it in its holster and fastening it securely.

Soldiers were flooding into the garages and as his company arrived so the vehicles began to get moved out onto the hardstanding in front of the huge hangars; Land Rovers, support vehicles, trucks, all began to get deployed. The air was filled with the deafening roar of dozens of huge engines and was thick with the blue smog of diesel fumes. Trailers were hitched up and filled with jerrycans of fuel, rations and boxes of ammo but it was all happening in an orderly fashion. No headless chicken impressions – everyone knew exactly what they had to do and got on with it without fuss or preamble. Slowly the garages emptied and the parade square filled with orderly ranks of vehicles, kit and men. As Seb was driven onto the square in his Land Rover he saw the CO pacing along one edge of the vast open space, the threatened stopwatch in evidence in his right hand.

The rain had resumed again and, although the scene was impressive, there was, thought Seb, a slight air of dispirited resentment in the assembled troops; a sullenness. He knew the soldiers didn't mind the idea of going out on exercise – it was the day job, after all. But having their weekend wrecked because the CO could bugger them about on a whim...that was something else.

Seb's driver pulled on the handbrake of his vehicle and cut the engine. On either side other vehicles were lining up. He looked at his own company and judged they were about two-thirds present. He glanced at his watch; just over an hour and a half since the original call. Not bad, not bad at all. Of course, if the last troops were hideously slow to arrive it could yet go to rat-shit, but assuming things went to plan, B Company was on course to acquit itself very well.

'I've got a bet going, sir,' said Seb's driver. 'Me and my mates reckon that whatever time we post getting everyone on the square and ready to deploy, the CO will tell us we're no good. We could be there in record time and he'll still tell us we're shit.'

'Hmm,' said Seb. 'I couldn't possibly comment.'

'Just saying, sir, that's all.'

'Maybe you shouldn't, Evans.'

'Well...we'll see, shan't we, sir,' said Evans cheerfully, not the least concerned by Seb's implied criticism of his view.

Seb climbed out of his vehicle and leaving the door open he stood on the sill to give himself an extra foot of height in order to survey the scene. It was impressive. Almost a whole battalion of men and machines. He wouldn't want to have to face this lot as the enemy.

'Hi, Seb.'

He glanced down from his vantage point. 'Sam. This is a rotten way to spend a weekend with your fiancé.'

She shrugged. 'Tell me about it. The exigencies of service,' she said, quoting the army's get-out clause. 'Army speak for "Don't bitch if you get mucked about".'

Seb laughed. 'Exactly.'

'I had a call from Luke to say he and Maddy have taken the kids out for a pub lunch. It's OK for some,' she added with a hint of bitterness. 'Do you think Maddy will be all right about him staying on at yours if we do end up deploying?'

'Of *course* she will. I've already texted her warning her that you and I mightn't be back for supper. I expect she'll be glad to have some company rather than facing a Saturday evening on her own.'

Sam didn't look completely convinced. 'But she hardly knows Luke.' She shrugged. 'I just feel it's a bit of an imposition.'

Seb glanced at his watch. 'Look, supposing I gave Maddy a quick call to make sure. I'm positive she'd be horrified if she knew you and Luke felt awkward about this.'

He called Maddy and had a brief conversation.

'As I suspected. And quite apart from anything else, she's got a fridge full of food that needs eating and she's relying on Luke to do his best to stop it from going to waste.'

Sam smiled at him. 'Aw, Maddy is a sweetie and that's great.' She sighed and looked at the leaden sky. 'A buggered-up weekend and rain – just wonderful.'

Ten minutes later Seb's CSM reported that all of B Company was present and correct and fifteen minutes after that the RSM's stentorian voice silenced the gathered troops. The CO climbed onto the saluting base by the flagpole at the edge of the square.

'Two hours and ten minutes,' he said, brandishing his stopwatch. 'Two hours and ten minutes,' he repeated.

Not bad, thought Seb. Evans was about to be proved wrong.

'Some of you may think that's acceptable.'

Well . . . thought Seb.

'Let me tell you it isn't. It's a bloody disgrace. Call your-selves professional soldiers? Well, you're not. You are a shambles. Had you managed to be ready for deployment in under two hours I would have stood you down until Monday but as it is it seems to me you need all the training you can get. So we are moving out to the ranges right now. I will be holding a CO's O Group at eighteen hundred hours for company commanders and further orders will be issued then. Right then, move out.'

Seb opened the passenger door and climbed in. His driver looked at him.

'Don't say a word,' said Seb.

'No, sir. Of course not, sir. Wouldn't dream of it.'

And as the vast convoy of vehicles formed up and began to move off the parade square towards the ranges the heavens opened and the rain began to sheet down.

Just brilliant, thought Seb, just fucking brilliant.

Chapter 36

At Winterspring Ducis the weekend for the Collins family wasn't going any better than Seb's, although they, at least, had the advantage of being indoors and not stuck out in the drizzle. But that was the *only* good thing they had going for them, as the atmosphere in the house seethed with the twins' resentment at being deprived of their phones and iPads. In turn, their bad humour rubbed off on their parents and in a small house with only one living room, everyone was snapping and sniping at everyone else.

Mike retreated behind the paper and Susie was in the kitchen with the ironing while the girls slobbed on the sofa watching weekend TV.

'Can't you turn that rubbish off?' moaned Mike, turning the pages of his paper noisily.

'Like we've got anything else to do,' snapped Katie. 'We can't exactly chat to our friends,' she added, pointedly.

'Besides, we like *Saturday Kitchen*,' said Ella.

'So why do you never help out in ours?'

'Because Mum listens to Radio 4, which is lame,' said Katie.

'It wouldn't hurt you to try and improve your minds instead of watching stuff designed for the lowest common denominator.'

Ella rolled her eyes and reached for the remote. She pressed the volume control and turned the sound up a notch.

Mike flung his paper on the floor and lunged for the remote, snatching it out of Ella's hand before she realised his intent. He pressed the off button and the TV screen went blank.

'You...you...' Ella saw the look on her father's face and didn't continue with her plan to tell him what she thought of him *and* his parenting skills. 'Come on, Katie.'

The pair stamped upstairs and the slam of a door reverberated round the house.

Susie came out of the kitchen. 'What now?' she asked with a tired sigh.

'Nothing,' said Mike.

'It must have been something.'

'Don't you start. I'm just trying to bring some sense of discipline and order to this house.'

'Implying that I don't?'

'I didn't say that.'

Susie glared at him. The phone rang. Susie stamped across the sitting room and snatched up the handset. 'Yes,' she snapped. 'Oh, of course.' She turned to her husband. 'It's for you.'

She handed Mike the phone and retreated to the kitchen.

A couple of minutes later Mike came to the kitchen door. 'I've got to go out. There are three villages over at Ashton-cum-Bavant way that have just been issued with a severe flood warning by the Environment Agency and they want me down at the incident room. It's all looking quite serious.'

'Saved by the bell.'

'Hardly. I didn't plan this, Susie.'

'No, I know.' She sighed. 'When do you think you'll be back?'

'I can't say.' Mike glanced out of the window. 'I can't see the rain stopping anytime soon.'

'No, well, take care. Floods are dodgy things.'

Mike nodded. 'Hopefully it'll be a case of prevention rather than... well, "cure" isn't the right word but you know what I mean. Maybe damage limitation...' He trailed off.

'Well, just you take care anyway. No heroics or anything like that.'

He nodded and picked up his car keys before heading off. Susie returned to the kitchen but before she picked up the next garment on the ironing pile, she twiddled the tuning knob on her portable radio until she found the local station. She needed to know what was going on – especially now that Mike was going to be in the thick of it.

The girls, sitting on Katie's bed, watched their father drive away, the wheels of his car throwing up arcs of water off the sodden tarmac.

'So,' said Katie, as she turned back from the window and leaned against the wall behind the bed, 'where do you think he's gone?'

Ella shrugged. 'Don't know, don't care. More importantly, do think he'll be gone long?'

Katie shook her head and got off the bed. 'Hang on, I'll find out.' She crossed the room and pattered down the stairs. A couple of minutes later she was back in the bedroom.

'Mum says he's been called out to a flood. She's got no idea when he'll be back.'

'And Mum's doing the ironing?'

Katie nodded and threw herself back on the duvet.

As Katie settled herself back into a comfortable position

Ella stood up. 'I'm going to try and find my phone. I bet it's in their bedroom.'

'You can't.' Katie's eyes were wide at the audacity of her sister's plan.

'Why not? They're our phones.' She reached out her hand to pull her twin upright. 'Come on, before Mum finishes the ironing and brings the clothes upstairs to put them away.'

'But . . . but she'll see it's missing.'

'Why? If she thinks they're hidden she won't go checking they're still there every five minutes.'

'I suppose.' Reluctantly Katie got off the bed.

'You keep a lookout to make sure she's still ironing while I have a rummage.'

Katie sat on the top step listening to the muted sound of the DJ's voice on the local radio followed by some crappy old country and western singer and, interspersed with the jangling banjo and wailing guitar, she could hear the thump and pffft of the steam iron on the board. Behind her she could hear the faint sound of drawers being slid out and then gently shut again. Every time there was a pause in the rhythm of the iron Katie held her breath, listening for her mother's footsteps crossing the sitting room, worrying in case she mightn't hear them on the carpet, and then feeling sick with relief when she heard the thump-thump of the iron once again.

She jumped out of her skin when Ella touched her on her shoulder and only just managed to suppress a shriek.

She spun round, about to have a go at her twin, but stopped when she saw Ella brandishing a phone.

'You found it?' she said, scrambling to her feet.

'Shhh.' Ella dragged her back to the bedroom and shut the door. 'It was in Mum's undies drawer along with our iPads.'

Katie nodded. But it was all right for her sister – back in communication with the rest of the world. She wasn't.

'I'm not going to keep it,' said Ella, as if she read her twin's thoughts. 'But now we know where they are, we can take them and use them when we want. We just have to be careful, that's all.' Her thumb skimmed across the screen.

'Who are you texting?'

'Ali.'

'Why? We can't go out, we're grounded.'

Ella looked up, her thumbs stilled. 'You can stay here if you want. I'm not, I'm going out.'

'But what'll Mum say?'

'Whatever she likes. What's the worst she can do? She already thinks she's got our iPads and phones but she's not as clever as she thinks she is. And if she stops our allowances, well, we'll just help ourselves. She hasn't noticed anything so far.'

'Maybe.'

'We can be downstairs and out the door before Mum even knows it.'

'But what about coming back?'

Ella narrowed her eyes. 'You scared or something?'

'No...no, of course not.'

'Good, because I want a ciggie.' Her phone trilled. She looked at the latest message. 'And, Ali says if we bring a fiver with us he can let us have a packet of ten.' She stared at her sister. 'So I suggest that while I put the phone back you find Mum's bag.'

Katie hesitated.

'Oh go on. Just nick a fiver. It's only two pound fifty each – hardly anything. A bus fare and school lunch is almost as much as that.'

'OK then.' Katie felt less than happy but she crept downstairs anyway. Halfway down the straight flight of stairs she paused and hung over the banister to look around the living room. It was empty but her mother's bag was on the sofa, and it would be visible from the kitchen should her mother turn around. Slowly she tiptoed down the remaining stairs, across the room and then casually sat down next to it. With a firm eye on her mother's back view, standing by the board in front of the sink, Katie clicked up the spring catch on the front of the bag and flipped open the flap. Susie's wallet was on the top. Katie eased it out of the bag and opened it. Her mother put the iron back on its stand with a bang and Katie's pulse rate went ballistic. She stared at her mother's back, frozen in horror, the wallet in her hand. If her mother turned round…but her mother had stopped to fold up the T-shirt she'd just pressed before picking up a blouse and carrying on. Katie sagged with relief. As fast as she could she flicked through the bits and pieces in the notes compartment at the back. There was a twenty and nothing else. She checked the change purse – a couple of pound coins and some small change, but not another three quid's worth. Making a decision, Katie picked out the twenty pound note and stuffed it up her sleeve before putting everything back as she'd found it and tiptoeing back to her sister.

She showed Ella her spoils.

'You took *how much*? You dimwit! She's bound to notice that. Can't I trust you to do anything?'

'It was that or nothing.' Katie glared at her twin but her shoulders went down. Maybe she *had* messed up.

'There must have been something smaller.'

'There wasn't. If you're so clever you go and do it, *OK*?' Katie pushed her face towards Ella's, daring her to push the issue.

'You did leave *some* money in her purse, didn't you?'

Katie nodded.

'Then you'd better hope Mum doesn't notice after all.'

'You too. You're in this as much as I am.'

The two girls slipped down the stairs, grabbed their out-door coats off the pegs by the porch, and a set of keys that hung on a nearby hook, before opening the front door as quietly as they could. They slipped out. Katie put the key in the outside lock and pulled the door shut before letting the catch drop back into place so they didn't have to slam it shut. Their exit had been almost silent.

'Nice one, sis,' said Ella.

'Thank you. See, I'm not such a dimwit.'

'No, sorry.'

They jogged down the garden path and over the concrete bridge that crossed the drainage ditch. The water was swirling along it at a ferocious rate but since the scare earlier in the year the water authority had cleared the banks of under-growth and dredged it and had assured the residents that the problem wouldn't occur again. The girls glanced at it out of curiosity but ran on, unconcerned.

Dodging the raindrops the two sisters raced up the road towards the corner. Ali and his pals were waiting for them.

'Got the dosh?' he said by way of a greeting.

Katie held out the twenty. 'It's all we've got. Can you change it?'

Ali looked at the note with contempt. 'What do you think I am? A fucking bank?' He waved the fags at them. 'Do you want them or not?'

Ella made a grab for them but Ali swished them out of reach. 'Hand over the cash and they're yours.'

'But...this is enough for four packs,' said Katie.

'Or,' said Ali, 'it's enough for this pack and something else. Something a bit special.'

'Like?' said Ella.

'Like this.' Ali produced a tobacco pouch from his pocket and some cigarette papers.

Both girls' eyes widened. They knew what they were being offered.

'Wanna try some?' said Ali.

Katie and Ella looked at each other. This was dodgy, dangerous and illegal. Of *course* they wanted to try. They nodded.

'But not here,' said Ali. 'If you go past the bus shelter there's a field on the left. Through the gate is a disused stable. Meet us there, five minutes.' He twitched the twenty out of Katie's hand and casually tossed the smokes at her in return. Katie fumbled the catch and they dropped in a puddle at her feet.

'Butterfingers,' sneered Ali as he and his mates swaggered down the road, hands in their pockets, strides jaunty, towards the bus stop.

Katie and Ella huddled together, feeling apprehensive and thrilled in equal measure at what they were about to do.

'What do you think it'll be like?' asked Ella.

'It'll be...cool, I suppose. We'll chill out, be relaxed.' Katie shrugged. 'It'll be fun.' She said it with false bravado and hoped her sister wouldn't detect it.

'I suppose.' Ella wasn't as good at dissembling as her sister and for once it sounded as if her confidence was deserting her. 'D'you think Mum'll be able to tell?'

'Doubt it. Like she knows anything about drugs.'

'Yeah, but even so?'

'You getting cold feet? After I nicked all the money?'

'No,' said Ella hastily. 'Come on, the five minutes must be up.'

They both knew they weren't but hurried down the road before either of them could change their minds.

Chapter 37

Katie and Ella slipped through the gate into the field and saw the ramshackle shed in the far corner, nestled into an overgrown hawthorn hedge, the branches of which had grown into straggly canopy that spread over the roof. The pair trudged through the knee-high mix of nettles, thistles and dead grass, stumbling over tussocks and avoiding getting stung till they reached the door. They knocked.

'Who is it?' asked a wary voice.

'Us,' said Katie and Ella in unison.

The door opened and a funny, sweet, smoky smell wafted out into the wet air. The girls slipped inside, into the dank gloom. In the low light they could see the glowing tip of a spliff and then, as their eyes adjusted, they could see the three lads lounging around on some sacks that covered what might have been hay, or straw. It was hardly a comfortable hideout but at least it was dry.

'Anyone see you coming here?'

The girls looked at each other. They hadn't thought to check they weren't being followed although the only person who might have done was their mother and she, as far as they knew, was unaware of their departure.

'No,' they said.

'Good. Only you're a bit young to be getting in trouble with the pigs,' said Ali. 'Your mummy and daddy would be well upset if that happened, wouldn't they,' he added with a sneer.

Katie swallowed. She hadn't thought about the consequences of getting caught by the authorities – only what her mum might think.

'Well, that's *not* going to happen, so why don't you give us what we've paid for.' She eyed him coolly, despite the fact her heart was pounding.

Ali looked at her with something that almost verged on respect and reached for his tobacco pouch. 'Here, I rolled a spliff for you and Ella.' He passed a rough-and-ready rollie to Katie. 'You know what to do?'

Risking looking foolish Katie decided it was best to come clean. 'Apart from sparking up, you mean? No.'

'Take a drag, hold it as long as possible before you exhale and enjoy the ride.'

'Ride?' The word slipped out before Katie could help it.

'Chill, it's not like Special K or magic mushrooms. It's cool. You'll enjoy it.'

Trying to keep her hand steady Katie took the spliff and put it to her lips. Ali flicked his lighter and Katie leant forward to meet the flame. She took a drag. The smoke tasted quite different from the Benson and Hedges she was used to. She took the smoke down into her lungs and passed the cigarette to Ella who followed her example. After half a minute she blew the smoke out. And…and…? And not a lot, if she was honest. She held her hand out and took back the rollie and repeated the process. She wasn't sure what she expected but it was a bloody sight more than this. But she did feel calmer, more relaxed. She took a third drag. God, this whole set-up was funny; her, her sis and three lads in a stable. It was almost like a scene out of a primary school nativity play. All they needed was a donkey and a manger and they'd be sorted. She started to giggle.

Seb got out of his Land Rover and stretched. The journey from the barracks to their exercise on the Plain hadn't been that far but the suspension on the vehicle wasn't brilliant and that, coupled with the rain, meant that his driver had been unable to pick his way around the worst of the ruts and bumps once they got off the beaten track. Seb felt as if he'd spent the last hour in the drum of a cement mixer. Around him his soldiers were already digging in, making slit trenches and creating defensive positions. The earth they dug out was more mud than soil and dripped off their spades, splatting wetly onto the ground as they tipped it off their shovels. Their ponchos and waterproof jackets were keeping the worst of the weather off them but even so everyone looked soaked and miserable. A couple of the troops, sheltering under a bivouac made out of waterproof ponchos, had got a brew on and were handing out mugs of hot tea.

'Want one, sir?' called the squaddie overseeing the process.

Seb nodded. 'I'll get my mug.' He walked round to the back of the Land Rover and opened his Bergen. He found his mug easily, packed where it always was in one of the side pockets. He trudged back across the sodden grass that was rapidly turning into a bog, feeling a certain amount of empathy with the soldiers on the Western Front. Not that he was being shelled and shot at...

He handed over his mug and the soldier slopped a dark beige liquid into it.

'And it's fresh milk, sir. We'll be on condensed again tomorrow but we might as well make use of fresh rations while we have them.' He held up a jam jar containing sugar and a teaspoon that had obviously been used to stir numerous cups already. Seb shook his head and slurped gratefully at his drink before walking off to find his platoon commanders and check the deployment of his soldiers before it got dark.

As he wandered round the company lines he sensed that his troops were far from happy. He tried to chivvy them along and cheer them up but they were having none of it. Eventually he turned to his sergeant major.

'What's the matter with them? I know the weather sucks but we've all been out in worse and they're not usually this miserable.'

'No...well.'

'Sergeant Major?'

Riley shrugged. 'Morale's low across the battalion. You know how it's been since...'

'Since?' prompted Seb.

'Nothing, sir.'

'Come on, man. Spit it out.'

'Since the new CO came,' mumbled Riley.

Seb nodded. 'And the new RSM isn't a bundle of laughs, is he.'

Riley shook his head. 'At least Jenks had a sense of humour.'

'What's it like in the sergeants' mess?'

'You don't want to know, sir. The wife won't attend functions any more. She says the heart's gone out of it, now Horrocks is in charge. He's a right stickler for the rules.'

Seb was saddened. He remembered the time the warrant officers and sergeants had invited officers to Christmas drinks at their mess. Or rather, he remembered some of it. Quite a lot was a blur.

No, thought Seb, the new RSM was a cold fish and as for the CO...It seemed the least transgression got the soldiers on a fizzer. No wonder the troops were fed up and Seb didn't really blame them.

Once he'd visited as many of his troops as possible – a word of encouragement here, a joke there – and checked everyone was pulling their weight and knuckling down to their allotted tasks, dusk had fallen – although given how gloomy the day had been it was hard to appreciate that the sun had just about set. He still had a couple of hours before he was due to present himself at the CO's O Group at six that evening, his driver was digging their slit trench and there wasn't much he could do now till he had to brief his troops once he'd got his orders from Colonel Rayner. Seb pulled up the collar on his multicam jacket and reached into an inside pocket. He checked the connectivity of his phone; two bars – it ought to be enough. He dialled home.

'Hello, sweetie,' he said when the phone was answered.

'Erm...it's Luke.'

'Shit. Sorry, Luke. And I'm sorry your weekend with Sam has been trashed.'

'Yeah, well...Maddy asked me to pick up the phone as she's changing Rose's nappy...' There was a pause. 'Did you hear that?'

'No.'

'Maddy was shouting she'll be two ticks. Ah, here she comes.'

There was a pause then a muffled clatter as the phone changed hands.

'Seb!'

'I didn't mean to disturb you.'

'No, it's fine.'

'I've just called Luke "sweetie".'

'Bless. I expect he'll get over it. I imagine, as he's in the army, he's been called worse. How's things?'

'Wet, cold, miserable.'

'I can imagine. Still, you're the one who joined the infantry not the Tank Regiment. Just think, you could be tucked up in a nice warm Challenger tank if you'd made a different choice.'

'I tell you, leaving the Hertfordshires and joining some other lot is becoming increasingly tempting.'

'But you'll feel differently when the weather perks up. It can't go on raining like this for ever.'

'It's not the weather that's pissing me off, it's Rayner. And he and his sidekick Horrocks have pissed off the troops too. I've never seen the lads so low. I know they've been a bit morose lately, that morale hasn't been top-notch, but I put it down to the shit weather. Normally they perk up when they get to do proper soldiering like this. But not this time. If anything, being on exercise has made it worse.'

'That's a shame.'

'It's more than a shame, it's not right. Anyway, you don't need my problems. I just rang to have a quick chat, tell you we've all made it out to the ranges in one piece, that sort of stuff.'

'That's fine. Good to hear from you.'

'And I need to ask you to say goodbye to Luke from me too. He'll be long gone by the time we get back...'

'He's off after breakfast tomorrow – going to get an early start for the drive back to his barracks. He said that much as he loves our place there's not much point in hanging around now Sam's not here.'

'And then you'll be all on your own.'

'Huh,' said Maddy, 'like I'm not used to that.'

'I'll try and make it up when I get back.'

'Yeah, yeah. Don't worry, I know it's not your fault. But bloody Rayner could hardly have picked a worse weekend weather-wise, could he?'

As Mike's car approached Ashton-cum-Bavant the weather deteriorated markedly. The tarmac was slick, the gutters at the sides of the road were swilling with water, any potholes were hubcap deep and the few pedestrians around were racing to find shelter. Despite the fact that it was supposed to be broad daylight his headlights had automatically come on. It was, thought Mike, the sort of day to be at home, in front of the fire, with the paper, *not* out in the back of beyond. And, instead of the papers for a bit of reading material, he had with him his laptop from work and a bunch of files. Being relatively new to the job Mike didn't want to rely on his memory alone for all the emergency procedures so he'd dashed into the office on the way to the RV to collect anything he thought might be relevant or helpful. Well, that was his official excuse for wanting the files – the one he'd given the security chap manning the entrance to the council offices. His other reason for wanting the files was more Machiavellian; those months working for Rayner hadn't been entirely wasted. Given the cavalier way Rob had dismissed all his assessments of the emergency planning budget, all his plans for flood defences, all his careful evaluations of weather patterns and risks, he did not want anything untoward to happen to any of those papers if any shit hit the fan later. If anyone was going to get the blame for lack of foresight it wasn't going to be him. No way.

He drove on through the teeming rain, past the cricket pitch and the village green and then past a sensational country house with a 'Sold' sign planted in the front garden. He glanced at it – it was the sort of place he might have aspired to if his career hadn't hit the buffers. All right, he admitted to himself, maybe not on that scale. But it was definitely the sort of place Susie had hankered after; he'd seen her flicking through copies of *Country Life* in the officers' mess – in the days when she'd been a member, not an employee – and reading the details of the swanky houses that commanded a double page advert and which had 'price on application' written in the copy; code for 'if you have to ask the price you can't afford it'.

Mike sighed and turned his attention back to the road, driving on carefully towards the RV with the police and emergency services. A mile outside the village he saw a barrier across the road. *Floods*. No shit, Sherlock, he thought. And he'd tried to tell that twat Rob about the need for flood defences along the Bavant, he couldn't have spelt it out more clearly in his report but Rob had dismissed just about every word; they'd had a 'full and frank exchange of views', as diplomats were wont to call a stonking great row, finishing with Rob informing him that if he didn't improve his attitude he might have to 'take matters further'. Yeah, well, who's been proved right now? thought Mike. Not that he could feel any satisfaction about the victory – not given the misery that was probably being generated along this stretch of river.

Beside the barrier a police car was parked. Mike drew up alongside and got out to talk to the coppers.

'Don't even think of going down that road, sir,' said the constable behind the wheel. 'There's a dip about half a mile along and the water is six foot deep. We've already had to get two cars dragged out. That's why we're here – to make sure no other muppets try it.'

'It's all right, officer,' said Mike. 'I'm the emergency planning officer and I have no intention of adding to the chaos. I just wondered if you know the best way to get to the bronze commander's RV. It's supposed to be at the pub in Upper Bavant.'

The constable in the car assumed a slightly more deferential attitude. 'I see, sir. Your best way is back through the village, turn left at the junction and head through Bavant Hinton. Not sure where the pub is in Upper Bavant but I can radio ahead that you're on the way and get someone to meet you in the village.'

'No, no, that's fine. Once I get past Bavant Hinton I'm sure I'll be able to find my way. Thanks.'

Mike splashed back to his car and slid into the driver's seat. He didn't envy the policemen. He thought he was being hard done by but at least he had something to do – he wasn't stuck in a car watching the weather chuck it down. He was just about to start the engine when his mobile rang. He pulled it out of his pocket and checked to see who the caller was. Susie.

'Hi, hon.'

'The little buggers have skedaddled.'

'Who?'

'Who do you think?' Her voice was shrill with indignation and annoyance. 'Ella and Katie, of course.'

Mike sighed. Little minxes. 'Any idea where they've gone?'

'They're probably out with those dreadful boys they've been hanging around with. Although I doubt if they're *out* exactly, in this weather. They must be indoors, somewhere.'

'Do you know where these lads live?'

'No. Somewhere around here but I don't know where exactly. I don't fancy knocking on random doors in case I strike lucky.'

'And with no mobiles you can't order them back home.'

'As if they'd obey me,' said Susie. 'Mike, they're out of control.'

Well, not completely but they were heading that way. 'They're just—'

'They're just impossible,' snapped Susie.

'Look, I expect they'll be back soon. And they can't have gone far.'

'No. No, you're right. And you've got enough on your plate without me adding to your worries.'

'Keep me in the picture. By text,' he added. 'I may be a bit busy to talk in a while.'

'Yes, I'm sorry. Hope it's all sorted soon.'

Fat chance, thought Mike. What the copper had told him about the level of flooding on the Upper Bavant road had been a bit of a facer; things were obviously more dire than he thought. He wondered what else was going to be in store for him – a lot more of the same and possibly worse, he suspected. He put his phone back in his pocket and drove on towards his rendezvous with the bronze commander.

Chapter 38

Maddy and Luke had got back to her quarter at around two and Maddy hoped they could all settle down in front of the gas fire, watch the sport on the TV and enjoy an idle, restful afternoon. But Nathan had had other ideas and Maddy had found that she'd spent the entire time trying to keep him amused. Every time she stopped he threatened to throw a tantrum and Maddy, not wishing to see Luke's afternoon ruined by screams and tears – and that would just be her – ended up being run ragged. It wasn't that she didn't want Luke to think she was a dreadful parent who had a child from hell, she also didn't want Nate to be some sort of dire aversion therapy designed to put Luke off fatherhood for life. Finally it had been time for the children's supper and bath and she decided she must have done something right during the preceding hours when Luke offered to read Nathan his bedtime story while Maddy settled Rose. Maddy could hear the shrieks of delight as Luke hammed up the book he was reading. He'd make a great dad, she thought, as she switched off Rose's light and went downstairs to make supper. She only hoped that the army didn't make it impossible for Luke and Sam to get together enough to keep their relationship going. One cliché might suggest that distance made the heart grow fonder, but Maddy knew from bitter personal experience that the counterpart – out of sight, out of mind – was just as true.

She opened the door of her fridge and contemplated the huge chicken she'd bought to feed her house guests for lunch the next day. If she cooked it as planned, she thought, there wasn't going to be much chance of her and the two kids getting through that in a couple of sittings. The leftovers would be epic and she and the children would be eating chicken for a week. While chicken was nice, she also liked a varied diet. Maybe she ought to joint it and think of different things to do with the bird; she'd checked the freezer and there wasn't a hope in hell of cramming it in so she'd have to do something with it before the 'use by' date. In the meantime, she needed to get on with tonight's supper for her and Luke – fish pie.

She heard Luke coming down the stairs – she needed to crack on if they were going to eat before eight. She pulled out the bag of smoked haddock and another one of cod, shut the fridge door and turned.

'Hi, Luke, I was just about to start supper. Fancy a glass of something?'

'Only if you're going to join me.'

'Hell, yes. And thanks for reading Nate his bedtime story. You are a wonder.'

'But it was great to revisit *The Very Hungry Caterpillar*. It's an age since I read it.'

'Not much call for it at Sandhurst.'

Luke laughed. 'Not a lot. The required reading was rather more serious.'

'Beer?'

He nodded. Maddy reopened the fridge and passed Luke a can of Spitfire. He popped the tab.

'There's a glass in the cupboard behind you. And if you could pass me a wine glass...'

Luke got out the glasses and passed one to Maddy. He went over to the kitchen window and peered out at the darkness, past the drops of rain running down the glass.

'Poor old Sam and Seb – out in this.'

'I know, vile weather.' Maddy poured herself a glass of white from the fridge. 'It's been a rotten autumn.'

Luke took a sip of beer. 'We had a big exercise in Germany in September, out in the field, and it wasn't too bad. Can't think why your CO chose November for an exercise.'

Maddy started to peel potatoes. 'Because he can.'

Luke picked up on her tone of voice and looked at her. 'You don't like him.'

Maddy shook her head. 'And his wife is a piece of work too.'

'Sam's not a fan of them, either.'

Maddy told Luke what Seb had told her in his earlier phone call.

'That's not good,' said Luke.

Maddy shrugged and cut the peeled potatoes into chunks before dropping them into a pan of water. 'But there's nothing we can do. Let's not worry about it.' But she did worry about it. Jack – and to a slightly lesser degree, Camilla – seemed to be getting increasingly dictatorial in the way they treated 1 Herts; like it was their own fiefdom and all the officers and men were their serfs. Maddy worried that someone was going to lash out and she just hoped to God it wasn't Seb. But she was sure someone would get pushed too far and probably in the not too distant future.

*

Susie paced up and down the sitting room. It was getting late and the girls weren't back. OK, it was only half six but it was pitch dark, it was still raining, and, when all was said and done, they were only twelve. She was tempted to go out with a torch and call for them, but would it do any good? Maybe confiscating their phones hadn't been such a good idea after all.

She consoled herself with the knowledge that they would be together so if something bad had befallen one of them the other would have come to get help. Realistically, she told herself, they were probably safe and warm and with friends and putting off coming home because of the trouble they were likely to be in. They were *not*, Susie thought firmly, under a lorry on the main road at the bottom of the hill nor had they been abducted by white slavers. And where was Mike? What was happening with him? God, today was turning out to be a nightmare.

She heard the click of a key in the lock. Mike, or the girls? The door opened and there were the twins. She told herself not to raise her voice, to remain calm. She would not have a row with them, she would not lose her temper but, dear God, it was going to be tough.

'Good, you're back in time for supper.'

The twins exchanged a look and then giggled.

'This is no laughing matter,' said Susie, struggling to maintain her calm.

'No, Mum,' said Katie, her mouth twitching.

'We won't wait for your father. I have no idea when he's going to be home.'

At this perfectly ordinary sentence both girls burst into laughter again.

'What is the matter with you?' Susie demanded.

But her daughters just laughed all the more.

Susie wanted to shake them but she didn't have the energy to have a full scale row with them, not without Mike's back-up. She stamped off into the kitchen and fetched the casserole out of the oven and put it on the table.

'Come and eat,' she told the twins as she fetched a bowl of mash to accompany it.

'Not hungry,' said Ella.

Susie turned. 'But you didn't have lunch.'

'So?' said Katie with a shrug.

'*So* you can have supper. You must eat something.'

The two girls slouched over to the table and sat down while Susie began to dish up. Silence reigned while she dolloped beef stew and dumplings onto their plates

'Aren't you going to ask us where we've been?' said Ella taking a spoonful of mash and dropping it, with a splat, onto her plate.

'No,' said Susie. 'Frankly, I'm not sure I care.' It was a huge lie but she wasn't going to give them the satisfaction of letting them know how worried she'd been.

The girls exchanged a glance. Susie ignored them and ate her stew while the girls picked at theirs. It was a pretty miserable meal because Susie was well aware that her indifference was worrying the girls more than if there had been a row. They weren't expecting it and it was unsettling them.

Finally, Susie cleared her plate. 'I am going to have a cup of tea and then I am going to have a soak in the bath,' she told them. 'If you want to use the bathroom I suggest you do so now.'

Again the girls exchanged a look and they trailed upstairs as Susie cleared the table and wished, for the umpteenth time that day, that she had something stronger in the house than tea.

After Maddy had fed Luke and she was pottering about in the kitchen clearing up, she thought again about the enormous chicken she'd bought. It was ridiculous to cook it for herself but it wasn't going to last till Seb got back. She made a decision, picked up the phone and dialled Jenna's number.

'Hi, Jen,' she said when it was answered.

'Hi, Mads, how's tricks?'

'Apart from being mightily pissed off at what the CO's done now, you mean?'

'Yup, apart from bloody Rayner. Dan and I had so much planned for the weekend and it's all gone to rat-shit now.'

'Same here – *and* I had Sam Lewis and her fiancé to stay and, now she's gone, Luke has decided he might as well go back to his own unit. Can't say I blame him; I can't imagine that if I were young and single I'd want to be trapped in a house with two toddlers.'

'No,' said Jenna. 'You have a point.'

'Anyway, that's the reason I'm ringing. How about you and Eliot come over here for roast chicken tomorrow? Unless, of course, you've got food in your fridge which is going to go to waste.'

'Come off it, Mads – me? Food in the fridge? Domestic goddess? And so yes, we'd love to come along.'

'Brilliant, see you then. About midday.'

'Perfect.'

Mike trudged out of the pub and down the steps that led down the steep slope to the road and then crossed it to look at the river Bavant. He lit his path with a powerful flashlight which made the falling rain glow white, like showers of sparks in a steel foundry. And the noise of the rushing water was at an industrial level too. Mike could barely hear himself think as the river thundered alongside the road. He splashed through the puddles in his wellingtons till he reached the white railings that separated the road from the river bank and shone his torch on the rushing water. In the summer, this was a beauty spot and visitors flocked to the pub to sit at the outside tables, basking in the sun, supping on good local beers and watching the little chalk stream drift by. Kids could play in it, paddling in the ankle-deep water off the pebbly beaches at its edge, dipping jam jars for minnows and sticklebacks, and the grassy banks were a haven for wild flowers and butterflies. But not now. Now the river was a muddy torrent, made worse with branches of trees being swept down from upstream, and which threatened to make things worse as they got caught in the low bridges that crossed it at intervals, impeding the water and causing it to back up.

Mike switched the beam of his torch from the water to illuminate the black and white stick, put there by the Environment Agency to measure the water level. A metre and a half. Maybe not so very deep for some rivers but this was a dangerously high level for this one; a level which threatened the safety of all the villages along its course and the livelihood of the farmers in the valley. It was now pretty obvious that it was a question of *when* it burst its banks and not *if*. Mike turned around and clumped up the steps back to the pub. Outside, in the car park to the side, were several police cars, a couple of fire engines and a satellite van from a TV station which Mike had to weave between to get to the door of the public bar where they had set up their HQ. He shouldered it open, switching off his torch as he entered the warm fug of the country inn.

'It's getting worse,' he told one of the policemen as he took off his dripping waterproofs in the small lobby.

A senior police officer came over. 'Worse, did I hear you say?'

'Up another ten centimetres, by my estimation. I think we ought to get the army out to help with sandbags. We simply haven't the manpower for this – the police and the fire brigade are stretched to the limit as it is. The guys we've co-opted from the refuse disposal companies are doing their best at the depot but...'

'Bin men?' asked the chief inspector.

Mike nodded. 'Yeah, we suspend refuse collections and transfer the manpower to this. The guys are happy to help and the overtime they're going to earn will be fantastic. Besides, I think people would rather have dry houses than empty bins, don't you?'

'Makes sense, I suppose. Do you really need more manpower if the Grundon chaps are already doing the job?'

Mike nodded. 'It's getting pretty desperate in places. As I said, the guys are doing their best but we just can't keep up with demand. It's not just filling the sandbags, it's distributing them. If we leave them for householders to collect you get the people who snaffle dozens more than they need. We need people to ration them out and we need boots on the ground to do that. If you can go to gold command and ask...' He willed the chief inspector to agree with him.

The chief inspector scratched his chin. 'OK, I'll take a look. Can I borrow your torch?'

Mike hoped the policeman would see reason when he'd been down to the river himself. He handed over his flashlight then scrubbed his boots on the large doormat. No point in making the flagstones of the pub worse than they already were – a dozen or so policemen tramping in and out in muddy boots had left the place looking more like a cow byre than a hostelry.

He went into the public bar which had been transformed into an operations room with maps pinned up on the walls and whiteboards showing the hotspots at greatest risk of immediate flooding and the evacuation centres for the threatened villages written on them in marker pens. Numbers for the RVS and local loo hire companies were also prominent. It seemed to Mike that, with the exception of a labour force to fill and distribute sandbags, most of the immediate bases had been covered.

A couple of minutes later the chief inspector was back with him.

'You're right, I've never seen the river like that before.' He picked up the phone and started dialling. 'Time to ruin a few soldiers' weekends.'

Chapter 39

Seb and his soldiers, loaded up with all their kit, were trailing around the hills and valleys of Salisbury Plain on a pointless map-reading exercise – or at least, Seb and his sergeant major felt it was pointless.

'It's as if, having crashed us all out he couldn't think of anything else to do with us,' grumbled Seb to Mr Riley.

Riley pulled at the straps of his Bergen to hitch it higher onto his shoulders and peered at the compass he held in his hand. 'What a way to spend Saturday night, eh? Getting wet through and sleep deprived all in one hit.'

'Just think, if we weren't doing this we could be sitting at home, in front of the fire, with a glass of wine and watching the TV.'

'Never mind, sir, we'll appreciate it all the more when we get the opportunity again.'

'Like when you stop banging your head against a brick wall?'

'That's it, sir.'

Behind them the hundred and fifty soldiers of B Company straggled along, heads down against the persistent drizzle, some of them yomping in silence, some of them muttering to their buddies about this or that but all of them fed up and disconsolate.

Seb's radio headset cracked into life. 'Hello, all stations, hello, all stations, this is zero, return to base immediately, return to base immediately. Acknowledge, over.'

One by one all the sub units of the battalion responded to the order as Seb halted his troops and got them to gather round.

'It seems we're to go back. I've no idea why but the CO has ordered that we return to base.' A swell of derogatory remarks along the theme of piss-ups being badly organised in breweries ran through the ranks which Seb pretended he didn't hear. He felt much the same way himself as he and his men about-turned and headed back the way they'd come.

An hour later, sodden, miserable and tired, Seb and his men came back to the point they'd left a couple of hours earlier. As they trudged back into their company position the men rolled their heavy Bergens off their backs and began remaking their bashers for some sort of shelter or lighting up their hexi burners to get a brew on.

'Want one, sir?' said a soldier waving an empty mug at Seb.

'Later,' he replied. 'Got to go to another O group.'

'Righty-oh.'

Seb rummaged in his Bergen for his mug and a note-book and pencil and, having given the soldier the former, he tramped off to where the CO was about to issue more orders to his subordinates.

The officers were gathering around the CO's Land Rover. Seb stood next to his second in command.

Andy, the adjutant, joined them. 'The CO will have a word when everyone's here,' he told them.

'Many left to arrive?' asked Seb.

Andy checked the millboard in his hand. 'Just a couple

and I've heard on the net they're nearly back here – just a few minutes out now. I'd better tell the CO that we're nearly all assembled.'

They watched Andy move off to talk to his boss. Over the muted hubbub of the quiet conversations going on around them Seb heard the CO's voice cutting across the noise.

'This is ridiculous. They're late. Everyone should have got here by now.'

'But, sir, they may have travelled further in the time than the other companies, which is why they're taking longer to get back.'

'Rubbish. They're just slacking. Five extra duties to the 2IC and ten to the OC.'

Andy scribbled a note on his clipboard.

Will raised an eyebrow at Seb. 'Always a brickbat at the ready, never a bouquet. And Andy's probably right; I bet they zoomed off and now they've got much further to get back. No wonder morale is shit if the CO won't see basic stuff like that.'

Seb recalled what his CSM had said about everyone being fed up. 1 Herts had once been a pretty happy battalion – it was anything but these days. Although, that said, the atmosphere in B Company HQ had lightened up a lot over the past weeks now that Will seemed to have accepted having Seb as his boss and Caro and Maddy were back on speaking terms.

'You know, Seb,' said Will, quietly, 'this exercise is making the Grand Old Duke of York look like he knew what he was doing. Talk about shambolic.'

'It seems a trifle unplanned,' agreed Seb.

'Unplanned? That's a prize understatement.'

'Shh,' said Seb, not because he disagreed with Will but because Will's voice was getting louder.

The final two officers panted up to the assembled group to be greeted by Andy with the glad tidings. Seb could tell by their expressions they were not impressed with their summary and unwarranted punishments.

In front of them the CO climbed onto the lowered tailgate of his vehicle to be visible to everyone.

'Can you all hear me?' was his opening line.

'Unfortunately, yes,' said Will very quietly to Seb.

Seb studied his toecaps while he got his face under control.

'I have just received a communication from Brigade,' continued the CO, 'requiring us to terminate this exercise immediately—'

'Thank fuck for that, there is a God,' whispered Will.

'—and to proceed to the river Bavant which is in danger of bursting its banks. The local flood defences are inadequate and the blue light services are already stretched to capacity so 1 Herts is being deployed to help out. To this end we are moving to grid six-seven-nine, five-three-seven, where we are to RV with the bronze commander at the scene.'

'Well, at least we'll be doing something useful,' muttered Will, 'instead of being toy soldiers being pushed around by a spoilt brat who doesn't know how to play nicely.'

Seb's toecaps got interesting again.

'So everyone is to move out of here as soon as possible, normal convoy regulations as per standard operating procedures are to be observed at all times when travelling on the public highways. To avoid congestion at the RV, drivers are to debus their troops on arrival at the scene and then follow the directions given to them by the emergency services as to where to park up. I will appraise the situation on arrival and then I'll hold another O group at the RV at...' the CO looked at his watch, '...oh-four-hundred hours. Is that all perfectly clear?'

'Sir,' assented his officers before they moved off back to their company lines.

Seb collected his promised cuppa and then asked Mr Riley to gather together his platoon and section commanders. Ten minutes later, he was repeating the CO's orders to them and almost no time after that his soldiers were racing around, backfilling their trenches, dismantling the recently erected bashers and forming chain gangs to get as much kit, as fast as possible, back on the trucks. However, as everyone was wet, cold and tired and it was pitch dark as well, things didn't go as efficiently as they might have and removing all traces of their occupancy of that bit of Salisbury Plain ranges took longer than Seb, mindful that the CO was feeling liberal with the extra-duty punishments, was entirely happy with. Finally, though, everything was loaded up, all weapons accounted for, all soldiers present and correct and the convoy of B Company vehicles began to move off, along the range roads to the main metalled road and relative civilisation.

Seb jumped into his vehicle followed by Mr Riley. The cab of the Land Rover was wonderfully warm as his driver had had the engine running and the heater on. Instantly the windscreen began to fog up as the steam from two damp bodies condensed on it. Seb leaned forwards and increased the heat and the fan speed to counteract it and the extra warmth made him yawn hugely.

'Tired, sir?' asked his driver.

'Knackered.'

'Should've done what I did, boss.'

'Which was?'

'Grab a bunch of zeds in the back of my Rover instead of going out on that stupid map-reading exercise.'

Seb looked at his driver. 'And the order was for *every* soldier to take part.'

'You didn't notice...' there was a slight pause, '...boss,' added the driver, giving Seb a broad grin.

Seb had to suck in his cheeks. 'I could have you on a charge for that.'

'You *could*. But given that if *I* can't map-read, given my trade and years of experience, things have come to a pretty pass. And besides which, I reckoned I'd be more use rested than in the sort of shag-order you're in now – with all due respect, sir.'

Seb nodded. The insubordination was epic – but so was the level of logic. Besides, he was too knackered to take the matter further.

He sighed. 'No, you're right and I'm too tired to argue.'

'Good. So I suggest you and Mr Riley get in some shut-eye while I get us all to the destination.'

Seb nodded. 'Good idea.' He pulled his beret forwards to cover his eyes and fell asleep before they'd gone another half-mile. Mr Riley followed suit almost as quickly.

Chapter 40

Mike was beginning to feel the effects of sleeplessness and went to the urn in the corner to grab yet another cup of coffee. His brain was jangling with caffeine but every other bit of him was bone weary – weary and cold. A tipper truck of sand had been delivered to the village of Upper Bavant along with a load of sacks and he'd been helping, like every other available able-bodied person, to fill sandbags and load them onto trailers being dragged by local farmers' tractors and taken to the most threatened sites along the river bank. And it wasn't just shoring up the banks that they were doing. Never had the old naval cry of 'man the pumps' been more appropriate, only now the pumps were diesel driven.

He wriggled his toes in his damp socks; what he would give to be dry. His clothes, damp and clammy, stuck to him and chafed his crotch and armpits. Mike told himself to man up. At least he was somewhere warm and dry and had a warm dry house to go home to – when he did finally get to go home. The people in the Bavant valley, whose houses were flooded, were looking at months and months of dealing with sodden furniture, soaked carpets and ruined plaster and electrics. And furthermore, he had access to hot coffee, he thought as he took a slurp. Things could be so much worse.

Outside he heard the sound of engines and the shouts of

men. He tramped over to the windows and peered out. The cavalry had arrived! Well, maybe not the cavalry but the army at any rate, and not a moment too soon. Mike hadn't realised quite how much pressure he'd been under, trying to juggle everything with too few volunteers, until the sense of utter relief swept through him at the sight of several hundred more pairs of hands arriving.

He took another swig of coffee before padding across the stone floor to the door, thrusting his feet into his rubber boots and heading back out into the filthy weather. On the road below the pub, soldiers were jumping out of the backs of trucks and Land Rovers into the now ankle-deep water. As the vehicles emptied the trucks were driven away to the village rugby club car park, the largest area of hardstanding in the immediate area, and the soldiers milled around outside looking for direction and someone to tell them where they were wanted most.

Mike ran halfway down the steps and hollered. 'Listen up!' The chat began to subside. 'Oi! Silence,' he roared, using his old parade square voice.

Silence fell, apart from the background thunder of the river. 'Mike?'

Mike peered at the figure pushing his way through the throng of soldiers and recognised the approaching figure. 'Seb?'

'Hi, buddy,' said Seb as he reached Mike and shook him warmly by the hand.

'Hey, am I glad to see you and B Company.'

'Glad to be of assistance. You tell us what you want us to do and we're ready and willing.'

'Seb, it's filling and moving sandbags. We've volunteers doing their best but it's not enough. The sand and the sacks have been delivered; they're at the farm up the lane there.' Mike gestured to the small road that ran off the main road about twenty yards further along. 'We've got the local farmers to take them on trailers to the worst affected places but there are dozens of other places at risk. Honestly, Seb, we're talking about fighting losing battles here.'

'Mike, 1 Herts doesn't lose battles. If we can turn the tide we will.' Seb turned to his troops. 'OK men, I want 1 and 2 Platoons to fill the sandbags and the rest of you are to remain here to be deployed by Major Collins as he sees fit. Over to you, Mike.'

Mike shouted instructions as to where the soldiers were to report and then watched as half of his ex-company marched off to the farm.

He turned back to the remaining troops and began to address them. 'I need chain gangs at a number of locations. I want section commanders to report to bronze HQ, which is here in the pub, for the grid references where we need you the most and then each section is to report to one of those hotspots. I'll leave it to section commanders to sort out who is going where.'

Another Land Rover drew up near the steps, sending a bow wave of water over the soldiers' boots. They muttered amongst themselves in irritation. Mike watched as his old adversary, Rayner, opened the door and stood on the sill – keeping his feet dry. Seb and Mike exchanged a look.

'You – you there.' Rayner beckoned to Mike imperiously.

'Colonel Rayner,' said Mike, coldly. 'You've managed to get here...' The unsaid word 'finally' hung in the air.

'Ah,' said Rayner, obviously recognising to whom he was speaking. '*Mr* Collins.'

The two glared at each other.

'Right,' continued Rayner, 'thank you for what you've done, Collins. If you bring me up to speed I'll take over.'

Mike felt his eyes widen at the audacity of Rayner's statement. 'With all due respect, Colonel, that isn't how it works,' he said.

'Don't be ridiculous.'

The soldiers gathered caught the vibe of poisonous antipathy and began to eavesdrop openly at the exchange going on. Seb stepped in.

'Colonel, Mike...I think we'd be better discussing this in your operations room, Mike.' Mike understood what Seb meant. 'And meanwhile,' Seb said with a raised voice, 'section commanders, you need to get the relevant grid references.' He grabbed Mike's arm and tugged him back up the steps.

'Don't let him wind you up. This is your show,' advised Seb quietly, 'not his.'

'I hate that man,' said Mike. 'And just when I think I've see the back of him, he rocks up again. I don't fucking believe it.'

They reached the door of the pub and Mike kicked off his boots as he went in. Seb, encumbered with complicated laces, just brushed his thoroughly but although he might have got the mud off, the fabric remained sodden. He squelched into the public bar.

A couple of seconds later the section commanders trooped in.

'Over here, guys,' called one of the police officers.

The NCOs did as they were bidden and gathered around the large-scale map of the area. Seb and Mike stood behind them to listen to the briefing.

'OK,' said the policeman, 'the black pins mark the worst affected areas. This is where we need you guys as soon as the others have got a decent supply of sandbags ready for you to use.'

'Just a moment,' called Rayner from the door of the room. 'Excuse me, this is now an army operation. I'll do the briefing, thank you.'

The police officer looked at Rayner with incredulity before saying, 'And you're au fait with the situation, are you, sir?'

'I will be when you've brought me up to speed. Once I know what's what, I'll pass the information on.'

'Wasting valuable time,' said Mike, no longer able to contain himself.

'I beg your pardon.' The colonel turned and gave Mike a basilisk stare.

'You heard me. Let's cut to the chase, we haven't got the time to say this twice, we need boots on the ground and we need them now.' Mike turned back to the police officer. 'Carry on, Inspector McAlpine,' he instructed.

'As I was saying—' said the colonel.

'Colonel, I regret to tell you this, but you are not in command in this situation. I am.' Mike couldn't have been any clearer and his voice was steely.

'You are junior to me, Collins, don't you forget it.'

The last straw. The last *fucking* straw. Mike cracked. 'I am *not* your subordinate, I am a civilian and emergency planning officer and you have no authority over me *at all*. If you don't do as you are bloody told I will have the police remove you from the scene.' His rage was partly driven by adrenalin because although he knew he was in the right there was a part of him that told him he couldn't speak to a lieutenant colonel like this. Except that he was.

Beside him he heard Seb take a sharp intake of breath.

The colonel's lips went white with rage. 'I'll have you remember who you are speaking to.'

Mike raised an eyebrow and then turned to the inspector.

Keeping his voice as calm as possible to disguise an internal turmoil, he said, 'Dave, can you get your officers to remove this man from the building? He is impeding operations.'

'Certainly, Mike.' The police inspector gestured to two of his men who began to approach the colonel.

Rayner glared about him as he backed away from the approaching policemen. 'You'll regret this, Collins,' he snarled, before he headed towards the door. 'I shall be making a full report to the district council, the county council and the brigade,' he shot before he exited the pub, slamming the door behind him.

In the corner of the pub the policemen resumed their briefing of the section commanders. Mike shut his eyes and took a long breath, opening them again when Seb clapped him on the shoulder.

'Well done,' said Seb.

Mike shook his head. 'Bang goes another job.' He could feel his shoulders sagging with dejection. He *really* shouldn't have done that. He gazed at the bottles behind the bar wistfully.

'That's not going to happen. I for one will stand up for you and so will the policemen here. Rayner was throwing his weight around with absolutely no authority.'

'Maybe. I just wish I could be so certain. Susie and I don't need any more bad luck.'

'More bad luck?' said Seb.

Mike nodded. 'You have no idea. I'll fill you in when this is over. That is, if you want to know.'

'Of course I do. I didn't know things had been so tough.'

Mike shrugged. 'At least we're better off than the folks hereabouts. And us gassing isn't helping them. Come on, let's get out there and lend a hand.'

Chapter 41

When Susie woke up the next morning the first thing she was aware of was the sound of rain still pattering against the windows. Then she remembered Mike was out dealing with flood defences – being OIC sandbags wasn't such a joke any more – and finally she remembered about her daughters' truancy the previous afternoon and evening. With a groan, as everything piled into her brain, she rolled onto her back and gazed at the ceiling. Why was life so utterly shit? she wondered.

In order to help blot out the vileness of her own circumstances she leaned over and hit the 'on' button on the bedside radio and switched on the light. The sound of a seventies pop classic filled the bedroom and as the chorus faded away the presenter from the local radio station announced that they were going live to a report from the Bavant valley. Susie pricked up her ears.

The report started off with a vivid description of the river and then narrowed down to stories of flooded houses, pensioners being rescued by the fire service, the centres where the locals were being given beds, shelter and food and the heroic work of locally based soldiers who were trying to stop the terrible situation getting worse.

'And with that,' said the female radio journalist, 'back to Andy in the warmth of our studio.'

At least, thought Susie, there was no mention of any casualties which meant Mike might be wet, cold and miserable but he was still fine. And, given the terrible situation of some of the locals, she had precious little to bitch about. Yes, the twins were being a nightmare at the moment but they were nearly teenagers so probably no worse than many other girls of the same age, they could do with more money, she hankered after a nicer house and Mike certainly deserved a better paid job, but compared to what other people had going on...no, she needed to be grateful for what she had and stop moaning.

It might be only seven in the morning on a Sunday but she needed tea. Susie swung her legs out of bed and stood up, glancing out of the window as she did. Shit a brick! She could see from the light of a street lamp that half of the front garden was under water. The concrete bridge had water flowing over it and water was racing down their road, towards the fields at the end, in a flood that must have been almost a foot deep. Susie ran down the stairs and opened the front door. The water would have to rise another foot or two before things became really critical so the house was safe for the time being but for how long? She slammed the door again, put the kettle on then went to the computer in the corner of the sitting room and switched it on. When she'd made her tea she returned to it and Googled 'flood warnings'.

Thank God for the Internet, she thought as the Met Office flood-warning site filled the screen. Quickly she bunged in her postcode. *Be prepared*, warned the site. Susie flopped back in the office chair and took a sip of tea as she stared at the computer. Be prepared? What did that mean? Blow up the water wings? Leave? Move their possessions upstairs? Susie swivelled her chair around and looked at their furniture.

Could she and the two girls get that lot upstairs? Some of it, obviously; the TV, the coffee table, the computer, the smaller stuff maybe, but the three-piece suite, the fridge freezer or the washing machine? No way. And there was another question Susie wanted answering – how much worse might it get?

She picked up her mobile. She knew Mike would be busy but hell, if he didn't have the answer, who would? Besides, how long would it take him to answer her question? She dialled his number. She listened to it ring and ring before she got diverted to voicemail. Bum. She left a brief message and then sent a text and when she'd done that she went and woke up the twins.

Peremptorily she flicked on the light switches in both rooms and then entered each room in turn to shake her daughters by the shoulders, telling them that she didn't care it was the weekend, there was an emergency.

'Wha . . .' said Katie, the first twin she woke, as she rubbed her eyes.

'Gerroff,' was Ella's response.

'The house is about to be flooded,' snapped Susie from the landing where she had flicked back a curtain to see what the water level was doing.

That woke them up.

'How, when?' said Katie.

Ella jumped out of bed and looked out of her window at the view over the almost pitch-dark Downs to the rear of the house. 'No, it isn't,' she said, frowning.

'Check the stream at the front,' said Susie.

Both girls padded out onto the landing and stood beside their mother. They froze when they saw what was happening outside.

'What are we going to do?' asked Katie.

354

'First, you're going to help me move everything we possibly can upstairs. I've left messages with Daddy to see if it's feasible for us to get out of the village. I don't know how bad it is around about. If it *is* possible to leave, I'm going to ring Maddy and see if we can stay with her; if it isn't we'll have to camp upstairs until either the floods go down or someone comes and rescues us.'

Both girls looked genuinely frightened. 'And what if they don't?' whispered Ella.

'They will,' said Susie. 'We'll be safe if we stay put and we'll only try and leave if I can be absolutely sure we can get out. The last time that stream almost flooded it was only this bit of the village that was affected because of the spring up the hill from us. If you remember the rest of the village was fine, it was just this estate that almost went under. This time though, the flooding isn't the result of a freak cloudburst, so I don't know.' She shook her head.

'So, you mean, everywhere could be flooded,' said Katie.

Susie gave her daughters a hug – the previous evening's shenanigans forgotten now something more serious had taken her attention. She felt helpless and useless in the face of such a potential disaster but there was nothing she could do to influence events. She could, however, with the help of the twins, try and save some of their possessions if the water did make it into their house.

'I don't know. We've got to hope it isn't. And in the meantime we've got to try and save what we can here, not that we *will* get flooded but better safe than sorry.' She smiled at her daughters with false confidence, trying to allay any fears they might have. 'So get dressed and I'll make you both a cuppa and then we must get busy.'

Ten minutes later she and Ella were busy hauling books,

the computer, and anything they could physically lift up the stairs. Susie put Katie in charge of stacking things in the spare room.

'Got to try and get as much as we can in here,' she instructed her daughter, 'so be as neat as possible and put the heavy stuff on the floor and pile the lighter stuff on top.'

Normally Susie might have expected Katie to make some sort of snarky comment back at her about grandmothers and eggs or some such, but on this occasion she just nodded meekly.

For the first half-hour Susie peered out of the sitting room window every few minutes to judge if the water level was getting higher. She couldn't tell if it was – or not significantly anyway, but equally it wasn't receding either. And it was still raining so Susie wondered if the ground could absorb any more water at all, or if any falling higher up was going to run straight off the Downs and exacerbate things. However, if any good was coming out of this horrid situation it was that the girls were being absolute stars; both of them really grafting without any sort of complaint at all. And then she was too busy to keep monitoring the water and concentrated on lugging everything portable upstairs. By the time they'd finished several hours had passed and they were exhausted. The three of them knelt on the sofa – one of the things they couldn't manoeuvre up the stairs, even though they'd tried – and leaned on the back of it to peer out of the window.

'I'm sure it's higher,' said Katie.

'I think so too,' said Ella.

Susie thought it was *a lot* higher – several feet nearer the house – but she didn't voice her thoughts; she didn't want to worry the girls unduly. In fact, she reckoned the water only had to rise by another few inches and it might come over the doorstep – or worse, up the drains. 'Maybe just a smidge,' she lied. 'Now, I think we could all do with some breakfast.' As she got off the sofa the lights went out.

The three looked at each other.

'That's breakfast stuffed, then,' said Susie.

Susie heard her phone trill. Eagerly, she grabbed it. Mike, at last.

'Hi, Mike,' she said. 'I need advice.'

'About? I'm really busy here, Suse, can't it wait?'

'No. I think the house may be about to get flooded and the power's just gone off. The girls and I have managed to move what we can upstairs but if the water comes in I really don't want to be trapped here. I need to know if the road from here to Warminster is passable. If it is, I want to take the girls to Maddy's.'

There was a pause as Mike took in what his wife had told him. 'The roads between you and Maddy's are OK as far as I know, as long as you avoid the Bavant valley. How bad is the stream with you?'

'Almost up to the doorstep.'

'You'd be better staying put.'

'I'll only go if I'm sure we can make it. But I don't fancy camping upstairs with no heating or hot food. And for how long?'

'No, I see your point. Look, I've got to go but don't do anything rash. Promise me. Don't take any risks. It isn't worth it to avoid being cold and hungry for a day or so if the worst comes to the worst.'

'No, I understand. I promise to be sensible. Love you.'

'Love you too.'

As Susie severed the connection she wondered why they'd both felt the need to say those last words. She gave herself a shake – they were not 'last words'. She was being a drama queen even thinking like that.

'What do you reckon, girls? Is it time to ask Maddy if she'll have us?' The pair nodded, gravely. 'Then, grab what you need for a couple of nights, plus your uniforms, school stuff... I'll give her a bell. Oh, and pack your kit in backpacks. We can't carry suitcases to the car, not in these conditions.'

'Mum,' said Katie. 'I know things aren't good but can El and I have our phones back? Please?'

Suddenly, in the scheme of things, the girls' recent behaviour seemed pretty minor in comparison. 'I suppose,' said Susie. 'But don't think that the matter of you and Ella smoking won't be addressed when things get back to normal.' If things got back to normal...

The girls scampered upstairs to pack as Susie rang Maddy. She explained the situation.

'And now the power's gone.'

'Susie, that's awful. Of *course*, you can come round. Do you want to bring anything from your freezer?'

Susie gave a hollow laugh. 'Maddy, I'd love to but I think it's going to be tricky enough getting me, the girls and the clothes we stand up in, across that wretched stream to the car without lugging frozen food too. No, kind offer, Mads, but it'll just have to be a part of the insurance claim if the worst comes to the worst.'

'OK. But promise me you'll go carefully and I'll see you in a while.'

As soon as Susie ended the call she went to grab a few essentials for herself and get the girls phones out of their hiding place. She looked at their iPads and considered relenting about those too. Maybe, given how much of a terrific help the girls had been she ought to. No, she decided: phones, yes;

iPads, no. Five minutes later the three of them were huddling in the rain on the doorstep wondering how best they could get to the car without endangering themselves.

Katie glanced up the road. 'I wonder if Ali's family is OK,' she said.

'I'm sure they are,' said Susie briskly. 'Besides, I've got enough worries of my own without wondering how other people are coping. Now, come on.'

Chapter 42

As Susie was working out how to get to her car without getting anything other than her feet wet, Seb was knee-deep by the bridge at Lower Bavant, not far from the pub where his wife and Luke had had lunch the previous day, only now the pub was a foot underwater and the road that led to it was all but impassable; the situation was likely to be made worse because of a large tree branch which had been swept downstream and which had fetched up in the middle of the old three-arch bridge that crossed the river at this point. Seb could feel the tug of the water as it swirled past his legs and every step had to be taken with extreme care. One slip and he could easily be swept away, but he put that thought from his mind as he leaned forward, one hand hanging on to the stonework of the bridge while, with his free hand, he tried to grab the wedged branch. The last thing the Bavant needed was a blockage and for the water to back up more than it was. Sludge-coloured water, which had the consistency of soup, raged under the shoulder-high arches and swirled violently past the old stone supports. With every minute more vegetation, more rubbish, carried by the flood, caught in the branch: plastic fertiliser sacks, carrier bags, cardboard, a milk crate were all festooned in the twigs like some hellish Christmas decorations but together they made the water jam the branch even more firmly under the bridge.

Seb became aware of another sound although it was almost drowned out by the eardrum-battering roar of the river. He reckoned his hearing had been subjected to quieter jet engines than this racket. However, he was concentrating hard on reaching the branch and he couldn't afford distractions. He didn't dare go further into the river; the force of the water was already almost enough to sweep him off his feet – another inch or two deeper and he was pretty certain the flow would be too strong for him to keep his balance. Clutching the parapet even tighter he leaned further, as far as he could without overbalancing, stretching, but still his fingers, cold and numb, couldn't grasp the branch properly. He managed to touch a twig and gripped it but as he yanked on it, it broke. Bugger.

Then he felt the sleeve of his jacket being tugged. He turned and looked. More by lip reading than through his hearing he saw a soldier standing just above him on the bridge saying, 'Sir, sir.' The soldier said something else but Seb couldn't hear. He shook his head and grabbing the parapet with his other hand he clung to the old stones as he made his way carefully to the bank and clambered up the slight incline till he was on the road. It was then that he recognised the soldier. Perkins. Lee Perkins, the one who'd been married to Jenna, the hairdresser. Seb didn't know he'd been posted back in – not that he ought to have done as Perkins, to his certain knowledge, hadn't come back to rejoin B Company...Not that now was the moment to be thinking of such trivial stuff.

'What is it, Perkins?' he yelled at the top of his voice.

Perkins bent his head to be close to Seb's. 'Sir, you should be roped on. I've got one in my vehicle.'

Perkins was right, of course. Seb knew he'd been taking a risk. He nodded. 'All right. Can you fetch it?'

Perkins jogged off and Seb stamped his feet in a vain effort to restore circulation. The rain was still drizzling down; not heavy but relentless and penetrating. Seb had been in some pretty inhospitable places in the world and had soldiered under some miserable conditions but, he thought, this was taking the piss. He saw a vehicle approaching – Perkins with his Land Rover and the rope, no doubt. The Land Rover puttered to a halt next to him, the tyres sending mini bow waves slooshing through the puddles and the driver's window wound down.

'Sir, you all right, sir?'

That wasn't Perkins's voice. Seb bent down and peered in. 'Hello.' It took him a second to recognise the face, then he twigged. 'It's Armstrong, isn't it? Sergeant Armstrong?'

'Yes, that's me, sir. From the LAD.'

Shit, the bloke Jenna Perkins had been shagging when he'd called around with the bad news about her husband. The *ex*-husband who was about to reappear with the rope. 'What can I do for you, Armstrong?'

'Actually, I was wondering if you were OK – stuck out here on your own.'

'I'm fine. Waiting for some support.'

'That's OK. As long as you're all right.'

Another vehicle drew up alongside Armstrong's Land Rover. This time it was Perkins.

'Off you go, then, Armstrong, mustn't keep you.' But it was too late. Perkins was already out of his Rover and heading round the front of the bonnet, a hefty length of rope coiled over his shoulder.

'No, mate, you stay,' Perkins said. He put his hand on the wing mirror to emphasise his words. He turned to Seb.

'We could use a hand.' He let the rope slip off his shoulder. 'To be honest, boss, I don't think you'll be able to haul that branch out by yourself; not given the weight of water holding it against the bridge.'

Seb knew Perkins was probably right but, equally, Armstrong probably wasn't the person he would have chosen to assist them – not given the shared history – but what alternative was there? 'Good point,' he said.

Lee bent down and peered into the vehicle. 'Sarge, could you give us a hand? That's if you're not wanted elsewhere.'

'Sure. I'll just park up.'

Jeez, thought Seb, this was all he needed. Not that, as far as he was aware, the two guys knew each other but if they realised their connection it could make things very tricky indeed. Still, the potentially tricky relationship between Armstrong and Perkins wasn't the priority right now. Right now they needed to clear the branch from the river.

Seb studied the river, the bridge and the mass of vegetation that was damming the flow. It was obvious that the branch had the potential to do two things: firstly it was going to make the water back up and cause this section of the Bavant to flood; and secondly the additional weight of water had the potential to damage the bridge, or even destroy it. And even as Seb watched, more flotsam and jetsam came thundering downstream only to get caught in the branch, thus exacerbating the situation. With every minute that passed, clearing this obstacle was getting more and more tricky.

Seb formulated a plan. There was plenty of rope so he would be tied to the Land Rover with one length and Perkins or Armstrong could belay him out to the tree where he would tie a second length to the thickest section, whereupon the Land Rover could drag the branch free of the bridge. Simples.

Or, at least, it seemed so in theory.

He explained his plan to his two subordinates.

'With all due respect, sir,' said Armstrong, 'you're the biggest and strongest and if anyone should belay someone else it should be you.'

Armstrong's comment made sense, of course it did, but Seb was uneasy about putting his juniors in a potentially dodgy situation. The river was a maelstrom and he couldn't ask them to do something he wouldn't do himself.

'Don't be a prat, sir,' said Armstrong as Seb paused before answering. 'You know what I'm saying makes sense.'

'And it isn't as if you haven't already had a go,' added Perkins.

Seb nodded. 'OK. So which of you is going to take the plunge?'

'Me,' said Perkins. 'I'm the lightest.'

Again Seb nodded. He took the rope off Perkins and extracted his pocket knife from his webbing. Deftly he measured out a couple of metres of rope and cut a length off before he tied it around his own waist and then fixed the other end to the Rover's tow bar. He repeated the exercise but this time cutting off a good twenty-metre length of rope. He tied one end to the back of the nearest Land Rover and, wrapping the rope around his right arm, across his back, over his left shoulder and round his left arm, he then passed the free end to Perkins to tie around his waist. The last, remaining, length of rope, he also passed to Perkins.

'When you get to the branch, tie this as firmly as you can and then I'll haul you back to dry land. Once we've got you safe we'll use the Rover to pull the whole thing out of the water. Well, that's the plan.'

'And what about me, guv?' asked Armstrong.

'You just get ready to help me out if I need a hand. And drive the Rover when we need it.' Seb looked at his tiny team. 'All set?'

Perkins nodded and began to head slowly towards the river bank while Seb paid out the rope. Perkins got to the edge of the water, turned and gave Seb a thumbs up and then stepped into the torrent. In two paces he was up to his knees and Seb could tell the soldier was having to battle to keep his footing. Having been in the river himself, Seb was only too aware of the bone-numbing chill of the water and the force of the current. He didn't envy Perkins a jot.

Suddenly Perkins disappeared and Seb was yanked off his feet. He landed with a sickening thump on his coccyx, the rope around his waist so tight he could barely breathe, and he was twisted round so his head was facing the river, in completely the wrong position to regain purchase with his feet.

'Armstrong,' he shouted in near panic. He tried to get to his knees but the weight of Perkins being dragged by the current was too much for him.

'Armstrong!'

He felt another pair of hands on the belay rope, taking some of the strain and the weight. Seb managed to get his feet under him and kneel up. He leaned back to get further leverage. The rope was burning the palms of his hands and was wrapped so tight about them he worried his knuckles might get crushed. And as for the pressure around his upper arms where the rope was wound around him . . . it was excruciating. But that was nothing to what Perkins must be experiencing, being battered and half-drowned in the seething Bavant river.

Seb redoubled his efforts as did Armstrong. Even over the thundering of the nearby water, Seb could hear the sergeant grunting with exertion as he heaved on the rope, his feet scrabbling on the muddy bank to keep his balance. Suddenly they could see a white disc in the water – Perkins' head, just above the raging river. They could see him gasping for air and then some of the strain came off the rope. He must have regained his footing.

Then he slipped again and disappeared. Seb heaved on the rope to do his level best to drag Perkins out of the water as Armstrong ran to the bank. He watched in horror as Armstrong waded into the maelstrom, then, when he was ankle deep, the sergeant wrapped his arm around the rope and waded out further. Now Seb had the weight of two bodies hanging on the belay line and no way could he try and pull the men out of the water. All he could do was stop them from being carried further downstream – or stop Perkins. If Armstrong lost his grip...

Seb watched, horror-struck, as Armstrong fought his way into the river, following the line, reaching for Perkins with his free hand. Where was the lad? thought Seb, desperation mounting with each passing second. How long had the corporal been under the water? Thirty seconds? A minute? No, it had to be longer. How long did it take to drown? He pushed that thought aside. He was *not* going to contemplate that possibility. He turned his concentration back to watching Armstrong, now bending down in the water, reaching forward... had he found Perkins? Had he got him? Yes!

He watched Armstrong bodily lift Perkins clear of the water. Instantly Seb braced himself and began to haul on the rope as step by step, Armstrong began to drag Perkins towards the bank. Seb did his level best to help with the deadweight of the casualty and, finally, the pair reached the bank and Armstrong pushed Perkins onto the land. With

Perkins' weight off the line, Seb was able to uncoil the rope and run forward to help.

'Is he breathing?' he yelled at Armstrong.

Armstrong, his chest heaving from his exertions, shook his head. 'Dunno, boss.'

'I'll start on the CPR – you call an ambulance.'

Seb flipped Perkins over and pushed his chin back to clear his airway before checking for a pulse. He couldn't feel anything so he switched from the pulse in Perkins' wrist to the pulse point in his neck. Still nothing. Seb pinched Perkins' nose and started breathing into his mouth. He gave the corporal several breaths before he began the chest compressions. Push, push, push and in his head he heard the Bee Gees' 'Staying Alive'. Push, push, push, push, *staying alive, staying alive...*

'Sir, my phone's fucked. Think it must have got water in it.'

Seb rocked back on his heels and rummaged in his inside pocket. He chucked it at the sergeant. 'Try mine.'

He went back to the compressions. Shit, it was hard work and double shit, he should have been counting. Thirty compressions then four breaths was the technique he'd been taught, and he'd no idea how many compressions he'd done. He took a break and did the breathing then back to the pumping. This time he counted and breathed into Perkins' mouth at the appropriate moment.

'How's he doing?'

Seb stared up at Armstrong as he returned to the compressions. 'Nothing yet.'

'The ambulance is on its way.'

'Good.'

'Want me to give it a go?'

'Let me finish this thirty off and do the mouth-to mouth.'

A few seconds later he handed over the pumping to Armstrong. His hands were right beside Perkins' name tape, stitched just above the breast pocket of his combats. There was no way he would miss it.

'Perkins?' he said to Seb.

Seb nodded.

'Jenna's Perkins?'

Seb nodded again.

'Blimey.' He carried on with the compressions before stopping after half a minute or so to administer mouth-to-mouth. He resumed pumping. 'How long do we go on for, boss?'

'Until we get a result or paramedics take over.'

'Do you think we'll succeed?'

'We are *not* going to fail. That is *not* an option.'

'No, boss.' Armstrong did a few more pumps. 'Jenna might not have been the best wife to this guy but she was fond of him, I know that. She won't forgive me if I fuck this up.'

He was about to bend forward to do mouth-to-mouth a second time when Perkins' chest heaved and water trickled from his mouth followed by a weak cough. Swiftly Armstrong rolled him on his side and more water poured out. Perkins coughed more and dragged in a big shuddering breath.

Armstrong closed his eyes and sighed heavily. 'Thank God for that.' He opened his eyes and stared at Seb, his face pale with tiredness and worry.

'Amen to that,' replied Seb with feeling. He leaned forward and looked at Perkins. 'Hey, buddy, how're you feeling?'

Perkins shook his head.

'Rough?'

Perkins nodded.

'You gave us a bit of a fright there.'

Perkins coughed again.

'You owe Sergeant Armstrong here a drink,' said Seb. 'I reckon he saved your life.'

Perkins switched his gaze to Armstrong and made an attempt at a smile. 'Thanks,' he mouthed and then gave Armstrong a weak thumbs-up.

Seb got to his feet. 'I don't know about you but I'm freezing.'

He went over to the vehicle and switched on the engine, thoughts of winching the branch out of the river long forgotten. He leaned in to the cab and flicked the heater switch up to full, before he returned to the other two soldiers.

'Give it a minute or two and we can go and sit in the cab – get a bit of warmth till the ambulance gets here.'

Chapter 43

Susie and the girls looked at the filthy water as it swirled across the road in front of them. After managing to reach the car and escaping out of the village they had all relaxed, thinking that it would be plain sailing to get to Maddy's. And so it had been – right up to this moment because, in front of the car, water was bubbling out of the drains at the side of the road and pouring over the tarmac. A stretch of the highway, a good two hundred yards long, was under water and Susie couldn't tell how deep it was. She clutched the steering wheel and stared at the scene. Did she dare risk trying to get through it? The water streamed into the drainage ditches on either side but still the level seemed to be rising. Even as she watched, the flood inched closer to her bonnet. It could be just a few inches deep or it could be a couple of feet and, if it were the latter, there was no way her little car would be able to make it through. Mike's exhortation not to take risks rang in her ears.

'Now what?' said Katie.

Susie shrugged. 'I'm trying to think if there's another way round. Ella?' Susie swivelled around in the driver's seat. 'Could you take a look in the seat-back pocket and see if there's a book of maps in there?'

There was the sound of rummaging and rustling. 'Not a thing.'

'The back parcel shelf?'

More rustling. 'Nothing.'

Susie sighed. And Mike had the satnav. And that was another problem with moving house a lot – you never really got to know your surroundings. Susie was certain that there had to be another way to Warminster, some back road or other, one that ran over higher ground and wouldn't be flooded, but she didn't know it. The only roads she knew were the routes that she travelled along on a regular basis. Maybe if she had a four-by-four she'd risk trying to continue but her little run-about was not the car to try to ford a flood in.

'We'll have to go back.'

'Mum,' the girls wailed in unison.

'But the house, the electrics,' added Ella.

'It's too dangerous. If we get halfway and get stranded things might get really dodgy. It's just not worth the risk. The house might be cold and you won't get a roast lunch but it'll be dry and safe.'

Both her daughters looked unhappy but even they could see that their mother had a point.

Susie picked up her phone from where she'd put it in the pocket behind the gear lever and pressed the contacts icon. She scrolled down the list to Maddy's number and hit 'dial'.

'Hi, Mads,' she said when it was picked up.

'Hiya, Susie. You on your way over? I've got Jenna arriving in a minute.'

'That's the thing, Mads, I'm going to have to cry off.'

'No! Why?'

'I can't make it. The main road is flooded and I daren't risk trying to ford it. Not with the girls in the car.'

'No. Is it that bad?'

'To be honest I don't know how bad it is, but if I get

halfway and have a problem...and maybe if I had something a bit more robust...'

'I'll come and get you. What's the point of Seb and me owning a four-by-four if most of the time I just use it for the weekly shop? Let's face it, the supermarket car park doesn't often require low-ratio gears.'

'But Maddy, you can't—'

'I can. When Jenna arrives she can look after the kids and I'll come and get you. So, that's settled then,' said Maddy, firmly. 'I suggest you find somewhere safe where you can park the car up and I'll come and find you.'

'If you're sure.' Susie was still very doubtful as to the wisdom. 'And if you change your mind when you see the flooding, you are *not* to risk it. Promise?'

'Promise. I know it's only a crappy old Mitsubishi but it's got lots of grunt – well, Seb says so. What do I know about cars? Anyway, I'll be with you in about half an hour – just as soon as Jenna gets here.'

Susie disconnected. 'Looks like we will be getting a chicken dinner after all.' She switched on the engine again. 'I'm just going to find a lay-by to park in and then we'll wait for Maddy to come and get us.'

Instantly the twins perked up no end.

Susie executed a three-point turn and headed back along the road, peering through the windscreen so as not to miss a lay-by or parking bay where she could safely dump her car. It was the middle of the morning but the light was so bad she was forced to switch her headlights on. She couldn't remember ever seeing such terrible weather. No wonder half of the county was drowning. She drove carefully back the way she'd come, along the deserted road until she came to a section with a wide flat verge. This'll do, she thought as she pulled off the road.

'And now, we wait,' she said to the girls as she switched the engine off.

Mike rubbed his hand wearily across his face and wondered when things might calm down enough for him to be able to grab some shut-eye. He'd had an attempt at getting his head down a couple of hours previously but Rob had come in and flapped around making ridiculous comments about how this flood was completely unforeseen and how no amount of emergency planning could have prepared anyone for it. At which point Mike had quietly reminded him that he'd tried to.

Rob had stared at him for a good five seconds as he took on board what Mike had said. 'Ah, yes, that report.'

Mike nodded. '"That report",' he agreed. 'That report', he added silently, that I sent to you and which, when I later checked, you'd signed off with the comments *no further action* and another, longer comment which implied that I was at worst scaremongering and at best being overcautious. Given the current situation, 'that report' and the subsequent comments were going to leave Rob in a pretty poor light.

Shortly afterwards Rob had scurried off looking, Mike thought, more than a little shifty and he wondered if Rob might have gone back to the council offices to retrieve – or destroy – the incriminating paperwork. Good luck with that, matey-boy, thought Mike as he glanced at his briefcase containing the files he'd liberated from the office.

But his encounter with Rob had banished all hope of a nap back then, and he'd been on the go since. So, he wondered, what were his chances of getting a power-nap now? Absolutely zero, he decided. The flood situation was getting worse and more and more homes were being evacuated

373

although, in some respects, other things were getting better as the emergency procedures began to kick in and more and more volunteers and organisations came on board; the evacuation centres now all had extra loos, generators had been delivered to where they were needed, the Plymouth Brethren and the RVS had set up emergency catering and soup kitchens and, with the army filling and shifting sandbags, at least the population knew that everything that *could* humanly be done to try and protect them *was* being done. But even with all those things sorted out, he really couldn't afford to stand himself down – not yet, at any rate.

He got up from his seat and made his way over to the coffee urn. Another cup might keep him going just a bit longer. He had to bring the police chief superintendent up to date about the situation as it stood now and he needed his wits about him if he was to write a comprehensive and comprehensible briefing paper.

'Ah, Collins, there you are.'

Oh, gawd. Bloody Rayner again – just what he didn't need. Mike turned. 'Colonel, what can I do for you?' Then he added, 'I'm just about to get myself some coffee, would you like one?'

'No time for coffee breaks, Collins. Work to be done.'

Mike ignored him and poured a mug anyway. 'Really? According to my team, we have pretty much got all bases covered.' He added milk to his brew.

Rayner shook his head. 'That was always your problem, Mike, lack of attention to detail. "Pretty much" implies that there are still outstanding areas of concern.'

Mike stared at Rayner, willing himself not to rise to the bait. As calmly as he could he asked, 'And what details would those be, details I haven't paid enough attention to?'

'The accident at the bridge. That could have been a fatality.'

'But it wasn't. Seb Fanshaw and Sergeant Armstrong's actions were exemplary and Perkins is on his way to hospital to be checked over. And besides, it wasn't a detail that was overlooked by my team, it was an accident that happened while Seb was trying to clear the waterway.'

'You should have given instruction to my men not to take risks.'

'From my understanding, Colonel, Seb was roped on, as was Perkins. They were not taking risks, they were reacting to the situation on the ground. And besides, it is not my job to micro-manage every situation as it happens and develops. Judgement calls on the ground have to be made by the people who are dealing with them; the officers and NCOs.'

'Typical,' said Rayner. 'No wonder the army let you go; you're still refusing to take proper responsibility for events.'

Mike was aware that a couple of police officers in the corner of the pub had stopped their own conversation and were listening to his.

He lowered his voice. 'I don't know what your game is, Colonel, but how I run my department and this particular emergency are none of your business. And now, as I have to brief the chief super prior to a press conference, I suggest you find something useful to do rather than stand here, irritating me.'

'You can't talk to me like that. I'll have you for insub-ordination.'

Mike shook his head slowly. This man was the bloody limit. 'Colonel, as I said before, I am not your subordinate and, what's more, I owe you no allegiance. I have things to do. Goodbye.' Mike turned away but was pulled back round by a hand on his shoulder.

'Don't you dare turn your back on me,' snarled Rayner.

Mike narrowed his eyes. 'I will do as I damn well please.' His voice was low and menacing. He turned again and this time Rayner grabbed his arm.

Over in the corner a policeman got to his feet. 'Is this man bothering you, Mike?'

'You stay out of it,' Rayner shouted across the room.

'Looks like he's assaulting you,' said the policeman.

'Don't be ridiculous,' said Rayner.

'Then remove your hand,' said Mike.

'I'll do more than that, I'll remove my men.'

It was Mike's turn to say, 'Don't be ridiculous.' Then he followed it with, 'Besides, you don't have the authority.'

The colonel's eyes were looking dangerously wild. 'Don't you tell me what I can and cannot do.' His voice was getting higher in pitch.

The copper moved closer. 'Come along, sir, before things get out of hand.'

Rayner rounded on the policeman. 'What are you implying?'

'Colonel,' said the copper, 'either you calm down or I'll be forced to remove you from the premises. Which is it to be?'

Rayner's mouth worked as he tried to formulate an answer before he turned on his heel and stormed out. Twice in one day, thought Mike. The man had to be deranged. For the first time since he'd been made redundant he was thankful he was no longer a part of 1 Herts and he pitied the poor buggers who were.

He went back to the table where he'd been working and picked up his pen ready to make a start on the report for the chief super.

'Hello, Mike.'

He dropped his pen in irritation. Not another interruption. He looked up and saw Seb. His attitude changed in an instant.

'Seb! How's Perkins? Thank God you and Armstrong got him out of the river.'

'It was mainly Armstrong, Mike. He's the one who risked his own life to save Perkins. All a bit ironic given that it was Armstrong who Jenna Perkins was having an affair with when Perkins got trashed in Afghanistan.'

'It probably makes them about even, then.'

Seb nodded in agreement. 'And to answer your question, Perkins is going to be fine. Armstrong went with him to the hospital, just for a bit of moral support.'

Mike's eyebrows shot up. 'Is that wise... given the past?'

'I don't think they're going to kick off. As you said, honours are about even now.'

'That's something. I need all the good news I can get.'

'You sound as if you've been having a bad time.'

Mike snorted. 'Not as bad as Perkins, obviously, but I've just had Rayner in here blaming me for what happened to him.'

Seb's forehead creased. 'What?'

'I know, the man's bonkers. Seriously, Seb, he's got a screw loose.'

'Tell me something I didn't know.'

'You've had trouble?'

'Nothing seriously career-threatening but...' Seb shrugged. 'How long have you got? And Maddy's fallen out with his wife.'

'Maddy? But she never falls out with anyone.'

'She has now. She and Camilla are at daggers drawn. And put it this way, I won't complain when I get posted out and I think half the battalion feels the same way. You're well out of it.'

'As I am beginning to appreciate.'

'Now, the reason for taking up your valuable time is that I came to borrow a phone. I lent my mobile to Armstrong and I haven't got it back.'

'Sure, be my guest.' Mike handed over his own mobile to Seb. 'I don't have Maddy's number on it though.'

'And I have no idea what her mobile one is. That's the problem with mobiles – you just press buttons. Just as well I know the landline one.' Seb dialled home.

'Who's that?' he asked when the phone was answered. 'Jenna? Can I have a word with Maddy?'

Mike tried to carry on with his report but couldn't help earwigging Seb's half of the conversation.

'Gone to get Susie? Why?...Oh, oh I see. Can you get her to ring Mike's phone when they get back? I haven't got mine with me...No, long story. I need to know they're safe...Yes...Yes, of course...By the way, I know he's not your husband any more, but Lee's in hospital.' Mike listened to Seb obviously calming down an upset Jenna. 'And it was your chap who rescued him...No, I know, you couldn't make it up...OK...That's fine...Bye.'

'So?' said Mike.

'Maddy's gone out in the four-by-four to get Susie and the girls who are trapped on the wrong side of a stretch of flooding.'

'Bugger. I knew Susie was planning on going to Maddy's – she was seriously afraid our house might flood. She'd moved stuff upstairs and everything. And then the final straw was a power cut.'

'The one that's affected half the houses in the area.'

'Exactly. So she decided to bail out. But I'm not happy that Maddy's involved and out in this.' Mike looked at Seb's face. 'And you're not either.'

'Maddy won't do anything reckless though, and neither will Susie. I'm sure they'll be all right.'

'Yeah. Yeah, of course. And they're on main roads. They'll be fine.'

The two men stared at each other, both trying to convince themselves that they were right.

After Seb had left, Mike returned to his briefing document, trying to concentrate and not worry about the plight of his wife, his children and Maddy. But given what he knew about the developing situation across the area, it was an uphill task.

Chapter 44

Jenna was sitting on the floor of Maddy's sitting room playing with Eliot, Rose and Nathan when there was a hammering at the door. She jumped up and rushed to answer it. Maybe it was Maddy back with Susie and her twins. She flung it open before she gave thought to the fact that Maddy would have used her door key.

It was that snooty cow, the CO's wife.

'Jenna? What on earth are *you* doing here? This is an officer's quarter.'

'And I'm Maddy's friend. I'm here for lunch.'

There was a sniff as Camilla Rayner took in the information. 'Lunch? Here?'

Jenna couldn't be bothered to reply. Nor was she going to invite the old bag over the threshold. 'Well?'

'I want to speak to Maddy.'

'She's not here.'

'I thought you said she's giving you lunch.'

'She is but she's had to go out. She's fetching Susie Collins who's stuck in the floods.'

'Is she now. When she returns I need to speak to her – about the community centre.'

'On a Sunday? Can't it wait till the weekend's over?'

There was a small snort from Mrs Rayner. 'I can't see why

380

the fact it is the weekend has any bearing on the subject. It isn't as if she works.'

And you, thought Jenna, are the sort who gives housewives and mothers a bad name. Not work! As if Maddy sat around loafing all day with two kids under four. And that was before she dealt with the sort of crap that Camilla pushed her way.

'I'll tell her.' Jenna began to shut the door.

'And you say Susie Collins is coming here too.'

Jenna nodded.

'Hmmm. I want to talk to her too. No need to pass on the message. I'll come back later – nothing like killing two birds with one stone.'

Camilla turned on her heel and swept off back down the path. There was something nasty, thought Jenna, about the way Camilla had said the word 'killing'.

Maddy drove her car along the road out of Warminster. So far so good, she thought, although she was a bit concerned that she seemed to be the only vehicle on the road to Winterspring Ducis. She pushed the 'on' button on the radio and then pressed the preset for the local radio station. An old Queen number filled the car with music. Maddy bowled along the road, the windscreen wipers flicking back and forth out of time to the music, which became too irritating, so she switched off the radio. Besides, there wasn't any traffic news on a weekend, was there? After about fifteen minutes she came to where the water was flowing across the road. The flood, steely-grey and intimidating, spread from field to field and over the tarmac. Maddy brought her car to a halt, her front wheels just a few feet short of the water, and pulled on the handbrake. She stared at the obstruction. How deep was it? she wondered. Did she have the driving skills to negotiate this? Did the car have sufficient ground clearance? From a deep memory she dredged the fact that she mustn't ease off the accelerator once she committed herself to driving through. She had to keep the exhaust gases pumping out the back to stop water flooding back into the engine. Whether it was the truth or an urban myth, she didn't know, but it was the only information she had.

As she sat contemplating her options and the risks a white van came along the road behind her. Like her, the driver paused, but then he overtook her parked vehicle and drove slowly into the water. He hadn't gone more than thirty or forty yards when he must have hit a lower-lying piece of road and the water suddenly went from being hubcap high to bonnet high. The van stopped abruptly. Maddy sent up a silent prayer of thanks that she hadn't continued.

As she watched, the van driver climbed out of his cab and waded slowly in the thigh-deep water back towards her. She hoped to God he didn't lose his footing. It didn't look as if there was much of a current but who knew, and she really didn't want to be a witness to a tragedy. Gripping the steering wheel and willing the man on, she saw the water he was battling through sink to knee level then ankle level as he neared her. She breathed a sigh of relief as she leaned over and pushed open the passenger door.

'Thanks, missus,' the bloke said as he leaned in. 'But you don't want me messing up your car. I'm soaked through.'

Maddy glanced at the back seat on which were toys, biscuit crumbs, used tissues and other bits and bobs of rubbish left by two small children. 'Mess it up? I think that horse has long since left the stable.'

The van driver climbed in gratefully.

'Look, I've just got to make a quick call, then is there anywhere I can drop you?'

'I was trying to get to me mum's in Salisbury but that's not going to happen. Where are you going?'

'Back to Warminster, I suppose.' Maddy got her phone out and rang Susie.

'Bad news, Susie. A van's just tried to get through the flood and failed. I daren't risk it. I think it's much deeper than it looks. If the van couldn't make it I doubt if I can.'

'Is your friend on the other side of this?' interrupted the van driver.

Maddy nodded. 'Hang on a sec, Susie.'

'If she can get to Ashton-cum-Bavant,' said her new companion, 'we could go round the back way and meet her there. When we had floods around here ten years ago that was the one village in the Bavant valley that never got cut off.'

'You sure?'

'I'm a delivery driver, I know *all* the roads around here.'

'Can you give my friend directions – and me for that matter?'

'Sure.'

'Susie,' said Maddy into her phone. 'I rescued the van driver and he's got a plan. I'm putting him on the phone now.' She passed over her mobile.

Swiftly, the driver ascertained from Susie exactly where she was on the road and which way she was facing before giving her instructions.

'You sure you've got that?' he said. He listened as Susie repeated his directions. 'Right, now if there's a problem on the Bavant Hinton road you'll have to call it a day but if you get to the Admiral Nelson pub safely you should be all right to get to Ashton-cum-Bavant. I suggest you head for the village green; you can't miss it. OK?' He handed the phone back to Maddy.

'I'll see you there. I hope,' she added. 'But no risk-taking.'

'Deal,' Susie said.

Maddy pressed the screen to end the call, started the car and executed a neat three-point turn. 'Right,' she said. 'Where to now?'

'I'll tell you the way as we go.'

'And when we've picked up my friend where do you want to go?'

'Nah – you're all right. I've got a mate in the village, I'll go to his.'

'That's funny, I've know someone who's just moved there too. Must be a popular place.'

'Dunno about popular but it doesn't flood so that's got to be a bonus. Left here, missus.'

Maddy stopped talking and concentrated on driving down the narrow unfamiliar lanes. In nice weather and in the summer it might be quite pretty, but right now, as she drove under sodden trees that arched over the road in a rather menacing way, she felt nothing but a sense of vague unease. Apart from anything else, she was in a car with a completely strange man, in the back of beyond, with floods all around. What on earth had she been thinking of when she offered him a lift?

Mike finished writing his briefing for the chief superintendent and read back through it, checking he'd covered all the main issues that had had to be addressed since the Bavant had burst its banks and the Bavant valley drainage system had been overwhelmed. He glanced at his watch – good, all done and an hour or so to spare. He looked longingly at one of the pub's easy chairs. Thirty minutes. Just thirty minutes' zizz was all he asked for. He headed over to the chair and slumped into it. God, he was knackered.

'Wake me up at eleven thirty,' he told the coppers, directing operations at the other end of the pub.

'Sure thing boss,' one called back.

Within seconds of him leaning back in the chair and putting his feet up on a nearby table he was fast asleep. On the table, a few yards away, his phone buzzed, unanswered.

'Don't know where your dad is,' said Susie. 'He's not answering his phone but I expect he's run off his feet.' She'd wanted to ring him and tell him of her change of plans. She thought about sending him a text but she changed her mind. She was crap at texting and Mike presumably had more important things to do than worry about his wife taking a bit of a detour to meet up with her friend. She slung the phone in the dashboard pocket behind the gearstick, put the car in gear and headed back the way she'd just come, looking out for the right turn that Maddy's random van driver had assured her would take her to a village where they could rendezvous. Not that Maddy actually had to give her a lift now because, if the driver was right, she could bypass the flood via this little village and head on to Warminster, but maybe he reckoned that, with her being a woman, she wouldn't be able to remember all the directions for the complete journey. He could be right, she thought, the ones for half the journey were complicated enough. A mile along the road she found the turning and headed off the main road onto a narrow lane. She eyed her new route warily. He'd better be right about this road not flooding, she thought. She didn't fancy reversing back up this lane if she couldn't get through.

Carefully she drove on, the hedgerows on either side brushing the paintwork of the car. Every few hundred yards there were passing places but there was nowhere that offered an opportunity to execute a three-point turn if she had to retrace her tracks. She began to feel more and more apprehensive about the route. And face it, she thought, neither she nor Maddy knew anything at all about the van driver. He might have been lying through his teeth about his local knowledge; thinking it a huge joke to send some poor woman and her kids traipsing halfway across Wiltshire. Susie began to wish she'd just turned around and headed back to her house.

'Where are we, Mum?' said Katie.

'On our way to meet Maddy,' said Susie as brightly as she could.

'But where *are* we?'

'Darling, I can't give you a grid reference.'

'Are we lost?'

Of course not. Now let me concentrate, I have to remember the nice man's directions.'

A hundred yards further on, she came to a fork in the road. Turn left, she told herself. Right at the next one. But doubts assailed her. She was sure that the instructions she'd repeated back to the van driver had been left, right, straight on, left, left, straight on...But now she wondered if she'd misremembered. Might it have been *right*, left, straight on, left, left...? No. She was sure she'd been right the first time. If only the buggers round here thought to put up a few signposts. She headed left.

*

'Where do you want dropping?' said Maddy as they passed the boundary sign for Ashton-cum-Bavant.

'The pub'll do, thanks. Just around this corner and it's on the left. My mate lives just along from it.'

'OK.' Maddy looked at the village. So far she didn't recognise any of it. Obviously, the last time she'd been through it, with Luke, they must have come in on a different road.

The pub was exactly where her passenger promised it would be and he climbed squelchily out into the rain. Maddy glanced at the floor mat, glistening with water, and wondered how difficult it was to dry out a car.

'Thanks, missus. Hope you meet your friend all right. And you know your way back home.'

'I'll be fine.'

It was only after her passenger had gone that she realised she hadn't a clue what he was called or where to find him again. Oh well.

Maddy drove down to the village green where all the roads into and out of the village met, and saw Rollo's house. Now she recognised the village and if, no...*when* Susie found her way to the village she couldn't miss the green. As Maddy parked up she looked across to Rollo's house. The lights were on and it was tempting to drop in and say hello but she didn't want to miss Susie. She glanced at her watch. If Susie got to her in the next ten minutes or so she could get them all back to hers in ample time to get the chicken on for lunch. Good, she thought, as she settled herself more comfortably in her seat.

'Mike...Mike! Mike, wake up.'

Mike opened his eyes blearily. It took him a second or two to work out where he was.

'Mike, it's eleven thirty.'

'Oh…yes. Thanks.' He swung his feet off the table and stretched. His neck clicked uncomfortably and his left foot had pins and needles. He supposed the short sleep might have done him some good but, right now, he felt rougher than ever. He staggered to his feet and stamped to try and get the circulation going in his legs. Right, time for another shot of caffeine before he headed up to the rugby club where the press conference was scheduled to take place. The chief super wanted him there early to go through the brief with him before he faced the reporters and the cameras. Mike went to the urn in the corner and poured himself a coffee before wandering over to the team controlling their assets on the ground; the guys with the sandbags, the local volunteers and the emergency services.

'How's it going?' he asked as he sipped his drink.

'No dramas – well, nothing unexpected. Nothing we haven't been able to cope with. The river levels haven't got much worse and the Met Office reckons the rain is going to ease off later today so, hopefully, by tomorrow, things will start to get better rather than worse.'

Mike nodded. 'And the evacuation centres?'

'Most people have found other places to go; friends, family and the like. Of course there's a few with nowhere else but the Plymouth Brethren are making sure they are as comfortable as possible. You know what the British are like; everyone is being pretty stoic. Lots of stiff upper lips and Blitz spirit.'

'Hmm,' said Mike. 'They probably won't be so braced up when they get back to their homes and see the damage.' He took another slug of his coffee.

'Umm, another thing. We've had a request from gold for waders and some high-vis jackets. New if possible.'

'New? What's wrong with issuing stuff from stores?'

'Just passing on the message.'

'See what is available. I imagine we'll have some kit that's never been used. If not, just try and clean some up so it looks new. How about that?'

'I suppose...'

'Right, well, I haven't got time for trivia like that, not when I've got to meet the chief super. Mustn't keep the top brass waiting.'

He downed the rest of his drink in two large gulps, grabbed his paper and his waterproof jacket and headed out, into the rain, through the pub car park and up the hill to the rugby club. Left behind, on the table in the pub, his phone buzzed again.

Chapter 45

Susie tried to stem the increasing feeling of complete panic. She'd been driving for nearly thirty minutes and from what the van driver had told her the journey should have only taken about ten. She had no idea where she was, the directions now made no sense at all and to cap it all the petrol warning light had come on.

She stopped the car, not caring if she completely blocked the road. Tough if someone wanted to get past. In fact, if someone wanted to get past she'd be just thrilled – she could ask directions back to the main road. Stuff a roast chicken lunch, stuff being in a warm house, all she wanted right now was to be back in Winterspring Ducis.

'Are we lost, Mummy?' asked Ella in a slightly shaky voice from the back seat.

Susie turned around and nodded. ''Fraid so, hon. I passed a gate to a field back there, I'm going to turn around and head back to the main road. Sorry, sweetie, but I think we'd be better off going back home.'

Ella nodded.

'But if we're lost,' said Katie, 'how do you know how to find the main road?'

'I'm sure we'll come across it sooner or later. And anyway, I shall knock on the door of the first house I find and get new directions. I'm sure there's bound to be a Good Samaritan around here somewhere. I'm just going to ring Maddy and tell her not to worry and to go home herself.' She picked her phone out of its pocket and called Maddy. No point in keeping the poor woman hanging around any longer. She waited for the phone to start ringing, but nothing. What? She looked at the screen; typical, no bars, no signal to be had here.

'Girls, have either of you got a signal?'

'Mum, we haven't got anything,' said Ella. 'Our phones haven't been charged since you took them so the batteries are flat.'

'Oh.' Bugger. 'OK, I'll turn around, drive back a way. There must be somewhere around here where we can get a phone call through.' She handed Katie her mobile. 'Shout if you get a signal and I'll stop the car.'

She switched the engine back on and, looking over her shoulder, reversed back up the lane to the gate and turned the car around. All she wanted now was to find that blasted main road and get back to the relative safety of her own home. Even if it had been flooded, and was cold and damp and miserable, it would be better than sitting out here, miles from anywhere and low on petrol.

The rugby club was packed out, thronged with press representing newspapers, television and radio. On his way to the clubhouse Mike had passed half a dozen vans with satellite dishes on their roofs ready to beam the stories back to London, or wherever, ready for the next newscast. Inside, at the far end of the room from the door and the bar which stretched the width of the room, a couple of portable lights had been positioned either side of the long table from which the chief superintendent would make his report of the latest situation and then answer questions. The table had been covered in a blue cloth and in front of the chief super's seat was a battery of microphones, most of which had the broadcasters' logos clipped to them. Between him and the table were rows of chairs seating dozens and dozens of reporters.

Mike squeezed down the side of the players' bar, stepping over cables, briefcases and legs to make his way to the front. He looked about him. Where was the chief super? He collared a constable standing nearby.

'Where's the boss?' he asked.

'Been held up. He won't be here for another thirty minutes.'

'Thirty minutes?' Mike looked at the crowd in front of him. 'This lot won't be happy. Can you get hold of him and ask him if he wants to issue some sort of statement to keep this lot quiet till he can get here?'

'I'll call the station, sir, find out how the land lies.'

That wasn't quite what Mike had asked him to do but it would suffice in the short term. A couple of minutes later the constable came back to Mike with an answer.

'OK, sir, they passed on a message. He said could you do the press briefing? He says you probably know more than he does and if we wait for him to get here, the chances are the TV news reporters will miss the one o'clock news slot and they won't be happy.'

Mike suddenly knew what a deer in the headlights must feel like. Brief this lot?! He stared at the faces in front of him and realised one or two of them were familiar. He mightn't be able to put names to them but he'd seen them often enough on his TV in the evening. As he looked he noticed several of the assembled journalists were looking at their watches. In a few minutes those with tight deadlines to deliver an up-to-the-minute report of the situation would get anxious.

Mike took a deep breath. He could do this. He would feel more comfortable if he could have a stiffener first but that wasn't an option. He moved to stand behind the chair in the centre of the table and held up his hand.

'Ladies and gentlemen,' he began. The hubbub in the room died away and someone threw the switch for the lamps. Mike was half blinded for a few seconds. Sheesh, they were bright. 'Ladies and gentlemen, as you can see I am not the chief superintendent. My name is Mike Collins and I am the emergency planning officer for Winterspring District Council.' Now he'd got going, he began to feel more at ease. He pulled the chair out and sat down, then he moved the chief super's nameplate off the table and put his notes down in its place. Digital cameras flashed, red lights appeared on handheld film cameras and pens started to race across notebooks. Mike took another deep breath and began. 'So, the situation is this…'

Maddy was getting increasingly fraught. Where the hell was Susie? She should have been here ages ago. She glanced at her watch for the umpteenth time. Forty-five minutes. This was now ridiculous and worse, really worrying. Where *was* she?

Maddy picked up her phone and tried to call Susie.

'The person you are trying to call is unable to answer their phone right now,' an automatic message told her. Well, that's no bloody good, thought Maddy. She sighed and called Jenna instead.

'Maddy! Where are you? I was expecting you back ages ago.'

'I'm still waiting for Susie.'

'You mean she hasn't got to you yet?'

'No, and I can't get hold of her.'

'You're joking.'

'I only wish I was. I'm going to ring Seb to see if he can get some guys out looking for her.'

'You can't,' said Jenna.

'I'm not with you.'

'Seb phoned here earlier. He says if you need him, you've got to get Mike Collins to pass a message because he's lost his phone.'

'He's *what*?' Maddy screeched, frustration and worry finally making her lose it.

'Hey, Mads, I'm just the messenger.'

'But that's hopeless. I haven't got Mike's number, only Susie's, and I can't get hold of Susie...Oh shit, this is getting worse and worse.' Maddy reviewed the situation. 'OK, I'm going to come home. I've got a mate who lives here so I'll ask him to keep a lookout for Susie and tell her how to get to ours. There's nothing I can do, stuck here. In the meantime, if you can bung that chicken in the oven so that lunch can be served before it's time for supper, I'd be very grateful.'

'Sure thing, Mads. See you in a little while.'

Maddy chucked her phone on the passenger seat and drove to the other side of the green and Rollo's house. She parked the car in his drive and raced past the elegant façade of the country house to the front door where she hauled on the bell-pull. Trust Rollo, she thought, not to have an ordinary electric doorbell like most of the rest of the population of the country. She sheltered under the beautiful shell porch until the door was finally answered.

'Maddy!' He sounded pleased to see her.

'Sorry to spoil things but this isn't a social call, Rollo, and I'm not stopping.'

'You can still step inside in the dry.'

Maddy did and was instantly gobsmacked by the chequerboard-tiled hall with its grand staircase and beautiful proportions. So much for her army quarter, she thought, before she explained the situation. 'So can I ask you to keep a weather eye out for this car – a green Golf? And if she does get here can you give her directions from here to my place?'

'Of course, Maddy. Anything for you, you know that.'

'Good, then I must be going.'

'So soon? Don't you want to see round my new pad?'

Of course Maddy did but not today. 'Another time. Tell you what, I'll come to the house-warming. I have no doubt it'll be one helluva party.'

'You have no idea of the plans I'm making.'

Maddy opened the door again. 'A green Golf. Don't forget. And if she appears you're to ring me. Understand?'

She returned to her car and as she put the key in the lock she saw Rollo waving goodbye to her. What he needed, she thought, was a wife. As she pulled away she began to wonder if she knew anyone who might be suitable. Stop it, she told herself. He was *not* good husband material. Mind you, she thought, given some of Seb's track record, what exactly *did* constitute good husband material?

When she got back and let herself into her house, she found a scene of relative tranquillity with Eliot asleep on Jenna's lap, while Rose and Nathan were sat on the floor each with a biscuit and a drink watching *Peppa Pig*.

'Hiya,' she said.

'Shh, Mummy,' remonstrated Nathan before he returned his attention to his favourite TV programme.

'Hang on,' whispered Jenna, moving Eliot so he draped

over her shoulder and hauling herself out of the chair. She and Maddy went into the kitchen.

'The chicken's on,' said Jenna as she reached for the kettle. 'Tea?'

Maddy looked at the kitchen clock. 'Given the morning I've had, I think it's time for something stronger.'

'Go for it,' said Jenna.

Maddy opened the fridge and got out a bottle of white wine. She offered it to Jenna.

'Yes, please,' she said. 'So what is happening about Susie?'

'I don't know. I can't get hold of her, I can't get hold of anyone who can, I can't even get hold of my husband and I'm worried sick. I've just got to hope she'll be all right.'

Chapter 46

S usie stared at the road ahead in horror and at the water which covered it from side to side.

'Oh no,' she whispered.

'It wasn't like this before,' said Ella.

'If we came this way – but we may not have done. I'll turn around again; see if we can find another way.' Susie felt panic rise in her again. She had to stay calm for the children's sake. It wasn't fair to them to let them know just how worried she was. 'Has my phone got a signal yet?'

'Nothing,' said Katie.

'Well, I'm sure we'll get one again soon.' For the second time that morning Susie put the car in reverse and backed down the narrow lane. It was tricky trying to steer down the centre of the tarmac; there was very little leeway for the least deviation and Susie went painfully slowly. After several hundred yards she found another gateway into a field and swung the car backwards into the gap.

There was a sickening thump and crunch and the back of the car slumped at a crazy angle.

'Mum!' shrieked Ella and Katie.

Susie froze. Oh fucking hell, she thought. 'It's probably nothing,' she said. 'I've probably just hit a stone or something.' Her hands were shaking, she noticed, as she switched off the engine. She clambered out of the car awkwardly; the silly angle that it was at didn't help matters. Praying that it was nothing serious she made her way to the back of the car. Nothing serious? Oh no, it was desperately serious. She shut her eyes – how on earth had she not seen the ditch? How could she have missed it? The rear wheel had gone into it and the bodywork of the Golf now rested on the sodden bank. The car wasn't going to be going anywhere – not now, not without a tractor or a recovery vehicle to tow it out. Susie wanted to cry.

The *Peppa Pig* DVD finished and was ejected from the machine.

'Aw,' complained Nathan. He stumped across the room on his chubby legs and took it out of the slot ready to put it back in its box.

Jenna, still cradling a sleeping Eliot while Maddy pottered around in the kitchen preparing vegetables, picked up the remote and flicked through the channels. She went past the BBC news channel and her finger froze on the button.

'Mads. Mads! Come in here.'

Maddy dashed through.

'Look!'

Maddy did and there on the screen was Mike Collins, holding forth to dozens of the nation's pressmen and women.

'Blimey,' she said.

The two women listened as Mike took questions about the state of the floods, the number of people evacuated, the arrangements for the evacuees and predictions for the coming days.

'He sounded quite the man of the moment,' said Maddy, as the newscaster introduced the next story.

'Pretty impressive,' agreed Jenna.

'Susie ought to be here, watching this with us.'

Jenna nodded. 'Ought you to try her again?'

'I did, just a while ago. Nothing.'

'Do you think we ought to ring the police?'

'And tell them what? We don't even know where she is. For all we know she might be safe at home.'

'If she were at home she'd be answering her phone,' Jenna reasoned. 'She gets a signal up at Winterspring Ducis. Unless she's run out of battery.'

Maddy dithered. Was she being overdramatic about the possible plight of her friend? The police presumably had more than enough to do without her adding to the burden by reporting Susie missing. But then, if she didn't and something happened to Susie and the girls, she'd never be able to live with herself. She was on the brink of picking up the phone when someone hammered at the door.

'What the...?' Maddy was perplexed. Who would bang on the door and ignore a perfectly serviceable doorbell?

'Ahh,' said Jenna. 'Forgot to tell you, Camilla wants to see you.'

'Camilla?' Maddy headed for the front door and opened it. 'Camilla.' She faked a smile of greeting. 'What can I do for you?'

'I want to talk to you about the community centre files. There are some missing.'

Maddy folded her arms; she wasn't having her Sunday interrupted for this. No way. Camilla might sleep, eat and breathe the army twenty-four-seven but Maddy had a life. 'You know, now really isn't a good time. I've got a friend here for lunch and I am seriously worried about Susie and her daughters who were also due to join us. They were supposed to meet me earlier and they never turned up. So, to be honest, the last thing I want to do right now is worry about some missing file. I'm sure it's something that can wait till Monday.'

'Well, really,' said Camilla, taken aback and disapproving of Maddy's attitude.

'Sorry, but that's how it is.' Maddy started to shut the door. 'Although...are you in contact with the colonel?'

Camilla nodded.

'And he's out helping with the floods, like the rest of the battalion?'

Camilla nodded again. 'But I don't see—'

Maddy held her hand up to silence her. 'Good. I need to get a message about Susie through to Mike. Seb's lost his phone and I don't have Mike's mobile number so, presumably, Jack might be able to help with that.'

'You want Jack to phone Mike?' Camilla looked down her nose at Maddy.

'Well, yes. Or talk to him, or send a runner with a cleft stick. Camilla, really I don't care how Jack communicates with Mike but he needs to know that Susie might be stuck out there in the floods. I'm really worried, Camilla.'

'But why should Jack do something for a man who has given him nothing but trouble?'

'For God's sake, Camilla, I have no idea what you're on about and even if I did understand we're not talking about some petty squabble between two grown men, but about a woman and her children who might be in danger.' Maddy was tempted to tell Camilla to grow up but decided that might be a step too far.

Camilla leaned closer towards Maddy. 'Do you realise that Mike has done his best to humiliate and undermine Jack?'

From what Maddy knew of Jack she thought he was perfectly capable of humiliating himself. 'But how? How could Mike do that; he's nothing to do with Jack or the army any more.'

'He's the emergency planning officer and, according to Jack, he's been behaving like some jumped-up little Hitler. Jack's in charge of 1 Herts and yet Mike seems to think *he* should direct operations at the flood, not Jack. And what authority has Mike got for that, tell me that?'

'I...I...' Maddy was at a complete loss. 'But isn't that his job?'

'How on earth can someone like Mike order round Jack?'

The way Camilla put it, she made Mike sound like he was some sort of plebeian imbecile trying to direct affairs of state, not an expert in his field managing extra resources.

'Look, Camilla, I don't want to get involved in this and I don't care what is going on between your husband and Susie's but it doesn't alter the fact that I think she's in real danger and the only way I seem to have of getting a message to the people on the ground is via your husband. So are you going to help or aren't you?'

Camilla stared at her and for a second Maddy thought she was going to refuse. 'If I must.'

Maddy just managed to stop herself rolling her eyes in exasperation. 'And I'll come round to yours on Monday to talk about the community centre, promise.' She had to placate the old bat somehow.

'Good, see that you do. Ten o'clock.' And with that, Camilla swept off. Maddy longed to call after her to remember to phone Jack about Susie but felt that it might just antagonise her into being contrary. Maddy didn't trust Camilla as far as she could spit.

'Will she do it?' asked Jenna, leaning against the sitting room door.

Maddy shrugged. 'If she's got the least conscience she will.'

Jenna snorted. 'If I were you, I'd report it to the police – just in case. Better safe than sorry, if you ask me.'

Mike finished the press conference and forced himself not to slump back in his seat as the reporters and cameramen filed back out of the rugby club bar. The TV and radio guys had buggered off some twenty minutes earlier to get the story back to their respective studios for the one o'clock slot but the print and other forms of media had stuck around asking further questions for some time. And now he felt absolutely wrung out, although he didn't think it would be terribly professional to allow his exhaustion to show publicly. It was partly lack of sleep but it was also because of the stress of being thrust into the limelight at no notice and being expected to handle a difficult situation with no experience of doing anything like it in the past. Trying not to yawn he gathered his papers together and then stood up ready to follow the last of the throng from the room.

'Well done, mate,' said the police constable he'd spoken to earlier.

'Thanks, you really think so?'

'The press are happy, you made sense, everyone understands what's being done to help the victims...I'd say that's a result.'

Mike felt a surge of relief that he'd really got things right. Thank goodness he'd not made a fool of himself in front of TV cameras and the nation's press. He headed for the door and the path down to the pub.

Outside the club it was still raining – no surprise there, he thought – and despite the fact it was still early afternoon it was already twilight. Down by the river, emergency lights were blazing as the army and volunteers continued to battle the floods with sandbags and Mike had no doubt that all along the Bavant valley the scene was being repeated. No one, he thought, could possibly say that everything that was humanly possible wasn't being done for the locals.

Wearily he pushed open the front door of the pub and headed back in to the warm and dry. The first thing he noticed, as he kicked off his wellingtons in the porch, was the noise level. A terrific hubbub of voices was cascading out of the bar. How come there were so many more people than when he left to do the press conference just forty minutes earlier? Where had they all come from? He pushed open the inner door to the saloon bar. Well, the noise level matched the number of people he saw – no mistake there. The place was chock full. Mike squeezed through the door and began to push his way back to the table he'd been working at before he'd left.

'ID, mate.'

'What?' Mike was confused – why on earth did someone want his ID? He looked in the direction the voice had come from.

'ID,' the voice repeated. It was a policeman. Then Mike noticed the copper's stab vest and the logo emblazoned across the front. He wasn't from the local constabulary but the Metropolitan Police. What the hell...?

'Sorry,' said Mike, 'can I ask why?'

The constable sighed. 'Security.'

'I gathered that,' said Mike, 'but I've been working from this pub for twenty-four hours now and no one has wanted it yet.'

'Maybe, but I want it now.'

Mike hauled out his lanyard from under his jacket and showed the constable his council pass.

'Thank you, sir.'

Mike pushed his way further into the room. In the corner, where the maps were pinned to noticeboards, he could see the chief super holding forth. So, the boss had managed to get here, at last. Mike wondered briefly what had held him up and then he clocked just who the chief was briefing. Bloody hell – the prime minister. The PM in a high-vis jacket and waders. Well, that explained the need for those and why new ones had been so important. And it also explained why he'd suddenly had to deputise at the press briefing. And no wonder there was security on the door.

Mike ducked away from the VIPs, the hangers-on and the brown-nosers all congregated around the politician. And – oh God, wouldn't you just know it – Colonel Rayner; trust him to try and cosy up to the prime minister. He found his way back to his corner and chucked his papers down. He'd been hoping to get another few minutes' shut-eye but fat chance with this circus going on around him. To keep himself awake he glanced at his phone. There was a missed call from Susie and another from Jack Rayner – like he was going to return *that* one. If that git wanted to talk to him he could walk across the bar and do it. Instead he returned Susie's. Straight to voicemail and there was no point in trying the kids' phones – not since he'd confiscated them himself. He hoped to goodness she'd got through to Maddy's. Of course she had. He'd have heard if she hadn't.

'Mike, can I have a word?'

Mike looked up to see the chief superintendent standing beside him. He dropped his phone back on the table.

'Of course, sir. What can I do for you?'

'I hear the press briefing went very well.'

'Thank you, sir. Of course, they weren't a tough audience. It wasn't as if I was in the frame for anything illegal or immoral, so no nasty questions, no curve-balls or anything like that.'

'Even so, Mike…' The chief super clapped him on the shoulder. 'And the PM would like a word, too. He caught the gist of your press briefing on the radio on his way down here. He was impressed.'

Blimey, praise indeed. Mike only wished Rayner had heard the compliment getting passed on, and then he checked himself for being so infantile. What did it matter what Rayner thought, anyway?

The chief super led Mike through the crowd of people, who parted as he approached as if he were Moses.

'Sir,' he said, when he reached the familiar figure, 'you wanted to meet Mike Collins.'

The PM stuck out his hand and grasped Mike's warmly. 'Mike, good to meet you. I can't tell you how impressed I was by the way you handled the press conference. Done like a true pro.' He laughed self-deprecatingly. 'And I should know. I'm also told that the smooth running of this operation is largely down to your planning.'

Mike could feel himself blushing and out of the corner of his eye he could see Rayner positively hopping with frustration that he wasn't being included in this conversation. 'Thank you, sir. I suppose I was lucky with my background.'

'Which was?' The PM sounded genuinely interested, but a bit of Mike wondered if it was a front that professional politicians were adept at putting on. Either way, he could hardly ignore the question.

'Ex-army, Prime Minister.'

'The army's loss is Winterspring District Council's gain, I'd say.'

'Thank you, sir. Not that it was desperately difficult to sort things out. Basically I made sure the essentials were in place—'

'Which were? interrupted the PM.

'Oh, er, shelter for the evacuees, food, power and sanitation – plenty of water and portaloos. And the teams working here have been utterly brilliant and tireless in sorting all of that out.'

'Even so, people get stressed and upset in these circumstances and I haven't heard much in the way of complaints.'

'With all due respect, sir, I think people are too busy at the moment, trying to keep the worst of the disaster at bay, to worry about complaining. I bet they will when it's all over. But in the meantime we're trying to keep everyone as well-informed as possible. Generally, as long as people know what's going on, or what's being done on their behalf, they stay calmer. It's being kept in the dark that gets people's goat. We've been careful to make sure as many of the victims as possible know what the emergency services have been doing on their behalf, and to inform people what they can do to help themselves, and, more importantly, what they can do to help others. People like to feel as if they are making a contribution – they feel valued. It all helps.'

'All I can say, Mike, is that it's worked. Well done. I'm proud to be a member of a country where we have inspirational chaps like you working on our behalf.'

The prime minister was led away by the chief super to meet other people who had been helping out with the floods and Mike was left with a warm glow at the words of praise.

Of course, he realised about a minute later, this had been praise from a professional politician – he would say such stuff, wouldn't he? – but, even so, it couldn't do any harm where his future was concerned.

He watched the PM's retreating back view and Jack Rayner, trying to muscle his way forward to have a word, but the PM's close protection officers thwarted that attempt, much to Mike's amusement. He turned away. Now that his moment in the sun was over, maybe he could get a few minutes' rest uninterrupted. Mike made his way back to his corner, right away from the PM's entourage, and sat down. He shut his eyes. Just five minutes...

'I see you were busy sucking up just now.'

Mike snapped his eyes open. Rayner. There's a surprise, he thought.

'I wasn't "sucking up",' he replied.

'It looked like it from where I was standing.'

Mike was very tempted to retort with, *And where was that? Out in the cold, right on the edge?* but decided it wasn't worth it. 'Look, Colonel, I am very tired. I've had a couple of hours' sleep at the most in the last twenty-four, so unless it's important could we leave this till another time?'

'If that's what you want. I was going to pass on some information but...' Jack smiled nastily, '...as you're too tired, it can wait.'

Momentarily Mike wondered what the information might be and he was tempted to ask what it was. But, fuck it. He'd rather get his head down than spend any more time at all talking to this git. 'Later then.' He hoped Jack got the hint.

'As you wish.'

Mike shut his eyes and was out for the count in a nano-second.

Chapter 47

'**M**um, I'm cold.'

'Me too,' said Ella.

'I know, darlings, I am too. And if the car wasn't kaput I'd switch the engine on to get the heater going.'

'Try, Mummy.' Katie's teeth were actually chattering.

Susie turned the key in the ignition again and the car coughed and spluttered but the engine refused to fire. She'd had several goes at getting it going, trying for thirty seconds at a time to get the engine to turn over, but the car wasn't going to play ball. Obviously, when she'd dropped the back end into the ditch the damage extended further than just bending a rear wing but Susie didn't know enough about cars to understand that ploughing the exhaust pipe into a bank and blocking it made it impossible for the engine to work.

'What have you got in your backpacks?' she said. 'Let's put on as many layers as we can.'

Ella, in the back seat, passed Katie's backpack forwards and unzipped her own. The girls extricated their school sweatshirts which they put under their hoodies and then put their anoraks back on top.

'Better?' said Susie.

'A bit,' they admitted.

Susie looked through the car windscreen at the encroaching

water. It had been down by the bend in the road a while ago and now the flood was only about twenty yards away. It wasn't deep – maybe only a few inches – but it was creeping closer and closer and who knew how deep it would end up once they were in the thick of it.

'Do you think we'll be here all night?' asked Katie.

'Goodness, no,' said Susie with false confidence. 'I bet half of the Wiltshire police force is out looking for us by now.'

'Do you think?'

Susie nodded. 'And it won't be dark for ages yet,' she added, more to reassure herself rather than her daughters. But as she said it she noticed the light was fading fast, the colours were starting to leach out of the already drab countryside. She glanced at the car clock. Three o'clock. At this end of November there was only about another hour left of useable daylight.

'Why haven't we seen any cars? asked Ella.

Why indeed, although Susie suspected it was because all the roads round and about were now flooded. 'It's not a very nice day to be out and about, is it? I expect most people have decided to stay indoors today.'

'I wish we had,' said Katie.

You and me both, thought Susie. 'It'll be something to tell your classmates on Monday.'

'If we get rescued,' said Ella.

'Of course we will.'

'But what if no one comes before it gets dark?'

'Well, we'll just have to put on *all* our spare clothes and snuggle down here for the night. But it won't come to that.'

'Won't it?'

'No.' And she hoped her own mounting feeling of panic didn't show in her voice.

'Mike. Mike!'

Mike opened his eyes and instantly he was alert. He glanced at his watch – three thirty – and then looked at the nearest window. It was getting quite dark outside. Another night of misery for the poor people of the Bavant valley. He yawned as the last vestige of sleep left him. He looked at the constable who'd woken him. 'You shouldn't have let me sleep so long. I only needed a power-nap.'

The police officer didn't look convinced. 'I'd have let you sleep longer, mate, but we've had a misper report.'

'Misper?'

'Missing person. A Mrs Susie Collins. Any rela—'

'Susie? That's my wife.' Mike felt a stab of worry punch him.

'Oh. She was reported missing an hour or so ago – by a Mrs...' The constable consulted his notebook.

'Fanshaw,' supplied Mike.

The constable looked up. 'That's right, sir. Anyway, we've had patrols out looking for her but they've not found any sign yet.'

That nugget of information wasn't helping Mike's blood pressure. He picked up his phone. Seb had called Maddy from his phone – the number would be in the call log. He scrolled through the menu till he found what he wanted and hit the icon.

'Maddy. It's Mike.'

'Oh, Mike. Have they found her?'

'No. Have you any idea where she might be?'

Maddy told him the story of the flood and the van driver and the planned rendezvous in Ashton-cum-Bavant.

'So she could be anywhere?' he said.

'Only south of that road, I would think,' said Maddy, with logic. 'Mike, you will keep me in the picture, won't you?'

Mike promised to, then he rang off and strode across the pub to where the maps of the area were. He squinted at the main one, his finger tracing the road from Winterspring Ducis to Warminster, and then south to the village of Ashton-cum-Bavant. The area Susie had to be in wasn't huge. The trouble was, floodwater now affected quite a sizeable chunk of it.

The chief superintendent joined him. 'I've just heard the news, Mike. I'm sorry.'

'It's a worry, certainly,' said Mike, trying to sound calm when he was anything but.

'We're going to task the helicopter.'

Mike was about to ask if it was necessary, but only because it seemed such a drastic step and he didn't really want to admit, even to himself, that his wife and children might be in serious danger. Instead, he just nodded and tried not to think about his family, out in the near-dark, in the pouring rain, cold, frightened and alone.

He busied himself with looking at the latest reports from the Environment Agency about the water levels and the forecast from the Met Office. He tried to find some positives in what they were saying but it was a struggle. The rain was set to continue through most of the night, although not as heavily, and the rivers were still rising but not as fast. The only conclusion Mike could draw was that things were set to get marginally worse before they got better. But how much worse?

'Mike?'

He put the briefing papers back on the table and looked around. Who wanted him now? Talking of things getting worse...

'Rob. What can I do for you?' he said.

'You didn't tell me the prime minister was here?' Rob glared at him.

Oh, for fuck's sake. Another twat who felt they ought to have been introduced. Mike counted to three.

'Well?' insisted Rob.

'I didn't know myself he was going to be here. I got back from standing in for the chief super at the press briefing and there he was.'

Rob's face indicated he didn't believe a word he'd said. 'Come off it.'

Mike had had enough. 'Do you know, Rob, I really don't care what you believe. I'm too tired and too busy to play games.' He turned back to the reports on his table.

'I hope you told him that the district council has done everything possible to try and mitigate the effect of a flood like this.'

Mike thought about the files in his briefcase, the peremptorily dismissed report about future flood defence planning, and nearly pointed out that while *he'd* done as much as he could, Rob had done the reverse. Instead he just said, 'The question didn't arise. All the PM wanted to know was what was actually happening and what we were doing to help those affected.'

'Oh.' Rob didn't look particularly placated – not that Mike cared one way or the other. 'Just as long as the council doesn't come out of this in a bad light. It wouldn't do, you know.'

Mike knew exactly what Rob was getting at and it wasn't the council he was worried about but his own poor judgement. 'No, Rob. I know what you mean.'

Oh yes.

Susie sat in the back of the car, cuddling her daughters, trying to keep them warm by holding them close to her. She wished she had a rug or a thermos or anything that she could offer them to help keep them warm but they'd left the house in such a rush she hadn't thought about an emergency like this. The only good thing, she thought, was they were still dry. She leaned across Katie and rubbed condensation off the window but it was so dark outside now she couldn't see a blind thing. She wondered what the water level was doing.

'Mum,' said Ella. 'My feet are wet.'

Susie froze. 'What?' She put her hand down and touched the mats in the footwell. Ella was right; the mats were sodden. Now things were getting really serious. She leaned forwards, squeezing herself between the two front seats and turned the headlight knob. Light beamed out across the road – or rather, where the road should have been. Instead they seemed to be in the middle of a lake.

Fuck, she thought as she sat back down on the back seat.

'What are we going to do, Mummy?' said Katie in a very shaky voice.

'Nothing much we can do,' said Susie. 'But someone will come along. Even if we have to stay here all night.' She put her arms back round her daughters and gave them both a cuddle. 'We may get a bit wet and we may get a bit cold but people survive much worse than this. We'll be all right. And I bet there are people out looking for us, lots and lots of people.'

'You think?' said Ella. She didn't sound at all convinced.

'Absolutely positive.'

'Mummy...?' said Katie.

'Yes, sweetie.'

'Is this punishment for being naughty?'

For a second Susie was dumbfounded. Why on *earth* would Katie think that? 'Of course not. Besides, it's not just us in this pickle, is it? Half the county is underwater and I can't believe all those poor people did something dreadful. Anyway, you haven't been so very naughty – not in the great scheme of things.'

'We have, though,' said Ella.

'I don't think smoking the odd ciggy deserves this.'

'But it wasn't just that,' said Katie.

'Maybe not, but I don't think we need to talk about it right now.'

'But we do,' insisted Katie.

'Like?' asked Susie.

'Like...' Katie dried up.

'Like we nicked money off you, Mummy,' said Ella.

Oh. Susie hadn't expected that.

'And we smoked pot,' said Katie.

Shit. Susie was at a complete loss. She had no idea what to say. The silence continued.

'Mum?' said Katie. She sounded close to tears.

'Sorry,' said Susie. 'Sorry, just...well, what you've owned up to is bit of a facer.'

'Are you really angry?' said Ella.

'More a bit shocked, really.'

'Are you going to tell Daddy?' asked Katie.

'I think I ought to, don't you?' On either side of her she felt the girls nod their heads. 'And I know he'll be a bit disappointed.' Susie raised her eyes. Disappointed? He was going to go ballistic. 'But if you never do any of those things again, he'll get over it.' Eventually.

'Do you think?' said Ella.

'We've all made mistakes. Done things we oughtn't to have done. It's learning from these things that's important.'

Silence fell. Susie wondered just how she'd break the news to Mike – if she got the chance to, that was. The silence stretched on. She wondered about suggesting they all sang to keep their spirits up but she wasn't sure whether it smacked of desperation or if it was just lame.

'We're not going to die, are we, Mummy?' said Ella after some minutes.

'No, no we're not. Trust me.'

Susie hoped to God she was going to be proved right.

And then the battery, run down by Susie's repeated attempts to start the car, finally ran out of juice and the headlights dimmed and went out.

Seb strode into the operations centre. He was wet and cold and utterly knackered – filling and shifting sandbags was exhausting and he hadn't had the chance to dry out properly after getting soaked at the river. He made his way over to where Mike was standing, by the maps of the area.

'Hi, Mike. Tell me the rumour I've heard about your missus isn't true.' But a proper look at Mike's exhausted and haggard face told him it was and Mike's weary nod confirmed it. 'God, I am so sorry.'

'They've scrambled the helicopter. I keep telling myself they'll be OK, but that business with Perkins was a close call. It brings it all home just how dangerous floods can be. I couldn't bear it if anything happened to them.'

'It won't.'

'But they've been missing for five hours now. Five hours.'

Seb patted Mike on the shoulder. 'You must be worried sick.'

Mike nodded. He gave a mirthless bark of laughter. 'I'm so worried I don't even want a drink. That's got to be a first.'

'Shit, I don't know what to say.'

'There's nothing to say, not till we find out what the situation is. One way or the other,' he added glumly. 'Thank God, Maddy rang the police to alert them that Susie was missing.'

'Talking of Maddy, can I give her another call?'

'Be my guest.' Mike handed over his mobile.

Five seconds later Seb was talking to her.

'You must be sitting on the phone, you answered it so quickly,' he said to her.

'I am. I'm so worried. Any news?'

'Not a sausage. And well done you, for reporting it to the police.'

'So didn't Jack Rayner pass the news on?'

'Rayner? Should he have done?'

'I had Camilla round earlier – I asked her to tell her husband. What with you having lost your phone and me not having Mike's number, I didn't know how to let you know Susie never arrived here. I asked her to help.' Maddy snorted in disgust. 'It appears she couldn't be bothered.'

'Jesus H,' said Seb. 'Look, I've got to go. I'll ring as soon as I know anything, promise.' He severed the connection and turned to Mike. 'You'll never guess what Maddy just told me . . .'

Mike's eyes narrowed as Seb finished the tale. 'I missed a call from him earlier so maybe he did try and pass on the news.' But his tone of voice suggested he didn't really believe this. 'And then when I saw him face to face later he was mad at me because the PM spoke to me not him. He said he had some information but that it could wait. He wouldn't . . . I mean, not even Rayner . . .'

Seb shook his head. 'I wouldn't put it past him.' As Seb said that, Rayner entered the pub, shaking water off his jacket and pulling his sodden beret off his head. 'Let's ask him, shall we?' Seb and Mike approached him.

'A word, please, Jack.'

Rayner looked daggers at Mike for calling him by his first name.

'Can it wait?' he snapped. 'I'm cold and tired and I'd like some coffee.'

'Actually, it can't,' said Mike. 'I expect my wife is cold and wet – and my children too.'

Rayner looked shifty. 'I don't understand.'

'Maddy asked your wife to pass a message to tell me Susie hadn't arrived at her house,' said Mike. Seb thought he sounded remarkably calm. If it had been him, he'd have probably had Rayner by the throat.

'I don't know what you mean,' blustered the colonel.

'I think you do. Maddy has just told us herself. So either Camilla didn't think the information was important enough to pass on, or you didn't. Either way, whichever of you is responsible, I think you are both utterly despicable.' Mike turned on his heel and left Rayner standing there with his mouth open.

'Seb,' said Rayner after a pause of a few seconds. 'Seb, I tried to tell Mike but he was too busy throwing his weight around. He wouldn't listen to me. You believe me, don't you? You know I wouldn't do anything like that.'

Seb didn't trust himself to answer and followed Mike across the room.

Susie had moved back into the driver's seat and was sitting with her feet on the passenger seat while the girls sat sideways on in the back, leaning against the doors with their knees crooked and their feet in the middle. Under them three inches of water sloshed around in the footwell while their breath fogged in the freezing air inside the car.

'What'll happen when the water reaches us?' said Katie.

'We'll get wet,' said Susie. 'But it won't come to that. The water will stop rising soon enough, you'll see. The rain has already eased off.'

'Not much,' said Ella, gloomily.

Susie checked her phone again.

'A signal isn't just going to magically appear,' said Katie.

Susie sighed. 'Maybe.'

She stared at her phone and thought about using the torch app to try and send some sort of signal – but to who? There hadn't been a sign of life around here for hours. And despite the lack of signal, she was wary of running her phone battery, as well as the car battery, down completely. Somehow, the fact that her phone still functioned gave her a crumb of comfort and to waste its power on the tiny off-chance that there was someone, out there in the darkness, who might just spot a glimmer of light seemed too remote to be worth considering. No, better to preserve this one resource, she thought, even if she wasn't entirely sure of her own logic. Disconsolately she put the phone back on the dashboard and stared out into the dark soggy evening. For a second she wondered if the light from the screen had left a residual image burned on her retina. A hundred yards away it looked as if there was light shining off the wet trees in a nearby copse. Then she realised there *was* a light shining off the leaves. And then she heard the wokka-wokka noise of helicopter rotors and saw the light came from a spotlight attached to the chopper.

As quickly as she could she swung her legs round and opened the car door.

'Mum,' the girls stated to protest before they heard what their mother had spotted.

Susie almost fell out of the car as she sploshed into the calf-deep, freezing water. She pressed her phone and then hit the torch app. Was the light bright enough? Would they see it? They had to, they just had to.

Chapter 48

Camilla was sitting on the sofa in her sitting room listening to opera and reading a book when she heard the front door slam open and then slam shut again.

'Jack?'

Nothing.

Camilla got up and went into the hall and saw her husband standing there, peeling off his wet combat jacket. Filthy water was dripping onto the fawn carpet.

'Darling, could you do that—'

'Don't you fucking start,' he snarled.

'Jack!'

He glared at her. 'What?'

'You're making a mess on the carpet.'

'Am I really?' he sneered. 'Like I care. Like I care about anything to do with the army.'

'Jack?'

He shook his head. 'Get me a drink. A Scotch – a big one.'

'Would you like some supper?'

Jack sighed. 'Maybe later. Right now I need a drink.' He sat down on the hall chair and began to unlace his sodden boots.

Camilla went into the dining room and got a tumbler out of the sideboard and then poured Jack a hefty slug of whisky from the decanter. Wordlessly she returned to the hall and handed it to him before heading upstairs. A couple of minutes later she returned with a warm towel from the airing cupboard and his dressing gown.

'Take your wet things off and come and sit down. The fire's lit. You'll feel better when you're warm and dry.'

Jack drained his glass. 'Get me another.'

Camilla was about to ask him if he thought this was wise when she saw the look in his eyes. She did as she was told. She consoled herself, on her return to the hall, that he seemed to be taking her advice about getting out of his soaked clothing and was towelling his semi-naked body down before he slipped on his dressing gown and pulled the cord tight round his waist.

'Want to tell me about it?' she asked.

Jack shook his head. 'Where do I start?'

Camilla led the way into the sitting room expecting Jack to follow her but he veered off into the dining room and, when he rejoined her, he was clutching the whisky decanter.

'They're all bastards and as for Mike Collins – if I still commanded him I'd have him court-martialled for gross insubordination, disobeying an order, dereliction of duty... and... and... I'd throw the book at him.' Jack took another slug of Scotch before he sat down.

'What happened?'

'I've already told you he thinks that as some jumped-up pathetic little council dogsbody he had the right to throw his weight about and command my troops. *My* troops!' Camilla nodded. 'And when I pointed out to him that he had no such authority he threatened to have me arrested.'

Camilla nodded again, her face a mask of disapproval.

'Well, it didn't end there. The PM came to visit the site, flew down from London, and Collins actually prevented me from talking to him. I mean, not that I wanted to for my own sake, but I felt it was important that someone represented the soldiers and told him what a fantastic job the lads were doing. But no, Collins was too busy sucking up and grabbing all the glory for himself.'

'Well, what can you expect from a family like theirs? The things I heard about what their daughters got up to at boarding school...'

'And as for bloody Seb Fanshaw.' Jack swilled some more whisky.

'Well, the Fanshaws...' Camilla sniffed. 'Maddy hangs out with other ranks' wives.'

'She does *what*?'

'She had that woman who runs the hairdressers over for lunch today. I mean, really!'

'In an officers' quarter?'

Camilla nodded.

'I'll have to have a word with Seb. Fraternising – it never ends well. Maybe I was wrong in recommending him for promotion. It was a mistake. A big mistake.' Jack emptied his glass and poured in more whisky. 'I don't see why they're all against me. Getting anything done in this regiment is like pushing water uphill. All the officers seem determined to undermine me. Seb and Mike even accused me of jeopardising Susie Collins' safety. They said I deliberately hadn't told them she was missing.'

Camilla snorted. 'How could they! Like you'd do anything like that.'

'Exactly. I tried to tell Mike but he was too busy arse-licking the PM to want to bother to listen to anything I had to say. Well, he's only got himself to blame.' Jack drank some more. 'They all hate me. It's jealousy, that's what it is.

Jealousy. And spite. You understand that, Camilla. You know I only want the best for the regiment and its men. You know commanding this regiment isn't some sort of personal ego trip.' He took another gulp. 'It's all hard work and no thanks. No thanks at all.'

'No, darling. They don't deserve you. None of them do.'

'Well, I'll show them. I'll show the bastards. They're not going to grind me down. I'm going to demand a posting – see how they like it when they get someone else. Someone who doesn't have the vision and leadership skills that I have.'

'Will they allow you to move on?' Camilla was hoping this was the whisky talking and that in the cold, sober light of morning Jack would have a different view; she really couldn't face another move in under a year.

'Hah, well if they don't I'll tell them to shove it. I'm not working with a bunch of back-stabbing, disloyal shysters. I'm too good for this place and it's about time they bloody well recognised it.'

Camilla bit her lip. 'Yes dear,' she said quietly.

Shivering with bone-aching cold Susie frantically waved her phone above her head, hoping the pilot would spot the tiny torchlight. Agonisingly she watched the spotlight pan over the countryside. It seemed as if it was being pointed anywhere but at her car. She knew there was no point in shouting; no one would hear her above the racket of the engines. The light shone on the trees in a nearby copse and Susie wept with frustration. Why the hell would they be in a wood? They'd been travelling by car, on a *road*. Why didn't they search along the road? But slowly the light drifted off the trees, along the hedge and towards her. Susie jumped up and down in the almost knee-high water, waving her phone like a woman possessed, forgetting the fact that she was almost numb with cold, just concentrating on the approaching light, willing it to see her, see the car...

And then she was in its glare. The light was blinding. It was like being dazzled by the sun and she had to look away, her eyes clenched shut as the downwash of the rotor blades swept over her, kicking up a fine spray of water and enveloping her in a paraffin-scented haze of aviation fuel exhaust fumes. Relief washed over her with an intensity she didn't know was possible, and with it came the realisation of how perilous their situation had been. For all her brave talk that the worst they might experience was being a bit cold and wet, Susie knew in her heart that the reality had been a sight more serious than that – and the fact that a helicopter was now involved served to underline it. Tears began to roll down her cheeks – she could now allow herself to acknowledge the danger she'd allowed them to get in.

The twins scrambled out of the car and sploshed through the freezing water to stand beside her. Susie put her arms around them as the helicopter hovered overhead. She gave them a reassuring squeeze. Their eyes adjusted to the brilliance of the searchlight and they were able to gaze up at the underside of the giant Sea King. Silhouetted against the light they saw a man on a wire being winched down towards them. He inched lower, rotating slightly as he descended. A minute later he was standing beside them in the water. He gave Susie a thumbs up then tapped Ella on the shoulder. Susie gave Ella a reassuring nod as the winchman looped her daughter onto the rope then she was gone; being lifted into the air and safety. A couple of minutes later Katie was whisked upwards and then it was Susie's turn.

A surge of fear engulfed her, despite the fact she was being rescued, as she felt herself being swung upwards, the horizon expanding madly with every metre of altitude. The strap under her arms was so tight it was hard to breathe and the noise as they got closer to the aircraft became even more deafening and then she felt arms tugging at her backwards, dragging her onto a cold metal floor, her legs banging against the edge of the doorway and then she was half sitting, half lying on the floor of the chopper staring up at a couple of men who were wearing helmets and coveralls. Once she was disentangled from the winch she was lifted to her feet, wrapped in a space blanket and led to a seat like a canvas deckchair, attached to the frame of the aircraft and strapped in securely. Her daughters were already sitting there, also wrapped in silver blankets and still shivering. As Susie sat down, the side door was slammed shut and the cabin heating cranked up to full blast. She wanted to hug her daughters, to reassure herself, as much as them, that it was all going to be all right but the space blankets and the harnesses made it impossible, so she had to contend herself with patting their legs and smiling. The twins smiled back, a little wanly but with warmth. Then both the girls, separately but together, each took a hand and held it tight. Susie had a sense that their terrible experience might have shifted the family dynamic quite significantly, and for the better. They were going to be all right – but in a more important, longer-lasting way than the helicopter rescue meant.

The relief when the radio message from the police helicopter came through to the bronze command operations room was tangible. Mike turned away from the crowd of people, his mouth working, and blew his nose. Seb clapped him on the shoulder.

'I'm so pleased for you, mate,' he said.

Mike swallowed before he answered. 'You don't know quite how worried you are, until you feel the relief.'

'I can imagine. But Susie and the kids are safe now, that's the thing. They're being taken to the evacuation centre but the helicopter is landing on the rugby pitch – only place locally that's easily accessible and big enough. ETA in about ten minutes. I'll organise transport to get them to the centre – unless you want to do that?'

'No, you carry on, Seb. The way I feel at the moment I don't think I'm capable of organising anything.'

'I'm not surprised. What with everything else *and* your family in danger . . . well, I think anyone would struggle.'

Seb made his way over to the main operations hub, organised a police Range Rover to collect Mike and then take the family down to the next village and the evacuation centre.

'Thanks, Seb,' said Mike, gathering up his coat and mobile. 'Don't know when I'll get back here. I'm sure the team can hold the fort – as long as Rayner doesn't keep sticking his oar in.' He looked around. 'And talking of Rayner, where is he?'

Seb shrugged. Like he cared. 'I should think he's slunk away back under his stone. You know, I'm still finding it hard to believe that he or Camilla could be so utterly vile.'

'Beggars belief doesn't it.'

A police officer entered the room and signalled to Mike that the helicopter was about to land.

'Give my love to Susie,' said Seb as Mike left. 'And let's hope she and the kids are suffering from nothing worse than a nasty fright.'

Mike nodded. 'Thanks, Seb.'

As Mike left the room, Dan Armstrong came in.

'How's Perkins?' asked Seb. With so much that had happened since they'd been recalled off the exercise on Salisbury Plain, Seb found it hard to believe that it had only been that morning when he, Perkins and Armstrong had tried to clear the river Bavant of the branch.

'He's OK, boss. They're keeping him in overnight, just to be on the safe side, but he's pretty chipper, all things considered.'

'And, um, how did you and he get on?'

'At the risk of making a comment in bad taste – considering what happened to Perkins – we both agreed it was water under the bridge.'

Seb laughed. 'Very bad taste. But it's good you're both behaving like grown-ups.'

Armstrong pulled a mobile out of his pocket. 'And I think this is yours.'

Seb nodded. 'Good. At least now I can phone my wife and tell her Susie is safe.'

'Who's safe? What have I missed?'

Seb explained to Armstrong about the drama involving Mike's wife.

'Well,' said Armstrong, 'thank goodness it ended well. But no thanks to Rayner, it seems.'

'I can't be sure what he did was deliberate,' said Seb, carefully.

Armstrong snorted. 'You may not be sure. There's plenty in the battalion who would beg to differ where that man is concerned. Seriously, if it had been Rayner who'd been swept away in the river I, for one, wouldn't have jumped in.'

*

427

Susie detected a change in the motion of the helicopter and realised they were coming into land. She wondered where it would be – not that she cared, she was pathetically grateful to be in the warm and dry. The helicopter seemed to be hovering although it swayed from side to side somewhat alarmingly and then there was a sizeable bump and a jolt. Almost instantly the tone of the engine noise changed as the pilot throttled back.

One of the chaps in coveralls unclipped his harness and jumped to his feet and seconds later the big side door slid back to reveal what looked like a car park – and rain. The crewman jumped out while his colleague helped the three members of the Collins family unclip their own harnesses and make their way to the exit. Overhead the rotors still swooshed round and the engines still roared as one by one they stepped onto the narrow metal step and then down onto land. And there was Mike and flashlights popping and a mic was thrust in her face and she was asked how she felt. But she ignored that and threw her arms around her husband's neck and hugged him, and as the two girls clung to his arms he gathered them to him while the snappers and a couple of TV cameramen recorded the touching reunion.

The next morning, when Maddy threw back the curtains, she could see stars in the still-dark sky and although the ground still glistened in the light from the street lamps it wasn't raining. Blimey, she thought, and then wondered if the next thing she'd see would be a dove bearing an olive branch. Perhaps the worst of the weather was over. She padded across the landing where she could hear Rose was playing in her cot and Nathan seemed to be telling himself some sort of story. She smiled.

She attended to Rose first and deftly got her into a dry nappy and then took Nathan to the loo for an early morning wee before they all went downstairs so she could make herself and Jenna a cup of tea. She popped Rose in her high chair while Nathan climbed onto one of the kitchen chairs.

'Where's Daddy?' asked Nathan.

'Daddy's being a proper soldier today. Daddy's been helping people.'

'When's he coming back?'

'I don't know. Soon, I hope.'

Maddy gave the children half a banana each to eat while she took Jenna's tea up to her.

'Morning, Jen,' she said as she opened her friend's door. 'It's stopped raining.'

'At blooming last.' Jenna was snuggled under the covers, cuddling Eliot, the travel cot standing empty at the foot of the bed. 'I'm going to have to crack on a bit this morning if I'm going to get to the salon on time. I need to get some stuff from home. Let's face it, when I came over for lunch yesterday we didn't plan on me staying the night.'

'I'm jolly glad you did. Why don't I look after Eliot while you go home and get what you need?'

'Would you? That'd be brilliant.'

'Just as long as you're back before nine thirty – I've got to get Nathan to playgroup and then go and see Camilla, remember.'

'I'll be back before nine. I've got a salon to run.'

At nine fifty-five Maddy made her way along the road, with Rose strapped in her pushchair, ready for a meeting with Camilla. Jenna had been as good as her word and had zipped home to sort herself and had returned in record time and now Eliot was in the crèche, Nathan was at the playgroup and Jenna was at the salon. And Maddy had even had time to see if she could find any files regarding the community centre that Camilla thought she might have. And the answer was, Maddy was pretty certain, no she hadn't. It still wasn't raining and Maddy felt that after the chaos of the last couple of days, order was restored. And if it wasn't for this meeting with Camilla, Maddy would be feeling pretty OK with life in general.

On the dot of ten, Maddy rang Camilla's doorbell. When Camilla opened the door, Maddy was shocked. The woman looked terrible. Her hair was unbrushed and she'd obviously been crying. Maddy mightn't like Camilla but whatever she felt about her, she was obviously suffering and Maddy wasn't heartless.

'Camilla, what on earth...?'

'It's Jack. He says he wants to resign his commission.'

'He *what*?'

'Resign,' repeated Camilla. 'He came home last night, said he hated the army, hated the people he worked with, drank half a bottle of Scotch and this morning he's gone to see General Pemberton-Blake. He wanted a posting but that's been refused categorically so now he's gone to the general to offer his resignation. Maddy, if he does that what'll happen to us?'

Maddy bit back the comment that it would be exactly the same as had happened to Mike and Susie Collins. 'The general mightn't accept Jack's resignation.'

'But what if he does?'

'You'll have to make a fresh start.'

'But I couldn't.'

Maddy couldn't help herself any more. 'Susie Collins did.'

Camilla bristled. 'Don't you dare mention that woman's name to me. It's her husband who is responsible for all this. According to Jack, he undermined him at every turn, he refused to respect the proper chain of command and the last straw came when he deliberately took all the credit for the operation when he spoke to the PM and implied Jack had had nothing to do with anything.'

'I'm sure it wasn't like that.'

'Huh. What do you know?'

'I know what Seb told me.'

'Oh well...if Seb told you.' The sneer was tangible. 'That confirms everything Jack told me. Seb hasn't exactly done his best to support Jack, has he?'

'I...but...'

'Don't you deny it. For a start, he dragged his feet over that business with the mess. And you were no help either.'

'Me?'

'I don't know what you've been saying about me around the patch but no one is willing to replace you on my committees.'

'I've said *nothing* about you, Camilla. Nothing whatso-ever. And,' said Maddy resisting the urge to jab her finger in the air, '*and*, if you recall, you decided to find people to replace me without even having the common courtesy to tell me you no longer wanted my services. I heard that you'd sacked me via the grapevine. So don't you go bad-mouthing me. I'm sorry, Camilla, I'm sorry for your troubles, but I don't think I am the person to help you.'

Camilla looked down her nose at Maddy. 'Typical.'

'Goodbye, Camilla.'

Maddy almost ran down the garden path and was still trembling with anger and indignation when she got back to her own house.

Chapter 49

Jenna was twiddling her thumbs in her salon. Business was slack. OK, Mondays were never that busy but she only had one appointment that morning and until then she had nothing much to do. And she wasn't much looking forward to the one appointment she did have because it was that old biddy, Mrs Laycock. She wasn't a barrel of laughs at the best of times and since she'd realised just who Jenna was she'd always managed to make some snide comment or other when she came to get her hair done. Jenna would have told her where to get off if it wasn't for the fact that she couldn't afford to alienate any of the few customers that she did have. She'd tidied the shelves, she'd rearranged the display of products, she'd refolded all the towels and even hoovered the floor and now...she looked about her. No, there really was nothing left that needed doing. She picked up a magazine and flicked idly through it. She'd go home if it wasn't for the fact that she had to be here in case someone popped in to make a booking. She sighed again, put the magazine down and wandered over to the window. At least the sun was still shining, which made a change. She could hardly remember the last time it had been nice enough to take Eliot to the play park and give him a go on the swings. Maybe she'd do that when she picked him up from the crèche.

'Excuse me.'

Jenna swung round. Blimey. 'Chrissie.'

'Can I come in?'

'Free country.'

'I know...it's just, well...I was a bit bitchy the last time I was here.'

Jenna knew a peace offering when she saw one. 'You didn't say nothing I didn't deserve.'

'Oh.'

'Anyway, how's Lee? I hear he's been in the wars.'

'That's why I'm here. Your Dan saved his life.'

'Then thank him, not me. I wasn't nothing to do with it.'

'We will, honest. But I thought I ought to say sorry to you. What happened between you and Lee isn't any of my business.'

Jenna shrugged. 'Except I nicked his savings – savings that I expect the pair of you could do with.'

'Maybe. Shit happens but there's more important things in life. What happened at the weekend taught me that.'

'Maybe.'

'So I'd like to make an appointment.'

'Yeah, sure. When?'

'Now? Can you fit me in?

Jenna looked around the salon. Was Chrissie taking the piss? 'Not sure about that. As you can see, I'm pretty pushed.'

Chrissie looked crestfallen. 'No, well, I can see you don't want dealings with me. I understand.'

'Joke,' said Jenna. 'I was joking. Of *course* I'll do your hair. Cut and blow dry?'

Chrissie nodded.

When Mrs Laycock turned up for her appointment thirty minutes later she was astonished to see Jenna and Chrissie chatting like they were the best of mates.

'And I'll tell everyone that you're a genius,' said Chrissie as she paid. 'I can't believe how good you are at cutting.'

'Cheers, babe. You do that.'

Maybe, thought Jenna, having Chrissie onside would give her salon the boost it needed. One thing was sure, it couldn't do any harm.

Mike pulled up on Springhill Road and applied the handbrake.

He gazed at their house, trying to judge how bad the situation might be when he got through the front door, steeling himself for the worst and hoping it wasn't going to be like that. His family really didn't need another knock-back. But the evidence that the entire road had suffered was right there in front of him. There was a clear tidemark on the wall, about three inches above the doorstep, and their neighbours were already hard at work stacking furniture and ruined carpets outside in their gardens. No, his family were flood victims – just like so many others. And on top of everything else.

No point in just looking at it, thought Mike. He needed to know exactly how bad the damage was, he needed the file which contained the details of their house insurance and he'd promised to get a case full of clean dry clothes for Susie and the girls. The Fanshaws had been wonderful and, as soon as Maddy and Seb had heard that Springhill had suffered they told Mike to bring his family over to theirs.

'I know you'll get proper rented accommodation soon,' Maddy had said to Susie who had phoned her from the evacuation centre to fill her in on the details of the day before, 'and I know it'll be a bit cramped, but for a few days, just while you get sorted out, we'd love to have you.'

And so Mike had left his family at Maddy's while he'd

trekked over to their house to assess their plight. And, he thought, it wasn't looking hopeful. He turned the key in the lock and peered inside. An inch-thick slick of mud and water covered the carpets and the smell was disgusting – raw sewage, he surmised – but the water damage didn't seem to have got above the skirting boards. He wandered through to the kitchen to see how bad it was in there. Much the same, only he reckoned the white goods were all beyond repair. As he was gazing at the freezer and considering the wisdom of opening it, his phone rang. He looked at the screen which displayed a number rather than a name but he pressed the answer button regardless.

'Is that Mike Collins?' said a voice.

'Speaking,' he said warily. He'd had more than enough calls about his PPI claim or his non-existent whiplash injury.

'This is Guy Manning speaking. I am PPS to Leon Rochester.'

PPS – was that like PPI? Or was this some revolting spammer already trying to make money out of his misfortune with some insurance wheeze? 'I'm sorry,' said Mike tersely, 'I've no idea what you are talking about. Goodbye,' and he hit the disconnect button.

He'd barely put his phone back in his pocket when it rang again.

Shit, this bloke had some nerve.

'Whatever it is, I am *not* interested,' he snapped.

'Mr Collins, please listen. I am ringing from the Department of Environment, Farming and Rural Affairs.'

'Defra?'

'Yes. I'm Guy Manning. I am the permanent private secretary to Leon Rochester.'

'And who's he?'

'The secretary of state at Defra.'

'Oh.' Oh God, yes, he did know that, of course he did. In his defence he had more things on his mind right now than the composition of the Cabinet. Besides, what the fuck did a government department want with him?

'Is this a good time to call?' asked Guy.

'To be honest, I'm standing in my house which was flooded over the weekend so it's not great.'

'I'm sorry to hear that and I promise I won't keep you. The secretary of state asked me to call to find out when it would be convenient for you to meet with him.'

'Meet the secretary of state? Me?'

'Yes. The PM suggested he ought to talk to you – about emergency planning, flood defences, that sort of thing. He'll want to be briefed on the whole picture from the budget to manpower management to long-term planning – the whole thing. The PM said that, while we all know that floods happen, the way the local authorities cope with the disaster is the key. He thought the Bavant valley flood was a shining example of how to get it right.'

'The PM,' repeated Mike. 'The PM said that? And the minister wants the whole picture?' He fell silent as he considered this praise.

He heard Guy sigh. 'So…a date?'

'Look, Guy, I'm sorry I'm being a bit slow on the uptake but I've had hardly any sleep for forty-eight hours, and on top of the fact that my house has been flooded, last night my wife and twin daughters had to be rescued by helicopter.'

'Goodness, you should have said. But they're all right now?'

'They're fine.'

'So about this meeting…'

'Yes.'

'Could you make tomorrow? It really is quite urgent.'

'I'll have to clear it with my boss.'

'Do that.' Guy added, 'Please,' as an afterthought.

'I'll call you back.'

'Thank you. I'll give you the number of my direct line.'

'Hang on.' Mike cast about him and found a half-written shopping list and a biro on the counter. He took the number down. 'I'll get back to you as soon as I can,' he promised as he ended the call. But before he could do anything about confirming the meeting or asking for the time off he needed to concentrate on sorting out some kit for his family and finding the house insurance details. He picked his way over the slime that covered the carpet to the stairs and went up to the bedrooms. He had to admire what Susie and the girls had done before they left. They'd salvaged so much stuff; they must have worked so hard. Maybe the girls weren't so bad after all. Before he got out a suitcase he went to Susie's dressing table and found their iPads and chargers. They deserved to have them back – as a thank you.

Susie was on the sofa in Maddy's sitting room staring out of the window. It was lovely to be there and back on the patch, and it was wonderful to be warm and dry but...but for the time being her family didn't even have a home and they couldn't stay at Maddy's for long – there really wasn't the space and it would be no time at all before everyone had had enough of everyone else's company. And anyway, the sooner they had their own front door again the sooner they could start getting back to normal, or as normal as things could become under the circumstances. Maybe things would seem more normal when the girls went back to school and she returned to work. Everyone had been very insistent that they needed to take things easy for a while; a day, maybe two, just to make sure they weren't suffering any nasty after-effects from their ordeal, but Susie wasn't sure about the wisdom of this. All it did was give them time to brood. She thought that if they were busy doing things the quicker they'd be able to put it behind them, but Seb, Maddy and Mike had been adamant.

'You've had a lousy twenty-four hours. Get your strength up for a couple of days, here with Maddy,' Mike had said. He hadn't even allowed her to go with him to check out the house. 'No point in upsetting yourself when you're already feeling a bit fragile.'

She tried to argue that he'd had an equally awful time but Mike wouldn't hear of it. So she was stuck here, on the sofa, wondering how bad the house might be, her imagination going into overdrive, and with nothing to do to take her mind off it. Meanwhile she could hear Maddy bustling about upstairs, changing the sheets on the double bed after Jenna's stay and moving Rose's cot into Nathan's room so the twins could be fitted into the other room.

'It's a bit unfair making Nathan and Rose share, isn't it?' Susie had protested.

'Don't be silly,' said Maddy. 'It's only for a couple of days. Just till we get you fixed up.'

And Susie's offer of help to make up the beds had been soundly rebuffed.

'You're done in,' Maddy had said. 'You spent last night on a camp bed in a village hall, you can't have had any sleep, so now I want you to put your feet up and take it easy.'

And, if Susie had been honest with herself, she was knackered and she didn't have the strength to argue let alone do much more. So now she was waiting for a call from Mike with the news of what she could expect to find when she did go over to Springhill Road, and nothing much else to do except to wonder what the future might hold – and from her current perspective, it was a future that wasn't looking very rosy. Redundancy, lack of employment, lack of credit rating and now *this*. More than their fair share, thought Susie, grimly.

'Mum?'

Susie looked up. The twins were peering round the door.

'Mum, can we have a word?'

'Darlings, you don't have to ask that, of *course* you can have a word.'

The pair sidled in. 'Mum,' began Ella, 'about what we told you last night.'

'About the money,' added Katie.

'And the pot.'

'Shhh,' said Susie. 'I think we've all realised that, in the great scheme of things, it's not that important. There are far worse things out there that we'll have to contend with.'

'But it *is* important,' said Ella.

Katie nodded earnestly. 'The thing is...are you going to tell Dad?'

Susie considered the request. 'Ah.'

The two girls stared at her, their brows deeply furrowed, worry etched into every soft little line.

'No,' said Susie, coming to a decision. 'No, I won't.' The twins sagged with relief. 'But,' she added. Her daughters straightened up again. '*But*, if you ever do anything like that *ever* again, he'll be the first to know everything. Do I make myself clear?'

The pair nodded gravely.

'No smoking, no dope, no stealing, no lying, no cheating... understand?'

Ella and Katie nodded again.

'Come here,' said Susie. She patted the sofa cushions on either side of her. The girls sat. 'I'm not being mean and I don't want to sound as if I am nagging, but you two are capable of so much, and smoking and taking drugs isn't going to help you achieve anything. I know you hate your school, I know it's been difficult for you but you should be able to rise above the kind of kids who think that underachievement is some kind of badge of honour. It isn't.'

'Suppose not,' said Ella.

'And there must be kids in the school who are brainy and get top marks.'

Katie shrugged. 'Maybe.'

'So why don't you hang out with them? I don't think, in your hearts, you want to end up with no qualifications, no prospects and no jobs. But if you hang around with the Alis of this world, smoking and doing drugs, you'll be going the right way about it.'

Another shrug, another 'maybe'. Then, 'But the brainy kids aren't popular.'

Susie thought about this. 'I expect they are with each other.'

'Suppose.'

'Think about it,' said Susie. 'And we won't be going back to our old house for a while so, if you want to make a break from your old gang, this is the perfect time to do it.'

She was aware of her daughters exchanging a look. She hoped the message had got home.

Chapter 50

Mike decided that, before he took the suitcase of kit back to Maddy's house, he ought to speak to Rob about his summons to London; besides, it wasn't much of a detour to go via the office. He strode across the open-plan workspace to his boss's desk.

'A word, if I may, Rob.'

'Mike?' Rob looked up from his computer screen and then at his watch. 'You're late.'

No enquiry after the health of his wife and daughters, he noticed. 'I've been at my house, finding out how bad the damage is. And seeing as how I spent my entire weekend dealing with the floods and the problems of the folk in the Bavant valley, I think I can be allowed today off in lieu to deal with my own ones.'

'I suppose,' said Rob, grudgingly.

'And I shall want tomorrow off too.'

Rob shook his head. 'Much as I realise that being flooded is a challenge you feel you have to overcome—'

Mike interrupted. 'Rob, being flooded isn't a fucking *challenge*, it's a nightmare. And I don't need tomorrow off for that. I'm wanted at Defra.'

'Defra?'

Mike nodded. 'In London.'

'I know where Defra is,' Rob snapped. 'And why do I only know about this now?'

'Because I only took the call from the minister's office in the last hour.'

'The minister?' Rob looked annoyed before he drew his diary across his desk and flicked it open. 'Just as well I'm free tomorrow so I can come with you.'

'No need, they didn't ask for you.'

Rob's lips tightened. 'An oversight, probably.'

Mike shrugged. Much as it pained him to consider the idea, Rob might possibly be right – after all, he was his boss. Besides, Rob was already sore about not meeting the PM and it wouldn't do to piss him off further about Defra. Mike might find his current job beneath his capabilities but it *was* a job and with everything else going on, he needed to keep it. He pulled out the scrap of paper from his pocket with Guy's number on it. 'OK – ring this chap. Guy Manning, he's the PPS to the secretary of state.'

He went back to his desk and left Rob to make the call. Two minutes later he saw Rob beckoning him back.

'I've given permission for you to go. I won't be required.'

Mike kept his face impassive. No need to look smug, he told himself. 'Good. Thank you.'

'I want a full report on your return.'

'Naturally.'

'By the way, I wanted to check some budgetary figures for the emergency planning but I couldn't find the files.'

'Sorry. I took them with me at the weekend. Being new to the job, I wanted to be sure that I implemented all the correct procedures and so forth . . . Wasn't sure I am sufficiently au fait with the job to want to rely on my memory.' Which wasn't completely true but it would suffice for the time being.

His other reasons were not for sharing.

'Fine,' said Rob, although from his tone Mike could tell it patently wasn't. 'Where are they now?'

'To be honest, I'm not sure. With all the worry about my family I clean forgot about them.' Which was a lie, because he knew, full well, they were in his car. But he'd need them tomorrow for the meeting and, before that, he needed to extract a great deal of information out of them and...well, he still had to make up his mind about what to do about Rob's dismissal of his report on the possibility of flooding in their administrative area. The truth was that Rob's attitude had no bearing on what had happened; no way could anything have been done in time to avert the situation, but it was the *principle* that was important. The fact that Rob had treated his suggestions with such contempt. And now such high-level people wanted his – *his!* – opinion he could make himself look brilliant simply by producing that report. But – and it was a giant *but* – if he did, he would automatically drop Rob right in it. Much as he loathed Rob it wasn't in Mike's psyche to behave like such a bastard. He was pretty sure that at some point there would be an inquiry into the reason for the devastating floods and while he wasn't prepared to point the finger of blame at anyone, he wanted his own personal insurance policy just in case accusations got bandied about. He mightn't be prepared to do the dirty but if the shit started to hit the fan he wanted his own position bombproofed. No, he'd remove the report from the file...but he'd tuck it away, for safe-keeping. Just in case.

'I want them found,' said Rob.

'Of course. They're probably at the pub. The bronze command team is still using it for the last of the clearing up. I'll make sure they're put somewhere safe till I can collect them. I'll bring them in on Wednesday. OK?'

Rob looked placated. 'And don't forget that report on your meeting.'

The next evening, Mike got off the London train at Westbury station and made his way to the car park. He thought about ringing his wife but decided that it would be more fun to see her reaction face to face. He plipped his car key and saw the indicator lights flash in response. Two minutes later he was heading out of the car park and through the town centre.

'You're early,' said Maddy when she opened her front door to him.

'The meeting took less time than I thought. Where's Susie?'

'Don't be cross with her but she popped into the mess to make sure nothing is going horribly wrong without her guiding hand. Seb tried to stop her but she said she'd worry about things if she didn't. She promised only to be gone for an hour.'

'And the twins?'

'Up in their room. So,' said Maddy, 'what was it like to walk along the corridors of power?'

'They had nicer paintings on the walls than we get in the council offices. And a minion served us tea and biscuits so I didn't have to put coins in a machine.'

Maddy laughed. 'Blimey – there's posh.' The doorbell rang. 'That'll be Susie.'

Mike felt ridiculously pleased that he'd be able to share his good news in a few seconds. He almost ran to the front door to let in his wife.

'Hi, darling,' she said, stepping inside. She gave him a quick kiss on the cheek. 'How was London?' She undid her coat and hung it on the hall stand. 'I'm gasping for a cuppa.

Put the kettle on, there's a love. Hi, Maddy. I trust the girls behaved while I was out?'

'They were fine. Don't worry about them, I want to hear about Mike's trip.'

Mike moved to the kitchen. 'London was interesting,' he told them both.

'Really?' said Susie. 'You never said that when you had that job at the MoD.'

He filled the kettle and flicked on the switch.

'Maybe not, but...well...I assumed the minister just wanted to pick my brains.'

'And?' said Maddy.

'Well, he did. But there was something else.' He paused for effect.

'For God's sake,' said Susie, 'just spit it out, will you?'

'It turned out to be a bit more than that. They offered me a consultancy post with a ridiculous annual retainer and a really generous sum for every day they actually employ me.' He grinned inanely.

'Employ you?' said Susie.

'It's not such a mad idea. Other people have.'

'I know, darling, I know. It's just...it's London. What about your current job? And the house?'

'I don't think either of those is going to be a problem.'

'And,' said Maddy, 'if it's not a rude question, what's a "ridiculous" annual retainer?'

'Just over a hundred k a year.'

Susie and Maddy looked at each other.

'Bloody hell,' said Maddy.

'Shit a brick,' said Susie.

'It almost looks as if that dreadful flood might have done us a bit of a favour.'

Chapter 51

As Seb drove the family car into Ashton-cum-Bavant village, Maddy was assailed with flashbacks of events six months previously when she'd last been in the village. Then, the weather had been appalling; rain, gales, lowering cloud but now it was bright and clear. The trees were sporting the vibrant lush green of spring growth, the birds were singing, flowers bloomed...the perfect English idyll. And the floods were pretty much forgotten now, apart from the poor folks still battling with repairs, renovations and their insurance companies.

Maddy glanced across at Rollo's grand mansion. And to think that she'd tried to protect Susie from hearing about his new place when she was facing having to live in Springhill Road and that awful house. Back then no one would have dreamed for a minute that she and Mike would end up as his neighbours and, despite the fact she was so thrilled that things had worked out for the Collinses, she couldn't help feeling horribly envious. Would she and Seb ever be able to afford a place of their own in such a lovely location? All she could see for herself was a succession of endless quarters – some nicer than others, but never accommodation that anyone in their right mind would class as 'wonderful' or 'desirable' – and precious little opportunity to save for a deposit for a house because the kids' boarding school fees would gobble up every last penny. She sighed. Maybe, despite everything, Susie and Mike were the lucky ones.

'Which way now?' asked Seb, breaking into her thoughts.

'Next left,' said Maddy.

Seb took the turn and the two of them peered at the names on the gates. This was, noted Maddy, the sort of village where houses had names, not numbers. And what houses... lovely half-timbered cottages with thatched roofs and proper country gardens – the sort which later would be filled with delphiniums and hollyhocks, lavender and stocks, the sort which foreign tourists oohed and aahed over as they passed through, brought here by their tour operators to see 'the prettiest village in England'. These were houses which appeared on the property porn shows and which Maddy knew she could never aspire to live in.

'Here,' she said spotting *Lower End* in clear black lettering on a five-bar gate.

Seb swung their four-by-four into the wide gravel drive that swept up to a double garage. To the side was a two-storey house with dormers in the thatch and mullioned windows. The porch – also thatched – was adorned with bunting and pretty hanging baskets flanked each side. Maddy was green.

Nathan scrambled out of the car while Maddy unbuckled Rose and lifted her down to toddle after her brother. A sign stuck in a flower bed exhorted them to 'Use the side gate'.

'This way,' said Maddy, grasping Rose by the hand and leading her along a path, through an ancient brick arch. She pushed open the wrought iron gate and stepped into the back garden.

Susie almost skipped across the lawn to meet them.

'Sorry we're a bit late,' apologised Maddy.

447

'Not at all, not at all,' said Susie. 'I'm so pleased you could make it. And that you agreed to come early so we could have a proper catch-up first.'

'Wouldn't have missed your house-warming for the world – or the catch-up. We've hardly seen each other for months.' Maddy gazed at the immaculate lawn, the herbaceous border, the beautiful Victorian conservatory tacked onto the back of the house, the huge pond, the weeping willow... 'Bit of a change from Springhill Road.'

Susie nodded. 'God that place was grim. I tried to make the best of it but, frankly, it would have been no great loss to the world if the whole place had been swept away.' She turned to Seb. 'I think you'll find Mike in the conservatory, making sure the bar is sorted for the barbecue. He could probably do with a hand.'

Seb didn't need telling twice and strode across the lawn to find his old boss.

'I bet the girls love it here,' said Maddy, still admiring the gardens.

'They do. And they're in the den with a stack of *Peppa Pig* DVDs for the little ones.'

'*Peppa Pig*,' yelled Nathan.

''Eppa,' crowed Rose.

Maddy followed Susie into the house. The interior was as wonderful as the outside, filled with bright rugs, vases of lilies and elegant soft-furnishings.

'Oh, Susie. I am trying hard to keep the green-eyed monster under control but I am failing miserably.'

Susie grinned. 'We have been incredibly lucky.'

'And that's not a phrase you'd have said a year ago.'

'No.'

They reached the den where Katie and Ella were marshalling

Maddy's two onto giant floor cushions in front of the big TV. Katie picked up the remote and instantly Nathan and Rose were in the thrall of Peppa.

'You be good,' said Maddy to her children, who didn't even acknowledge their mother had spoken. 'Come and find me if you need me,' she told the girls. They nodded.

'Guided tour?' offered Susie.

'Thought you'd never ask.'

Susie led Maddy towards the ancient, uneven, polished oak stairs.

'How are they settling in at their new school?'

'It's a sea-change from Winterspring Comp. They're a bit behind – mainly because they completely marked time when they were at the comp – but they're trying really hard to catch up. I tell you something, those months made them realise how lucky they are to be getting such a good education. And they fit in to this new school. Before, they had the wrong accents, wrong ethos, wrong background. And they tried to make it better by hanging around with the wrong crowd – the kids who think smoking, underage drinking and the like is cool.'

'Susie!'

Susie looked Maddy in the eye as they stood on the landing. 'And the rest. Not,' she added, 'that Mike knows – or he doesn't know yet. I suppose I can hardly blame them, given the way things were in the past with Mike and me. Hardly grade-A role models. As always, it's more than likely a case of "I blame the parents".'

'You can't take the blame for everything, Susie.'

'No?'

'No. Drinking, smoking, it's what kids do these days.'

'Really? I'm sure there's an awful lot who don't. Anyway, I've got to hope that now they're at their lovely day school it won't happen again. Actually, it better *hadn't* happen again; I have warned them of the consequences if they do because, if there are any more reports about them being disruptive or badly behaved, I've threatened to tell their father everything. That's enough to keep them working like little Trojans.'

'So you're certain they did those things – smoking, drinking…'

'Certain? God, yes. They coughed to everything when we were stuck in the floods. So we've drawn a line in the sand and agreed to forget about it and I've promised it'll stay that way unless they put so much as a toenail across that line. If they do…' Susie rolled her eyes and drew her hand across her throat. 'Please don't tell Seb. I'm sure he'd be the soul of discretion but…well, male loyalty and that stuff. So, unless it all goes horribly wrong, I'd rather it was only you and me in the know.'

'Crikey,' said Maddy. 'I'm a bit surprised you even told me.'

Susie shrugged. 'I think we know too much about each other's buried bodies for me to keep anything from you.'

Maddy grinned. 'You can say that again.'

Susie changed the subject and started to show Maddy the first of the five bedrooms upstairs and the twins' transgressions were forgotten as Maddy was blown away by the lovely ancient beams that ran across the ceilings, the thickness of the walls, the mullioned windows and the neat little en suites that the previous owners had shoehorned into the rooms.

They clattered downstairs again and, having made sure the girls and Maddy's kids were still OK, Susie took Maddy into the kitchen which was a modern extension and which would have made Jamie Oliver jealous, let alone someone who was stuck with an army kitchen in a less than modern quarter.

'Drink?' offered Susie.

Maddy nodded. 'White wine, if you've got it.'

Susie got out two glasses.

Maddy's eyebrows shot up. 'Susie?'

'No – still on the wagon. But I prefer to drink soda water out of a wine glass. Maybe it's because I can kid myself it's a proper drink.'

'And Mike?'

'He had a couple of monstrous tumbles off the wagon but…' Susie rapped her knuckles on the big scrubbed pine table in the middle of the floor, before she took two bottles out of the fridge and poured Maddy's drink and then her own. 'Cheers.'

The two women clinked glasses.

'Now then, what happened to Rayner?' asked Susie.

'Well.' Maddy put her glass down on the table. 'His resignation was accepted but it was decided that he couldn't stay on because, well…I think the powers that be decided he'd gone a bit bonkers.'

'A *bit*?'

'Indeed. So he got sent on gardening leave quick sharp and Camilla was livid. All her aspirations to being Lady Rayner when Jack made it onto the army board.'

'As if,' interrupted Susie.

'They were each as delusional as the other, I reckon. Anyway, the rumour is that he's running some company that sells carpets.'

'Carpets?'

'So I've heard. I can't imagine Camilla is very happy – no one to boss around, no one to lord it over.'

'How have the mighty fallen.'

'I am a great believer in karma,' said Maddy. 'He was

such a shit to everyone and made so many lives difficult it was bound to catch up with him in the end.'

'I don't think people always get what they deserve,' said Susie.

Maddy knew Susie was thinking about Mike's redundancy and the disasters that had followed on from it. 'But you did in the end, Susie. This wonderful house is payback for what you did for me, when Seb was in Kenya and I was dealing with the bunny-boiler.'

Susie shook her head. 'I still can't believe things came right like they did. I tell you something, Maddy, talk about a roller-coaster ride. If you want epic highs and abysmal lows, just spend a year with the Collins family.'

Maddy laughed. 'Which is why you get the "for better, for worse" bit in the marriage vows. I think we'd all prefer to take the "better", "riches" and "health" bits and sod the negatives.'

'On the other hand, Mike and I are such a team now. We've had our disagreements but when you've come through what we have...' Susie sighed. 'Not that I'd recommend it but we've got a superglued bond now.'

Maddy leaned across the table and gave her friend's hand a squeeze. 'I am so pleased. Really. Envious, of course,' she added with a laugh, 'but really pleased. I do miss you being my neighbour though. And you working in the mess. It's not the same without you around.'

'But that was always the way with the army – people come and go, in and out of your life. Much as I hated it when we left and I thought I'd never get used to being a civvy, it's not so bad when you get used to it. I don't mean it's "not so bad" because we've got this.' Susie waved her glass to indicate the house. 'But I can plant perennials in my garden, I don't automatically know what my neighbours do for a living – or what their pay grade is – but I know they'll be staying put and not moving out in a year or less. I've even joined the local WI.'

Maddy squealed with laughter. 'You? The WI?!'

'It's grand. I love it.'

'So you can recommend civvy street then, can you?'

'Abso-bloody-lutely.'

HOW TO GET YOUR FREE EBOOK

SOLDIERS' WIVES

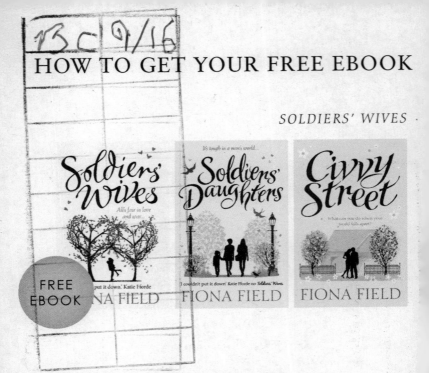

FREE EBOOK

TO CLAIM YOUR FREE EBOOK OF *SOLDIERS' WIVES*

1. FIND THE CODE

   This is the last word on page 252 of this book, preceded by `HOZ-`, for example `HOZ-code`

2. GO TO HEADOFZEUS.COM/FREEBOOK

   Enter your code when prompted

3. FOLLOW THE INSTRUCTIONS

   Enjoy your free eBook of *SOLDIERS' WIVES*

Offer closes on 1st February 2017. Offer excludes residents of United States and Canada.
Terms and conditions can be found at headofzeus.com/ebookoffertc